I0612668

The Coal'd War

Alan Thompson

Published by New Generation Publishing in 2013

First Edition

www.newgeneration-publishing.com

 New Generation Publishing

This book is dedicated to my two Sons, Mark and Adrian, my Daughter Ashlie and my Grandchildren from a very proud Dad and Grandad.

Prologue

On a January night in 1981 the door of the sanctum sanctorum of the Politburo meeting room in Moscow's Great Kremlin Palace opened exposing a clutch of four gloomy old men. Two equally old and grim faced aides helped them on with their coats before handing them their scarves, hats and gloves. The four then made their way in silence down the wide, carpeted staircase and through to a side door leading to four massive, chauffeur driven, Russian built, black limousines.

The car carrying Yuri Plakinov, the newly appointed head of the KGB, was the first to leave. He was slumped back into the luxurious leather of the rear seat impervious to the many coloured reflections of the wet road stones beneath as his car moved quietly across Red Square. Despite the comfort of the car Plakinov shuddered from the brief exposure to the cold he had experienced in the short walk from the side door to his vehicle. His reflections were as grey and cold as the winter night as his mind mulled uneasily over the report he and the other three leaders of the Soviet Union had just been listening to.

The journey to Plakinov's apartment took less than three minutes. His comfortable first floor apartment was situated only a few hundred yards from Red Square. As the car drew up outside the main entrance to the building the guard telephoned his apartment. After making his way up the wide curving staircase he was met on the landing by his assistant, Li Sarich. He shuffled past her.

'Good evening comrade!'

'I am in no mood for stupid pleasantries' Plakinov replied.

'I apologise comrade. I didn't mean to …'

Her words were cut short as he scowled; 'Get me a drink.'

Having shed his coat, hat and scarf on the nearest chair Yuri Plakinov made his way across the room without a word. She automatically responded to his order by placing a cut glass tumbler together with a bottle of single malt Scotch whiskey on a table by the side of his favourite chair. Having experienced such moods before, she left the main room and sat in the next room with the door left slightly ajar.

At first she watched and waited like a young gazelle sniffing for danger as Plakinov stared ahead with unseeing eyes. His position was altered only occasionally when he picked up his drink from time to time or refilled his glass. Eventually he fell asleep.

Just after five in the morning Li woke to the sound of Plakinov shouting her name. Stepping out of her bed she called 'I'll be with you in a moment.'

As she came out of her room Plakinov shouted.

'Telephone Cheslav and Andrei, tell them I want to see them here; now!'

'But it is very early comrade' she protested.

'Never mind that, I want them here, now! In my apartment office' he demanded.

Li went to his office and telephoned the two men who were Plakinov's personal assistants and bodyguards. Both enjoyed the rank of KGB colonel.

Forty-five minutes later two tall and agile men arrived at the door of the apartment. Both smiled and greeted Li who by this time was wearing trousers and a jumper. She returned their smiles and greetings as she showed them into Plakinov's office where he sat behind his desk awaiting their arrival. Li held the door handle as the two men passed her then she left closing the door gently as she went.

With the door closed Plakinov swept the open palm of his hand across his body indicating that the men should sit.

When his guests were seated he stood up saying 'Komrads!' Then he walked around his desk in the spacious office and stood before a large map of the world situated in the middle of the wall opposite.

Cheslav and Andrei swung around in their swivel chairs to face the map.

'Komrads' Plakinov repeated as he picked up a long wooden pointer.

'Our Leader has given us the task of creating economic difficulties for our enemies in Western Europe. In the past we have spread our resources. As from today I want to concentrate all of our efforts on one target; England. Let me tell you why.'

As he spoke Plakinov dragged the pointer across the map to illustrate his point-The United Kingdom was to Europe what Cuba was to have been to the United States in 1963.

Placing his thumbs behind crimson coloured shoulder braces that supported his trousers Plakinov stared at his two man audience for a second before returning to sit at his desk.

'You both know me well. You have both served me well. I have few secrets from you' as he spoke he put his elbows on the desk and crossed his arms so that his hands rested on his shoulders with his head protruding from between his hands.

Before speaking again he stared at his two colonels for a few seconds in turn.

'This plan' he began 'has to work. We begin to assemble the people and the finance as of now and we will work together daily to ensure that we make no mistakes. Nothing has to be overlooked. No mention of this project has to be made in any company or to any individual. You will both spend some time each day improving your ability to read and speak the English language.'

Chapter 1

In November 1983 a delegation of Polish Miners arrived at the Central Station in Newcastle upon Tyne. They were the guests of a delegation from the Northumberland branch of the Coal Miners Union of Great Britain, known as the CMU who were waiting on the platform to meet them.

The Polish group consisted of six representatives of the Polish coal miners union, a representative from the Polish Embassy Trade Section in London and two interpreters. One of the interpreters was called Gennardy Mardosov.

When the train came to a standstill the two groups came together on the station platform. Gennardy Mardosov made straight for Tony Hartill. Both men were smiling broadly as they greeted one another with warm handshakes.

'Tony my friend, are you still asking so many questions?' said Gennardy.

Tony's colleagues laughed at Gennardy's friendly jibe and Gennardy translated to his group who then joined in the laughter and pointed at Tony who grinned and absorbed the attention.

Sharing the burden of luggage between them the group made their way to the waiting coach that took them on the short journey to Miner's Hall the regional headquarters.

Inside the hall they took coffee and biscuits into a conference room and sat round a long, highly polished conference table. When they were all assembled Ray Mullaney the Northumberland area secretary entered accompanied by Albert Markham the national general secretary and Owen Williams the Member of

Parliament for the Northumberland mining constituency of Winsbreck. Everyone stood up and applauded until Albert Markham indicated that they resume their seats.

Ray Mullaney then stood up and welcomed the assembly. On the wall behind him hung the red flag of the Soviet Union flanked by pictures of Joseph Stalin and Lenin.

'Well comrades!' he began 'We all know one another from the excellent visit we had to Poland last year when most of us met for the first time.' He paused whilst Gennardy interpreted before continuing; 'Miners are miners wherever they are in the world and whatever they dig for. Miners everywhere get a raw deal and hopefully exchanges such as this will lead to a better world for all miners. As you will remember from Poland when our leader Albert and our good friend Owen joined us for a few hours they told the best jokes and so I will ask Albert to say just a few words because I know they are short of time' he paused for a moment then added 'Komrads, Albert Markham.'

Albert Markham stood up and told the assembly that a pole in English meant something straight strong and upright and there was much in common between an English pole and a Polish miner.

'You are straight, strong and upright' he told an appreciative audience who responded with warm applause.

After a short speech Markham and Williams left with the Polish embassy official.

When they had gone Ray Mullaney surprised everyone by announcing that instead of being accommodated in a city hotel, arrangements had been made for the guests to be accommodated in the homes of those delegates who had visited Poland from Britain the previous year.

That way, Mullaney boasted, 'You will enjoy some genuine Geordie hospitality.'

The representative from the Polish Embassy in London had earlier objected to this arrangement but he was assured that this was the way the CMU wanted to cement relations. Mullaney assuaged his protestations by insisting that they were all comrades and world socialism would be better served in this way.

Tony Hartill volunteered to host Gennardy and one of the Polish miners.

During the following six days delegates met in the mornings and made collective visits to coal mines and sightseeing tours of the area. In the evenings they went back to the homes of their hosts and firm friendships were established.

The visit to Britain was to change the outlook of Gennardy Mardasov forever.

On the first day a casual visit to the local Supermarket left Gennardy and the Polish Miners astounded. Initially they thought that the store was a propaganda stunt to impress them. They asked if they could pick up packages to make sure that there was something in them. They were incredulous that ordinary British people, coal miners included, could actually buy whatever they desired. As the customers rolled their trolleys up to the checkout Gennardy was close to tears in a state of anger, pleasure and wonder.

'If the people at home could see this' he said involuntarily. Tony Harthill overheard him and said. 'Pardon'

'So much food!' replied Gennardy almost whispering. 'I have never seen so much food.'

In the late afternoon they called at a shop on the corner of a street not far from Tony's house.

Gennardy asked 'What is this place Tony?'

'It's a shop!' replied Tony quizzically. 'I have just called to get some cigarettes for Maggie and a bottle of whisky for us.' he smiled as he finished his sentence.

'Everything here!' said Gennardy as he looked around the colourful shelves all packed with goods. 'What is it here for?'

'What is it here for?' repeated Tony.

'Well it is here because this man Abdulla.' He paused as he acknowledged Abdulla, the proprietor of Asian extraction, 'owns the shop and buys in goods to sell to the local people.'

After the goods were paid for Abdulla said 'Cheerio Tony.' And the two men left the shop.

Outside Gennardy said 'How does this man have this shop.'

'Because he wants to I suppose' said Tony.

'In England can anyone have a shop?' asked Gennardy.

'Of course' Tony replied 'Why shouldn't they?'

Gennardy's questions continued all the way to Tony's home.

That night they all met up at a local Pub where they had a pint of beer before going on to the Equality Club where the visitors enjoyed a reception the likes of which they had never heard of let alone experienced. Gennardy was completely overwhelmed but he stayed the course of alcoholic indulgence unlike some of his delegation

The evening went over quickly. Everyone seemed to be joking and happy. About 10.30 Tony Hartill declared that it was time to leave and get to sleep so that they were fresh for the next morning. On their return Tony's wife, Maggie, put out a cheese board and some biscuits then she went to bed.

Tony got out the bottle of whisky and gave Gennardy a nip with his supper before turning in. Gennardy had had more food during the two first days than he would normally have in a week in Minsk. He patted his stomach and gave a long sigh staring at Tony as he did so.

'I know now why Abdulla is such a fat man. He has to sell some of the food or he would be even fatter.' Gennardy joked then went on; 'You do not understand how much good luck you have had to be living like this.'

Tony replied, 'Oh! I don't know we live a pretty ordinary life I suppose.'

'You call this ordinary? I think you are a very lucky man Tony, my friend.'

'Well I am pleased to know that you like it here.' Tony said with deliberate slowness to help Gennardy to understand. He need not have bothered because although Gennardy had a difficult time with the local accent, he had little difficulty in understanding Tony who spoke the accent with clear diction.

Suddenly Gennardy looked at Tony and said.

'Do you remember when we were at the club and the men there were making amusement of me.'

'Of course I do.' The look on Gennardy's face prompted him to further comment. 'Don't be offended the lads were joking with you.'

'I understand this.' said Gennardy. 'I like all the joking but I told them we put the first man in space and a Russian inventor invented television. What I told them was true. Why did they say all those things about Russian fairytales? I do not understand this, why fairytales?'

'I don't see why it is so important.' said Tony.

'It is so important to me Tony because I think I have believed many lies before now and I am not stupid and

12

I do not like people treating me as stupid.' Gennardy's voice was raised and his face was red with the combination of alcohol and anger.

'Look Gennardy! No one wishes to offend you. Anyone can see that you are not stupid. It's obvious. You're just a bit drunk.' Tony replied and tried to laugh off Gennardy's concern.

Gennardy became sentimental. 'Tony, my friend, I want to tell you about what it is really like in the Soviet Union. What you saw when you came to Poland was very good by our standards. Everything is put on especially for you to give good impression. Until your friends told tonight that this Scottish man called Baird invented the television I have believed all my life that it was a Russian who invented it. I always used to wonder why it was that; in the Soviet Union all of the good things were done by Russians. Why no inventors from Belarus or the Ukraine or the Caucasus? Tony how many lies have I believed all these years? And also our Miners in Poland and the Ukraine! They have nothing!'

Tony Harthill was not sure that he was qualified to listen to this jumbled confessional and he suggested that they turn in for the night. Gennardy apologised and hoped he had not offended the wonderful hospitality afforded him. Tony reassured him and eventually they went to their beds.

The following morning Gennardy was again anxious to ensure that he had not offended his host and was quickly reassured. Despite the reassurance, before they left the house he drew Tony aside and said 'Tony! Last night! I said some things! You will not say my thoughts to anyone?

'Of course not' Tony said reassuringly patting him on the back.

The Polish miner couldn't understand a word of what was being said and concentrated on his breakfast as though he'd never eaten before.

The following day after the group visited a local pit Tony took his charges to the centre of the city of Newcastle upon Tyne. The main shopping thoroughfares were brightly illuminated with the electric light from the Christmas decorations and the streets were thronged with people going about their business. Gennardy and the Polish miner were like children as they walked past the windows of the shops and stores staring at the festive displays.

That night Tony arranged a game of snooker in the home of his old friend Bill Robinson. Gennardy loved the large green baize snooker board and the fun and joking that went on during the evening. Some of Bill's other pals had come over to meet Gennardy and they all had a few drinks from the built-in bar. Bill's wife laid out some delicious savoury snacks and they all had a wonderful evening.

The Polish miner just wanted to eat and drink so Tony said 'Right Lads. You're here tonight to watch the very first international snooker match between Belarus and England. Tonight I am Anton Hartillinov an adopted son of Belarus who will partner Gennardy Mardosov in a match against Great Britain.'

Until that night Gennardy had never held a snooker cue but he loved the game, the atmosphere and the constant joking.

The match was won by Belarus by arrangement with the opposition and encapsulated in friendship and laughter. Gennardy was fascinated by the game and overwhelmed with the hospitality. It was a night he would never forget.

When they arrived back at Tony's house Gennardy took hold of Tony's hand and shook it with the words:

'Tony my friend I have had such a wonderful time. I did not realise that life could be so much fun. I hope that we shall always be friends. You may think me odd perhaps but I will tell you that never in my life have I had a friend. When I was a boy I could share my feelings with my mother and my father. Now my only friend is my Grandmother. I will tell her all about Ashington and my friend Tony when I return. She will like that.'

Tony was embarrassed by this unexpected confession.

'Aye, Well! As long as you've enjoyed yourself, I'm pleased' he said awkwardly clapping his hand on Gennardy's shoulder.

Gennardy's confession prompted Tony to realise that he and Gennardy had more in common than Gennardy might realise. He was a reluctant miner living in a society that the world was passing by whilst Gennardy was living in a society that had been passed by.

Each day of the visit the two men looked forward to the evenings when they would sit together till the early hours of the morning talking about their lives and their future.

They discussed the events that had influenced their views and how they had grown up in contrasting cultures.

One night Tony told Gennardy about the time in 1956 when the uprising against the communists took place in Hungary:

'I remember sitting in the house listening to the radio with my Mother. I can still hear the desperate appeals made by Budapest radio. In my mind I have a vivid picture of a young Hungarian man trapped in an upstairs room appealing to the western world for help as the Russian tanks swept down the streets of Budapest crushing all resistance.' Tony paused, his eyes staring into the distance as though he could see the man, before continuing

'I can still hear his young voice appealing; this is Hungary calling! This is Hungary calling! The West must come to help us.' Tony paused again then went on

'In my mind I can see the man speaking calmly as he clutches the microphone knowing that his message is going out to the world. At the same time he knows that heavily armed Russian soldiers are making their way up the staircase as they close in on him. At any moment his short life will come to an end in a burst of machine gun fire. If he is not killed he knows that he will be incarcerated forever in appalling conditions.'

Gennardy listened staring at Tony as though he too was there.

When Tony finished his story he looked about awkwardly before suggesting that it was time to turn in for the night. Gennardy said he knew of the story but not the way Tony had told it.

Over a few short days, Tony and Gennardy talked openly and earnestly. It was often well through the night when they dragged themselves off to their beds. Each night Tony's wife would awaken with the words, 'What the hell have you two been talking about. D'yu know what time it is?'

The more Tony and Gennardy talked the more Gennardy wanted to know about Tony and his friend Bill. Tony found himself going over his life and telling Gennardy how fate and coincidence had brought him and Bill together so often since the days when Bill Robinson had left Woodhill colliery all those years ago.

He related a tale about one such situation that took place in Wiltshire when Bill Robinson was doing his Military Service in the Royal Air Force in 1957. He had just completed his basic training and the squad was given the weekend off. On the Friday night the lads had gone to the nearby village of Wilton to drink the local ale. In a pub there Bill had chatted up the Barmaid and was quite pleased with himself but by the end of the night they had all had too much to drink and when the bar was closed a very drunk William Robinson waited for the Barmaid. Having stepped outside into the night air Bill was feeling the effects of the local apple cider called scrumpy and by the time the pair had reached the front gate of the girl's house Bill was hard pressed to speak coherently let alone make advances. The last bus back to the camp had already left and a taxi was too expensive so the girl loaned Bill her bicycle on the understanding that he returned it the following day. Bill navigated an erratic exit from Wilton and cycled wildly along a country lane shouting his head off in incomprehensible shouts calling into question the birthright of all military officers wherever they may be. Suddenly bright lights shone from behind him and he turned his head to find its origins. The bicycle with Bill went straight into a hawthorn hedge where the bike lodged allowing Bill to free fall into the field beyond. The occupants of the vehicle were Military Policemen who loaded an unconscious Aircraftsman Robinson and a Ladies cycle into the rear of their landrover vehicle. One of those Military Policemen was Tony Hartill on his very first outing after his transfer from the Royal Artillery which he had joined the previous year just after his twenty first birthday.

Bill got 'clink' and 'jankers' for punishment but the two men met for a quiet drink and good laugh before Bill was posted to Germany where he served most of his national service.

Gennardy loved the tale and envied the friendship between the two men.

When Bill Robinson arrived in Germany the country was still recovering from the Second World War and the German people had got used to working hard in an attempt to put their lives together again. During his time in Germany Bill became friendly with a young German of the same age who was doing his best to learn English. The young German, Klaus, invited Bill to the home of his girlfriend's parents with whom he lived; Klaus had lost both parents at different times during the war.

The girlfriend introduced Bill to her parents and a bond was formed between her father, Yurgen, and Herr Robinson, as her father called Bill initially. The bond was the result of a common interest in furniture and carpentry. Yurgen was manufacturing first quality hardwood furniture to meet the demand generated from the growing prosperity of the people. As the years went by, more and more Germans had disposable income and Yurgens business prospered. When his military service ended Bill married Yurgen's daughter and started a new life for himself selling Yurgens furniture in London. Yurgen thought it a good decision.

With a £200 loan from an old aunt, a £500 loan from a London bank manager and extended credit from Yurgen, Bill rented a small ground floor building in Hackney Wharf, London and went into business. Like Yurgen's business, Bills business flourished and seventeen years later he sold it leaving him in a comfortable situation for the rest of his days providing he invested well.

Bill and his wife and family moved back to his native North East and settled in the small seaside village where his roots were. He then started a new business having secured a franchise from the emerging Japanese photocopier companies. This business grew at a bewildering rate under his guidance and the commitment of his first recruit who was to become Sales Drector and his second recruit who became his Technical Services Director. By 1983 he operated a 'management by exception' style which gave him the time to indulge his other interests. From time to time he would meet with Tony for a few drinks or a game of snooker and enjoy wide ranging discussions and common interests.

Gennardy wanted to know about Tony's exploits so he explained to Gennardy that during his army career every day was an education and he got around the world until he was wounded: He was in Cyprus in 1963 during the Greek Cypriot EOKA terrorist campaign travelling between the towns of Limassol and Paphos when a landmine exploded beneath his jeep. The Sergeant with whom he was travelling died by the roadside a few minutes after the explosion.

After weeks spent in a military hospital Tony made a full recovery but was obliged to leave the army because of a hearing defect. Having to leave the forces was a bitter pill to swallow. He returned home to Woodhill to his wife who had borne him his third son just after the explosion in Cyprus. At first his intention was to move abroad and begin a new life but his wife was adamant in her refusal to consider such an action.

As Tony told the story he wondered, not for the first time, if he had done the right thing in marrying her when she had found herself pregnant at the age of nineteen. He wasn't quite eighteen at the time and in the confusion and conflicting advice he was married before he knew it. To all outward appearances Tony's Mother had gone along with it and she never interfered. His Mother was always helpful but he suspected that she was very disappointed.

The only work in the area that paid reasonably well was at the pit and Tony found himself back there working as an Electrician. By 1969 half of the sixty seven pits in the Northumberland coalfield area had been closed and many miners and their families had moved to collieries in the midlands. The Nottingham coalfield attracted most families. By this time Tony was the Treasurer of Woodhill Miners Union. The job taught him a variety of disciplines and he enjoyed the camaraderie, the ribbing and good natured banter which was one of the great benefits of working within the mining industry.

On the evening before his departure Gennardy told Tony about his Grandmother and the story of his Grandfather's disappearance. This was the first time Gennardy had ever told the story to anyone.

The disillusionment with socialism that had evolved in Tony's thinking over the years became absolute as he and Gennardy talked. Tony imagined how he would feel if the roles were reversed. It made him more determined to work within the trade union and Labour movement to bring about social justice without revolutionary socialism.

When the time came for his guests to leave Tony and Gennardy shook hands earnestly and both vowed that they would try to keep in touch despite the communications problems that existed between their two worlds. They both knew that there was a good chance that they would never see each other again.

Two and a half weeks later Tony Hartill arrived at the Equality Working Men's club at the invitation of his Union Secretary, Ray Mullaney. The club was one of twenty eight similar establishments in the coal town of Ashington. The weather in the North East of England had produced a cold wet day with a stiff breeze from the North making it seem even colder. Both men were wearing waterproof jackets and caps to protect them from the rain and cold.

'Thanks for coming over Tony.' said Mullaney as he guided his guest into a small side lounge that had no customers. 'What will you have?'

'I'll have a pint of Scotch.' he replied.

'What about a little'un to go with it? Keep the cold out!'

'No thanks Ray. Drinking in the middle of the day is not for me. I like my beer at the weekends.'

'Aye you've always been a bit different from the rest of us.' Ray commented as he made his way to the bar. 'Most of us can take a drink at any time; could be your last as they say.'

Tony looked at his watch and then turned his head looking around the room with which he was so familiar.

The club had been a pair of large sandstone fronted houses with large bay windows and a roof of Welsh slate. Extensions had been added to accommodate a concert room and a large bar. Other rooms offered snooker and pool tables.

As Mullaney returned with the drinks Tony Hartill commented, 'Ah didn't realise how shabby this room is. Look at the state of the place.' He went on as he pointed to the chipped tables, the worn materials on the chairs and the bare patches in the carpet.'

Mullaney ignored the observations as he made himself comfortable and looked straight at Tony waiting to see his reaction to the news he had.

'They're shutting Woodhill Tony. The announcement is to be made tomorrow morning.'

Tony leaned back in his chair. His body sagged.

The two men sat in silence looking straight across

the small table at each other before Mullaney continued.

'The government plans to shut another twenty pits. That means that we are losing nearly twenty four thousand members. We need to make a stand. If we continue to lose members at this rate the union will be powerless.'

'What do you mean by a stand Ray? I'll tell you what you mean. Strike action! That's what you mean. Well it's not on' came the reply.

'And why not it's our only weapon.' said Mullaney looking at Tony Hartill through narrowed eyes.'

'In the first place, you know as well as me, Woodhill has been worked out for years. What's the point in striking to keep pits open if they're knackered. And in the second place the people who bear the pain and hardship of strike action are the men; the miners themselves' Tony Hartill stuck his chin out towards Mullaney as he spoke. 'And they are the people who elected us to look after their interests.'

'Well whose interests do you think we're looking after?' said Mullaney becoming irritated.

'Not the Miners. And that's for certain.' Tony quickly replied.

'We had a strike eight years ago and we won.' said Mullaney swelling with pride.

'Won, What do you mean won? Some of the lads were still paying off their debts years later.'

Realising he was beginning to shout Tony Hartill lowered his voice.

'Look Ray, the world is changing, and changing fast. We need to use the strike threat but keep the miners in work and pay. Coal will never need hundreds of thousands of miners again technology has...'

Mullaney interjected scowling. 'I might have known whose side you were on. You've always been the same.

Why can't you be like the rest of the lads and tow the union line'

'You mean tow your line' he replied.

'The union can do without smart arses like you pal' said Mullaney pointing his finger at his guest.

'Why is it that you always start to threaten when you can't get your own way' asked Tony Hartill. 'As Regional Secretary you are the top man around here Ray, the men need bloody leadership. We need to think this through. We need a different strategy.'

Ray Mullaney reached over to pick up his coat as he said.

'I'm off!'

'Suit yourself.' Said a grim faced Tony Hartill.

Mullaney made his way to the main bar.

He was a member of the club committee a position that entitled him to twenty free pints of beer a week plus the occasional 'perk' from the Steward who managed the club under the instructions of the club committee.

Mullaney never talked. He shouted everything and rarely was without a smile as though he was always pleased with himself. His largesse was as big as his red face and ample belly.

Unusually, on this occasion the florid features of Mullaney were in repose and for once he sat on his own in a corner of the bar. A group of three retired coal miners sat playing dominoes at the other end of the room. A pint of beer was within easy reach of each participant. A couple of younger men stood at the bar drinking pints of beer prior to going home to get some sleep before beginning work down the pit that night in the fore shift. A third fore shift worker entered the bar and shouted 'Aye lads', 'Aye Ray' in a loud voice. Everyone responded with an 'Aye.'

Ray Mullaney responded with a wide automatic smile and in an even louder voice 'Ya havin a couple afore ye gan te bed then.'

'Aye, two or three pints then off te bed for a few hours before ah put the next shift in'

Both men laughed loudly.

'Aye lad' they both said in unison.

Mullaney was pleased that the man did not join him. Unlike normal times he wanted to be on his own. He wanted to think. Thinking seemed easier with a pint of beer in his hand and he had a lot to think about.

Apart from being a 'committee man' in the Equality Club and a local Labour Councillor Mullaney was also the Area Secretary of the Coal Miners Union, the CMU, of Great Britain. The previous night he had returned from the monthly national meeting of Area Secretaries and Chairmen at the Doncaster headquarters in South Yorkshire. The agenda had been gone through over two days and three very enjoyable nights when the beer had flowed and an agreeable mixed company had, 'put the icing on the cake', as Mullaney would boast. What had distressed him when he had had time to digest it was the half-hour private conversation he had had with the National General Secretary, Albert Markham.

Albert Markham and Ray Mullaney went back a long way. Both had an interest in Revolutionary Socialism. *'Marxism fulfilled'* Albert had called it many years previously.

They had met originally at Summer Schools organised by the CMU and the Labour Party.

In those days they were just a couple of young lads encouraged by others to take an interest in Union affairs. Since so few of the Union members had taken a similar interest the two had soon found themselves in a situation where their careers, their passions and their personal wellbeing were wrapped up in the Trade Union and Labour movement. Both were groomed as public speakers and became familiar with the history of the Trade Union movement, British Constitution and the workings of National and Local Government. Both had shown flair and had steadily made progress; but whilst Ray had done well Albert Markham had discovered his own power in oratory. As a public speaker Albert was in a class of his own. He came to believe that his oratory was a force of unlimited power. Because of his abilities Albert had become the youngest General Secretary in the history of the CMU; once elected Albert embarked upon his own agenda.

As Ray had entered Albert's office Albert held his hand out to be shaken as though they had not seen each other for ages.

'Aye Ray' said Albert, 'How's things in the North East neck of the woods?'

'Much the same' said Ray. 'No problems really, the lads back the Union to the hilt. Only thing is we have shrunk in membership. Numbers are well down again and when those bloody Tories are through we'll have no bloody pits left to keep the Union alive.'

'Aye, they think they've got us by the balls Ray'

'Ah expect not' said Ray. 'Ahm not prepared to sit back and let those Tory Capitalist bastards ruin us.'

'Well said Ray'. Albert replied.

Albert Markham never touched alcohol but he recognised the desire of Ray to have a glass in his hand whenever possible. 'A *little un* before dinner' Markham said as he poured whisky into an ample tumbler and passed it to Ray who introduced a small amount of lemonade. 'Single malt whiskey Eh Albert, nothing but the best Eh'

Markham did not drink but he could not see the

point of adding lemonade to single malt whisky. He did not respond.

'Grand drop of stuff this'

'Aye it is that Ray' came Markham's reply.

Ray was always relaxed in the company of Albert. He felt doubly so in the deep leather chair with his right hand holding the tumbler as it rested on his knee.

By contrast Albert was never at ease or relaxed in any company though he disguised the fact very well through masterly practised care. He pulled up a simple, straight backed, chair and sat facing Ray just a couple of feet in front of him.

Alberts drawn face seemed luminous to Ray as he sat staring straight into it. His florid features looked up slightly at Albert whilst Albert stared down at him. Ray suddenly felt a little uneasy.

Albert started talking. 'The time is now Ray to put those Tory bastards in their place.'

Nothing was more appealing to Ray Mullaney than the thought of 'putting those bastards in their place'. As Mullaney had looked into the face of Markham that night the slight uneasiness felt by him turned to a mixture of joy and panic as he realised that Albert was planning to challenge the British Government and its leader, Prime Minister, Margaret Thatcher.

Albert explained that the whole of the working class was to be involved, but that the detail was to be kept a secret until the very last minute. The trusted few which included a swollen with pride Ray Mullaney would be advised of the detail as events unfolded. 'Keep your lads worked up a bit Ray.' Markham had said. 'They tend to be less militant in Northumberland than the other areas so keep the buggers on their toes'.

'Don't worry' said Ray 'I'll not let you down. Tony Hartill's the only one who ever gets in the way and I'll stitch him up.'

As Ray Mullaney sat in the Equality club that lunchtime his pride was diluted with fear. He wanted to talk it over with someone but that was out of the question. This was serious stuff! Ray was never the one to be on the losing side and he wanted some assurance that the plan for a general strike was likely to succeed bringing about the revolutionary victory of the working class and a forever Socialist Britain. 'Or did he?'

After all he could retire in five years time when he was sixty. He had a good salary, an excellent pension and lots of other perks and these things couldn't be taken away from him whatever happened. Ray decided not to put his head above the parapet but to go along with things as usual. Whatever happened he would see to it that he was safe. All he had to do was agitate in private, with a few reliable hard men, and appear to be caring and responsible in public.

Chapter 2

The joy that British Prime Minister Margaret Thatcher felt in May 1983 after winning her second General Election was overshadowed by the battle with the Coal Miners that she felt was bound to come.

The former Prime Minister James Callaghan had briefed her when she was the Leader of the opposition before becoming Prime Minister herself. Ironically Callaghan had lost the election after endless and often mindless strikes by the Trade Union movement culminating in what was to be labelled: 'The winter of discontent' during the dark winter months of 1978 and 1979 when workers were called out on strike by their union leaders, ad nausea. The consequences of the strike had been awful with people being unable to bury their dead and refuse lying uncollected in the streets for weeks on end.

Western Governments were well aware that the Russians would use every opportunity to destabilise the Western democracies and those countries that were supportive of the West.

British Intelligence sources in the USSR and elsewhere round the world reported back to London. The information and signals were analysed and processed in the usual manner. Important Intelligence was communicated to the Prime Minister's office and then to the cabinet by Mrs Thatcher. Nothing of any significance regarding the destabilisation of Britain was noted.

The 'destabilisation theory' or 'European Cuba Theory' as it was sometimes called was not new to the leaders and strategists of the European governments and especially the British Government.

Albert Markham's activities in South Yorkshire had

not gone unnoticed in 1974 when he had led militant miners and others into a ferocious campaign of strikes and mass picketing. On the contrary insurrection from within was being constantly monitored.

With Markham now heading the CMU collective wisdom of successive governments concluded that the European Cuba Theory strategy was more likely to be attempted.

When the highly respected Jack Gorton had retired as National General Secretary of the CMU he had actively campaigned to stop Albert Markham succeeding him. He was unsuccessful and advised the then Prime Minister Callaghan that Markham had his own agenda. Callaghan respectfully accepted Gorton's advice but he had already made his mind up that if and when Markham and his colleagues decided to attempt to hold the country to ransom by calling the miners out on strike; the country would be ready. Callaghan had ordered the National Coal Board to increase its reserve coal stocks as quickly as discretion allowed. This was done and on her succession to the Prime Minister's office Margaret Thatcher had accelerated that policy so that by 1983 almost 50 Million metric tonnes of coal stocks stood on British Soil. Even with these stocks Thatcher knew that an all out prolonged strike by the miners under the spell of Markham would be an almighty tussle.

In December 1983, just three weeks after the visit by Gennardy and the Polish miners, Owen Williams was given House of Commons clearance to visit trade union leaders in Checkoslovakia. This was an annual event and considered a matter of routine. Ostensibly Williams was there as a member of the House of Commons attempting to improve Britain's tenuous links with the

Eastern European countries. He was to be away eight days. After flying to West Berlin he took a taxi to the border crossing known as Checkpoint Charlie that was the most famous crossing point along the line known as the iron curtain that divided Eastern Europe and Western Europe. He left his taxi and walked past the American guards and then the East German Border Police on the other side where he was met by a man and a woman and ushered into an official car before being driven off.

Operating inside Eastern Germany was difficult for Western Intelligence but the reports that came back stated that Williams had not been seen by their contacts in the East German city of Leipzig where Williams was supposed to meet Trade Union leaders from Eastern Europe.

On his return to London Williams complained that he had been confined to bed for several days when he had first arrived in Liepzig. This story was to explain his non-appearance at official gatherings during the first few days. He knew that his absence would not go unheeded and he had made a point of appearing with the East German miner's leaders on the day before his return. This appearance together with a picture and a small article in the East Berlin Newspaper reporting his indisposition was cover for the real purpose of his visit

That same week all enquirers for Markham were advised that he was in a meeting and he would return the call as soon as possible if no one else could deal with it. Callers were further advised that it could be a day or two before their call was returned since Mr Markham was so busy.

In fact Williams had been flown straight out of Berlin to Minsk, the capital of Belarus and Markham had gone by ferry from Liverpool to Dublin where he had a meeting with a long standing Irish Republican contact who was a go-between and a passport fixer.

Markham had got through British Customs at Liverpool and Irish customs in Dublin. His passport had his profession down as Mining Engineer and he had changed his name and his hairstyle, he wore bifocal spectacles and darkened his normally fair hair and eyebrows. The passport was recently stolen and genuine; only the photograph was changed. After his meeting in Dublin he flew to Paris and on to Vienna where he was met and taken by car over the border to Bratislava. A Russian military transport aircraft then flew him to Minsk.

The meetings in Minsk began as soon as Markham arrived. Williams was already there. Plakinov wanted to see his man eyeball to eyeball, he also wanted to go over all of the plans; particularly the assurance that no involvement by the Soviet Union could be proven. Markham was to be furnished with huge sums of cash in Sterling and hiding the trail and source of this cash was critical if an embarrassing diplomatic incident was to be avoided. Interference by a foreign power was dangerous.

Although it was risky having the two men in Minsk Plakinov wanted to meet Markham in order to confirm his own instincts and assess the judgement of his chosen man.

They were all staying in the Orbital Hotel on the outskirts of Minsk. The Orbital was Minsk's newest and finest building. Three of the ten floors were booked for this meeting. The first floor was empty. The accommodation for Plakinov's entourage and the meeting room was on the second floor and the third floor was also empty. The lift attendant was not

31

allowed to stop at floors one, two or three and armed guards attended the main staircase and the fire escape staircase.

The three men met regularly for sessions lasting one to two hours with two of Plakinov's interpreters. By late afternoon on the second day Plakinov was satisfied and happy. He invited his two guests, together with his own team, to a little party with some entertainment that evening.

Plakinov's entourage arrived in the huge hotel restaurant from their rooms on the second floor and took their places around three large round tables immediately before the stage. Plakinov and his special guests were already sitting round a large circular table that was placed a few yards to the left of the stage. A fine net curtain was hung round the table from the ceiling offering privacy. A group of singers, musicians and dancers provided traditional Russian entertainment.

The other guests included some off duty security guards, the hotel manager, Plakinov's assistants and a stand by interpreter who had been sent for the previous day when one of Plakinov's regular interpreters had complained of feeling ill. As it happened the services of the stand-by interpreter were never used and he found himself sitting next to a young woman.

'I am very pleased to be here.' He said to her.

'My name is Gennardy Mardosov.'

'I know!' replied the woman. 'I made the arrangements for this party; acting on Komrad Plakinov's instructions; of course. My name is Li Sarich.'

The two shook hands.

Li then introduced Gennardy by his first name to the others on the table.

Everyone said 'Welcome Komrad' and went on talking eating and drinking. They all seemed to know one another.

'Are you enjoying this assignment?' asked Li.

'Well I have had nothing to do so far but I appreciate the invitation to the party.'

'Komrad Plakinov is very happy and he wants to celebrate.'

'I am privileged.' said Gennardy deferentially.

There was a pause before Gennardy said.

'You must work in Moscow most of the time.'

'Yes I do,' she replied 'but I don't come from there. I'm from Mongolia. I'm not Mongolian it's because my parents settled there.'

'That's amazing!' Gennardy replied. 'My parents were stationed in the Capital, Ulan Bator. I spent part of my childhood there.'

'I can speak some Mongolian Chinese.' said Gennardy.

'So do I.' replied Li. 'Besides, I have Mongolian blood. Just a little I think!'

The two began to speak in the strange dialect peculiar to Ulan Bator. Li was thrilled and she enjoyed the company of this man of many parts.

Gennardy found Li very attractive. He was pleased to sit by her and teased her a little with his knowledge of Mongolia. Li was thrilled. It was not often that she had the opportunity to speak her own language and have a light hearted conversation with a man unafraid to pay attention to her.

The food and drink was lavish and everyone was feeling comfortable with the pleasure of enjoying such good food taken with Rumanian wine or Vodka or both.

Gennardy drank little. To be unavailable through the influence of alcohol could have serious consequences. Li also drank little for the same reason but nevertheless as the evening wore on they both relaxed and chatted comfortably.

During their conversation Li commented on Plakinov's appreciation of western products, particularly special Scotch whisky and clothes. Gennardy gently boasted that he had been to England. He decided against promoting it too much and said it was all right but Russia was mother earth for all comrades.

At this point Li confided in a low voice that the two men behind the net curtain were from Britain. Gennardy was surprised that someone in her position should divulge information so offhandedly. On the other hand he had been called in at short notice because he was an interpreter with an impeccable record of service so her indiscretion was hardly important.

Plakinov was well pleased with himself. He was impressed with the meticulous detail in the plan of action shown to him by Markham. His only real concern was in finding the large sums of money Markham demanded to ensure that he could carry out the plan. Overall he was in high spirits.

As the party went on Plakinov appeared from behind the curtain with one of the entertainers, a mature looking woman wearing an off shoulder white blouse as part of her central European gypsy dress. The guests cheered and everyone clapped to the music as the couple danced around the stage. Clearly enjoying himself Plakinov stopped as the music ended and beckoned to someone else behind the curtain to join him. A few moments later Albert Markham and partner danced their way across to the Plakinov dancing partnership and attempted to emulate the entertainers dancing beside them.

Gennardy Mardasov gaped in disbelief when he saw

Markham.

'Markham with Plakinov?' he thought.

Gennardy glanced at Li as the two couples were exposed to his view. Like those round him he clapped his hands in time with the music and looked away from the people on the stage and at the people on his table smiling as he did so to encourage the idea that he was enjoying the evening as much as them. In fact his pulse was pounding in his ears. He knew that he was in a dangerous situation if Markham saw him and recognised him.

Gennardy continued to smile and move his head in unison with the others at his table whilst his brain raced. The song and the band seemed to last such a long time. He lifted his napkin up to his face and glanced at the stage again to see a sweating and panting Plakinov dancing alongside Owen Williams who had also emerged to join in the festivities.

Eventually the music stopped and the three conspirators returned behind their curtain to the applause of the others. Gennardy cheered and applauded as hard as anyone whilst keeping his head turned.

'That was good to see people dancing and having such a good time. Comrad Plakinov must be very happy to amuse his friends so much.' Li commented.

'Yes!' replied Gennardy. 'Good food, plenty to drink and some good Russian music. What more could anyone ask for.'

There was a pause in their conversation whilst Li used her fork to toy with a morsel of food on her plate.

'Do you dance?' she asked suddenly turning to look at Gennardy.

'Well, yes I do' he replied 'We should make a new rule that everyone should dance for at least half an hour every day.'

Li laughed at the idea of such frivolity saying 'what a wonderful thought.' Then she said. 'Do they dance much in London?'

'I think so' Gennardy replied 'I saw some people dancing in England but I haven't been to London.'

Li then casually said 'Komrad Plakinov is going to London next year to honour Komrad Markham as a Hero of the Soviet Union.

Gennardy was hard put to hide his incredulity, not only at her indiscretion but also the content. Shortly afterwards the assembled company were advised that their host and his guests had left and the party ended.

The following day Gennardy had no commitments. He had hardly slept. His mind going over and over the same thoughts: No one could get to Plakinov without the business being very serious. Plakinov in London! Handing out Soviet awards! Impossible!

Yet Li had been matter of fact. She couldn't have invented the idea. Gennardy knew that he had stumbled into a dangerous situation. Knowing what he did could be extremely dangerous. It was probable that the identities of Plakinov's British guests were unknown to everyone at that party except him and Li. He could disappear without trace if there was the slightest suspicion by Plakinov and his cronies that there was even the possibility of a breach in security. He had been called in to the Orbital in an emergency without any special security clearance. The meeting obviously had top secret classification. He had been given the assignment at short notice; but would he have been given the assignment if Plakinov and his immediate personal security team knew that he had been to England and he was aware of the identity and position of Plakinov's guests? Furthermore there were rivals in his office in Minsk who would be quite happy to ingratiate themselves with senior officers at Gennardy's expense if they discovered his secret.

When the party was over he had shaken hands with Li and thanked her for being such a good companion. It was obvious to him that she had enjoyed herself and he was sure that he had struck a chord with her but a romantic connection was not high on his agenda. He felt insecure. He had walked away from the Orbital hotel feeling very vulnerable and his thoughts ranged over his trip to England a few months earlier.

He couldn't stop comparing the warm, comfortable houses that he had been in during his short visit as a guest of Tony Hartill. Each house had its own independent central heating system supplemented by a coal or gas fire in the lounge. All of the floors in the houses were covered in fitted carpets and he imagined what it would be like if he was going home to such luxury.

Since his return to Minsk the temperature had rarely risen above freezing point and the bitter northerly winds seemed to drill the cold into his bones. Too often he and his fellow citizens were without heat and electricity because of endless power failures.

Gennardy felt insecure and friendless and he was cold and he was hungry and he was angry.

Chapter 3

A month after Tony Hartill's meeting with Mullaney in the Equality club Woodhill colliery was closed.

Tony was standing in the pit yard as the last cage rose to the earth's surface from the black depths he had got to know so well. With scores of others he stood watching as the men in orange overalls who had made their final examination of the underground workings, left the cage that had been lifted up the shaft for the last time. The throng of men and women stood as though commanded to do so like sailors watching their ship sinking into the cold waters of a dark ocean. All eyes looked up at the huge wheel that had taken men and coal up and down the shaft for over fifty years. They all knew that it would never turn again.

Tony couldn't help asking himself what it had all been for.

In his head he could hear the voices of the men below chiding one another in fearful language and no one took offence. He could hear the laughter. He could hear the cries of pain from the men he'd seen injured. He remembered his first day at a junction in the pit when a man walked out of the darkness escorted by his `marrer' (colleague). The man wore no helmet. His head was swathed in bandages till it looked like a Sikh turban. Blood seeped through the turban and the man's filthy shirt and trousers was covered in his blood. He could hear the voice of his friend Bill Robinson shouting to nobody in the gloom 'Oh God get me out of this hellhole'

Vivid recollections of his own first day down in the pit came to him as though it was yesterday. He was fifteen and on returning home after work he had told his mother all about his day. She had told him to write a story about it and instead he had written a poem for her that he could still recite, word for word. His mother was still proud of that poem. As he stood he recited it to himself.

Up in the morn when the light kisses dawn
along on a bike to the pit
Follow the path that follows the line
where the coal wagons sit

Filled with excitement yet terror and fright
in to get changed with the rest
who tease and rib with never a slight
each having withstood the test.

Up to the pit head and through the airlock
into the flat on the crown
sitting on haunches or 'honkers' they call them
as the miners wait to go down.

A steel rope is flashing coming up at high speed
lifting a cage from the depths
clashing and clanking with ear splitting noise
till the cage comes to rest on the keps.

Earth's oldest smells mix with cigarette smoke
as the miners suck strong the last draw
then they enter the cage which will carry them off
to caverns beneath the earth's floor.

'Quick'; into the cage all packed in there tight
wearing a battery and a hat with a light
the keps are withdrawn and the cage starts to fall
and weightlessness happens and voices can't call

It falls down forever; Dear God; will it brake
will the man in the winding house stay wide awake?
or will he forget and the cage falls to hell
and no one will know of their thoughts as they fell.

Tony Hartill could not remember the last time he
had cried but at that moment the lump in his throat
could not be swallowed. He shuffled his feet, as if on a
signal others did the same, and then they all moved
slowly away. Two women standing nearby wept
openly.

Tony's father had always impressed upon him the
belief that all of life was a conspiracy against working
people; particularly the coal miner's. Tony's Mother
was always annoyed by what she called the prejudiced
over simplifications of her husband. She emphasised
the power of knowledge and the dangers of prejudice.
She was religious and a devout Methodist as were her
parents. Her father had been a Methodist Minister.

'I came from stock who founded the Labour and
Trade Union movement.' she would say when she
became annoyed. 'We are supposed to be working for a
society free from ignorance, poverty and prejudice' she
would declare.

Mrs Hartill never really argued or contradicted her
husband. That was futile. It just made things worse.
Instead she would go on to raise some positive topic of
conversation which was more objective than subjective
in an attempt to retain harmony and bring
enlightenment by her example.

As an avid reader she would borrow and read at
least two books a week from the lending Library
despite her busy days. Tony too had got into the habit
of reading and he and his mother would try to find

words that the other could not spell. Although he did not realise it at the time he had his Mother to thank for a home based education that taught him to learn.

The coal mining communities were a man's world where everything revolved around pit work. Like most of the kids he went to school with Tony looked forward to the day he could go down the pit to join the army of men working in their own nationalised coal mines.

The reality was not at all as he imagined it.

Shortly after his fifteenth birthday, he joined the National Coal Board. After a three month training scheme he was assigned to work in Woodhill. A Deputy Overman took him underground to a junction where four tunnels converged. One of the tunnels was on a steep incline and wagons (tubs they were called) full of coal were pulled out of three horizontal tunnels and disconnected on a landing before being transferred to the inclined tunnel. They were lowered down the incline to the bottom of the shaft where they were then transferred in a cage to the surface. The tubs were more than a metre long, a metre wide and above waist high. They were hauled along by a wire rope. A heavy metal clip called a hambone because of its shape was attached to the wire rope and a chain from the hambone was connected to the tub. Tony's job was to attach or detach these hambone clips from the steel haulage wire rope that pulled them along or lowered them down the slope.

Quite often the tubs would be derailed throwing up clouds of choking dust through which it was impossible to see. Electrical lighting in the pit was poor at the best of times and only junctions and landings were illuminated.

To put the derailed tubs back on the rails involved pushing your backside against the tub and attempting to nudge it back into position. The miners doing this job wore an `arse flapper' - a piece of rubber and canvass conveyor belting which was suspended from the miner's trouser belt to protect the lower back. At first the task seemed impossible but experienced miners would show how it was done. After a while the newcomers got the hang of it.

Sometimes full tubs would come off the rails (off the way) when being lowered down the incline. Hambone chains would snap and the tubs would hurtle down the steep gradient crashing into others, breaking more hambone chains, and then the wire rope would lash wildly across the inclined tunnel with a force which could easily decapitate a man. At the same time tubs flew off the rails in all directions hitting the tunnel roof sometimes and crashing into the empty tubs being hauled up the incline on the other set of rails parallel to those on which the full tubs travelled. When these incidents occurred, the choking dust thrown around by the endless collisions and impacts meant that all that could be seen by the miner from the light of his cap lamp was light reflecting off tens of thousands of glittering dust particles dancing before his eyes. Miners would stumble into a manhole for refuge and wait until the choking dust settled by which time coal and stone dust filled every exposed body cavity. When the mayhem subsided the men would emerge from the security of the manholes and come out to put things right in the eerie silence that followed the deafening explosive hell. Then the cursing would begin and go on unendingly until the men and boys made the system operational again. Despite the cursing and the awful work the men were good-humoured and cheerful and there was always a good feeling of shared adversity among them. Tony decided that the men liked the pit because each man was dependent upon his fellows and they were a family of men determined not to let each other down. It made sense; after all, their lives could depend upon it.

Despite hating every moment in the pit Tony Hartill endured the next six months without complaint, waiting, hoping and praying that he would be offered an apprenticeship by the National Coal Board that would remove him from his living hell as he saw it. Before going to work in the pit he had not realised that there were no toilets in a coal mine. There was nowhere to wash hands. When it was time to eat he sat on a box and ate his 'bait' where he worked.

Despite the camaraderie and the wages he found it hard to tolerate.

The only solace that Tony enjoyed from his initiation into mining was his friendship with Bill Robinson, a young man of the same age working nearby. Bill would disconnect the hambones from the front of the sets of full tubs coming into the junction and Tony would connect the hambones to the wire at the back of the set to lower the tubs down the incline. After five months both lads got a message from 'on bank' (the surface) to see the Union Secretary. Tony was offered an apprenticeship as an Electrician, Bill was offered training as an Analytical Chemist. Tony was thrilled at the thought of getting away from those hambones and doing something where he could work with hand and head whereas Bill Robinson astounded everyone by turning down the best offer of the lot; the chance to train as a Chemist and go to University.

Despite his tender years Bill Robinson believed that nuclear energy would replace coal and that in the longer term the coal mines would become redundant. Two days previously he had accepted a job offer to train as an apprentice Mechanical Engineering Draftsman in Newcastle upon Tyne. He told a bemused

Colliery Manager and an even more bemused Union Secretary that he wanted to get as far away from coal mines as possible.

Although he had hated the pit Bill never lost his affection for the coal miners. Years later he would amuse friends and company by telling stories about his days as a miner: One such story was about the day the Union Secretary had told him that he had been selected to train as an Analytical Chemist. The Secretary had been unable to get his tongue around the word 'analytical' and in despair offered Bill the job as a Dust Sampler because it was easier to say.

Before the coal mining closures began coal mining was the primary industry and almost the whole economy was built around it. The most able people competed for a career in colliery management or a career in the Trade Union movement through the CMU. Many an able coal miner had become a Colliery Manager or a National, Regional or Area Secretary of the union. Some had taken the Union and Labour Party route to become prominent Councillors or Members of Parliament.

Once the pit closure programme began in the 1960's the most able people recognised that the career prospects were becoming increasingly limited and as a result ever more talented and able people moved away to areas and activities which had a long term potential. The result of this was that the nineteen seventies saw a clutch of, in the main, less able and more militant people being elected to prominent posts within the Union.

Tony Hartill was increasingly distressed by the quality of leadership to which the membership was subjected. He felt that all reason had been abandoned and replaced by a destructive dogma that he detested.

Despite the ongoing list of pit closures attendance at union meetings was poor. Those who retained the values of moderation and what was the best strategy to give the maximum return for the members were continuously shouted down and even threatened by those who supported the simplistic instant remedies floated by the likes of Ray Mullaney. By the end of the seventies the meetings had become a farce. They were all about national party politics and how only state intervention in all industrial processes was the only way that power could be available to the miners. At every union meeting a resolution would be passed demanding the sinking of new coal mines, more Government subsidies for coal and the nationalisation of more industries.

At the time of Gennardy's visit to England Tony was forty eight years old. As the years had gone by he had become more and more irritated with the leadership of the CMU and the same old Socialist propaganda. It was outdated and it was holding back progress. Gennardy's visit had reinforced his disillusionment with his life and environment. Furthermore too many long serving CMU officials were now living off the backs of fewer and fewer members. Membership was only a tiny fraction of what it had been twenty years before and he was angered by his belief that many union officials like Mullaney were exploiting the miners.

A regional conference of the CMU was scheduled for the first week in January 1984 to debate the future of the Coal mining industry and the strategy of the CMU. To get a resolution on the agenda at the conference it was necessary to move the resolution in a branch meeting and to have the resolution endorsed by a majority vote of those in attendance. Tony drafted a resolution calling for an open independent inquiry to produce a realistic policy for coal. If that meant further pit closures an economic regeneration programme would be drawn up to provide alternative training and an adequate compensation package for miners and investment in the declining coal field areas to bring new industries.

An attendance of nine members including officers was about the norm at most branch meetings. To win the resolution Tony reckoned that he would need about twelve members to vote for his resolution to guarantee a win. Ray Mullaney was almost certain to turn up and he would urge the members to vote against it and the nine would almost certainly do as he suggested.

In the days leading up to the meeting Tony thought he had persuaded almost forty members at Ellington to come to the meeting and support his resolution. He felt he had done enough until he arrived at the meeting room to find that only twelve of those who had promised to come were in attendance. Nevertheless if they all voted his way he would still win.

The Branch Chairman sat at the end of a long table covered in green baize material. Ashtrays were spread around the table and the air was filled with cigarette smoke even before the meeting began. Six members sat at the table either side of the Chairman and the Secretary sat on the opposite end. The other members sat in chairs behind those at the table.

After clearing his throat the Chairman opened the meeting commenting on the remarkably high attendance. As he did so he looked across at Mullaney who sat to his right and then to Tony Hartill who sat at the middle of the table on his left.

Normal business procedures were gone through in time honoured fashion until the Chairman announced the next item on the agenda which was a resolution to send to Regional Conference if passed.

'Tony Hartill to move' he announced 'Dickie Sanderson to Second.'

Tony opened his papers and looked at a list of the headings he planned to expand upon as he developed his argument. He had been talking for only a few minutes when a voice behind Mullaney shouted. 'We can all read. We've read the resolution and it's time to put it to the vote otherwise we'll be here all night listening to this junk.'

His interjection was punctured with expletives prompting the Chairman to caution the man with the words. 'Haway Harry! Tha's nee need to gan on like that'

'Whay man the buggers dead against his own union. We want to fight to keep the pits open and he's ask'in us to co-operate with the bloody Tories to shut them.'

A chorus of 'Aye Harry's right.' sounded off as one behind Mullaney.

Mullaney looked at Tony as he said. 'If we passed this rubbish we'd be the laughing stock of the union. If the other side get wind of this they'll say we're split and walk all over us. I'm asking you to withdraw the resolution.'

Suddenly there was a silence and a tension in the room that had everyone gripped. All eyes were on Tony. Tony's eyes stared straight into those of Mullaney across the table. Slowly he looked into the hostile eyes of the man to Mullaney's right and then to the next man and then into those of the men sitting behind Mullaney. Inside his ears he could feel his blood thumping through his head and his mouth was dry. His heart was pounding in his chest. He clenched his fists.

'There was a time.' He said quietly 'When this union was a legend for its commitment to social justice and fairness. It produced leaders who argued their point of view and who listened to those who disagreed: Leaders who dedicated their lives and their talents to furthering the interests of the miners. Our future as miners is bleak and I fervently believe that the British people will be prepared to give us as good deal. But that will not happen unless we reason our argument and explain our position and our desire for new jobs and a new local economy.'

Mullaney intervened. 'All this fancy talk is getting us nowhere. Do you think that Maggie Thatcher and all those pigs in London give a damn about us; Course not. This is the only thing they understand.' He went on as he looked at his fist shaking in the air.

'That's right Ray' came a chorus from behind Mullaney.

'No more talk. Put it to the vote Chairman.' bellowed the man sitting next to Mullaney.

Tony looked at the man and felt sick. He knew the man well. Rarely did he put a full week's work in. Most weeks he only worked three shifts and spent the rest of his time drinking in the club. His wife was often so bruised she wouldn't leave her home.

'All right then.' agreed Tony. 'We'll put it to the vote by secret ballot.'

'Show of hands!' said Mullaney. 'We need to know where everyone stands.'

Tony looked at the Chairman and quoted the rule book. 'The mover of a motion has the right to a secret ballot if he so wishes. Correct?'

'That's never happened before in my time.' said Mullaney.

Before he knew what he was saying Tony volunteered, 'Maybe we would be in much better shape 'in your time' if things were a little more democratic.' Tony regretted what he said as soon as he completed his sentence: He knew that he was just inflaming matters.

Mullaney glowered at him. 'I'll just bloody well remember that Mister.' he seethed.

The Secretary gave all those present a slip of plain paper and the Chairman declared:

'Right then, all those for the motion write yes on your slip, all those against write no, the Secretary will collect the slips.'

The few seconds it took to collect the slips hung like the cigarette smoke that ghosted its way in the electric light.

Mullaneys followers gasped as the voting was declared at eleven for the motion and ten against.

'Okay pal.' shouted Mullaney. 'But the number of votes for and against goes with the motion to the region. Tony resisted his desire to smile at his little victory as he said. 'That decision Mr Chairman is in dispute and I suggest we vote on that too by secret ballot.'

To Mullaney's disgust a sheepish looking Chairman said 'If we must so be it!'

The Secretary dealt out the slips again and the vote was the same, ten for and eleven against.

The Chairman called order and declared. 'That's it then. The motion moved by Tony Hartill is passed and the motion goes to region without the votes for and against; any other business.'

No one spoke so Tony smiled at the colleague to his left as he rose from his chair. At the same time the man sitting opposite to him lunged across the table grabbing his tie. The man pulled with all his strength pulling Tony's head across and down to the table. The man sitting next to Tony's assailant grabbed him shouting. 'Leave loose of the tie. Let go! Let Go.' He screamed.

Tony was helpless his head jerking up and down and unable to reach the man.

After a few seconds he couldn't get his breath and his arms were flailing desperately trying to get a purchase on his attacker.

The man holding the attacker put his arm around the man's neck pulling his head back until the man released his grip. Tony fell back in his chair gasping for breath and struggling to remove the stricture round his neck.

During this time the Chairman was shrieking at the top of his voice 'Stop! Stop! Get the Police. Stop it you crazy bastards.'

Suddenly there was silence except for the gasping breathing of Tony and his attacker. Every man was on his feet waiting for something else to happen. Eyes were on full alert as each man jerked his head from side to side looking for the next incident.

The Chairman mopped his brow and shuffled his portly frame towards the door.

'I want every man out of here in orderly fashion.' He shouted. Then looking at Mullaney he said. 'Ray, you stay with him.' pointing to Tony's assailant. Then he said. 'Tony! You get out first and don't hang around.'

No one spoke and the men filed out of the room in orderly fashion.

Tony was furious at being caught unawares. A physical assault was not something he had anticipated. He would have liked to report the matter to the Police but he knew that in the eyes of the men that would be counterproductive. Better still he would have liked an opportunity to give his assailant a lesson in hand to hand combat. As usual his instincts were frustrated. He consoled himself with the fact that he would get the opportunity now to put his motion to the Regional conference and then it would get some publicity.

In the weeks leading up to the regional conference

Tony worked hard on his speech. He would have twelve minutes to move the motion and his 'seconder' would have four minutes. The Union Library in Newcastle upon Tyne gave him a wealth of information on the history of the leaders over the years with copies of their speeches. The more recent history of pit closures showed that the mining industry had lost far more pits under Labour Governments than under the Tories but he decided not to point that out. He simply listed the number of pits that had been closed in each of the last three decades.

The city Library in Newcastle upon Tyne furnished him with a wealth of information on the reserves of gas and oil in the North Sea and elsewhere and he also investigated the prospects for alternative energy sources and the prospects for new industries.

Until he began his researches he did not realise how drastically the demand for coal had been reduced by the government act to reduce pollution by the programme to switch from coal fires to smokeless fuels for domestic heating and ironically even the miners had to convert to smokeless fuels. The whole of Winsbreck was to be a smoke free zone by the year 1990 and that programme was already taking place.

The most difficult part of his speech was keeping it within the twelve minutes. When he had finished it he asked his wife Maggie to listen to it but she wasn't interested so he telephoned Bill Robinson who invited him round to his house.

Bill was impressed with the research that had gone into the speech and complimented Tony with a job well done.

'I got wind of the branch meeting. Apparently some bloke didn't like the tie you were wearing.' said Bill sardonically.

Tony laughed. 'I love the way you interpret events. I

thought he was pulling my head off. In future I'm wearing those clip-on things.'

The two men sat comfortably in the company of one another. First of all discussing the contents of the speech and then just chatting. Bill always had some amusing anecdotes to cap a very rewarding evening. Tony was grateful that he was there as a bulwark in a hostile sea.

The regional Conference was held in the Headquarters of the Durham CMU. The building was grand by any architectural standards and had been built in the heyday of the CMU. The meeting room could accommodate over two hundred delegates but these days less than a quarter of that number participated.

When the agendas were circulated Tony was dismayed to find that his motion was last. Ironically almost all of the other motions were on relatively trivial matter with the exception of the first motion which was a call for all out strike action should the British Coal Industries attempt to close one more colliery.

In the event the debate over the first motion was allowed to run over it's allotted time by almost an hour as speaker after speaker went to the rostrum to say more or less the same thing in support of the motion.

Despite his protestations no time was allocated for his motion and this meant that it would never be aired at national level. Matters were made worse by the fact that Mullaney chaired the last of the four sessions held over the two day conference. Tony was filled with anger as he sat helplessly watching the procedure being manipulated to exclude him.

Just before the winding up session Mullaney looked across at Tony. His hands were together and resting on the table before him. The index and middle fingers of his right hand came up together as Tony looked in his direction. The self-satisfied smirk on the face of Mullaney made Tony Hartill want to smash his fist into it.

Chapter 4

By January 1984 Albert Markham was very pleased with himself. He had lulled the Board of the British Coal Industry (BCI) into a mood of optimism. The Board had a remit from the Government to make the coal industry more competitive and that meant fewer pits that were more efficient if it was to be a player in the energy market. This inevitably involved the closure of uneconomic and worked out pits.

The recently appointed Chairman of the Board, Harold Mark, was an autocratic businessman who had made his way to the top from humble beginnings. He operated a simple philosophy; 'if you are not in control, then you are out of control' and Harold Mark had concluded that the management of the coal industry had been out of control for decades.

The other element to his business success was his instinct with people; and he hated Markham.

Although Harold Mark was suspicious, both he and his board had been amazed at Markham's reaction when they had listed dozens of pits for possible closure.

Despite his distaste for Markham he was determined to do everything he could to avoid giving an excuse to swing the miners behind a policy of strike action. His remit included a commitment to do everything possible to avoid confrontation with the miners.

Markham and his three man delegation had come to London, listened to the proposals and had gone along with them. Believing that Markham and the CMU must have decided to accept that exhausted pits had to close the Board decided to include other pits and offer better compensation to the redundant miners. There was also an improved package of incentives for new industries to assist with the inevitable unemployment. Harold

Mark could only conclude that the CMU had decided to face up to the inevitable and he and his board felt relieved to say the least.

At the epicentre of support for Albert Markham was a large mining community in Yorkshire called Watts where the name Albert Markham was revered from Grannies to Grandchildren. He was considered to be a hero of the working class.

The amazement of the board of BCI was turned to astonishment when Markham had raised no argument against the closure of Watts; a farcically uneconomic pit that had been kept open for years because it was so politically emotive.

They were even more astonished the very next week when the closure was announced and Markham appeared on television.

Markham claimed that he knew nothing whatsoever about the proposed closure of Watts and a long list of other pits.

'It had been a bolt from the blue.' he claimed. 'This is yet another example of BCI duplicity.' No mention of the closure of Watts had ever been suggested and this was an attempt to provoke the people in the mining communities. This is another scandalous example of the Tory party lackeys attempting to grind the British Coal miners into humiliating submission.' ranted Markham.

Each time the interviewer asked a question Markham replied at length with a venomous appetite. The question was never answered. Instead Markham conveyed his own message with ease. From then on the electronic media and newspaper journalists were covering every detail of what Markham said. He was in his element. Markham the great communicator!

At home in his terraced colliery house in Ashington Tony Hartill watched Markham on television with as much astonishment as the Board of BCI.

Watts Colliery had been on a list of Collieries in a secret report prepared for Markham and the Regional Secretaries. This report had been commissioned by the executive of the CMU and published nearly a year before.

Several months before Tony had picked it up on a coffee table in Mullaneys office whilst paying a routine visit at CMU regional headquarters. Mullaney had gone out to make a phone call which he said was personal.

At the time Tony had thought little of it except that the document was marked CONFIDENTIAL on the front page. Tony hadn't seen the front page at first because the document was already opened at the last section concluding with the list of pits that Markham's advisers deemed exhausted. Watts was first on the list. Tony only saw 'CONFIDENTIAL' when he went to replace the report on the coffee table. He had decided to leave it as he found it and make no comment.

'What the hell is Markham up to' said Tony to no one in particular as he sat watching the BBC Six o' Clock news on television.

Markham knew that he couldn't call a strike without a ballot. By announcing that there was to be a ballot in March he reckoned he had enough time to stomp around the coal fields to ensure that the members voted yes. The next six weeks were hectic as the Regional Secretaries dedicated to Markham did all they could to guarantee the mandate from the membership.

Other Secretaries, particularly in the English midlands went through the procedures in the normal way and reported back their feeling that the outcome was far from certain. Markham went round the coalfields speaking to miners in packed halls. At each meeting the two hundred, or so, miners who turned up gave him a rapturous ovation and clapped him from the hall as he left. Markham thought it was in the bag.

It was then Markham's turn to be astonished. When all the votes were counted there was no clear- cut mandate for all out strike action despite the fact that much intimidation had taken place in some areas and some of that intimidation was not very subtle.

The miners from the Ashington and Ellington pits came to vote at the miner's hall in Ashington. Almost all of the miners eligible to vote came to exercise their right. They moved up in lines toward to a long table at the top of the hall where they were handed their voting slip. The scrutineers, including Mullaney, stood at the other side of the table and watched where every man placed his cross. Some of the men protested vigorously that the ballot was supposed to be secret. A few defiantly placed their cross in the 'NO' box and waved it in the face of Mullaney and the other scrutineers. Whilst all of this went on a group of men stood at the back of the hall and shouted; `Strike, Strike'. Outside of the hall there were posters everywhere with the words STRIKE -YES.

When the result was announced the whole country sighed with relief as did most of the miners. The result was a decisive NO to strike action.

Markham and Mullaney were distraught as were Markham's other 'Insiders'.

The reason for the NO vote was complex but some factors were clear. The majority of the older miners wanted the money offered in the redundancy package. Many of the younger members of the CMU realised that a future in mining was uncertain so it was better to make the break, take the money, and start afresh elsewhere. For others life meant the pit, the community and the union. Without these pillars of support, especially the CMU, which they believed to be the greatest Trade Union in the world, the closures would destroy the life that they had been content with. Certainties would disappear and how would they survive? For many of the Union Officials the pit closures meant the end of their careers.

The voting figures from the Northumberland coal field were against the strike call by a majority of three to two. Mullaney couldn't believe it.

In the biggest pit, Ellington, the miners had voted NO by a majority of ten to one.

Despite the vote a furious Markham concentrated all of his cold calculating determination to manufacture an opportunity. It was now or never. If he couldn't get the miners out then Plakinov would never trust him again and his opportunity would be lost forever! Much of the money from Plakinov was already on its way. Some was here already.

He also knew that the BCI would feel that, because of the vote, they could accelerate the closures. That would further weaken the CMU. Markham knew he had to act immediately.

Within a week of the vote Markham called a special meeting of Regional Secretaries and Chairmen. He explained that there were now special circumstances for bringing the men out. Knowledge he had obtained in a leaked memorandum from the Prime Minister to Harold Mark, explained that the Government had a secret agenda to put every pit in the country up for sale. The buyers could decide whether they wanted the pit for coal production or they could clear the site and sell the land for whatever purpose they wished. A masterful final speech by Markham ended with the words.

'The purposes and intentions of this evil Tory Government is not just about closing every pit in the land; it's about smashing the CMU, it's about smashing the Trade Union movement; it's about smashing the Labour movement and above all its about smashing the lives of working people everywhere. The Tories would smash the cradle of Socialism for decades. We havn't got time for another ballot so get the men out now.'

When Markham ended his speech most delegates were immediately on their feet. They cheered, clapped, shouted and waved their support but there were those who wanted to see evidence to support Markham's allegations.

Markham claimed that those who doubted him were questioning his trust and a shouting match ensued. The dissenting delegates left after having been shouted down by the majority who were in Markham's camp. Markham believed that those who stayed behind would do his bidding. He explained his strategy to the remaining delegates who then left to implement it.

Ray Mullaney had travelled to the meeting in the car of his Chairman Sandy Short. Sandy befitted his name. He was five feet three inches tall and rotund. Sandy had wanted to leave with the dissenters.

As the pair journeyed back they were shouting at each other. It had started from the moment they got into the car and Sandy said.

'That fucker's mad'

Ray stormed back at him. 'Well what are we supposed to do? Stand by and watch the Union disappear up Maggie Thatcher's arse.'

'Are you stupid Ray? We've just had a ballot and Albert lost by a street.' Sammy went on: 'In case you are still hypnotised by Alberts wonderful words the ballot in Northumberland was against striking by a distance longer than Newcastle fucking race course. You know as well as me that half of the miners in Northumberland work at Ellington Colliery and they opposed the strike with a ten to one majority.' He could hardly get his breath and paused before saying: 'Despite the ballot box intimidation.'

'Don't you realise that if we cannot get Ellington out it doesn't matter about the rest.'

Ray responded with his teeth clenched.

'We'll get Ellington out. We'll get the whole bloody lot out despite everything. We'll do exactly what Albert told us.'

They agreed to differ since both had very red faces, both were shouting and the car was swaying from side to side as Sandy drove up the motorway.

For the rest of the journey they hardly exchanged a word. Ray Mullaney was filled with anxiety thinking about what he'd promised Markham but he was determined to follow the instructions. He knew the men he could call on.

Sandy was filled with exasperation and deep concern. He believed that as a union official he was in for a rough ride unless they observed the wishes of the members. This time the members had not been easy to manipulate. Unlike Mullaney, Sandy Short was not privy to Markham's real agenda.

A day later the word went out that a special strike meeting was to be held in the Trade Union Hall in Ashington. The hall could hold about two hundred and fifty if all the fire regulations were ignored. On the night of the meeting the hall was packed out and another fifty men stood outside unable to get in. The majority of miners stayed away.

Mullaney attempted to emulate the speaking style of

Markham and used Markham's own words. The final sentences were shouted with his fists punching the air.

Mullaneys men, shouted constantly for strike action throughout the oration. Mullaney asked for a show of hands in support of immediate strike action. A lot of hands went up and those with their hands raised shouted 'Strike, Strike' Some of those outside took up the shout whilst others said to their marrers 'Listen to those stupid bastards.' Those in the Hall who had not raised their hands kept quiet believing that on this occasion discretion was the better part of valour.

Tony Hartill sat in the hall furious at the deception and manipulation. Sitting at the side of the top table from where Mullaney was speaking Tony waited for a lull in the noise before standing up. 'Wait, wait!' He shouted.

The noise in the hall subsided a little more as Tony continued. 'We've just had a ballot and if there is to be strike action we have to be consulted again.' As he spoke Mullaney looked at the men in the front row and nodded towards Tony. The men took up the chant 'Strike scab, strike scab!' Within seconds the noise was deafening and Tony's words were drowned.

It was impossible to be heard above the noise and so he stopped. Eventually the chanting became quieter and so he resumed his speech. As soon as he did so the chant went up again. The futility of trying to make a point was obvious by then and so Tony made his way out of the Hall. As he did so he glowered at Mullaney who had his hands clasped with two fingers sticking out.

Although the meeting in the hall had gone Mullaney's way to begin with things were not so good for the Picket that he had planned for the next day. After Tony Hartill had walked out of the meeting hall there was a general exodus despite the pleas of Mullaney for the men to stay. Only about seventy men remained to hear him appeal to them to form a picket and a core of only eleven of the men were prepared to man the picket line at Ellington. After much urging and cajoling a further ten agreed.

Mullaney was in a dilemma. He could not mount an effective picket at Ellington with so few men and since Ellington was the most productive pit it was essential to keep the miner's out. The vote against the strike by the Ellington men meant that he needed a substantial picket. Reverting to the only option open to him he spent that night and most of the next day organising men from Durham to provide the full round the clock complement he needed.

The next day all was quiet and everything continued as normal until at seven o' clock in the evening pickets appeared at the entrance to every pit in Northumberland and most pits in the country. At Ellington Mullaney, with over seventy pickets, mainly from Durham closed the colliery gates and stood outside waiting for when the buses and cars began to arrive at 8pm.

The miners together with the underground mining officials who were arriving for their shift all arrived as usual within minutes of one another to begin their shift. Few were aware of what had taken place in the Union Hall the previous evening. The sudden arrival of so many vehicles unable to get access to the colliery car park had blocked the road. The men in vehicles away from the gate had left their cars and buses to see what was happening creating a crowd of over three hundred people outside the pit. On the inside of the gate were those who had just finished their shift and wanted to get home.

Division and dissension underground was a situation that all miners dreaded. Bad blood between people in ordinary civilian life on the surface was bad. Underground it could spell disaster. Trust and goodwill between miner and miner is essential. To avoid conflict the bonhomie and friendly chiding in mining everywhere was an essential ingredient of life underground. Markham knew this as well as anyone and so he gambled on the historical legacies, loyalties and traditions of the CMU winning the day. No miner would want to break the picket. No miner would want to weaken the Union and destroy the work which had gone on over the decades by selfless leaders who had shown the very best of qualities in that leadership; tolerance, determination, fairness and brotherhood. The men facing the picket lines were in a dilemna because the other side of the equation was that Markham had broken the rule: No ballot, no strike!

The men argued and questioned the right of the pickets who responded by insisting that no one was to pass by order of the union. Eventually Mullaney decided to intervene. He stood on a box and called for order. As the throng became silent Mullaney explained that they should all go home and wait for further instructions until the situation was clarified. He went on to say that the Government had taken advantage of the miners and insisted that the action was in their best interests and all would become clear within a day or two. The pickets he declared would let no one pass. The miners knew that if they were going to work that night they would have to fight their way through. That was not an alternative. Almost all of the miners went home. A handful stayed behind to join the picket.

The following morning the radio announced the events of the previous night. The miners began to arrive for the day shift demanding an explanation or access to the pit. When they got to the main gates they realised, like their comrades who had gone in the night before, that there was a situation here which was going to be very difficult to resolve. A few were persuaded to join the picket lines. The majority, left to face the pickets were sickened by seeing some of the pickets kicking, punching and tearing at the clothes of those men, women and girls who worked in the offices. Hasty arrangements had been agreed to get them past the picket line with a police escort. Unfortunately no one had remembered to tell all of the pickets who assumed that they were attempting to break the picket. To defuse the situation the management told those who had got through the picket to go home until further notice. The terrified men and women walked silently away to the jeering pickets.

As the jeering subsided men on both sides of the picket line looked away in shame, embarrassed, as they watched women with ashen faces pass by with torn tights and wheals on their legs.

From then on the miners who weren't picketing stayed away from the pit anticipating a new ballot or some explanation of what was to happen. At most pits there was no leadership other than that given by the CMU and for too many of the miners the message from the CMU was not what they wanted to hear. The resulting vacuum was what Markham wished to exploit.

Markham had pulled off a remarkable feat by anticipating the reaction to the heavy picketing. The police had also been caught off guard since no warning had been given. The pickets had simply appeared throughout the country at the appointed hour and in the ensuing confusion, Markham's plan had worked well.

Chapter 5

After his initial reaction at seeing Markham with Plakinov Gennardy Mardosov reflected upon his life to date and on his future: He had almost come into contact with Markham in the Orbital Hotel through pure coincidence and since then he had been on edge.

Through no fault of his making he could find himself seen as a threat by the KGB, the Russian secret police. All it would take would be the discovery that he knew who Markham and Williams were. The fact that he had been to England could only compound his position as a perceived security risk.

He was so glad that he had not been called into the meetings when Markham was there. If Markham had recognised him, which was almost certain, then Plakinov and his aides would have insisted on him being subjected to a withering interrogation. Depending upon the level of security paranoia at the time he could even disappear. His conversation with Li could only make matters worse. And what if Li reported their conversation?

Usually he wasn't a nervous man but time and time again he found himself going over his conversation with Li and the implications of what he'd seen. He was having trouble getting to sleep at nights and he was always wondering if he was under surveillance.

Whenever he had the opportunity he would go for a walk in the centre of Minsk to relieve the tension he felt in his breast. The main street, the Leninstrasse, went in a straight line from one end of the city to the other making it easier to see if he was being followed.

The road was wide with broad pavements on either side. It had been designed and built by German prisoners after the Second World War. It would have been very imposing still had it not been so badly holed and neglected. As he walked along he compared his surroundings with the streets and buildings he had seen in England then his thoughts ranged over the events that had shaped the recent history of Minsk.

During the Second World War the German army had raced across the flat terrain of central Europe straight for Minsk as soon as Poland had fallen. The resistance from the poorly equipped and badly organised army of the USSR was fierce but their defeat was inevitable and Minsk was shelled and bombed unceasingly until the fragmented Soviet army retreated or surrendered.

Two years later when General Zukov's Soviet army finally broke through the German ring of steel surrounding Moscow one of the first objectives was Minsk. This time it was Soviet armour and air power doing the damage as their forces swept forward. By the time hostilities ceased in Belarus, Minsk was razed to the ground. Only one tiny area, about the size of two football pitches, was left standing. The people of Minsk who had stayed and survived were living in cellars accessed by holes in the rubble. As the German Army retreated they had orders to destroy everything that stood leaving nothing for the Soviet forces. They didn't quite manage to destroy everything but they came close.

The thousands of Germans taken prisoner were treated worse than animals and they died in thousands from exhaustion and malnutrition as they worked continuously to rebuild the city. For many years after the war the buildings, like the roads, were designed and built by slave labour from the defeated German army.

Everything was built from concrete and apart from some variation on the front of the buildings the design was monotonously repeated. As a consequence the city was a grey and soulless place with endless multi-storey, concrete, apartment blocks.

Each apartment consisted of two living rooms three metres by four metres. A door in the middle of the three metre long wall in each of the two rooms accessed a narrow passage. This in turn accessed three doors leading to a tiny area which contained a flush toilet, a slightly larger area which was the bathroom containing a 1 metre long bath and another room the same size as the bathroom that was the kitchen area.

These apartments became the standard design across the USSR from Minsk to Vladivostock seven thousand miles away.

The original intention had been for one family to have one apartment but in reality often two or three families shared. It was common for people to sleep in shifts and privacy was a rare luxury. By the nineteen eighties conditions in the apartments were more crowded than ever. Good accommodation was a rare luxury.

In Gennardy's thoughts he was always making comparisons with what he'd seen in England. Everything in Minsk now looked drab and colourless. The architecture he pondered was a reflection of his life in the USSR.

The home of Tony Hartill often came to mind. He loved the bathroom, the cleanliness of the toilet, the choice of soaps and shampoos having as much hot water as you wanted. Tony had two bedrooms in his home which were unused. Tony's parents shared a home that was even bigger than Tony's; and Bill Robinson's home was more like a small palace.

On occasion he would break his stride on Leninstrasse and stop. Looking around he would wonder; 'Could it be that he could hear the grim laughter of the ghosts of those German Soldiers as they looked down on Minsk and surveyed what they had left behind. Could this be their revenge?' He would then check again to see if he was being followed.

Gennardy still lived with his Grandmother who was in her seventies. She had made her tiny wooden home as comfortable as possible. Her house was about the size of a large garden shed and therefore easy to keep warm when she had logs to burn. He stayed with his Grandmother as much as possible because he did not qualify for a home in Minsk. As a result when it was necessary to live in Minsk he stayed the night mainly with girlfriends who shared with other family and friends. Sometimes he stayed with his college friend Sacha who was a ballet dancer and an actor with the Minsk Ballet and Opera Company. Sacha was the nearest thing he had to a friend but he could never open his mind to him.

Wherever he stayed Gennardy thought of Tony Hartill's house, the gas central heating, carpets on the floor, and warm comfortable beds. He yearned to return to such luxury; 'and the food. Oh! The food'!

Like so many of his countrymen Gennardy had decided that to get married and have children was out of the question. There was no where to live. A baby in an apartment which was shared by so many people involved endless rows, sleepless nights, filthy toilets and bathrooms, endless power cuts in the depth of winter and all the other myriad elements that can make life hell.

A few weeks after seeing Markham in the Orbital, Gennardy Mardasov hatched a plan. The concept was simple; he would go to live in England.

He shared his thoughts with his Grandmother, the one person he loved and trusted. They sat together one evening as they had done so many times and talked quietly and earnestly as they watched the wood burning in the tiny fireplace. Despite the comparative warmth of her little house they both wore their warmest clothes to protect them from the chilling drafts.

Outside the wind further chilled the ice capped, snow covered ground whilst inside the warmth and the smell from the burning logs created a relative haven for him to think.

'There is no future here for me and I am in danger just because of what I witnessed in the Orbital Hotel.' He told her. 'I cannot get married and have a family. Even my language teacher, Professor Nadov who has worked in the University in Minsk for twenty years has to share an apartment' he went on.

'I want a wife and I want to have your great grandchildren Nana. I want a place where they can grow up with a future'

His Grandmother nodded her understanding. She stretched her hand from under her shawl and gently patted the back of his hand as she told him not to worry about her. They caught each other's gaze. The candour in her eyes moved him.

'If I am successful Nana I will do everything I can to get news to you.' Gennardy stood up put his arm around her and kissed her gently on her brow. She smiled at him.

'I know that. I know that' she said.

Gennardy returned to his chair. There was a silence and then his Grandmother looked across at him before saying; 'Gennardy, whatever happens I shall die with a smile on my face believing you were successful. Hope can never die.'

Gennardy was close to tears. The underlying

defiance and anger that had been so characteristic of his Grandmothers life had given way to a quiet resignation and acceptance of her future. She sat on the wooden armchair that had been made for her by Gennardy's Grandfather when she had found herself pregnant all those years ago. Dozens of pieces of different types of woven material, gathered over the years were draped over the back and the arms of the chair to minimise draughts and retain the warmth.

Gennardy believed that when he left he would probably never see that kindly, timeworn face again. He looked at her as she adjusted the headscarf that framed her face. He smiled a little smile and pushed his fingers through his thick hair before he leaned forward and kissed her on either cheek. As he did so she said,

'You are a good man; just like your Grandfather'

The next morning Gennardy set out on his quest. There was no British Embassy or Consulate in Minsk. The only place where he could make a contact was in Moscow or Warsaw. He had no work in Poland and so he took the train to Moscow. As the train laboured for eight hours through the snow covered countryside Gennardy was deep in thought. He sat huddled in the corner of his compartment with his arms across the front of his coat to retain his body heat. The carriage heating system was defective and Gennardy was pleased that he had not made the journey through the night.

On arrival he took the famous Moscow underground to a suburb of the city and walked the half mile from the underground station to the apartment block which was his destination. He went up the familiar staircase layout, only the graffiti was different, and knocked on a third floor door with a coin. The door and door frame was covered in sheet steel to stop would be intruders from enjoying easy access.

After a few seconds the door opened slightly. A stout security chain limited the opening. Part of the face of a woman appeared in the slit.

'Is Irena in please?' said Gennardy. 'I would like to speak with Irena, Irena Kot'.

'Who wants her?' said the voice of a younger woman.

'Just tell her to come to the door if she is in please.'

'She isn't in' said the voice.

'I will call for her later' he replied.

'Who should I say has called?' enquired the woman.

'Its alright.' said Gennardy. 'I'll call later.'

Normally he would have given his name but not on this occasion and he knew the woman would not be able to give a good description of him because it was so dark in that gloomy passage.

He decided to wait at the bottom of the staircase just inside the entrance. Whether Irena was in or out she would have to pass him.

He waited for hours in the bitter cold. Occasionally he ran or walked up and down the staircase to keep warm and he ate the last of the black bread and fat pork that his Grandmother had given him. The darkness had come early with more snowfalls. The evening wore on. Hours later a frozen Gennardy heard some soft footsteps coming towards the staircase and this time it was Irena. Gennardy recognised the winter coat she was wearing and of which she was so proud.

'Irena' he called out quietly. Irena immediately stopped and slowly looked around.

'It's Gennardy Mardasov from Minsk.'

'Oh, Gennardy, you frightened me' she replied.

Gennardy was in luck. Not only was Irena pleased to see him she had one of the rooms in the apartment to herself for a few days.

The woman who had earlier answered the door had moved into the other apartment room with her boyfriend since its normal occupants were working away for a while. They kept themselves to themselves. This suited Gennardy and Irena who had shared many an opportunity to keep each other warm during long Russian winter nights when they had been working together.

Irena was also a Linguist with German as her special language. Before sleeping they exchanged stories of their work and travels. Irena wanted to know all about England. Gennardy thought it better not to convey too much enthusiasm for his visit despite Irena's unending questions.

When asked about his visit to Moscow he told her that things were quiet and he had been given a few days off. He told her that he had to phone his office at the Ministry for Information in Minsk each day in case something came up.

Casually he asked Irena if there were any cultural exchange groups from the west in Moscow at that time. She said there were two. One was a German exhibition showing off a range of West German glassware and pottery. Another Anglo - French stand in the main hotel just off Revolution Square was exhibiting tools for the motor car industry. Gennardy knew that such exhibitions and stands were meeting points for intelligence gathering on both sides of the iron curtain. He also knew that the places would be under strict surveillance.

The next morning Irena was up early to attend her assignment in Moscow. She spent a long time in the tiny bathroom then sat before a mirror in their room making up her face and grooming her hair. Now that she was approaching forty she was not as slim and shapely as she had been and it troubled her. She stood up and pressed her hand on her stomach as though trying to push it in and then she would slide her hands down her clothes from her waist to her thighs as though trying to accentuate her disappearing curves. As she went through her routine they talked about why they weren't married and about Gennardy's Grandmother and Irena's parents in Tambov who she saw only once a year. At her appointed time they were ready to leave. Irena put her arms around the neck of Gennardy and told him how she had enjoyed seeing him.

'I mustn't kiss you' she teased 'I might end up missing my train.'

They both laughed and left the apartment making arrangements to meet when Irena was returning from her work.

Gennardy accompanied her to the underground and travelled with her saying goodbye when she left the underground at the station before his in central Moscow. They had arranged to meet again late that afternoon and go back to her room together. She seemed very happy.

Making a contact was going to be difficult so Gennardy decided that instead of going into a hotel he would walk around the area and make his initial observations. He was quite confident that he would recognise someone who fitted the criteria he had decided on and early in the afternoon two men emerged from the hotel that was hosting the Anglo-French exhibition. One of them was what he was looking for.

Gennardy was instinctively sure that one of the two men he was following was British and the other almost certainly Russian. Gennardy tailed them to the 'Havana,' the most famous coffee shop in Moscow.

The clientele were mainly foreign, many of them accompanied by Russian officials. Gennardy didn't look too conspicuous despite being on his own. He sat at the table next to the two men he had followed and listened to their conversation. The two men spoke in English.

When the waiter came to ask him for his order he summoned up his best English accent and said loudly. 'I am waiting for a friend.'

The waiter then said, in Russian, 'I shall come back later then. Shall I?'

Gennardy had anticipated this answer by the waiter so he shrugged his shoulders and said 'Pardon!' in English as though the Russian language was foreign to him. The waiter was perplexed because he had guessed that Gennardy was a Russian.

Although Jeremy Smart appeared to give his full attention to his Russian companion he was very well aware of the solitary figure on the next table. He knew that the man was not British. It was obvious too that the waiter was perplexed because he had assumed the man was Russian. Smart wondered what this fellow was up to.

Jeremy Smart's Russian companion had his back to Gennardy so that he was unaware of the events taking place behind him. Eventually he indicated his intention to leave expecting Smart to do the same.

'I will sit here a little longer.' said Smart. 'I need to rest my legs and have another coffee.' The Russian said he would see him later and left.

Gennardy watched until the Russian had left before leaning slightly towards Smart and asking quietly if he could join him. Smart nodded his assent and said, 'of course.'

Each man waited for a moment expecting the other

to speak. Now that Gennardy had made a contact he wasn't sure how to start.

The waiter eyed both of them suspiciously and came over for the order. In a loud voice Smart said. 'And how long have you been over hear George? I haven't seen you for ages. What will you have?'

'Coffee would be fine.' said a relieved Gennardy.

'You look bloody frozen.' whispered Jeremy Smart.

Gennardy ignored the observation and said. 'Thank you for this; I must trust you I have no other choice'

'Trust me?' said Smart 'Why?'

'I know you are British and probably English. I have been to England. I have friends there. I can tell. I must trust you.' In his anxiety Gennardy's words suddenly tumbled out.

Then he paused and after a furtive scan of the room he leaned forward saying in a whisper. 'I have some very important information for you and a favour to ask.'

Jeremy Smart sipped his coffee, took his eyes from Gennardy and looked slowly around the coffee shop.

The Englishman unexpectedly stood up and Gennardy's pounding heart beat was banging in his ears.

'Shall we stretch our legs now do you think?'

Gennardy regained his composure and said slowly; 'Of course' before emptying his coffee cup and rising to his feet.

Smart was curious at this unusual situation. He was also very keen to know if this was some sort of game and he could not think of its purpose if it was. As Gennardy watched his host pay the bill he hoped and willed that he had not made a mistake and chosen the wrong person. Such a mistake could have dire consequences. It could cost him his life.

The observations that Gennardy had made over the years served him well. It was the man's clothes that had singled him out. He had made a good start. Not only was Jeremy Smart English he was working in the British Embassy.

Whatever Gennardy was up to Jeremy Smart could not tell; but one thing was for certain; to the best of his knowledge nothing like this had ever happened before. He was determined to get to the bottom of it but he also knew that the East / West intelligence game was a dangerous business; so why was this man risking his life, or was it some sort of set up?

When they were outside the coffee shop Jeremy Smart shook the hand of Gennardy and said. 'So nice to see you again George, can we meet here tomorrow at the same time so that we can talk properly.'

Gennardy masked his surprise saying, 'Yes of course' at that Smart smiled, turned on his heel, and walked off.

As Gennardy walked away his mind was in turmoil. He knew from his training as an interpreter that he should not make contact with 'evil people from the West', people, he had been told, who would take advantage of him at every opportunity. The penalties for breaking this rule were severe. He also knew that what he had been trained to believe was a lie. He had seen real prosperity on a scale he could never even have imagined. Tony Hartill was not a lie. Britain was not a lie. He had seen it with his own eyes.

Could he trust this man? He didn't even know his name. Why couldn't they have talked there and then?

As he made his way back to Irena's apartment he felt sure that he would be followed. To avoid any pursuers he made his way through a maze of streets and alleyways until he was sure that no one could have followed him. He had several hours to wait for Irena so made his way to the main railway station to get shelter and some warm food. There was nothing suspicious about a Russian reading the national newspaper, Pravda, whilst waiting for a train.

Late in the afternoon he took the train out of central Moscow that Irena would board at the next station as arranged. Gennardy saw Irena on the platform but did not join her. He sat in a different part of the train until it arrived at the station where she got off. They left the train at different points on the platform before meeting up outside the station.

'I thought you must have missed the train' said Irena.

'No problem' said Gennardy, 'I just did not see you in the station when the train left' he lied.

Gennardy was determined to avoid incriminating Irena in any way if he could.

'Well it's nice to know you are here and you will be keeping me warm again tonight' she said with a knowing look.

As they walked through the dark, bitter cold, suburb each with an arm round the other Gennardy was quiet. 'Well whatever happens I have lived a little and perhaps I may yet make a new and better life' he heard his voice saying in his head.

He thought of his Grandmother and that frankness on her face. He imagined her smiling as a young girl, full of vitality, full of vigour, full of love for his grandfather who was whisked away for inciting public unrest; all because he had complained about the activities of a corrupt Army officer who had cheated him and his fellow villagers out of their payments for feeding a company of soldiers.

'You are very quiet Genna. What are you thinking of?' said Irena.

'I am thinking of how warm you are in bed.' he replied prompting her to give him a little dig with her elbow.

The next day Gennardy made the same journey with Irena. He had told her that he was not sure that he could meet her that night because he may have to stay in central Moscow if he was required. As an interpreter herself Irena thought little of it. She knew that interpreters worked whenever they were asked to work.

Gennardy looked across the road to the coffee shop and to his relief his contact was there.

Jeremy Smart had taken a seat by the window with a view overlooking the street. He was just as pleased to see Gennardy. He casually finished his coffee, paid his bill, and left. As he came out of the cafe Gennardy approached and Jeremy said. 'Walk along with me. Don't worry everything is fine.'

They turned into a side street and then into another. A car door opened as they came up to it and Jeremy Smart told Gennardy to get in. Gennardy hoped against hope that the providers of the car were neither KGB nor the Moscow Police.

The car worked its way though several suburbs until the driver and the man who sat in the front passenger seat were sure they were not being followed. During the journey Jeremy Smart asked a lot of questions. Gennardy was asked to remove his coat and empty his pockets and he promptly complied. After half an hour the car suddenly stopped at the side of the pavement next to a large building. They left the car and Smart ushered Gennardy up some steps.

The building they entered was situated not far from the centre of Moscow close to the coffee shop where they had met. They had travelled in a full circle.

Gennardy knew the building. It was an accommodation block for mainly foreign long stay visitors.

Once inside Gennardy was shown into an apartment where he was introduced to a small, very sophisticated middle aged lady who said she was Miss Smith. She wore her hair up and her eyes were partly disguised by heavily framed spectacles. Gennardy wondered if there were lenses in the frames or just plain glass. There was not a lot of light in the room and he had the feeling that she was, at least, partly in disguise.

'Good morning Mr Mardosov' she said as she shook hands. 'Shall we enjoy the music of your wonderful composers as we talk?' As she spoke she depressed a button on a portable tape player.

The distinctive sounds of Tchaichovsky filled the room as she continued, 'I understand that you have some important information for us. Information, you believe, which simply cannot wait. If you are not an impostor, or a plant, and we obviously think you are neither of these, we will be pleased to hear what you have to say.'

She then turned and nodded to Jeremy Smart who left the room leaving Gennardy and his colleague sitting in comfortable chairs on either side of a low table.

Miss Smith sat with her back to the heavily curtained window so that her face was in silhouette.

Meanwhile Jeremy Smart who had left them with a 'see you both later' gone to sit with a man in the next room who was listening through earphones to every word that was being said. Smart picked up a spare set of earphones and the pair listened intently to the conversation they were recording.

Gennardy's mind was racing. This woman was

definitely English. She spoke like the Newsreaders he'd listened to on British television when he had stayed at Tony's house. There was no hint of an accent in her speech.

The perfume too, that perfume was not the heavy, cloying, sickly sweet stuff that was available to Russian women. These simple clues helped to persuade him that he had probably made a good contact.

In his short conversation with Jeremy Smart the day before Gennardy had quickly explained as much as he could. As a trained listener Smart had missed nothing and instinct told him that Gennardy was telling the truth.

Smart was part of the intelligence team in Moscow. His boss was on leave in England. On his return to the office he had made contact immediately with two of his colleagues to organise the interview with Gennardy. The three discussed the unusual situation and set up the arrangements. They worked all the time as though there was a Russian ear in every pocket and drawer. They believed that this guy was either very clever or very stupid or very desperate. It could be argued that they were right on all counts. Miss Smith opened with that very question.

'You are correct.' said Gennardy. 'I can tell you that I am desperate and that makes me stupid if taking this big risk is called stupid. Maybe I am clever and maybe not so clever.' He shrugged. 'Let me tell you.'

Gennardy had made his mind up that he had been lucky. His plan had worked at the first attempt and he had made contact with the British. He would soon have his deductions and doubts confirmed.

Gennardy poured out his story over a period of some three hours. After the first hour Miss Smith left the room after a man came in to replace her. The man brought tea and delicious sandwiches. He sat in Miss Smith's seat and asked Gennardy to continue. Gennardy knew then that one or more people were also listening. His interviewers changed places several times.

In the afternoon Miss Smith said 'We have no more questions and we believe you. However believing is one thing and having evidence is another, we need proof.'

By this time Gennardy was feeling exhausted from the endless questioning and cross-questioning. His inquisitors were well skilled in determining whether the story was consistent and they had been very thorough.

'Proof' said Gennardy, 'how proof?'

Gennardy almost passed out with anxiety when he heard how he was to get the proof.

'We want you to make contact with Li Saric again and use her to gain access to Plakinov's apartment. She lives in it with him. If you can get us information or if you can recruit Miss Saric we will get you to the West. You will become one of us.'

Gennardy was dumbfounded. He was tired and his self control and nervous system was on the limit.

'Are you playing games with me?' he shouted angrily.

Miss Smith lifted the index finger to her pursed lips and went 'shhh.'

Gennardy looked around frantically before continuing in a restrained voice.

'How do I say to Plakinov; Excuse me Mr Plakinov but my English friends have asked me to borrow the key to your apartment so that I can steal your papers!'

His hands flew up and down as he continued 'No problem Mr Mardosov replies Plakinov. Here are the keys. Help yourself. Tell the KGB to have the day off.'

Gennardy then sank into his chair and looked at his

inquisitors with contempt.

When they did not respond he searched for words before shouting, 'You tell me I am stupid. You are.......' Gennardy's eyes searched the room for the words as he stood up. 'Nuts'

Miss Smith smiled. Although she did not reply, she agreed with Gennardy. To put it in the mildest of terms the plan was audacious.

'May I suggest' she said quietly, 'that you contact Li Saric and use her to obtain some information.'

'Can you imagine what they would do if they caught her ...us?' said Gennardy feeling trapped. 'You are every bit as bad as them.' He went on in desperation.

'It is the oldest way of obtaining information.' said Miss Smith. 'You may find that she is so fond of you that it is surprisingly easy.'

Gennardy swallowed hard. They were so matter of fact about their request and he was certain that they meant every word of what they were asking. He needed time to think.

When the meeting ended Gennardy was restored to the streets of Moscow in the fading light. The air was freezing and he felt very lonely indeed.

By the time the interview was finished the tapes were being prepared for transportation to the British Embassy in Moscow and then on to London in a diplomatic bag. If the information on the tapes was true the British Intelligence team in Moscow had pulled off a little coup.

Chapter 6

The early spring of 1984 saw the United Kingdom at the beginning of what was to be a long and bitter dispute. Markham's Strategy was to get the miners out and keep them out by threat, coercion or any other tactic. He was confident that whenever trade unionists saw a picket line they would not cross it. If he could keep the pits unproductive until November the accumulated stocks of coal would be exhausted before the winter set in and the Government would make mistakes that would swing public opinion behind the miners. Hopefully they would fall into the trap of calling for Military assistance to keep the coal supplies moving. At that stage the Government would collapse because British Soldiers would not fire bullets at British Trade Unionists. In the ensuing chaos Markham would persuade working class people to focus on the real enemy, the Tory Government.

As Tony Hartill read the newspaper reports and watched the television news he was filled with anger. Anger at Markham, anger at the further duplicity of Mullaney, anger at the thought of divided mining communities. Anger that it had been so easy for Markham and Mullaney to persuade or frighten people into such unnecessary hardship. But anger was not enough he needed a strategy to bring common sense to the minds of the miners.

Tony made a list of all those he thought he could trust including his eldest son, Kevin, who lived a few doors away with his wife and young child. Kevin was a bright young man and happy with his lot. He enjoyed his social life revolving, as it did, largely round his wife and her two brothers and their wives. When Tony got to

Kevin's house he knocked at the back door and walked in as was the custom and practice. Front doors were rarely used and some hadn't been opened for years.

The back door led into the kitchen which in turn led into the living room. Kevin's wife was busy in the kitchen.

'Aye Sharon' he said in greeting.

'Aye Tony' she replied sullenly.

'What's the crack then?' he asked.

His question evoked no response.

The sound of conversation told Tony that Sharon and Kevin had company and, unusually, the door from the kitchen to the lounge was closed.

'Some of the lads and Kevin are having a meeting.' Sharon volunteered.

'I'm not surprised' said Tony. 'I've just been watching television and theres ructions on all over the country.'

Without further ado Tony turned the door handle and entered the lounge. Inside the room was full of young miners. Every seat was taken and others sat on the floor.

'Aye what's up then' said Tony.'

We're workin' oot who all those scabby bastards are who are trying to fuck the strike up, that's all' said a young lad who was sitting on the floor.

'Ah cannot fuck'in wait.' he went on 'to give them a good turn'in over. Ray Mullaneys right, we stand to lose everything just because of a few useless traitors.'

Tony Hartill was horrified. His eyes quickly switched across the room to see the reaction of Kevin. It was obvious from the expression on Kevin's face that he agreed with the speaker.

Knowing that the speaker was referring to him Tony slowly looked at each man as his eyes searched the room. Everyone was awaiting his response.

Having gathered his thoughts he began to speak; 'Look lads. This is a no win situation. For God's sake don't go throwing your weight about. We've been duped and tricked into staying away from the pit: And for what?'

Before Tony got any further another miner interposed.

'What are we supposed to do? Sit here like statues waiting for those Tory bastards to tek wha jobs.'

'Wha not gan doon without a fight and anybody who is not wi'us is against us.' shouted Kevin.

'Right' said a chorus of voices.

'That's right Kev. This is wor (our) Alamo. We either win or get wiped oot.'

It was then that Tony knew that Kevin was leading this group.

'Look Kevin, and listen all of you.' shouted Tony. 'The only way that this can be properly resolved is if we all vote and we all accept a majority decision. As long as we are split we are guaranteed to be the losers. Don't you see? We have always stuck together in the past. We must stick together again.'

'Answer me this then.' said another man 'If you want us all to stick together as one Union; how come your gann'in round trying to get people to join another Union.'

Tony looked earnestly at the speaker before replying; 'Who said I was trying to form another union? Mullaney will not have a ballot and the only way, I can see, to force a ballot is if we can make Mullaney and his supporters see common sense. If we can persuade him that he will lose out to a rival union he will be forced to think again. We must have unity.'

Another miner said, 'Well! Mr Hartill, some of us have just come back from a meeting with Ray Mullaney and he says you are a bloody traitor.'

As the man spoke his voice was rising and his agitation was obvious.

'You, Mister, Your'e one of them that's causing the bother. Either back us or fuck off.' to which there was loud shouts of support from the men in the room.

Above the clamour Tony shouted; 'I'm on your side, I'm trying to make you see sense.' As soon as he finished the sentence he regretted it.

'Look' he shouted, but before he could continue another voice said; 'No, you look! I've heard enough.' The man was stabbing the air with his finger as he spoke 'You! Either join us, and promise your full support, or bugger off.'

'Aye!' came a clamour of support for the speaker.

The room went quiet. Tony looked at the man who challenged him and then around the room until his eyes rested on Kevin. Everyone was waiting for the reply.

Kevin's eyes exhibited only contempt for the stance of his father. Tony was painfully wounded by the withering look of his son.

Knowing that further attempts to see his point of view was futile Tony gave up.

'I'll see you later.' said Tony to no one in particular as he left the room to shouts of 'Aye we've got your bloody card marked.' and 'Traitor.'

'See you Sharon' Tony said quietly as he walked through the kitchen and out of the back door.

He was angry and distraught. He was disillusioned and uncertain and very unhappy.

'What's the matter with you then.' was the greeting he received from his wife when he arrived at his home.

'I've just been along to our Kevin's and there's a meeting on. Can you believe it they're talking about going around threatening anyone who wants to go back to work; I tried talking to them but they cannot hear.'

'What else do you expect them to do? If ah was a man I'd do the same' she replied.

Tony stared at her briefly to allow time for her statement to be assimilated in his mind.

'So what your saying is; I'm not a man because I'm not prepared to physically threaten men that I have known and worked with all these years' answered Tony.

'Talk sense woman. Can't you see what's going to happen?' he went on.

'If they don't support the strike they're not worth knowing. Me Dad say's Kevin's doing the right thing' said Maggie 'and I agree with him' she shouted at the top of her voice sticking her finger into her chest for greater emphasis.

Tony didn't respond. He didn't want to talk about it any further. He also wondered why he went home at all these days to talk about anything.

He sat for a while wondering how many other similar meetings were taking place in the land. Eventually he said he was going for a walk and left the house.

The late evening air was crisp as he compared the stars shining against the black sky above the gloomy narrow lanes he knew so well. The lanes had a proper road surface now but once the tubs of coal had been pulled along narrow gauge railway lines to bring coal from the pit to heat the homes of the miners. At the bottom of every yard, next to the lane was a coal house with a small door half way up the wall through which the coal was transferred for daily domestic use. Next to the coal house was another unit called a midden to store the used ashes from the coal range.

Inevitably Tony was greeted by one of his marrers who

was walking his dog.

'Seen the news tonight, Tony' said the man.

'Aye, I have that' Tony replied.

'What a bloody mess we're in now! Aye! That Yorkshire pudd'in has done exactly what Joe Gorton said he would do. What are we going to do about it then' the man went on.

'Search me' said Tony.

'Search me too' said the man. 'It'll be like 1926 and 1972 all over again. We'll go back a lot worse off. No one ever wins with strikes. Look at the money we've lost already.'

'The trouble is that we're in a trap of our own making this time.' said Tony.

'What a bloody mess' the man said before walking on.

The effects of the, so-called, strike had still not fully impacted upon the minds of all of those involved. As the days passed and March gave way to April small gatherings were taking place everywhere and the miners positioned themselves into those who wanted to go back and the minority who wanted, or who were being persuaded, to keep them out. For the majority it wasn't so much of a strike as a dispute between an organised few who were prepared to resort to violence and the disorganised majority who saw their livelihoods held to ransom without a mandate. The frustration and the exasperation of those on both sides stoked anger and bitterness and endless arguments. Family relationships were strained even in families that were normally as close as any.

At first the men who wanted to work waited for the expected meetings to be called to get the matter thrashed out. Their demand for another ballot went unheeded. As the time went by they realised that the

Official Union Leaders had no intention of reverting to normal democratic procedures. Wives who had previously persuaded their husbands not to place their heads above the parapet for fear of intimidation, which had become a daily feature of the dispute, became less resolute about sitting on the fence. Many families had run out of money within a few weeks.

Each day the miners and their families along with most of the population watched television news broadcasts waiting for a resolution of some kind.

As April gave way to May most people understood which side they were on but no one wanted to take a lead. Then Tony Hartill's phone began to ring regularly.

'C'mon Tony; your a Union man. Call a meeting and we'll get something done'

'Ray Mullaney's your man for that' Tony would reply.

One of the difficulties of talking over the telephone was the suspicion that the conversation could be overheard. Information was only given when the other voice was recognised. The atmosphere was tense.

Around the country there were rumours of a new breakaway miners union. Tony's leading role in forming a new union began with the idea that it would force the CMU into a proper ballot. As that hope receded, the idea of being involved in a new union began to grow. Tony's involvement was only a suspicion by those who thought of him as an enemy and he didn't wish to incite them or advise them. Any concrete evidence his enemies could come by could be enough to threaten the security of anyone within his family. This was one of the unbearable consequences of the dispute. It caused him great distress and endless worry.

Tony had kept away from the Union offices to avoid

unnecessary and futile confrontations with those who were doing the picketing. He was very upset that his son Kevin was a devoted Mullaney supporter and very active on picket duty. At every opportunity he would try to reason with Kevin but it was difficult to arrange to meet him alone. The last time they'd been together Kevin's parting words were; 'You're a bloody traitor Fatha'.

Tony was so shocked that he was unable to reply. They could no longer relate and he was deeply hurt.

One morning in late April Tony went to the union offices to find the ground floor full of those who had come to be known as the *hit squad*. The men were drinking cans of export beer from cases standing against a wall. As He entered the room someone shouted to him.

'Only here for the beer Tony? Come to join us at last.'

Someone else said, 'Seen the light has he.' The atmosphere was surly. All heads had turned and he was asked what he wanted.

'Where's Ray?' he asked.

'Depends what you want him for' came the reply.

'That's my business' said Tony.

'Make an appointment Tony' someone said and they all laughed.

As Tony looked around the room he realised that of the twenty or so men there many were already the worse for the beer and it was just past eleven O'clock. Tony looked anxiously around for Kevin and was relieved to see that he wasn't there.

He knew most of the men there. They were mainly good blokes but amongst them were also some nut cases and 'workie tickets'. A handful Tony had never seen before.

He left and walked briskly up the street. Coming in the opposite direction was Ray Mullaney striding out in the crisp morning sunshine, chest out, head up, and flanked by two other men who looked very intimidating. Mullaney spotted Tony and looked around anxiously for a moment. Content that Tony was alone he regained his permanent smile.

Tony said. 'I need to speak to you Ray'

'What about!' came the reply.

'You know fine well. This is a bloody mess and there is no end to it. The men want another ballot at least' said Tony.

'Ballot my arse' said Mullaney; 'and as far as an end goes. Get yourself on the streets and get the Transport Workers and the Power workers out. That's the only way to end it.'

At that moment one of Ray's minders stabbed Tony in the chest with his forefinger before saying, with a thick Yorkshire accent, and when this is all over we'll remember those that helped and the scabs that didn't.'

Tony Hartill fumbled for words his heart was thumping in anger and anxiety. His instinct was to hit the man over the head but the man's bulk demanded that discretion was the better part of valour in this instance.

Realising that others were stopping on the street to listen Tony said. 'Don't you realise that if this continues we'll hardly have any pits left to go back to. By being split like this we'll wreck the Union, the pits and everything else'.

'That's all Capitalist crap from the newspapers' said Mullaney's other accomplice, also in a thick Yorkshire accent. Tony ignored him.

'When is there another meeting with the men to get things sorted out?' shouted Tony to Mullaney.

'Everything has been done by the book' lied

Mullaney in a loud voice for everyone to hear. 'Check the union rules.'

Unable to contain his rage at what he saw as the duplicity and the hypocrisy; Tony heard himself speaking in a clear, controlled, even voice as he looked Mullaney in the eye.

'You stupid, evil, conniving Bastard, Ray' to make sure he had the last word he turned and walked off.

Mullaney's everlasting smile had wilted as Tony had spoken. Quickly recovering his composure he shouted, 'Not much you can say to cowardly capitalist supporters like Tony Hartill.' to the disappearing back of Tony. One of those among the throng gathered to listen to the altercation was Bill Robinson.

The confrontation with Mullaney in the street simply motivated Tony Hartill to strive even harder to bring an end to the impasse'.

Much of his time was spent going to the homes of like-minded colleagues who could be relied upon and who were actively helping him. His activities were concentrated in two areas: Alleviation of hardship among the mining community and forcing the union to negotiate a deal that would bring an end to the dispute.

One night at dusk he went round to the home of Dickie Sanderson a dedicated union man who Tony liked and respected. Dickie was not lacking in courage and had supported Tony on many occasions.

Dickie lived in a terraced colliery house similar to that of Tony. As soon as he arrived, Dickie's wife said. 'He's in the room! I'll put the kettle on.'

The two men sat chatting together until Dickie's wife poured some tea and sat with them.

They finished their tea and Mrs Sanderson had picked up the cups to return them to the kitchen when there was a crash of metal in the yard outside and then an alarm went off in the house.

Dickie leapt out of his chair and went to the rear door where he picked up a garden fork and switched the electricity off at the main switch plunging the house in darkness.

Everything was silent. Dickie shouted. 'Tony! There's a spade by the front door.'

Tony went for the spade while Mrs Sanderson stood in the corner of the room clutching a drying cloth in the gloom. As her eyes grew accustomed to the darkness she surveyed the crockery she had dropped lying shattered on the floor.

The two men stood behind the rear door as Dickie said 'Right!' when you open the kitchen door I'll charge out and you follow up behind O.K?'

'O.K.' whispered Tony who quietly lifted the door latch and flung the door open.

Dickie dashed out of the door with Tony right behind him shouting 'Come on out ya' bastards.'

There was no one in the yard except a cat which was standing wide eyed in the corner of the yard with its tail in the air mee-owing for all it was worth.

'Heaven help us.' shouted Dickie. 'We must be a bundle of nerves. It's just a bloody cat. It must have jumped on the bin lid and knocked it setting the alarm off.'

'Thank goodness for that.' said a relieved Tony.

Back in the house all three tried to have a laugh but it was obvious that they were all shaken.

'When will all this end Tony.' said Dickie's wife. 'Everybody's on tenterhooks. You can't even go to the shops without wondering if the people you know are going to speak or ignore you.'

'I'll tell you what pet.' Dickie said to her. 'We'll all have a drop of that brandy that I got for Christmas.'

Although the incident had turned out to be only a perception of fear it further reinforced Tony's understanding of the stresses and strains that ordinary decent people were subjected to on a daily basis. He also realised that the perceived threat was much greater than the reality but the television reporting on daily news broadcasts exaggerated the perceived threat, particularly in the minds of those living in the coal field communities.

As the weeks went by organisation for the collection and distribution of money and goods became of paramount importance. Initially, in Northumberland, all monies and goods collected by the ad hoc organisations that sprang up was delivered to the miners hall in Ashington for distribution throughout the needy families in the South East Northumberland coal field area. The system was far from perfect but it brought a little comfort to many families who were having a very difficult time.

Tony Hartill and Dickie Sanderson were prime movers in organising the volunteers and initially differences about 'the strike' were subsumed for the common good. People from all walks of life contributed but overall the contributions did not make a huge impact.

Suddenly, one morning, to the surprise of the distribution groups a lorry arrived at the Trade Union Hall. The driver declared that he had a load of food for the miners. All available hands went to assist with the unloading. The cargo included sacks of wheat, rice and flour and cases of small cans of condensed milk. For some, such contributions were a very welcome supplement. Each family who wanted a share brought a container to the union hall or if they were unable to attend their share would be delivered. The volunteers were told that the food had come from Russia. Whether it had come from Russia or not Tony and his colleagues never really found out. The deliveries were erratic and no mention of the origins of the food or how it got there was ever confirmed.

The Russian food, as it was called, received a mixed reception in many ways. The wheat was unusable and of such poor quality that it was eventually fed to chickens. The flour and rice faired better with much of the rice being used to make a rice wine or spirit. The jokes and humour related to some of the activities of rice recipients helped to relieve the anxieties and uncertainties that haunted the communities.

Many of the miners refused to accept the donations from Russia and were furious at the implied associations between the miners and the USSR.

Tony and his colleagues had to listen patiently to the convictions of many genuinely held views. Some pro Markham and some vehemently opposed. Some were furious at what they saw as the humiliation of the CMU accepting food from Russian and Polish coal miners who were living from hand to mouth. Others who desperately wanted to return to work would have nothing to do with any union activities or any of the ad hoc relief organisations.

It was against this background that Tony Hartill and his colleagues found themselves at the centre of more controversy. The focus on relief for needy families had brought together a cross section of men and women who had set aside their allegiances or personal differences with the pros the anti's of whatever camp. They collected whatever they could and distributed among the colliery groups on a pro rata basis.

This altruistic accord was damaged and finally

smashed when Mullaney and his pro Markham camp decided that the distribution group should be directly under the control of the CMU. Mullaney was aware of the success and the popularity of the food distribution teams. He was concerned that people such as Tony Hartill had never picketed and were suspected of being involved in recruiting disenchanted CMU members to join the breakaway Union of Democratic Mineworkers or UDM.

A meeting was called and addressed by Mullaney who congratulated the work done by the distribution organisers and said he hoped they would continue with the new CMU distribution system. Not many of the volunteers turned up at the meeting since they were not interested in procedural matters. Tony Hartill had mustered a few to attend and as he looked around the room he realised that Mullaney had made sure that his supporters were in a considerable majority.

Tony Hartill stood up. There was silence in the hall. He looked at Mullaney.

'You have just stated that those who have done the distribution so far have done an excellent job. So why change the system?' he stated.

'It's the duty of the CMU to look after the best interests of the miners.' snarled Mullaney who then looked around his supporters with a sudden smile as though anticipating some acclamation.

'If that's the case why not have a proper democratic ballot on this matter and on one or two other pressing matters….'

Before Tony could finish his sentence he was interrupted by someone shouting. 'And when's the last time you stood on a picket line. Yarra scab Hartill.'

His friend Dickie Sanderson grabbed Tony by the arm saying. 'Don't waste your time Tony. Let's get out of here.'

The two began walking out of the room and others followed to jeers and shouts of 'Scab.' and 'Scabby Bastard.'

After that meeting each colliery or group operated independently with small teams of ad hoc units providing meals or distributing whatever came their way. Once again this was a symptom of the breakdown of unity and cohesion that had sustained the coal mining communities for decades.

The last straw for Tony Hartill had come towards the end of May. The dispute was at stalemate and the outcome was far from certain. The financial pressures and constraints on many of the families was awful causing tempers to flare and fists to fly in homes and within groups of family that had never known much dissension.

The CMU leadership was aware of the distress and they wanted to distribute cash to help. Rumours were in abundance that the CMU was preparing to pay out cash to the membership throughout the country as part of the strategy to strengthen the resolve of the miners. Many looked forward to the forthcoming financial help.

All union officials were summoned to a meeting in the union headquarters in Newcastle upon Tyne. Mullaney and the Chairman of the Durham area informed the delegates that two men from each pit were to be appointed to collect the cash. They would be advised of the rendezvous two hours before the men set off. £10.00 was to be made available per week per member. Distribution was up to each branch.

From the audience came the question. 'How much money does the CMU have?' to which Mullaney said.

'That's not our problem. There's more than enough. When we get the money we'll telephone to tell the branches to collect.'

'What if there isn't enough money for all the members' asked another questioner.

'Don't worry!' Mullaney's replied. 'Albert has everything in hand. If we just keep our powder dry it will all work out'

Another questioner shouted. 'Where's the money coming from?'

'Jesus.' shouted Mullaney. 'What's this? We've gone to a load of trouble to get the help you've all asked for and all I get is a load of stupid bloody questions. Do you want the money or not.'

'Ray's right.' said another voice. 'Let's stop buggering about and get on with the business. Personally I couldn't care where the money comes from.'

'Aye that's right.' said a supporter.

As a Treasurer of Northumberland CMU Tony Hartill had full entitlement to an invitation to the meeting in Newcastle upon Tyne. Those invited had been telephoned the previous day. Only those considered to be in full support of Markham's camp were asked. After the meeting Tony received a visit from a colleague who had just come back from the meeting asking why he wasn't there.

'Wasn't invited, knew nothing about it' said Tony.

'Where are we going?' asked the man who then said. 'I've never been so fed up in all my life. The other thing that I had to tell you was about the branch meeting. We are to have a branch meeting to finalise the list of all the members who are eligible to receive their £10.00.

'How will it be paid.' asked Tony.

'We collect it and then distribute it.' The man then went on to explain what had happened at the meeting in Newcastle and the questions Mullaney had refused to answer.

'By the way' the man said before he left. 'The branch meeting is tonight.'

'Tonight!' exclaimed Tony. 'But no one knows about it.'

'Well you know now.' said the man. 'I hope you'll be there to speak up.'

Once again Tony Hartill was a very angry man. He made six telephone calls. At each call he asked the man on the other end to go to the meeting and to telephone someone else asking them in turn to go to the meeting and make a further telephone call.

At the meeting he was pleasantly surprised by the support that he had when he saw the faces. His son Kevin was there but Tony received no acknowledgement from him; this hurt him deeply. Just before the meeting began Mullaney walked in with his minders.

Mullaney sat in the vacant chair next to where the empty Chairman's seat and declared. 'Kevin Hartill will Chair the meeting as Chairman of the strike committee. There's a lot of people here tonight who were not expected but no doubt our Chairman can cope with that.

Tony Hartill felt like screaming. Mullaney was relishing every moment. Tony was so embarrassed that he avoided any eye contact.

Kevin took the Chair next to Mullaney and opened the meeting.

'Item 1.' he said. 'The response for volunteers to picket has been good but we need more. Anybody wanting to join the Pickets see me; any questions?'

A general discussion followed on about avoiding VCP's (Vehicle Check Points) manned by the Police. No one on Tony's side got involved.

'Item 2, and this is important, headquarters has

made as much money available to us as they can. Support in money is coming in but in some cases we have to go to collect it. We cannot put it through a bank accounts cos' the Government could trace it. I need a volunteer to go with me to a rendezvous tomorrow to collect the first lot. We have nearly two thousand members here so I will be picking up £20,000 in cash. That's a lot of money so as well as the bloke with me I would appreciate a two car escort. Petrol will be paid and any damage to the car's, well we'll see you alright.' There was dead silence.

Mullaney broke the silence with. 'Kevin needs another two cars and three comrades; one to accompany each driver.' All ten members of the Strike committee volunteered.

Mullaney said. 'Thanks lads. The ones that don't go this week go next week. I notice there's an acute shortage of volunteers from some quarters.' as he looked across at Tony and his colleagues.

'Item 3.' said Kevin. 'We have as many weekend holidays in Ireland as we want for CMU members and their wives. We urgently need volunteers now to go this next weekend. All expenses paid.'

Kevin looked at Mullaney who said. 'Tell them.'

'Each couple will be expected to collect a large bundle of cash when they are there and bring it back. All the arrangements have been made. Two of our lads spent a week over there making the arrangement with a group who are supporting the Miners.'

The room fell silent as the import of what had just been said was assimilated. Men looked at one another and began murmuring before Dickie Sanderson said. 'I don't suppose you know who is supplying the money.'

'What difference where it comes from' said a member of the strike committee. 'We need the money to keep the strike gannin.'

'It makes a hell of a lot of difference.' shouted Tony. 'If the press get wind of this we'll be branded. We'll never get any support from the public. Use your brains for God's sake.'

Another man sitting behind Tony shouted. 'Are you telling us that you are taking money from the IRA'

'Nobody said that.' Mullaney shouted back.

'You don't need to say it. It's written all over your faces.' said the angry faced man. 'And I'll tell you something else. My son is over there with the British Army trying to keep the peace and so is your Brother.' He went on pointing to Kevin. 'You must all have sand for brains. I'm getting out of here. The man stood up and turned to leave. One by one the others followed until only the strike committee and Mullaney were left sitting in the room.

The next day on the instructions of Mullaney the strike committee were told to pass the word that the IRA connection was a malicious lie put out by the newly formed Union of Democratic Miners to discredit the CMU.

Tony Hartill and his colleagues knew different, one of the members of the strike committee who had sat behind Kevin the previous night waylaid Tony and Dickie Sanderson the following morning. 'I need to talk to you.' He said.

The man was known as a Mullaney supporter and so Dickie responded with. 'We heard enough from your lot last night.'

'That's what I want to talk to you about.' said the man. 'But not here.'

Tony looked at the man who appeared to be genuinely agitated. 'I'll tell you what. Meet me at my Mother's house in twenty minutes. I'll look out for you and let you straight in. Come to the back door.'

Twenty minutes later the man sat in the Hartill's

sitting room with Tony and Dickie Sanderson where he related the story behind the events of the meeting held the previous night.

'I just had to talk to somebody. I'm on this strike committee and I joined thinking I would help the cause on the Picket lines but two weeks ago I was on one of the flying picket trips to Nottingham. There was four bus loads of us. Some had their wives and kids with them to get past the Police manning the VCP's by pretending to be on a family day out. We left the women and kids in a Park and joined other pickets who had come in from everywhere. There was Scottish Miners, Welsh Miners and Miners from all over. Not all of them were Miners though; some of them were sympathisers. That's what they called themselves. Some of the battles were horrendous and some of the lads lost their heads. Some were pissed out of their heads and started throw'in bricks it was a bloody nightmare. Scores of them lined up armed with pick axe handles and charged at the police and the Nottingham men trying to get into the pit. Sometimes you didn't know who was who. Mind, the Police were no bloody angels either. Some of those buggers had a field day.'

The man paused before adding. 'Last night. That was the finish. Wor lass (his wife) said she wants away. She cannot stand any more of this. We cannot sleep at nights and when I do sleep I wake up with the nightmares. The trouble is that all our friends are up to their necks in this and we don't want to fall out with them. Hell if they knew I was here.'

'What do you want us to do.' asked Tony quietly.

'I don't really know.' replied the man. 'I'll tell you what though; Ah feel better for just gett'in it off me chest.'

'That IRA bit last night!' he continued. 'It was your

Kevin and another lad who set the deal up in Ireland. They were over there for nearly a week. Mullaney's the only one who knows the details. That finished me, but how do I get out though?'

Tony was stunned. He looked at the man in silence.

Dickie looked at Tony with consternation writ large upon his countenance.

Tony put his elbows on his knees and dropped his head in his hand. 'That's it then.' said Tony to no one in particular.

Dickie said to the man. 'Thanks for the information. I think you should just tell Mullaney or who ever you have to tell, that the stress is too much and that you resign from the strike committee. Then lie low till it's all over.'

'Thanks.' said the man. 'It's helped having someone to talk to. Sorry to be the bearer of bad news.'

Dickie saw the man out. 'Take care lad and good luck.' he said as they parted

Chapter 7

On arriving back in his native village Bill Robinson and his family had adapted to their new life in what was a completely different community and lifestyle to that in a terraced street in Islington.

Whilst in Islington he had taken an interest in local politics although he had never stood for office. He had also joined a 'Speakers Club'. This was a non-party political organisation that met in a pub called 'The Dun Cow' every Monday night and invited Speakers from all walks of life to give a twenty-minute speech followed by a few questions. The speaker would then be invited to stay whilst a member was asked to speak for ten minutes on a subject he'd been given the week before. The member was always subjected to the scathing wit of the guest speaker and his fellow members. Everyone listened attentively for a gaff or looked for an intervention that would introduce amusement and sometimes, great hilarity.

From time to time Members of Parliament would be invited and one Monday night in the late nineteen sixties the club members were wrapped in attention to a clever and witty twenty-minute statement by the Right Hon. Jo Grimond, Member of Parliament for the Orkney Islands.

His subject was about the state of Britain's heavy industries and the short-sightedness of the establishment in not addressing the problems of competing in a world which was to change significantly in the years to come. Jo Grimond was the leader of a small group of Liberal MP's who were elected to Parliament mainly from Britain's Celtic fringe. From then on Bill would read whatever he came across related to National Politics and became a Grimond devotee.

On returning to the North East of England Bill found a small band of Liberal supporters in his new constituency of Winsbreck and joined them.

Winsbreck District Council was formed under the local Government reorganisation of the early nineteen seventies and Winsbreck had returned a full complement of forty six Labour Councillors who had been largely unopposed at the elections.

Four years later the Liberals had won two seats and had come close to winning a further two. Again most of the seats were uncontested. Within a few months of the District Council elections a Labour Council member died who had represented a ward which had been almost won by a Liberal candidate.

A bye-election was called and after a lot of hard work polling day arrived with the Liberals feeling cautiously optimistic about winning the seat. Bill Robinson with the Liberal candidate and his team of helpers arrived at the school hall where the count was to be made. Over forty Labour Councillors and Labour Party workers were already in the hall standing in a group apart. The Conservatives also contested the seat. The Tory candidate and a team of six helpers wearing their blue rosettes stood in a group apart from the Labour group.

Eventually the Returning Officer announced a seventy one per cent turnout of voters. This was very high for a local election anywhere. Everyone was surprised at the size of the turnout and even more surprised by the events that followed.

The rules clearly stated that only a limited number of representatives were allowed in the count and each had to submit a form signed by a Justice of the Peace.

Bill and the Liberal candidate approached the

Returning Officer, who was also the Chief Executive of the Council, to complain that the Labour Party representation was excessive and a clear breach of election law. Critall the Chief Exective was clearly angry at this criticism of his management and the validity of the complaint was largely ignored.

He accused Bill and his colleagues of calling his professional ability into question. Bill Robinson told him that the procedure was a farce if the Labour Party could flout the rules and demanded that the Labour members in excess of the quota be expelled. Critall raged at Bill and told him to put his complaint in writing.

Rather than dare to even suggest the eviction of part of the Labour Group Critall told Bill that he was a troublemaker and he, Bill, would be expelled if he caused any more bother. The Liberal and Tory groups were flabbergasted. Worse was to come. As soon as the count began it became obvious that the Liberal candidate was winning in a landslide. In a state of panic the Labour Group milled, illegally, around the counting table disbelieving what they saw.

Only two scrutineers from each party were officially allowed to stand over the counting tables so Bill demanded that Crittall implement the rules. It was clear to that those counting the votes were becoming anxious; they were being jostled by Labour supporters, many the worse for too much alcohol, who were milling around the tables. Eventually the counting was stopped till the crowd milling around the table withdrew.

When order was restored the count went ahead. The result was obvious long before the announcement and insults from the Labour group were increasingly in evidence.

Realising they had lost, the Labour Councillors and

there supporters were ushered into a corner of the room where they sang the Red Flag over and over again. Eventually a very distressed Mr Crittall asked for silence before he, as Returning Officer, announced the result.

Although the Liberal group were delighted with their result they didn't cheer. The situation was ugly enough without making things worse. They were taken aback by the hostility so they decided to keep quiet to minimise further ugliness. To their further surprise the Tory agent too, began shouting at them; 'What right have you to stand. If you hadn't stood we would have got the vote and won.' The Liberal group said nothing. They agreed among themselves not to respond and asked the attendant policeman to see them safely out, as they began to leave a prominent Labour Councillor called Ray Mullaney shouted across the hall. 'I will personally promise you that this is the last election your lot ever win.'

In the years that followed the Councillor was unable to fulfil that promise.

By May 1983 Bill himself had become a Councillor. He was one of ten Liberal Councillors elected from every part of the Council district covering what was also the Winsbreck constituency.

Very few of the Labour Councillors spoke in the Council meetings. Bill recognised that many of them were self-conscious and found it difficult to express their view before a lot of people. In the main he liked them and outside the Council Chamber they were largely very decent people with good intentions. The same could not be said for some of those who spoke for them. Most statements came from just four or five Labour Councillors who would snarl through their vitriolic condemnation of everything except their

107

concept of 'pure' socialism.

What galled Bill was the continuing spiral of decline of Winsbreck. It seemed that despite the rhetoric no genuine attempt was being made to bring an alternative to coal mining. On one occasion one of the Labour councillors told him that the worse things got the harder people voted Labour. Another told him that prosperous people voted Tory and so everyone had to have the same so that everyone would vote Labour. Bill saw the naivety of these statements as a threat to the wellbeing of everyone in the coal field areas.

In the Council Chamber his attempts to bring some expertise and prospects for the future went unheeded.

'If ever a place needed inspiration for enterprise and innovation it was Winsbreck.' he argued. His calls fell on deaf ears. Such terms and words were outwith the philosophy of Winsbreck Socialism and could not be embraced by Winsbreck Council in any way.

Council Officers are normally obliged to avoid any Party Political bias. This was not the case in Winsbreck. Too many Officers were in place because of their allegiance to the views of the voluble oligarchy that made all the decisions. Very often Officers who had a statement to make which they thought may not go down well with Labour Group would begin with: 'Now you all know my political views. I have been a Socialist all my life, but of course my views have no bearing on this place or on the advice which I have to give you, however ....etc.' This blatant act of ingratiation with the Labour leadership was regularly denounced by Bill and his colleagues; always to no avail.

Professional standards were sacrificed for Officer job security and a peaceful life.

The Liberal Group wanted to assert themselves as a

political force with a set of policies to bring new industries and stimulate new businesses in the area. Although they paid lip service to this objective the Labour Group were quite content so long as they retained control. Whenever an initiative was suggested by the Liberals the snarling vitriol of Mullaney, and the CMU oligarchy that controlled the council would rally the Labour side to shouting abuse at the unfortunate Liberal spokesman who had provoked the response.

Many of the Liberal Councillors were intimidated by such occasions and so speaking on behalf of the Liberal Group was left to Bill Robinson and George Atkinson who had somehow immunised themselves from the abusive verbiage which was the stock in trade of the Winsbreck Labour leadership.

The electoral successes and a lot of helpful newspaper reports had made the Liberals in Winsbreck very prominent within the Liberal Party in the North East of England where success against Labour was hard won.

Several weeks into the miner's dispute Bill Robinson received a phone call from Daphne Galbraith who was the Regional Secretary of the Liberals. The gist of the call was: 'Bill, a CMU official from the Durham Coalfield has approached me to ask if we can help him and his colleagues get back to work.'

'How do we do that?' Bill asked.

Daphne went on. 'He seems to think that our Members in Parliament can approach the Government to ask for their help. Anyway I have met the bloke. He came to my house and told me he was in a Back to Work group and we were the only people they could think of who could possibly help.'

Bill pondered. 'It could be a set up of course, sounds very odd really but I suppose these guys are in a difficult situation. No money and the strike could go on for ages. They are obviously not getting any help from their Labour Party colleagues.' he said thinking aloud.

Daphne replied. 'He wouldn't leave a phone number but he said that if we left a number he would contact us. Is it all right if I give him your number and leave it to you? He said he would call at my house again tomorrow between six and seven.'

Bill said. 'OK. I'll let you know how I get on.'

The following night Bill's telephone rang and a voice said. 'Is that Bill Robinson from Winsbreck.'

'Yes' said Bill.

'I know you must think this thing is crazy but we are miners and genuine people who want to get back to work. If we don't get back soon we'll have no pits to go back to and most of us are skint already'

Bill agreed with him. 'Well I do appreciate the situation. I am living with it every day here. It is just about the only topic of conversation.'

'I know this seems a bit like James Bond and that but there are some real Loonies down here and we are in a difficult situation. Can we meet you soon?'

'What about' Bill asked 'how soon and who are you?'

'Tomorrow night.' replied the man 'and no names just yet.'

'No.' Bill said. 'Tomorrow night is too soon. I need time to think and sort something out. Telephone me here again tomorrow night and we'll talk about it again.'

At the same time the following night Bill answered the telephone and the easily recognised Durham accent asked if Bill would go to a place in County Durham to meet him and two others.

On receiving the first call Bill had gone to see his friend and Councillor, colleague, George Atkinson, who after a long discussion, agreed to accompany Bill if the man phoned back.

Two days later, on a Sunday night, they followed the caller's instructions and drove to Trimdon village in County Durham.

As requested Bill parked his Jaguar in the car park of the village pub just before dusk. He had given a description of the car and the registration number to the man during their telephone conversation.

After a few minutes three men came out of a house opposite. They got into a car and drove their car alongside Bill's in the car park.

One man, got out of their car, came across to Bill. `Bill Robinson?' he asked.

'It is.' Bill replied. 'This is my colleague George Atkinson.

'Can I get into your car and then you can follow me marrers car.'

'No problem' said Bill. 'But you sit in the front and my friend will sit in the back. 'O.K'

'O.K.' said the man.

'What's all this cloak and dagger stuff ?' said George from the back of the car.

'We cannot afford to take chances. But then again I suppose this is taking chances' said the man who was obviously nervous.

After they had driven about a mile the car in front pulled up outside the entrance to Trimdon Cricket Club. Bill followed suit and then a third car pulled up behind Bill's car. The man in Bill's car opened his car door and shouted to the driver of the first car.

'Drive in and blast your horn like hell if you see anything suspicious.'

All five men watched in silence as the car moved along the narrow road to the club house. The driver went into the building beckoning them to follow him back into the building after emerging a minute later.

The driver of the third car was asked to remain at

the cricket field entrance.

A few minutes later three of the men sat around a table inside a cosy upstairs room with a view across the whole ground.

Once inside the familiar Durham voice said. 'Sorry about all this but we can't be too careful.' He then introduced himself and his colleagues finishing with. 'The lad at the gate is my brother in law.'

Bill tried to make a mental note of the names before replying: 'Bill Robinson and George Atkinson.'

Bill opened by saying that he wasn't sure that there was any way in which they could do much to help. At this the men went into a long explanation about their circumstances and frustration and that they needed to get access to someone who would recognise that the miners did not want the strike. When Bill pointed out that the Durham miners had voted to strike his hosts all jumped in to say that at most collieries in the Durham area the vote was rigged.

One of them then revealed that he was a card holding member of the Communist Party of Great Britain; 'but!' he said. 'I am also a democrat and I can't stomach what is going on with Markham and his henchmen. This is a setup.'

'We've been completely stitched up' said one and the others nodded their confirmation.

After about an hour, at the request of their hosts, it was agreed that Bill and George Atkinson would report back and try to get a Liberal Member of Parliament to come to see them. They all shook hands and parted company.

Bill contacted Daphne who reported back to London. The proposition was taken seriously and arrangements were made to meet in the upstairs room of a large hotel just outside Durham City a week later.

Two Liberal Members of Parliament alighted from

the train in Durham Station at four in the afternoon and were met by Bill Robinson who drove them to the hotel. They went into the upstairs room and introductions were made. When Bill Robinson entered the room the first person he laid eyes on was Tony Hartill.

One of the men was a union official well acquainted with Tony with whom he had discussed the dispute at length. Tony had endorsed the contact that Daphne had given to the men and hence the phonecall to Bill Robinson. Inevitably someone said 'It's a small world.'

Bill Robinson said to Tony; 'You know I was going to get in touch with you when these guys asked us to come here but I thought you had enough on your plate. I should have known better.'

Whether this meeting had anything to do with it or not Tony Hartill and Bill Robinson would never be certain but from then on the campaign to get back to work seemed to gather momentum. Covert meetings, similar to that attended by the Liberal MP's, were taking place all over the country. The problem was that those who wanted a return to work were disorganised and unsure of their strength. No one wanted to be first in case the whole campaign crumbled under the weight of intimidation or events unforeseen. Small groups of men gathered in cells in each other's homes to give each other moral support and to discuss tactics.

Some of the miners had relations, or friends, who were policemen. For many policemen the thought of coming up against relatives and people they had known all their life was a nightmare. One of the things that came out of the Durham meeting was the fact that obstructing people who wanted to work was wrong and against the law so that, in theory at least, those who wanted to go to work had the right to do so. In these circumstances the Police were obliged to ensure freedom of movement.

Lifted by the knowledge that there were like-minded people all over the country Tony Hartill approached the local Police to find out how a back to work campaign could be organised. He then began making contacts with men who, he felt, would want to return to work. They were in two categories: Those who would defy the picket no matter what and those that would join the back to work once they had seen the evidence of some success and the level of support.

Only a minority belonged to the first category for obvious reasons. They didn't want to be called scab for the rest of their lives. They didn't want to fall out with friends and relations. Most were under pressure from wives and family who feared for their welfare. Feelings were running very high and serious injury was a possibility if things got ugly in a divided community. Even children were pitted against one another depending upon the views and actions of their respective families. The real tragedy was that the community had never ever before had any real divisions. This situation was less of a strike and more of a cat and mouse game between those who wanted to work and those who were determined to keep them out. Confusion and fear reigned everywhere.

By mid-May and for the first time since the dispute began Tony Hartill and a dozen others swept through the picket lines at the entrance to Ellington Colliery in a Mini bus escorted by Police. The trip became a daily event but it was no more than a gesture for once inside the pit yard the Mini-bus passengers sat around and waited to be taken out again.

At first the pickets were caught off guard but as more pickets arrived each morning and evening the times of arrival and departure were varied in an attempt make it difficult to man the picket. As the days went on the pickets became more aggressive and more numerous but there were suddenly two mini buses and then a fifty-seven seat bus.

Slowly the pickets and their leaders found out the names of those who were on the buses or who were suspected of being on the buses. From then on the situation for the named ones became very tense.

What the pickets couldn't discover was the identities of the bus drivers who had a tendency to move with the grace and pace of Olympic athletes. A long wooden baton was always positioned near the driver's seat and no one on the bus or coach was in any doubt of their intention to use it with effect if necessary. Some of the drivers drove the bus slowly through the pickets with one hand and fought with the pickets with their free hand through the open window of the driver's door. All doors on the bus were locked until the bus was clear of the lines. The driver's door was always locked. Tony marvelled at some of the tactics used by the drivers and memories of his training as a Militarily Policeman came flooding back. He was sure that some of these men had military training.

The tactic worked but the level of intimidation was so intense that the management asked for the attempted return to work to be called off temporarily. In the weeks and months that followed many of those in the return to work attempt were to endure some unpleasant experiences.

Apart from a brief honeymoon period on his return from Cyprus relations between Tony Hartill and his wife, Maggie, had blown hot and cold. Their second son, Richard, had joined the Army when he reached eighteen and the third son, Nigel, was at University. Nigel was named after the Military Police Sergeant who had died on the roadside in Cyprus just as he was born. The Sergeant did not have a family of his own and he had taken an acute interest in Tony's family.

Tony's Mother did not see too much of her Grandchildren when Tony was in the forces but when Tony came home Nigel spent a lot of time with Grandma' Hartill who introduced him to the magic of books. Grandma' Hartill and Tony were so proud of Nigels academic achievements as were Maggie and the rest of the family. Whenever Grandma' Hartill saw Maggie she would say 'You must be proud Maggie, you have three fine sons.'

And Maggie was proud. And so was Grandma' Hartill because the implication was that she had three fine Grandsons.

After endless arguments over Kevin's involvement with Mullaney, the pickets, and the trips to Ireland Tony found himself at loggerheads with Maggie and her large extended family and in turn their friends. Tony's involvement with the Police escorted coaches made relationships intolerable. Going back to the atmosphere in the three bedroomed terraced house that Tony and Maggie had shared all these years had become an effort of will. Maggie was spending more and more time with Kevin and his wife or with her parents or brothers and sisters who were solidly behind the strike.

Maggie had always been a moderate cigarette smoker. Over recent months her dependence on cigarettes had increased significantly and she was now chain smoking at a time when money was scarce. This caused arguments. Kevin and his wife now had virtually no income and to Tony's dismay they would not take any money from Tony to help out. This caused further arguments. Everything caused arguments and Tony found himself continually re-appraising his life and his future.

Quite often he would find himself asking 'Why don't I just join them or sit back and ignore the whole business?'

Returning from the pit in mid-May Tony arrived at his house to find it full of Maggie's relatives. As usual Tony walked in through the back door from the yard and as he entered the voices in the lounge subsided to silence. Maggie looked at Tony anxiously. She wanted to say something and words wouldn't come. Tony was just inside the kitchen door. Maggie stood with the same look of anxiety she had all those years ago when she had found herself pregnant. He remembered the relief and joyous happiness on her face when he told her he would not desert her. Her white teeth had gleamed, her smooth skin had glowed.

'Maggie! What's going on?' he said.

'Why can't you just be like everybody else.' she said quietly as she turned to step back into the lounge.

Inside every face was turned up to look at Tony. He looked around at them and for some reason he remembered a night in the Equality Club less than two years previously:

The Commander of a Royal Navy Destroyer, visiting Newcastle upon Tyne, had come to the club to receive a cheque for the Falklands war veterans.

Tony remembered the Commander flanked by two Junior Officers standing on the stage in the large concert room which was packed to capacity. Maggie's older sister was the principal organiser of the event. She had made a simple speech.

As the hushed audience listened she declared that the Club had raised seventeen hundred and eighty three pounds and fifty pence. Then to thunderous applause she handed the cheque over to Commander Bridges who shook her hand and kissed her on the cheek as everyone in the room clapped, cheered and whistled. The mouths of the three Officers had opened a little as the sum raised had been declared. Everyone in the room was shouting; 'Speech!'

Maggie's sister spoke briefly to the Commander who stepped up to the microphone. Fortunately he had to wait a moment or two for the cheering to die down. He had not anticipated such a large donation and he was obviously moved by the occasion.

Tony asked himself the question; 'How was it possible for people, who were so basically honourable and decent, to be duped and misled into a situation which at the end of the day would create only hardship and misery?' The answer eluded him.

As Tony feared, when he saw the gathering in the lounge, there was going to be a showdown.

'Nice to see you all here, it's a while since we all got together like this.' He said for the want of something to say.

'Don't you play smart-arse with us Mr Tony bloody Hartill' said Maggie's sister.

'This is mine and Maggie's home.' said Tony quietly.

Despite the fact that he wanted to scream at the top of his voice he went on, 'I am quite prepared to have a civilised discussion but I am not entering a shouting match so if we are going to talk we talk on my terms in my home.'

'What sort of home is this for Maggie.' said Tony's brother in law.

Kevin chipped in: 'You're making a bloody laughing stock of your own family. What sort of Fatha' are you.'

'Aye, and what sort of bloody husband' said Maggie's sister.

Tony recognised the futility of responding. He knew that whatever he said would quickly lead to a slanging match. He looked at his distraught wife. She didn't deserve all this pain and anguish. With the advancing years, the anguish and the endless taunts and family trials that had gone on over the last months Maggie looked awful. The happy green blue eyes of yesteryear were prematurely sunken and the skin surrounding them looked blue black. She sucked heavily on yet another cigarette. Her lined face stared at the floor.

Tony drew a deep breath and said, 'There doesn't seem to be any point to this. I think you should just leave us in peace; if you would?'

They looked at each other with sidelong glances. No one moved.

Tony looked around before leaving the room and then the house. As he walked up the narrow back lane shared by the long rows of back to back Colliery houses he realised that he did not know where he was going but he knew that he was never going back to the house he'd shared with Maggie. He decided to go to his Mother's house.

As always Tony's Mother was busy. Since the dispute she had called regularly at Tony's house and at the home of Kevin with what she called 'tasty bites'. These so-called tasty bites were usually substantial meals such as steak and kidney pie or hot pot. She would telephone Maggie or Kevin's wife and forewarn them of her arrival. Such food was very welcome because although hard times had not arrived completely there was no end in sight to the dispute and every contribution was welcome in every mining household. She knew that Tony was very upset at the relationship that had developed between him and Kevin and she believed that people were always more kindly disposed and conciliatory when they were well fed. As always, Tony's Mother was busy caring, smoothing, soothing and trying to heal.

Despite this the rift between Father and Son widened. Tony just wanted to put his arms around his son. He desperately wanted Kevin to know of the love he felt for him. He so desperately wanted that love to be reciprocated. He wanted it to conquer their differences. He just did not know how to do it.

One factor which was of great relief and comfort to Tony was the attitude of his own Father who subscribed totally with Tony's view; that the dispute could not and would not benefit anyone. Tony's Father had eventually left the pit when he was sixty-five years old. He had a modest pension, modest savings, and a modest home that he owned. He and Tony's Mother considered themselves to be very comfortable. For Tony the home of his parents was a refuge, a sane, clean and comfortable refuge.

Chapter 8

The train journey from Moscow to Minsk takes about eight hours. Gennardy had boarded the train about an hour previously and he found himself sharing the three-berth couchette with one other person who was in army uniform. The man was a colonel in the Polish army and the purple band round his cap indicated that he was in the Polish Intelligence service. The Officer opened a bottle of Vodka and handed the bottle to Gennardy who disguised his surprise at this uncharacteristic gesture and took a small swig. It was about midnight and after a brief conversation the man indicated that he would like to sleep. Gennardy responded by advising the man that he too wanted to sleep. The two released one of the bunks on the side of the compartment and the Colonel climbed up into it. Gennardy stretched out on the seat below that doubled as a seat and a bunk.

'I'm pleased there's some bloody heating on this train grunted the Colonel.'

'Da' Gennardy confirmed.

As Gennardy lay on the bunk in the gloom of the compartment the monotonous drumming rythm of steel wheels on steel rails clackety clacked. He desperately wanted to get some sleep himself but his mind was full of thoughts, ideas and suspicions.

'Was it a coincidence that he was sharing this compartment with an officer of Polish Intelligence?'

'It must be coincidence.' he advised himself.

Things had gone better than he had thought possible. At least he had made contact with the British. It had been much easier than he had imagined. Then he thought about Miss Smith's demand for proof.

He decided that the British didn't really care about him that much but he reckoned that they would keep their word as long as they got some information. His mind wandered on as he thought about Li and how he could contact her.

'Plakinov's office or apartment indeed, stupid people!' he thought.

Outside an intense frost lay on top of the deep snow covering the countryside. As the train plunged on down the line the bright moonlight glinted off the rails and off the frost. The world outside seemed to be bathed in a blue light and he thought about his parents who had lost their lives travelling on this very line between Moscow and Minsk. Then again he had not a shred of evidence to support that story.

'Had their really been a derailment? He would never know.'

Whatever happened he hoped that they were together because he was sure that they had loved one another. He thought about his childhood and how happy they were together. He remembered walking through the woods looking for wild mushrooms with each of his hands secure in the hand of his Mother and Father as they walked three abreast. He could hear his voice shouting. 'Swing me Mama. Swing me Dada.'

Gennardy pushed his hand to his brow and thrust his fingers through his thick hair then turned on his side cupping his ear in his hand to reduce the noise of the clickety clack. His thoughts meandered on until eventually he fell into a sleep of sorts.

About six in the morning the Officer swung himself down from the bunk above, opened the door of the compartment and stepped into the corridor of the train. Gennardy was immediately wide awake.

Russian passenger trains have a guard for every carriage with the job of feeding the little coal fired boiler to circulate heat through the compartments. The

Guard is also expected to report anything suspicious and he or she has the right to check the papers and luggage of passengers at will. Gennardy had travelled this journey many times but this time he was nervous. He felt as though everyone was aware of his guilty secrets despite the fact that he knew they couldn't be. The guard had checked his papers as he had got on the train and he had checked them again shortly after the train had left but everyone else had had their papers looked at a second time. He consoled himself with the thought that it was probably just the guard making himself important because he wanted to impress the Polish Officer.

The Officer returned muttering complaints about the cold in the toilet. Gennardy agreed with the grievance before making his way to the toilet at the end of the carriage. The noise of steel wheels on steel railway lines increased significantly as Gennardy closed the toilet door. The temperature inside the toilet area seemed to decrease in proportion to the increase in sound. Gennardy urinated into the steel bowl provided and pressed the pedal with his right foot whereon the flap at the bottom of the bowl opened. The contents released by Gennardy fell by the side of the railway track and at the same time freezing air rushed up through the bowl. Gennardy shuddered and quickly took his foot from the pedal. As he did so he caught his reflection in the cracked mirror above a washbasin. He wanted to wash his hands but there was no water let alone soap.

Looking at himself in the mirror he thought about the comfort and warmth and good food he had enjoyed at the home of Tony Hartill. He saw himself smiling into the mirror prompting him to examine his white and even teeth. He noticed that his face seemed drawn and it appeared thinner. He wasn't sure whether this was due to the anxiety of recent times or the fact that it was so early in the morning. Deciding that it was probably a bit of both as he took out a comb and drew his luxuriant hair to either side of the parting on the left hand side of his head.

He wondered if he would ever see Tony Hartill again. His own brown eyes reminded him of the sincerity that he had seen in the eyes of Tony when he had explained his feelings of betrayal during his visit to Ashington. He had never seen people so at ease with themselves. People who joked and laughed so much and made fun of one another with such enthusiasm. He shuddered again from the cold as he adjusted his clothes and decided that there was certain to be a beautiful woman in England who would take a fancy to an eligible bachelor from Belarus. As he pondered his reflection he said to the mirror. 'Hello lady. My name is Gennardy a man who is in good health and who stands 1.7 metres tall with good shoulders and a good physique.'

He decided that since he had done quite well in the USSR he should enjoy some success with women in England. The problem was how to get there?

Once again he was filled with resolve and purpose as he made his way back to the compartment. He pushed the sliding door open, entered, and sat down.

The Polish Colonel had replaced the upper bunk bed against the wall of the compartment and had started drinking vodka from the small bottle. He again offered it to Gennardy.

The last thing Gennardy fancied was Vodka at that time in the morning but he was not prepared to violate the hospitality of a Polish Intelligence Officer. Gennardy wiped the top of the bottle and took a small swig attempting to make it look like a large swig.

Conversations between strangers on trains within the USSR were not unheard of but such was the fear of inadvertently making a slip of the tongue that conversations were not commonplace and responses were carefully weighed.

Gennardy ventured an innocuous opening statement; 'Going home on leave then?'

The Colonel looked at him and said 'No; I have been to Moscow to discuss Poland. We have some subversive elements in Poland especially in Gdansk.' Gennardy ventured to say that he knew Gdansk reasonably well.

'As members of the Warsaw pact and comrades we are working with our Russian colleagues to do our best for our beloved Poland.' said the Colonel.

'General Jarolzelski, our Prime Minister, is determined to ensure that we work together to ensure that our respective motherlands are not contaminated by destructive influences.'

Recognising the official party speak; Gennardy ventured another contribution.

'Like you I have an interest in both of our Motherlands because Polish blood runs in my veins too. I speak Polish.'

The Colonel smiled and immediately switched to the Polish language. Without further ado he began to tell Gennardy about his wife who was a haematologist in Warsaw's principal hospital. He had a daughter who was twelve years old and he would like a son but their apartment was really too small for four. The post-war apartments in Poland were the same as those in Russia.

Gennardy sympathised. He knew the problem only too well and the Poles were slightly better off than their Russian counterparts and much better off than their Belarus counterparts; though he did not volunteer this knowledge.

Feeling comfortable speaking in Polish the Colonel talked about Poland and how the Polish and Russian governments were working together to find a way to quell the unrest being generated by subversives who had an underground network in Poland called Solidarnosc. Gennardy listened in silence for a long time as this thoughtful man who was built like an Olympic javelin thrower talked freely without incriminating himself in any way. The train began to slow as the dawn became a new day and shortly afterwards it arrived in Minsk.

The two strangers left the train and nodded their goodbyes and Gennardy made his way to the Minsk offices of the interior from which the Belarus Interpreters worked.

He had been away for several days and had telephoned his office daily. Despite this; such was his feeling of guilt, and his expectation of being found out, that he was expecting a barking command from somewhere shouting: 'Mardosov is no longer a comrade of the USSR; fellow comrades; look upon a traitor who has defiled the purity of the Peoples Republic.'

By contrast his appearance in the office evoked no response.

On leaving the train at the station in Minsk Gennardy had had the same sensation of fear and guilt as he walked along the gloomy platform. All the time he was waiting for a voice to say, 'Gennardy Mardosov, you are arrested for participating in anti Soviet activities.'

At first Gennardy felt so uncomfortable in his office that he believed his attempts to look perfectly normal were unlikely to deceive anyone. Then he realised that he was so indoctrinated into the belief that the system was certain to discover him he that he was unable to believe otherwise. Sitting at his shabby desk on his shabby chair he suddenly wanted to laugh hysterically at what he saw as the ease with which the Soviet system had brainwashed its people into a world of silence through fear, fear borne out of a system of betrayal of Mothers by Sons and Sons by Fathers.

Gennardy realised that the peoples of the USSR were little different from people anywhere. The only thing wrong was the system.

Everyone lived in fear in the USSR and not in hope. Yet even the Polish Intelligence Officer had within him some latent hope that this world of fear and hopelessness would end. Even if the perceived enemy that they were all so familiar with did prevail: 'Could life be less worthwhile?' Furthermore if the West was so awful and dangerous and corrupt and evil; 'Why was it that the people there were so obviously happy?'

Gennardy suddenly felt more powerful, more self-assured; he had travelled by train from Moscow to Belarus and gone to his office in Minsk after having met with British Intelligence. He had talked to people who were worlds apart from what he had been brought up to believe or indoctrinated to believe. What the hell! He had done it and the Polish Officer had given him an idea.

There were no Commissions on his desk. The winter weather assured that most appointments for interpreters were for times of the year when Business people, Politicians, Administrators or Bureaucrats were more certain of reaching their destination. Travel in the depths of winter was avoided whenever possible. Suddenly Gennardy felt more relaxed and somehow less on his own.

Although he could not confide his views or feelings

and aspirations with anyone he now felt that he understood the underlying mood and hopes of the peoples of the USSR. These hopes and aspirations were no different from the hopes and aspirations of the people of England except that they had achieved their hopes and aspirations to a much greater degree.

He thought again about his conversation with the Polish Colonel and he realised that whilst the man had the job of curbing and undermining the popularity of the Solidarity movement it was highly likely that his heart was not in it. He was a Pole before being a comrade and whilst he would never volunteer such heresy it was obvious to Gennardy that, what he had perceived as, the Colonel's discomfort justified such a conclusion.

The Interior Ministry offices were in the centre of Minsk just off the Leninstrasse. It was just like the other buildings, built by prisoners after World War ll.

Inside the shared office a dozen tables with tubular steel legs and frames were matched by a tubular steel framed chair which went with each table. Only a couple of tables were in use. The two users gave Gennardy a polite greeting and continued their allotted task. There was obviously no news or scandal.

The heating system was common to the whole building and hopelessly inadequate for the depths of a central European winter. As he sat at the table he used for his desk he did not remove his heavy ex-army greatcoat which had been altered and dyed black to demilitarise its appearance. He drew the coat closer around his body and thought of warm food. He went to the office of his boss, Anatoly Brok, who was out.

Brok didn't like Gennardy probably because his comely secretary did. She smiled at Gennardy explaining that her boss was at home ill and if anything important happened she was to telephone him.

'Have you anything important to tell Anatoly' she said as she grinned cheekily at Gennardy.

They both guessed that because it was even more quiet than usual Anatoly Brok was probably keeping himself as warm as possible in his bed throughout the dark days of winter like so many other citizens.

'I want an authorisation slip to collect my wages and also some vouchers for the canteen.'

The Secretary adjusted her small but ample body and reached into a drawer for the appropriate paperwork. Her lips were heavily painted in thick bright red lipstick and as she fiddled with the papers she looked up at Gennardy and smiled through the scarlet oval formed by her mouth. Gennardy returned her smile.

Everyone had so little to do in this land of full employment that when they had something to do to relieve the boredom it took ages. Eventually Gennardy was given the slips of paper and he went to the pay office where, after what seemed another age, he collected his roubles. He then went to the canteen where he gave a voucher in exchange for some black bread and a bowl of thin soup with large pieces of fat pork, potatoes and cabbage floating in it. After the soup he went back to the counter where he was given a plate which supported a piece of fat pork, a portion of cabbage and a pile of boiled potatoes. He took it back to his seat and ate every morsel before returning to the table in the big office used by the translators.

Ever since Miss Smith had asked Gennardy for proof his mind had been going over possibilities, implications, practicalities and contingencies. Ideas were forming in his mind and each time he came up with an idea he would ask himself what would happen if all went well and what contingencies he had if it all went wrong.

His constant concern revolved round the thought that he could possibly get the proof Miss Smith required and then be betrayed by British Intelligence in exchange for some favour. He was pleased that he had come back to Minsk to think things through. His mind was clearer now and whilst he was very frightened he had regained control of his fear.

Miss Smith and her colleague had not only questioned Gennardy exhaustively; they had also suggested that Gennardy was in a unique position because of his links with Li. Gennardy had reiterated the fact that he had only met Li on that one occasion. Furthermore, if he attempted to use her she would almost certainly advise Plakinov. Gennardy was in no-man's land.

Miss Smith had shrugged her shoulders and assured him that the only way she could guarantee his safe return to England, and obtain political asylum, was if she could show that he had made a significant contribution to the country he wished to live in.

Gennardy was not to know that what Miss Smith had told him was far from the truth but in the tangled world of espionage and intelligence truth is an abused word. Miss Smith wanted information and how acquisition of that information affected the lives of those who obtained it was of secondary consideration.

Without realising it Gennardy had sat at his table for a long time after he had eaten. His thoughts had ranged over so many factors and apart from several attempts to telephone Irena in Moscow he had sat and considered his situation. Telephone calls were free in the USSR and, whilst conversations generally tended to be short;

telephone conversations tended to lengthy. Eventually he got through to Irena who was surprised to hear from him so soon.

Yes he could stay with her for a couple of nights. After that she did not know until the others sharing could tell her when they would be back.

'We will not be as private as before.' she teased. 'Are you up to performing in public?' she laughed.

Gennardy chided her and put the phone down before standing up. As he did so he realised how stiff and cold he was. No matter; at least he knew what he was going to do.

He walked across to the office of the red-lipped secretary and entered.

'What do you want now Mr Gennardy Mardosov?' She said with her teeth smiling through the oval.

'I am expecting a big job which will take me to Leningrad and Murmansk via Moscow.' he advised her, 'and I would like an open train ticket and pass.'

'Surely you are not going to Murmansk at this time of the year' she replied.

'It all depends, he lied. I was asked to be prepared to go.'

Interpreters were privileged people and they were there to respond to requests from very senior officials and so Gennardy was given the appropriate forms to sign before pocketing the pass authorisation.

'See you soon' said Gennardy as he left the office. He was on his way to Minsk railway station to board a train for Moscow.

Chapter 9

Gennardy's inquisitors in British Intelligence had advised him that should he wish to make contact one of them would be walking along the pavement opposite the monument celebrating the achievements of Yuri Gagarin at some time between noon and the following half hour each day. Their contact would approach Gennardy. It would not necessarily be Miss Smith or Jeremy Smart.

Having taken the overnight train back to Moscow Gennardy arrived with some time to spare. He sat in the huge marble hall of the main Moscow underground station and read Pravda, the official Soviet daily newspaper before eating a meal similar to that he had the day before in Minsk. Fortified he set off and walked towards the monument. Within five minutes of his arrival a voice said in Russian. 'Have you dropped something?'

Gennardy replied. 'I didn't think I had.'

'Well done.' said Jeremy Smart. 'You remembered then.'

'It wasn't exactly difficult to remember' he replied.

'What do you want.' said Smart.

'Information on the movements of Plakinov and Li; I particularly want to know if Li goes somewhere in Moscow where I can make contact.'

The two men stood a short distance from one another in the raw dry cold of the Moscow mid-winter. They both stared with apparent interest at the massive bronze statue and its lengthy inscription.

'Plakinov`s movements are not advertised' said Jeremy sardonically, the right hand side of his mouth curling, slightly amused at his own comment.

Gennardy flashed him a glance. 'Please! Do not

132

make amusement with me Mr Smart.

I am already in much danger and you and your friends are much amused because you put me in worse danger. I did not expect the British to be the same as KGB'

Smart was in complete sympathy with Gennardy but it did not show. He knew the game.

Within a few minutes Gennardy had the bits of information he needed and he made his way directly to the huge Library of the People housed in one of Moscow's most beautiful buildings. It was an example of architecture built under the reign of the Czars to elevate Russian Imperial prestige.

Gennardy had been advised that Li used the library extensively; particularly when Plakinov was away. He was told that Plakinov's aides had recruited her as a research assistant, ostensibly for her educational achievements in the State University of Ulan Bator. One of Plakinov's regional officers had recommended her. The Officer had attended a ceremony where she had received an award from him on behalf of the People's Republic. Li's family had received certain privileges because of her promotion.

Anyone using the library had to pass through the huge reception area that opened up from the grand front entrance. The room had once been used for concerts and balls attended by the aristocracy. Massive chandeliers hung from the high ceiling. A line of pillars made of Italian marble stood in lines on either side of the entrance leading to the staircase. All around the pillars were clusters of tubular framed tables and chairs similar to those in Gennardy's office in Minsk; in such a magnificent setting the tables and chairs looked grotesque.

The library was used extensively and often groups of two or three people would sit at tables sharing the contents of a book or copying tracts of text by hand. Gennardy guessed that they were Academics and students. Around the grand hall large ornate doors opened up into rooms filled with books. At the opposite side of the main entrance was a huge curved marble staircase leading onto a balcony that ran around the grand hall. Off the balcony were rooms that corresponded to the rooms downstairs. No one could be unimpressed by the splendour despite the fact that it was in need of refurbishment. Not even the tasteless modern accoutrements could tarnish the majesty of the place.

About every fifty paces a middle aged or elderly lady would sit by the base of a pillar on her tubular steel framed chair and watch the people as they passed by. Occasionally one would rise from her chair and visit the lady in a nearby chair. There was nothing that went on that they would be unaware of Gennardy noted. In order not to be conspicuous Gennardy went through the unnecessarily complicated paperwork system, borrowed a book and took it to a seat by a table near the top of the huge staircase. From this point he could see people entering and leaving the library and most of the activities in the ballroom. He noticed a uniformed guard sitting inside a small cabin in the equivalent position on the other side of the staircase from where he sat.

The day went by slowly and sitting motionless for long spells allowed the cold to chill the bones so every forty minutes or so he went to the toilet nearby to get his blood circulating. Once inside he would swing his arms about and run up and down on the spot until the stiffness eased.

Late in the afternoon a small female figure stepped out of one of the side rooms downstairs and made her way to the desk. There she waited her turn whilst the two people before her were attended to. Gennardy immediately went to return his book. He wasn't sure but he thought it could be Li. She was better dressed than most Russians and that had attracted his attention though he could not be sure it was her.

The woman taking his book back seemed to be moving in slow motion. Gennardy felt like screaming at her to hurry. She was just about to conclude the simple transaction when her telephone rang. She picked up the telephone with an air of great self-importance and began to speak. Gennardy couldn't see the desk that the Li figure was at and he could do no more than stand there looking unconcerned despite the frustration and exasperation that had warmed him very quickly indeed.

After what seemed like a very long time the lady ended her call and replaced the receiver before making a comment to a lady watcher on a nearby chair. The call had been on matters trivial like so many phone calls. Slowly the desk lady completed the paperwork acknowledging the return of the book.

Resisting the tendency to race down the staircase he stepped lightly and quietly down and walked towards the main door. His head was turning as he went as though he was admiring the building. He was looking for the slender figure in the smart clothes and she wasn't there. She must be outside. As he stepped outside the main door the daylight was beginning to fade as the early dusk began. She was at the bottom of the steps. He stepped down quickly without appearing to rush and caught up to within a short distance of her and called 'Li'.

The figure stopped as though suddenly frozen. She did not turn to look to see who had called as he would have expected.

She said 'Who is that?' Do you remember me?' said Gennardy

'We met in Minsk at the Orbital Hotel'

Turning to look at Gennardy she was about to smile then her face frowned slightly and she looked all around her. Gennardy marvelled at her lovely face framed by the expensive black fir hat and the matching black fir collar trimming her expensive winter coat. In Gennardy's mind Li looked like what most Russian women would wish to look like.

'It's alright' said Gennardy, 'I was not certain that it was you. I saw you leaving the library and I didn't want to miss the chance to talk to you, if it was you; if you see what I mean.'

She looked all around her again before saying. 'What are you doing in Moscow?'

'Things are quiet in Minsk and so I thought I would brush up on the Russian and Polish rail systems. It's part of my job to know about them. Does that bore you?'

'Of course not' said Li looking around again.

'Will you be coming back to the Library?' asked Gennardy.

She began to say that Mr Plakinov was away and she had a day off. She got as far as Mister and stopped before saying; 'I will be coming back to the Library tomorrow.'

Gennardy asked 'May I sit with you.'

'Someone may see us' she said.

'We will speak in our Mongolian tongue and pretend we are an old married couple' he said reassuringly.

'You are a very silly man Gennardy Mardosov.' she said as she laughed behind her hand.

Then she said quickly in Mongolian 'I would love to

but it could be dangerous for you.'

'I am a good comrade otherwise I would not be an Interpreter.' said Gennardy.

'Besides you remembered my full name. I am flattered.'

'It is my job to remember names.' said Li biting her bottom lip and looking around as she did so.

'I will be in the Library at ten o' clock' she said as she turned and walked off.

Gennardy stepped out to find a hostelry where he could get some warm food before going to Irena's apartment. It was one thing to ask for a bed and another to ask to be fed as well. He wondered if he might find a little present for Irena. All in all he felt quite pleased with himself and Li looked so beautiful. As a child he had thought that his Mother was the most beautiful woman he had ever seen. Li reminded him of his Mother.

Li walked off to make the twenty-minute walk back to Plakinov's apartment. She was so excited. She had enjoyed talking to Gennardy in Minsk. So many people were afraid to talk to her because of who she worked for. 'Worked for' was hardly the right description. She was there because it satisfied the vanity of Plakinov who could tell his little circle of apparitchik that they were lovers and she was dedicated to him. On arrival in Moscow she had been in a room of her own adjacent to Plakinov's apartment. She had come prepared to work hard and to help the Soviet Union to bring about the Utopia promised in the latest five-year plan.

Plakinov had wanted a beautiful woman who was special to adorn his presence whenever he attended meetings. There were two reasons for this. He was bisexual with homosexual preferences and having Li around dispelled rumours regarding his true orientation.

The second reason was that his wife and family were aware of his tastes and having Li around gave them to believe that he had reformed his habits as he had assured them. His wife reasoned that it was better to have a husband in name only with a mistress rather than to have people know that she had a husband that preferred men to her.

The way things were arranged was the best compromise and it meant that Plakinov's wife would attend the few occasions when good citizen leaders of the USSR could parade their wives and families in public. To compliment these complex arrangements Plakinov also had Li to adorn the dinner table when he met privately with people he wished to impress. The arrangement had worked and model citizen Plakinov had eventually got the top job and his wife and family enjoyed the reflected prestige that that job gave to them.

Li entered the apartment block where she shared quarters with Plakinov. In the lobby entrance was a junior army officer who was an armed guard. Against the wall opposite his desk was a chair on which a lady observer sat. The guards and the ladies worked shifts. The list of security personnel was rarely changed and so Li knew them all by their first names and held little conversations with them on a regular basis. She was desperately lonely and the flimsy contact she had with the security people in the foyer was one of the things she looked forward to. It was obvious that the Officer guards were all attracted to her. In turn she was attracted to several of them. Sometimes she would tease the men by looking at them in the same way that they looked at her. At other times she tried to copy the images of the western women she saw daily in the western magazines in Plakinov's apartment. She knew which security women frowned on her little flirtations and which ones approved and so she would be selective in her timing.

On this occasion she radiated a smile as she passed through the door and nodded to each in turn as she made her way to the apartment.

When she had first been shown her room and en suite bathroom she had felt guilty at what she considered to be the excessive self-indulgence. Over time she had come to realise that the luxuries enjoyed by the decadent West were also available to those in high positions within the USSR and the hypocrisy was not lost on her. One thing was certain; a little bit of decadent luxury was wonderful and her bathroom had helped her to pass many a long lonely evening.

Li lay in the bath and wondered about Gennardy. She knew that she was sometimes followed when she went out. Often she would play a game with her pursuer and try to lose him. It was always a man and she often wondered why. She was a regular at the Library and she knew the security ladies. Any obvious association with a man would soon be spotted and reported.

The appointment with Gennardy was very exciting but she would have to be cautious.

After preparing some supper in Plakinov's kitchen she spent her night reading and imagining all sorts of possibilities and scenarios involving her meetings with Gennardy.

The following morning she left at her usual time and made her way to the Library. Gennardy was standing by the main entrance to the Library at the top of the steps. As she approached Gennardy she said 'Join me in the side room specialising in the Great Composers in five minutes.'

Unable to think of anything better to do he walked down the steps as though leaving. He then walked around the building before returning up the steps and through the main door where he made his way to the room that Li had used the day before.

Like Gennardy Li had all her winter clothes on despite being indoors. She sat at a shabby table in one corner of the room.

Gennardy walked purposely to a bookshelf, looked at the titles for a few moments, and removed a book taking it across to where Li sat. She looked up at him and went on reading. Gennardy looked at the lady sitting in the tubular framed chair by the door and nodded with a little smile. The security lady responded likewise.

'You know who I work for?' questioned Li.

'Yes' said Gennardy 'The KGB man who had the party in Minsk. You have a very good job; I think.'

'He's not a KGB man. He's the head of the KGB within the Soviet Union.'

'I know this,' Came his reply. Li looked into his face to ensure that Gennardy was sound in mind before saying: 'What do you want of me.'

'I want to talk to you to see what you think about music and life and how many children you would like and what you would eat if you could have anything to eat in the world; and that's just a few of the things I would like to know.'

She found Gennardy amusing. Most men she had met seemed to have little conversation unless they were encouraged to concentrate in the area between their knees and their belly button. In any case most of the men she had met were elderly. In her amusement she said as much to Gennardy and they both laughed out loud before restraining themselves in response to a fierce glance from the security lady. They then chatted quietly for half an hour before she whispered 'I will go to the park now at the back of the Library. Meet me there in 10 minutes and we can walk together.'

She stood up and so that the lady at the door could hear said; 'Goodbye it has been very nice to meet you, perhaps our paths may cross again soon.'

'Tomorrow, I hope.' said Gennardy so that the woman could hear. 'I shall be at the Library again tomorrow. I would like to join you again if you are here.'

Li saw the lady watching her and replied casually. 'I'm not sure that I will be here but if I am I would be happy to hear your views on a different composer.'

The lady at the door listened approvingly. Not enough people took serious music seriously she thought.

After a trip to the toilet, where he took time to warm himself up by swinging his arms out and across his chest, Gennardy strolled out of the Library and made his way to the park. Once inside the park Li advanced towards him said hello and gave her hand to him to shake. He took her hand as she said; 'The main path is very busy today because the sun is shining so we can talk as we walk and it will be warmer than sitting in the library.'

As she talked she kept looking around. Gennardy took a chance and said, 'are you looking for someone.'

Li shot him a quick glance. 'No, not really, it's just that some people may imagine all sorts of things when they see me with a stranger. That is why I shook hands with you, to advise any observers that we know each other on a formal basis.'

'Well we are not really strangers now; after all this is the third time we have met. Once in Minsk and twice today.' said Gennardy smiling.

'You make it sound like we are old friends.' Li laughed.

'Well; not old friends but new friends.' He replied.

Li responded with 'You have spoken a little about your journey to England. Tell me some more about it. It must have been very special for you.'

Gennardy began telling her his story guardedly but as he talked Li could see the enthusiasm he felt for the people and their lifestyle.

'I can confide a little secret,' said Li, 'and perhaps it is a bigger secret than I think but you see I work with Mr Plakinov and I have looked at many of their magazines which are delivered to various departments of KGB. Comrade Plakinov brings them to his apartment. My English is not thought to be very good but it is better than some people know so I have some knowledge of the West; mainly of Great Britain because Mr Plakinov likes the magazines from Britain the best.'

Gennardy said enthusiastically, 'But they have so many magazines. There are magazines about everything. They have shops selling only newspapers and magazines.'

Li looked at Gennardy with her eyes full of mischief. 'Most of the magazines I see from Plakinov's office are full of decadence.'

Gennardy pretended that he had not picked up her attempt to get a reaction. Western decadence was a big plank of Soviet propaganda against the West and so he replied, 'Well they seem to be able to write and say whatever they think.'

As they talked Gennardy was racking his brains to discover a way in which he could persuade this attractive and very intelligent, yet vulnerable, woman to

142

betray her powerful boss and her country. He knew too that if she helped him she would betray her family; she would know that some sort of revenge or retribution could be inflicted upon them. The only thing giving Gennardy a glimmer of hope was her obvious pleasure and even joy when they met.

Overall he was amazed at his achievements in contacting the British and then Li. He was also pleased that he had befriended her in the way he had. The difficult part of his task was how to approach her about getting access to information. In ordinary circumstances it would be difficult to gain a confidence and then exploit it. These were not normal circumstances and he had only a limited time.

Time was running out so he decided to attempt one more contact before making any final decisions on whether to take a chance and ask her directly for information. If that failed as he anticipated he would opt for his contingency plan.

The pair talked non-stop until Li said she must return to her office. To Gennardy's surprise she confirmed that she would meet him again on the following afternoon. They shook hands and smiled as they looked upon each other before they parted.

Gennardy was delighted with his progress. He had time to spend until he went back to Irena's apartment so he went in search of warm food and then returned to the shelter of the library where he spent the afternoon.

The British Airways scheduled flight from London to Moscow was taxiing into Moscow airport at about the same time as Gennardy was meeting Irena outside the tube station near her apartment. On board the aircraft was Humphrey Goodchild who was head of the

Agricultural Unit of the British Trade Section in the Moscow Embassy.

Like their Russian counterparts those in the trade section were closely linked with British Intelligence and everyone in the business knew it. The secret was not to get caught.

Humphrey Goodchild had not been caught by either side despite having been a double agent during and since the frenetic years following World War Two. At that time Plakinov and Goodchild had crossed paths regularly by accident and design. Both had been middle ranking army officers attached to units attempting to bring order from the chaos of a devastated Europe in cities such as Trieste, Vienna and Belgrade. In those days unwritten deals were made by representatives of both the Soviet Union and the Allies that sometimes brought joy and sometimes misery to hundreds of thousands of people vulnerable to exploitation of every kind. It was during these years that Plakinov had easily recruited Goodchild who reasoned that whatever you called the system; whether it was Capitalism or Communism, there had to be a ruling class and he wanted to be part of it, whichever side was victorious. Another reason, which cemented their mutuality, was their common sexual interests, discovered during a binge celebrating a deal involving tens of thousands of refugees.

Humphrey Goodchild was almost sixty years of age but he looked a few years younger. He was married with one daughter. His wife, Mary, and he had made an agreement many years before that he could pursue his career to his heart's content and she would lead her own life, which she did with discretion. In this way she could indulge her love of horses and run the twenty five-acre farm that she had inherited from her father. Mary and her daughter were very close sharing common interests partly financed through her husband's salary that dropped into their bank account every month from Her Majesty's Government. No scrutiny from counterintelligence or any other organisation could find even the hint of a blemish to warrant suspicion in the affairs of Officer Goodchild.

Goodchild was driven straight from Moscow airport to his office at the Embassy. There was not a lot on his desk. He quickly scanned the first page of each of the documents. He reached the report from Jean Donkin, alias Miss Smith, and read on in utter astonishment. Unlike the other documents this one was very long since a full transcript had been made from the tapes made during Gennardy's interrogation. Eventually Goodchild sat back in his large and comfortable desk chair to realise that it was very late and he hadn't finished. He went to the back of the document to read the summary and the action taken. His astonishment was intensified.

The summary read; Mardosov has agreed to approach Li Saric who works as a personal assistant to Yuri Plakinov, Head of the KGB, in an attempt to gain further information or evidence to support the information given in interview.

Beneath the summary was a hand written addendum bearing the current date that read; Mardosov has made contact with Li Saric. Further contact is anticipated.

The import of what Humphrey Goodchild had just read registered immediately; his eyes widened and his heart gave a massive thump sending his pulse rate to its limits. The only person who knew he was working for the Soviets was Plakinov since Plakinov's former bosses were now all dead. He was sure that Plakinov would have kept his word and referred to him by code name, Adria, only. The name Adria was a reference to shared experiences in towns and cities situated on the northern Adriatic coastline. 'However the woman Li, how much did she know?' Goodchild's feelings ranged from near panic to nausea. Surely he couldn't be within a few months of retirement with a small fortune sitting in a bank in Lucerne, Switzerland, only to find himself threatened by Plakinov's assistant.

Goodchild placed the documents in his desk before leaving the embassy and making his way to the National Hotel. The National was full of bars where members of foreign embassies and Consuls from all over the world met. It was a hive of intrigue and a focus for information both to inform and mislead. It was the best place in Moscow to use a telephone since the telephone lobby was always busy and the phones in constant use making the caller difficult to identify afterwards.

A rack of telephone booths lay just within the lobby. Goodchild spoke in perfect Russian with a Caucasian dialect that he had picked up from his tutor in a London Boarding school before going on to Cambridge University to read Balkan History. He had dialled a number given him by Plakinov that he had memorised. Identifying himself as Adria, he was passed on to another office. The phone rang out and a Plakinov aide said. 'Yes Adria' followed by 'and where do you go?'

'Trieste' said Goodchild.

'How can I help you' said the Aide.

'I must speak to Mr Plakinov immediately' replied Goodchild. The Aide apologised and advised him that Plakinov would not return to Moscow until late the following morning when he would be in his apartment office. Goodchild banged the telephone into the receiver in frustration. He would have to return to the hotel the following lunchtime to reach Plakinov directly.

The following morning Li prepared for the return of Plakinov. Working in his apartment office under the instructions of Li on weekdays was a young female soldier who was a typist together with a middle-aged army Sergeant who was there to answer the telephone and assist as a general clerk. The pair liked Li and attended to their duties on a daily basis in an atmosphere of warmth, comfort and luxury. They spoke little and only carried out duties as Li delegated them. Most of the work surrounding the enormous range of activities, worldwide, for which Plakinov was responsible, was carried out within the huge KGB building in the centre of Moscow. The apartment office was essentially for occasions when Plakinov wanted to spend time away from KGB headquarters so that his mind was clear and free from the irritations and distractions of so many people vying for attention.

Plakinov arrived at his office just before two o clock in the afternoon, much later than he had anticipated. He was tired and wanted a nap after a snack and a drink.

'Good afternoon Comrade Plakinov' said Li and her two colleagues as Plakinov walked into the outer office. He acknowledged them and then dismissed the two security men attending him.

Li followed him into his inner office.

'There are some phone calls for you.' she said 'Shall I call them back for you.'

'Just leave them for now.' he said 'I must have a little rest, anything urgent?'

'Your office telephoned about agent Adria' said Li, 'and he phoned himself, he said he would call back every half hour'

'hmmmm' murmured Plakinov.

'What will you be doing this afternoon' said Plakinov to Li.

'I was planning to go to the Library but it is not

147

important.'

'No, go to the Library if you want to; I shall not need anything. I must rest awhile' said Plakinov removing his jacket.

On his reply Li went to her room and put on the warm winter furs that Plakinov had bought for her. Emerging with only her face radiating from the warm winter garments she walked across the room and said her Goodbyes. Nothing could have forewarned Li of the permanence of those Goodbyes.

Plakinov waited for Adria, Humphrey Goodchild, to telephone. It was irregular and unusual for Adria to telephone so persistently. Eventually the telephone rang and the Sergeant advised Plakinov that he had a Mr Adria on the line. Plakinov moved across his office to his large desk, picked up the telephone and flicked a switch on the handset giving him a secure line.

'How are you my friend?' began the Russian.

'Yuri, I must speak to you immediately. A most unusual and bizarre situation has developed which could seriously jeopardise our positions. I do not want to talk about it on the telephone. We must meet now.'

The anxiety in Goodchild's voice was uncharacteristic which immediately alarmed Plakinov. Plakinov's irritation was characterised by the gesture of slowly lifting his left hand to his left ear lobe and stroking it between his thumb and folded forefinger. He was tired.

'What is this about?'

'Meet me in your room in the National Hotel in ten minutes. It is essential for both of us that you do so' demanded Goodchild.

Plakinov was now wide awake. This was unusual. 'Where are you' he asked of Goodchild.

'In the National Hotel by the telephone booths'

'Good, said Plakinov, then stay there.'

Plakinov was not in the habit of taking instructions from others but the concern in Goodchild's voice was worrying.

Twenty five minutes later a tall athletic looking hotel porter walked up to the Englishman standing by the telephone booth and with a slight bow enquired; 'Mr Goodchild?'

'Yes' came the reply. 'You will come with me please?'

Goodchild's eyes made a careful surveillance as he followed the man up a staircase to the first floor and along a little used corridor with a dead end. There was winter sunshine outside which transmitted bright light into the hotel window at the end of the corridor. The man walking before Goodchild was a moving silhouette as he walked towards the window before stopping in front of a door on the right hand side.

The man knocked at the door. It was opened immediately and the two went past the man who had opened it.

The room they entered was well decorated with a range of shades of green. The ornate plasterwork on the walls and ceiling was finely embellished in gold leaf emphasising the quality of the craftsmanship. A square of carpet covered the floor of the room otherwise it was devoid of furniture save for three simple chairs standing against a wall.

Goodchild was ushered through a solid mahogany double door into the room where Plakinov awaited him. This room was decorated exactly as the other, and there the comparison ended, for this room was lavishly furnished with the finest of handcrafted furniture made from dark polished hardwoods and matching coloured leather. Goodchild had been a guest in this room a couple of times before in more genial circumstances.

The room was part of a large suite that Plakinov kept for liaisons and special contacts. Few people outside of Plakinov's trusted aides knew of its existence. Plakinov had inherited it from his former boss who had rarely used it. Plakinov by contrast loved it and had made the most of it.

As soon as the door was closed Humphrey Goodchild launched into an explanation of why he was there. Plakinov listened intently and as he did so his head shook slowly from side to side as his unseeing eyes looked from object to object around the room and then back to Goodchild. Plakinov was utterly astounded.

As Goodchild talked Plakinov's mind was in overdrive. He constantly stroked his ear lobe as he listened and considered the ramifications and the implications.

Without warning he said to Goodchild 'That's enough for now. We must find them immediately. Perhaps no damage has been done yet.'

Plakinov opened the mahogany door leading to the ante-room and said Goodbye to Goodchild adding. 'Thank you for this! We will discuss again later.'

The hotel porter and his colleague rose automatically sweeping their fingers down their suits to remove any creases. Goodchild entered the corridor after seeing that it was empty and made his way back into the hotel foyer area before returning to his office.

Plakinov told his two security men to find Li. If they could find her at the Library then there was a strong possibility that Mardosov was nearby or even with her. One of the two had been with Plakinov in Minsk and so he could recognise him. He was sent to the Library whilst the other went to see the guard at the entrance to Plakinov's apartment. If Li had not returned to the apartment he was to join his colleague at the Library. Plakinov had stressed that no word of this incident was to be reported to anyone. He would be the biggest fool in Russia if word got out that the Head of the KGB was sharing his official apartment with a woman who was working with Western Intelligence.

That same afternoon Li and Gennardy had met and resumed their conversation. Gennardy had thought of an idea to sound her out. As soon as they met he came straight out with his rehearsed statement saying; 'I am worried about what I saw in Minsk which I was not supposed to see.'

Li looked straight at him for a second or two before realising what he was talking about.

Then to his astonishment she replied.

'No one there would know that you had recognised Comrade Markham. It was a pity that you did recognise him. If Plakinov had not drunk so much he would never have made such mistakes. When he is sober he would be very harsh with anyone else who did silly things that breach security. It just goes to show that he is human like everyone else.'

Gennardy said, 'How did you know that I recognised Markham? I was expecting you to ask me what I saw.'

'I was watching you when you looked across to where they were dancing. You nearly jumped out of your skin and then you reacted by...........' she didn't finish her sentence.

'But if you saw that I had recognised him perhaps someone else did.'

'I think not.' said Li. 'If they did they would have said something and I would probably have been questioned. After all I was talking to you.'

'Do you like him.' asked Gennardy.

'Like who?'

'Plakinov'

'I want to have a job for myself because of my talents and abilities and also because I want my own home one day. I think I will get these when I am promoted to a more important position. Comrade Plakinov rates me very highly and I think he will use me for more important work.'

The mind of Gennardy was racing now; 'But, if you saw that I recognised Markham then someone else may have observed me; as you did.'

Li looked at Gennardy for a second or two before saying, 'I doubt it. I have already told you. If anyone else had seen that you knew who Markham was they would have made a report about you immediately, most of the people there that night would do anything to ingratiate themselves with Plakinov and his subordinates. Everything is about favours and spying on one another. You know that as well as anyone.'

Gennardy knew she was right and felt relieved that he had got as far as he had without being caught. He shivered involuntarily suddenly pricked with fear before saying, 'And why do you not want to please Plakinov by reporting me?'

Again Li looked at Gennardy for a few seconds before saying, 'What good would it have done me? I would have got a pat on the head and you would have been interrogated. They would be so suspicious that they would take no chances. You could easily have been involved in an accident. Talking to you that night in Minsk was the nearest thing I have had to a good time since I left Mongolia. I left my home with such high hopes. Now I am a very lonely woman who lives in a luxurious apartment with an old man who prefers men.'

She paused and sighed.

'I am trapped until Plakinov is deposed or retired and then I too could be involved in an accident.'

Gennardy was amazed at her frankness.

Without realising it they had stopped walking and they were standing facing one another with their faces earnestly staring at each other, completely absorbed in their conversation. Their breaths mingled as they hung on the cold Moscow air like little puffs of steam.

Gennardy stretched his arms out to her. His heart was full of emotion and sympathy. He felt like screaming and he told her so. Li gave a little wan smile and suggested that screaming was inadvisable. They smiled together and at each other. Gennardy marvelled at the whiteness of her teeth. He wondered if his mother was somehow watching them. He felt desperately lonely too. Even more so since Li had abandoned all discretion. Her vulnerability frightened him and he felt ashamed that he was using her.

Li pushed his arms back to his sides looking round as she did so. She was amazed at what she had come out with. All that training and brainwashing had evaporated the first time she had an opportunity to have an unofficial conversation.

Plakinov's assistant, Li Saric, was nothing more than a liability she decided.

Li suddenly realised that the time she had spent with Gennardy had flown over and that they had the park virtually to themselves now that the sun had almost disappeared and the temperature had plummeted. She was anxious to return to her apartment before she was missed.

Gennardy looked frozen and he was. He was also anxious to know what to do next. He could hardly say to Li; 'Look Li I am a spy for the West and I want you to get me proof or evidence of the Plakinov-Markham plan'.

As they were leaving the Park through the main gate Gennardy's mind was in turmoil. Should he come straight out with it or arrange another meeting? It had to be another meeting, and then again he didn't want to jeopardise the future and possibly the life of Li. He decided that he would say Goodbye to Li and forget about Smart and Miss Smith and their ridiculous requests. He would revert to his contingency plan and find his way to the west by his own endeavours.

As they left the Park Gennardy put out his hand saying 'I will leave you now, perhaps we shall meet again someday.'

Li put her hand in his and quietly replied; 'I have enjoyed our little chats Gennardy; perhaps I will see you in the Library again. I will look out for you.'

Gennardy nodded and in a low voice said; 'I would like that.'

They smiled at each other and she walked away leaving him standing. She knew that he was watching her so she half turned and waved when she reached the corner a few seconds later. As she did so the Plakinov guard who had gone to the Library came around the corner walking at a pace close to running and nearly knocked Li over. When he realised who she was he grabbed at her and shouted. 'Ha! Got you! Comrade Plakinov wants to see you and that rat from Minsk. Where is he?'

The man had got behind Li and he was holding her upper arms bringing her elbows together behind her back. Gennardy was stunned for a moment his mind racing at the implications.

'They knew, how?'

'Who could have betrayed them? Who knew? How could they know? Li was as good as dead.'

Blood rushed to Gennardy's head and surged

through his body. He ran straight at the back of the man. Gennardy knew that he was probably no match for the guard who would certainly be trained and supremely fit. The man heard the feet of Gennardy pounding on the concrete pavement. Still clutching the writhing Li he managed a half turn to see who was bearing down on him. An instant later Gennardy collided with him. All three flew sideways before crashing to the ground. On contact the man instinctively released Li who was spun around before landing on her hands and knees.

Gennardy's was cushioned as he fell with the man whose head hit the pavement with a very loud thud. Gennardy's instinct was to lift the man up by his coat lapels and crash his head to the ground again but the man was unconscious at least for the moment. Gennardy pulled the zip down on the front of the man's leather jerkin before rolling him over and frantically extricating the gun from the shoulder holster inside. The man groaned slightly offering no resistance.

Gennardy looked wild eyed around and across the street where an elderly couple stood watching from the side of the pavement. When he looked at them they shuffled off. The handful of other people who had witnessed, or heard, the fracas went on their journeys. They obviously did not wish to be involved.

Gennardy stuck his hand down the back of the man's neck grabbing the collars of his clothes and pulled him off the pavement and onto a snow-covered part of the park. Placing the man with his back against a young tree he quickly released the man's trouser belt. He then pulled it off and used it to tie the man to the tree by his neck ensuring that the buckle was against the far side of the tree behind the man's head so that he could not reach.

As Gennardy was going about his task, a very

shaken, Li had got to her feet and stood looking at what was happening. Her mouth was opening and closing and she was gasping with fright and fear. Gennardy grabbed her hand in his and with the gun in his other hand he began to run into the Park urging Li on. After no more than a minute they stopped under a tree. They both looked wide-eyed at each other and all around them as they slowly got their breath back.

'Gennardy, what is happening? That man is Plakinov's personal security guard! What have you done?' gasped Li.

'I don't know exactly.' he replied. 'What I do know is that we are in terrible trouble and we have to get out of here somehow.'

'What will Plakinov say? What will I tell him? Oh! It will be terrible. I must go back and explain.'

'Look Li,' said Gennardy, 'if they catch us we are as good as dead, further than that I cannot think straight. We must find somewhere to hide.'

Li looked around and ran off. Within seconds Gennardy caught her and shook her by the shoulders. 'You can't go back! You can't go back!' he shouted at her 'you must come with me while I explain or you are as good as dead!'

Both calmed down and as they walked along the full import of their situation became crystal clear. Gennardy explained that they needed warmth and shelter and that there was no going back. 'Why! Why, Why' she kept asking and eventually she understood and fell silent.

Resigned to their situation they realised that Li had to get rid of those expensive furs. Plakinov would give instructions for them to be arrested and every officer, policeman and informer would be searching for them and her clothes would give them away.

At first Gennardy's only prospect for refuge was

Irena's place. He went on to tell Li that he had a friend who would put them up for the night but they had to get the underground.

Li suddenly said, 'If I get on the tube dressed like this the police will spot me immediately. And they are sure to be looking for me... us, by now.'

Gennardy agreed. Then said, 'But what choice have we.'

Li was very cool now. She was furious with Gennardy for turning her world into a nightmare but she knew that if she went back to Plakinov her future would be precarious and probably unbearable. Rumours persisted in some sophisticated circles of Moscow society that Plakinov delighted in consigning people he considered unacceptable to prostitution, whether they were male or female, for the benefit of military personnel in remote parts of the Soviet Union. People disappeared and to all intents and purposes they lost their identity in a life of misery devoid of purpose. Realistically such a fate was her best hope if she were caught alive by Plakinov's security service.

As Li contemplated her situation she was filled with wonder that she could be in a safe and comfortable world in the middle of what started out as a perfectly normal day and a few hours later find herself without a future, without any comforts, without anything at all. Her only hope lay in the vague ambitions of a man on the run who could speak foreign languages and who was contemplating the same awful possibilities as she was. At least they were on equal terms.

As the night wore on and their situation became more precarious they knew there was little hope of them reaching Irena's apartment without being discovered. Instead they made for the sidings and huge goods yard near to the main railway station in central

Moscow with which Gennardy was well acquainted. Eventually they found an unoccupied cabin with a supply of coal and a stove that would keep the cold out even on a January night in Moscow. The stove was opposite to the door and on the wall at each side of the cabin was a bench seat. Goods yard workmen had used the hut during the day so that the stove was still warm but inside the hut the temperature was only a few degrees warmer than the outside.

It took time to get the stove going again and it seemed ages before some real heat was forthcoming but come it did. Despite their weariness neither Gennardy nor Li could sleep in their tiny oasis of heat and temporary security. They sat side by side in the dark as close to the stove as they could.

In answer to Li's endless questions Gennardy began to explain how he had ended up talking to the British and the attempt he had made to ingratiate himself with Li in order to get himself a ticket to England. Li had never heard of anything so farfetched in all of her life and yet she knew that Gennardy was telling the truth.

Gennardy was convinced that the only possibility they had was to escape to the west using his contingency plan, the first part of which he explained to Li who thought it would work if they had the right equipment otherwise they would never survive the cold and hunger.

As the early hours of the morning crept on and the explanations and likely scenarios were explained each to the other Li suddenly realised that her knowledge about Plakinov and his establishment could be useful. Believing her to be harmless her boss had taken her into his confidence, probably more so than anyone else.

She knew that Gennardy's plan was their only chance. If he deserted her she would have no chance of escape; a slim chance was better than nothing.

'You know!' she said as they sat in the cabin assessing their prospects. 'All of this would never have happened if I had not believed that you really fancied me. Do I look like a fool? It doesn't matter now does it?'

Gennardy began to explain but Li stopped him immediately saying. 'Do not even begin to explain. From now on we are stuck together through necessity and nothing else. Maybe I am more valuable to you and the British than you are.'

She paused before going on. 'You will have a better chance with me. I will explain.'

The problem for Gennardy was that Li's plan and its execution seemed even more implausible than the events of the last few hours. She explained her thoughts to Gennardy who was amazed. As she was talking Li searched the bottom of her handbag and produced a key. She held it up triumphantly in the small light coming from the door of the stove before carefully replacing it in the same side pocket in the bottom of her bag.

At first Gennardy said it was far too risky but after a lot of questions he thought that it was as good a plan as any. In any case they had nothing to lose. As they considered the implications Gennardy wondered if Li was leading him into a trap and then decided that nothing could ever reinstate Plakinov's confidence in her and she would know that. He decided that her intentions must be genuine.

Despite the stress and precariousness of their situation they were both succumbing to the desire for sleep brought on by sheer exhaustion from the events of the previous few hours. They each stretched out on the comfortless forms on either side of the cabin. Surely it couldn't be less than six or seven hours since Li had parted company with Gennardy in the Park by the Library? It seemed a lifetime ago since Gennardy had rushed Plakinov's guard just outside the park. Li fell into a fitful sleep whilst Gennardy dozed waking regularly, ears pricked, and eyes searching in the limited light given off by the stove where the ashes fell.

Chapter 10

Gennardy opened the door of the stove slightly to look at his watch. It was just after two in the morning. A gentle nudge roused Li who looked around and then remembering her circumstances she sat up quickly. The expensive furs that Li was wearing would give the game away very quickly so they decided to turn them inside out to see how that looked. It was even worse with the pure silk lining shining in even this limited light. Gennardy tore out the lining from both the hat and the coat and Li wore them inside out. If accosted their best bet was to look like shift workers, going to, or returning from work.

The familiarity with the rail system that Gennardy had gained over the years stood them in good stead and they followed a pathway by the side of a rail line until they were less than a few hundred yards from the building which housed Plakinov's Moscow apartment. A brisk walk, along streets that were mainly deserted at that time in the morning, brought them to one of many architectural recesses along the side of the building that had been Li's home just twelve hours before. The recesses were about one and one half metres deep and went from the top of the ten-storey building to the bottom. The purpose of this feature was to allow more light into the rooms from windows at the side of the recess. The two window apertures on the ground floor immediately beneath Plakinov's apartment were built up and skimmed with cement. Stepping quickly from the pavement into a recess identified by Li they looked around to ensure they had not been seen. With her heart beat pounding in her ears Li fumbled in her bag for the key. Her hands were trembling with cold and fear. Standing on her toes she entered the key into a small hole in the top right hand corner of the window area. She turned the key a quarter of a turn until she heard a click and the door panel opened with a light push. They quickly entered into the black void before them. Once inside Li gently pushed against the door from the inside until it closed with a light clicking sound as the spring driven slide sprang back into its bolt hole.

The pair stood silently inside the door with the noise of their own heartbeat still pumping in their ears. As the strain and tension subsided and they listened for the slightest sound Gennardy found himself straining from laughing hysterically. He was simply incredulous at what he knew he was doing. It was as though someone else was doing it and he was watching.

Li broke the strained silence when she whispered. 'We will have to wait here until daylight breaks and then I will show you around. There is some secondary light in daytime so we will be able to see more easily.'

At least it was warm inside and so they slid down the wall to the floor and talked quietly as Li explained in detail the purpose of this secret place.

After the Second World War the apartment had been designed for the then head of the KGB. The specification included a full security system to accommodate all contingencies with a refuge and escape route. Factors taken into consideration included external threats from nuclear attack, conventional bombing and so on. Just as important was the prevention of assassination by rivals in the USSR and internal purges. From the inception of the Soviet Union the leaders had often found themselves victims of their own regime. Trotsky was one of the many. The long arm of Soviet revenge had found him in Mexico where he was killed with an ice axe.

No one in power left anything to chance if it was

avoidable and Plakinov was, in the main, pleased with the accoutrements of his inheritance.

The ground floor area on which Li and Gennardy were sitting was exactly the same area as Plakinov's apartment above. All of the external windows and doors of this ground floor apartment were filled with slabs of concrete. All of the wall areas were then covered in sheets of lead which were sandwiched between the outer wall and an additional internal wall. This had been built to give protection in the event of radiation following a nuclear attack.

Beneath this apartment was a bunker with communications systems, emergency rations and a supply of small arms. Plakinov had shown Li all around the bunker and he had mentioned the escape route but he had not shown her how it was accessed.

Apart from a sliding panel in Plakinov's office, the door that Li and Gennardy had entered was the only way in and out that she knew of. A quarter turn of the key on that door allowed entry and egress without the knowledge of anyone else. A half turn or more triggered a series of alarms indicating an unauthorised intruder. This was why Li had turned the key just sufficiently.

They chatted quietly until the darkness turned to gloom and eventually to daylight. Neither had eaten since lunchtime of the previous day and darting pangs of hunger reminded them of the fact. They each removed their footwear and made their way across the empty apartment to a door opening into a stairway leading down to the bunker built into the foundations of the building. The bunker was permanently lit with strip lights which gave off sufficient light to see where everything was. To switch on the main lights would light a diode on the security panel in the main entrance to the building. Li stressed that Gennardy was to take a seat and touch nothing.

Food, nourishment, was now the main concern of both Gennardy and Li. To be without regular meals for people who are used to feeding every few hours causes serious problems physically and psychologically and Li was weak with hunger. She was so tired and hungry that she was straining to maintain her concentration to ensure that she did not inadvertently expose their whereabouts.

Tiredness and hunger create a negative attitude. The desire to survive pulled on reserves of courage, determination and fortitude never previously experienced by the two fugitives. Both found that survival focuses the mind in a way that no other situation or condition can match. They also felt better that they were sharing the experience. It would have been even more difficult had they not had each other's company.

Having eaten some biscuits and drunk some bottled water Li and Gennardy suddenly felt better. They smiled and nodded at one another and trusted one another a little more. They dared to hope that together there was a chance that they would survive. Should they survive and achieve objectives that few of their countrymen could conceive, let alone understand, a new life beckoned. A life in England that was the beacon of Gennardy's ambitions would be available to them both.

The willpower to concentrate on every detail of their minute by minute existence was the key to achieving the seemingly impossible goal. For long hours they talked quietly of self-fulfilment and an imaginary world much fairer than that known to either of them in the USSR.

Li told Gennardy about the first time she had been brought to the bunker by Plakinov. At the time she had assumed that this was his attempt to seduce her into the acceptance of his desire for her. She was left with a feeling of relief and annoyance: Relief that this awful specimen of life had wanted her and was unable to fulfil that desire. Her annoyance emanated from her realisation that Plakinov did not find her irresistible and respond normally. As a consequence she was less powerful than if he had fallen madly in love with her. He had never approached her in that way again and she had simply become his ornament.

Plakinov had shown her how clever his predecessors had been in making arrangements for every contingency. She smiled to herself as she looked for more food; Plakinov would explode if he knew where she was right now. Gennardy asked what she was smiling at and when she told him they smiled at each other. 'Do you know.' she whispered. 'We may be within a few metres of Plakinov at this very moment.'

As Li searched she found a cupboard replete with small jars of emergency food supplies. They removed the tops and deliberately fed themselves slowly so as not to be ill. Between mouthfuls she told Gennardy about her short-lived love life with Plakinov. Gennardy smiled and shook his head. They decided that they were as safe as they could be since Plakinov rarely checked out his bunker. Having eaten they each lay on a bunk and took turns to sleep. The bunks afforded unimaginable comfort after the events of the last few hours.

By noon Gennardy was wide-awake and feeling fully recovered from his weariness. Li by contrast slept on for a further hour until Gennardy gently roused her. They ate some more of the food from the jars and replaced the lids before returning them to the cupboard. Now that they were rested and fed they felt stronger and began their preparations.

'We have to do two things' said Gennardy in a hushed voice. 'First we must prepare for an arduous journey overland that could take weeks. I have prepared a plan in my mind. The second thing we can do is to try to get some information out of Plakinov's office. Let us talk through the journey.'

Li said. 'I know we are going to Great Britain but how?'

'As I said, I have a plan but that plan will have to be flexible. I have thought about my travels as an Interpreter and I know the roads and the railway routes. This is my advantage. There will be problems and you must do as I tell you. Our first task is to get into Poland.'

Gennardy told her about the long conversation he had on the train to Minsk with the Polish Colonel. 'This man gave me an idea.' said Gennardy. 'We need help and the only place I can expect help from is Poland. Do not worry about it. We will worry about it when we get there. Right now we must carefully use what is available in this place to fight off the cold and the hunger and the security services.'

Li looked at him thoughtfully. 'Plakinov will leave no stone unturned till he finds us.'

'I know this.' replied Gennardy. 'He will never take me alive. He said grimly.'

'Promise me! You will not let them take me too.' pleaded Li.

Gennardy looked her straight in the eyes for several seconds before replying. He swallowed hard and pulled the gun from his pocket that he had taken from Plakinov's guard before saying; 'I promise.'

'Now!' whispered Gennardy more brightly. 'Let us

see what treasures Mr Plakinov has provided us with to help us on our journey.'

'Be careful.' urged Li. 'Make sure that that you do not bump into something and do not drop anything.'

After a while they had assembled an array of clothes and food and laid it on the bunk beds.

'We will start with clothes.' said Gennardy. 'These vests and trousers are American.' He pointed to the label. 'We will wear these next to our skin. They are called thermal.'

'Shall we not put another set in our bags?' asked Li.

'We will have to see how heavy our bags become. We may have to walk for long distances and we must have enough food. We must also take these plastic bags to keep the warmth inside.'

Gennardy unrolled one of the clear plastic bags to check the size. It was about one metre long and half a metre wide. 'I think these must come from the west too. I saw some like this in England.'

Eventually they each had a canvas bag with sturdy canvas carrying loops. Inside their bags, each had a lightweight sleeping bag and some food. Gennardy's bag had twice as much food as Li's; he also had twelve of the clear plastic bags, a ball of string and a knife.

They each stood up in turn and checked the weight of their bags. Gennardy said the bags were ideal because if they had a long walk they could carry the bags on their backs with their arms through the canvas loops.

Li gathered a few small items for her handbag.

'I think that this is all we can take.' said Gennardy quietly. 'The bags are unusual and may cause attention but we will have to take the risk. Now! Clothes! We need light warm clothes to put on top of the American vests and trousers and then we are ready.'

Having completed their preparations for their departure Gennardy found a pencil and under the instructions of Li he drew a plan of Plakinov's apartment above them. The process went well into the afternoon by which time Gennardy had a clear picture of the rooms, door positions and the disposition of furniture and security arrangements.

Since they were so close to Plakinov's office they could now enter it and just possibly gain the necessary evidence regarding Markham's visit or other information that they could barter for their escape.

With their shoes off the two made their way up into the ground floor void between the bunker and Plakinov's apartment. They then crossed the floor and crept up the set of concrete steps leading to the panel door that gave entrance into Plakinov's office. The air was warm and dry and heavy with the smell of concrete. They sat silently on the floor in the gloom outside the panel door each listening intently. Neither could hear any noise except the distant humming of a pump and the occasional muffled sound of a vehicle as it passed by the building.

The only other noise they could hear was the sound of their own gentle, panting breathing.

Since it was now Saturday Li knew that under normal circumstances it was most likely that Plakinov would be away. But these were not normal circumstances and she was attempting to predict Plakinov's actions. She knew that it was likely that the city police were looking for her since Plakinov controlled them indirectly. The internal security and intelligence unit would probably have been kept in the dark. Plakinov would probably wish to keep them out of it in case word fell into quarters that were possibly hostile to Plakinov. She decided that Plakinov would be at the KGB headquarters managing the hunt for her and

Gennardy.

Li told Gennardy that the Officer that Gennardy had tied to the tree was Andrei, one of Plakinov's bodyguard, who would by now have disclosed the little he knew-assuming that he had fully regained consciousness. On the other hand he could have died. Andrei was such a big and powerful man; he must have hit the ground with terrific force. They would have to assume that the former situation was the most likely and that Andrei had explained to Plakinov how he had apprehended Li before being charged down by Gennardy.

When Plakinov's security aides had gone looking for Gennardy the previous afternoon the second man, Cheslav, had got to Plakinov's apartment building and been advised that Li had not returned. Cheslav drew his tall body to its full height and stood breathlessly before the Security Officer on guard at reception. Looking down on him Cheslav insisted that he be accompanied to Plakinov's apartment. The Security Officer knew who Cheslav was but nevertheless insisted on seeing his authority to enter the apartment. The guard thought that there was every possibility that this was just another test of the security system. Whilst on the other hand Cheslav was obviously agitated.

Li's assistants, the Sergeant and the Clerk, were just preparing to leave. They confirmed that no one had been to the apartment since Comrade Plakinov had left about an hour before. Cheslav accompanied by the guard went into every room and after a quick look around they retreated to the main entrance reception where the guard resumed his duties without enquiring what it was all about. All he knew was that they were looking for Li.

Plakinov's man raced off for the Library to find and assist his colleague and friend Andrei. When he finally tracked him down he saw the large frame of Andrei being helped into a car by two policemen. On producing his identity card he used his authority to order the policemen to drive directly to KGB headquarters. During the drive the two policemen told the story of how they had been called to the park to find KGB comrade Andrei tied to a tree by his trouser belt. The two policemen explained how the belt been passed between his teeth with the buckle at the back of the tree making it unreachable and that was as much as they knew.

No one had come forward to say they had seen anything except the good citizen who had heard a man groaning. The man had stopped the passing police car after having investigated the source of the groans. Cheslav told the two policemen to find the man and bring him in. He was the only witness they had apart from the unfortunate Andrei who was in no position to relate anything.

Chapter 11

On arrival at KGB headquarters Cheslav immediately telephoned for a Doctor and then telephoned Plakinov. Plakinov was distraught. He had Andrei brought up to his own suite of offices where the stretcher on which he lay was placed upon a conference table. Cheslav went over his story in detail and Plakinov listened intently.

This Mardosov man was creating mayhem and he was either, extremely tough and able, or he was incredibly lucky. The chances of anyone knocking Andrei unconscious were remote. Andrei in the meanwhile was beginning to show signs of recovery but he was obviously unaware of what was going on.

The arrival of the Doctor brought a swift demand for Andrei to be transferred to the special military hospital in central Moscow. Plakinov insisted that no effort was to be spared in the care of his man and that he wished to speak to Andrei the moment that was possible. The unconscious security specialist was carefully transferred to a military ambulance which was driven with cautious haste to the waiting team of head injury specialists.

As the stretcher left Plakinov's suite he was giving instructions for the Chief of Police and his trusted KGB team to meet in his headquarter suite within one hour. It took a little longer for them all to assemble and those who were last were left in no doubt at Plakinov's displeasure.

The story he told them was simple; his beautiful comrade and colleague Li Saric had been abducted by an Interpreter from Minsk. The purpose of this abduction was not clear but what was clear was the fact that Plakinov wanted his beautiful mistress rescued and returned to him promptly. No effort was to be spared and a full operations centre was to be set up with those present in constant attendance to co-ordinate the operation. No one in the room was to leave the building until Li and her abductor were found. No effort was to be spared and no clue or piece of information was to be overlooked. Contingency plans arranged for other possibilities were to be fully implemented. Other arms of the administration of the USSR were to be told that a full alert had been arranged as a training excercise to test the system. Plakinov was sure that the Mardosov man and Li would be picked up in hours.

Li and Gennardy lay behind the door panel that led to Plakinov's apartment office. They had been there now for over half an hour. Gennardy was not an expert on hand guns and he was afraid that the gun he had taken from the security man could go off accidentally. He held it with his forefinger behind the trigger and looked at it constantly to reassure himself. He was not even sure if it was loaded.

Eventually the pair decided to enter Plakinovs office. Li pulled on a bar and part of a picture panel about two feet wide and five feet high swung silently open. They looked at each other then Li opened the door wide.

Gennardy followed Li as she stepped over the deep threshold. The room was beautifully furnished and full of light. As they had arranged Li went straight to where Plakinov kept his private files. She knew where they were since Plakinov had told her that on his signal, in an emergency, she was to destroy them in a petrolem fuelled incinerator which was built into the bunker beneath. This act of destruction was only to take place in the event of an instruction communicated by Plakinov himself. Li had therefore memorised the six digit lock code.

Li wanted to take the box containing the files to the bunker but Gennardy pointed out that he needed more light to read the contents. They settled for Li taking the box through the panel and handing Gennardy one file at a time so that he was in the light and still in a position to make a quick exit through the panel.

The first files handed to him were dossiers about high ranking Soviet Army Officers and other senior personnel from the Warsaw pact countries. Gennardy put them to aside. Halfway through the search he came upon a cover with *U.K. Embassy Moscow* written in large letters across the front. On opening this file he revealed the first of several sheets of paper showing photographs of U.K. Embassy staff with a note of their names, departments and possible contacts within the USSR. The sheet covering the Agricultural section showed a picture of Goodchild with a clear statement about his role as a servant of the USSR and the esteem with which the KGB held for him. Gennardy was horrified because immediately beneath the picture of Goodchild were pictures of Smart and Jean Donkin (Alias Miss Smith). Gennardy was suddenly sweating profusely. He had made contact with a British Agent who had a boss who was working for the KGB.

'God in Heaven' he unwittingly volunteered just like his Grandmother did. What a time to think of his Grandmother he thought.

'The British I contacted have a boss called Adria, his English name is Humphrey Goodchild, who is working with Plakinov and has been for over thirty years' Gennardy advised Li.

Li looked quickly across at Gennardy.

'Adria? That is the name of the man who was telephoning for Plakinov every half hour yesterday'

'Now we know why' said Gennardy.

'We must get out of Moscow. Plakinov knows

everything. He'll have us shot on sight. What a mess. What a terrible bloody mess.' Gennardy went on.

'You must get the file on Markham' said Li.

'What bloody use is that now' Gennardy retorted.

'When we get to England that file will be our passport for asylum.' Li insisted.

Gennardy looked at Li. He was silent for a moment and then said.

'I am so sorry that I got you into this awful mess Li. Everybody in the Soviet Union has a chance to be searching for us now.'

'I know;' said Li. 'but Plakinov is in a difficult position too. Think about it! He can hardly tell everyone that his personal assistant absconded with a wacky interpreter who wants to get his KGB secrets to take to England. They will be searching for us for sure but we could still be lucky. And remember your plan if you had been unable to get me to get you the information you wanted?'

Li went on in this vein whilst Gennardy looked at her and listened, his thoughts racing.

'You are right.' Gennardy confirmed.

'Let's get this evidence for the British and give it a try. It's the only chance we have.'

They continued to look for a file on Markham.

Eventually they came across a file called *The Socialist Republic of Britain.* The first few pages showed pictures of Albert Markham taken both in the U.K. and on the Soviet side of the Iron Curtain. They did not have time to read it. The light was fading fast and so Gennardy gave the Embassy file and the Markham file to Li whilst he put the rest back in the secure box. They were just about to put the secure box back in the cupboard within Plakinov's desk when Gennardy heard a noise. He froze and whispered to Li pointing through the room in the direction of the sound.

174

Three minutes before Gennardy had heard the noise one of the security ladies who normally sat with the guard at the entrance had been passing an unused door from the corridor that led to Plakinov's office when she thought she heard voices.

The door was locked and rarely used.

The woman placed her ear against it.

Sure enough she could just distinguish the voices of a man and a woman but she couldn't hear what they were saying.

The unusual excitement of Li not returning and the search by the KGB man had raised awareness, what had started out as another boring day had fuelled speculation and stimulated curiousity.

The security officer was very sceptical of the woman's claim until he too had gone up to the first floor and placed his ear to the door. He immediately returned to his desk to telephone his boss who was not available. Leaving an urgent message the guard took the key to Plakinov's apartment door and entered. It was then that Gennardy had been alarmed by a noise as the guard had fiddled with an unfamiliar lock.

Gennardy was even more alarmed when he heard the click of a light switch and saw the line of light beneath the door separating Plakinov's office from the rest of his apartment.

Gennardy didn't have time to put the box back so he passed it to Li on the other side of the void making too much noise as he did so.

The guard opened the door into Plakinov's office. He was surprised that the door was unlocked. He peered through the gloom before finding the light switch with his left hand. His body was trembling as his shaking right hand undid the catch on the gun holster hanging from his belt.

Gennardy and Li had not had time to close the panel door.

The door to Plakinov's office should have been locked. Plakinov must have been so anxious after speaking to Goodchild that he had forgotten to lock it as he left in a hurry for his rendezvous.

Li stood erect holding the two files with her back pressed hard against the wall inside the panel door. She was trying to breathe without making a sound but her breathing seemed to sound like a roar.

Gennardy had his face and the palms of his hands pressed against the wall on the opposite side of the panel door. He had placed the gun in his pocket to leave his arms free.

The two could hear the stertorous breathing of the guard who was advancing to the partly opened void. The guard pushed his pistol into the darkness of the opening as he tried to decide whether he was a hero or an idiot. He gently pushed the panel door with his free hand and narrowed his eyes as he blinked and peered into the darkness

As soon as Gennardy saw the collar on the man's uniform coming through the panel he grabbed at it with both hands just as the man raised his foot to come over the threshold.

Unbalanced the guard clutched at the air dropping his gun as he fell to the floor below squealing with pain and fright as his shoulder shattered on impact with the concrete.

Gennardy raced down the staircase using the light shining through the panel void to see. He shouted to the man to be quiet or he'd shoot him where on the anguished guard whimpered and groaned: 'My elbow, my shoulder, my arm.'

Gennardy undid the gunbelt from the wounded guard and pulled it between his teeth as he had done with Andrei. The man bit into the leather as the pain from his shattered elbow seared through his brain.

Grabbing the back of the man's collar Gennardy pulled him across the floor to the bunker entrance.

Li had followed Gennardy down the concrete steps and now she rushed back up the steps entered Plakinovs office, closed the door and went to replace the box then thought better of it. She didn't have time; someone could come at any moment. She quickly stepped over the threshold.

Her hands were trembling as she pushed the picture panel into place before feeling her way down the concrete steps to rejoin Gennardy at the entrance to the bunker.

'Oh! Gennardy I am almost passing out with fright.' Li panted.

'No more than I am' he replied.

'We must get out of here now. Get the two bags we packed and put his gun in the smaller one. You carry that one and I'll get the other' he ordered.

They left the wounded man propped against a wall as far from the concrete steps as possible. Li had taken a thick winter coat she had found in the bunker together with a heavy woolen hat.

Both had previously replaced their other clothes with the kit from the bunker wardrobe. Plakinov had unwittingly provided them with their immediate requirements.

Only the limited light from the open entrance to the bunker was available to guide them to the outer door. Li said her hands were trembling so much that she couldn't possibly operate the key. Gennardy took her instructions and felt for the keyhole before carefully turning the key through ninety degrees. Li pulled on the door from the inside and the freezing Moscow air rushed in as though seeking refuge from the cold.

The pair stepped into the darkness outside and stood for a moment before walking into the street.

Gennardy went first as they had agreed and Li stepped out to follow him. They both knew that Plakinov's people would probably be searching for a man accompanied by a woman so they walked apart.

Within minutes they were off the streets and walking alongside the railway line to the little hut they had shared the previous night. Inside they loaded the stove with coal and waited until the warmth from the stove raised the temperature. Gennardy kept looking at his watch and asking Li to do the same. Each time they looked they opened the stove door to provide some light. Somehow the hut was more welcoming than it had been the previous night. There prospects were still grim but at least they knew what they were about to attempt and what they were up against.

At one o clock in the morning they set off towards the central Moscow railway marshalling yards walking in the darkness of the shadows at the side of the railway line. Everything was covered in snow and a breeze carried light flurries through the bitterly cold night air.

When they got to within a few yards of a huge junction Gennardy told Li to wait by a shed whilst he reconnoitred the area.

He was waiting for the Moscow to Warsaw goods train that went off in the early hours of every morning pulling a mixture of trucks and wagons.

Gennardy knew that the engine crew and the train guards would be Polish civilians but there was always the possibility that the Russian military would be there in numbers if the train was being used for the shipment of military equipment.

As he got to the goods yard he could see the last of the wagons being shunted on to the end of the train.

The train was made up mainly with empty coal wagons returning to Warsaw to be refilled for the journey back to Moscow to fuel Moscow's electrical power stations.

Gennardy scanned the train to find a wagon that he and Li could travel on. At the back of the train were some covered wagons but they had sliding doors on the sides. Opening the sliding doors of these trucks was too risky and not easy when the train was moving; however slowly. They would have to gain access through the roof.

Gennardy went back for Li and deliberately positioned her at the beginning of a long slow bend so that they could get aboard the train out of sight of the driver and his crew. As the train pulled out of the goods yard the flurries of snow had cleared and Gennardy cursed as moonlight appeared through the gaps in the translucent clouds.

Li listened carefully as Gennardy once again rehearsed the procedure for stepping on to the steel step of the first wagon he had identified.

They stood waiting as first the engine and then the empty coal trucks groaned, squeeked, squealed and rattled by.

'Now!' shouted Gennardy.

Li stepped lightly onto the steel step of the truck and then onto the next before reaching the narrow platform at the back. Gennardy was keeping pace with the truck and handed Li her bag which she grabbed and held on to whilst Gennardy, bathed in an eerie, blue, shadowy light and breathing heavily with effort and concentration leapt onto the same step and clutched at the handrail. Gennardy's foot hit the step with the arch of his boot. His foot slid off the step forcing Gennardy to release the handrail. He hit the ground hard just inches from the rails.

Li's voice shouting an anguished, 'Gennardy,'

above the clamour of the noise of the wheels saturated Gennardy's senses.

He rolled over, leapt to his feet, and boarded the train three carriages further down. Li watched as he stood on the narrow platform holding onto a rail with one hand and clutching his heavy bag with the other. His chest was heaving with the exertion.

They could see each other standing motionless in the moonlight.

Gennardy removed his coatbelt which was difficult to do with gloves on. He slipped the belt through the handle of his bag and refastened the buckle. The loop made by the belt went over his head and he put one arm through so that his bag was on his back. With two hands free he made his way to the end of the truck and climbed the ladder above the couplings to the roof. His instinct was to slide along the roof on his belly in the direction of Li. He realised that if he did the grime collected by his coat would certainly attract attention later so he opted to make his way on his hands and knees.

The train was now picking up speed and the wind chill factor made his perilous journey even more arduous. Eventually he got to the end of the carriage where Li was almost frozen to the handrail and shouted down. Li looked up and closed her eyes with relief.

Without Gennardy she was a dead duck.

Turning round Gennardy released the cover on the roof to reveal the aperture which provided just enough space for an average sized person to get through. He looked in and could only make out the shadowy outline of what he thought must be canvas covered machinery. He pushed his bag through and went back for Li.

He took her bag and pushed it through the hole then helped her manoeuvre her stiff, cold body up the ladder and onto the roof.

Li was dropped gently inside the truck and Gennardy followed. They then proceeded to run up and down on the spot turning around in the dark as they did so and laughed and gasped after their strenuous and hard won accomplishment.

Plakinov's bunker had provided them with zipped body bags specially designed for Russian military personnel. The bags retained natural body heat keeping out the debilitating cold. They were so pleased to have them.

The two of them sat in their bags with their backs resting against the canvas covering the machinery.

Through the night they talked of their immediate contingency plans. Minsk was about six hours down the line and it would be daylight when they arrived. Li would ask questions beginning with; 'What if....?' and Gennardy would think through the answer.

They jollied each other along. On one occasion Gennardy said; 'Would you believe it? We have food, warmth and free transport courtesy of Yuri Plakinov and the government of the USSR.'

Li laughed and put her gloved hand over her nose to keep it from freezing; before shouting, 'We are on our way from Moscow.'

Through the night the pair talked when they were not dozing and once opened a jar of their precious food, courtesy of Plakinov's bunker.

The following morning the two railway truck passengers found themselves in Minsk railway yard being thrown back and forth as the trucks and wagons banged into one another in diminishing collisions before the train came to a halt.

Gennardy was keeping an eye on activities and to his horror he realised that the trucks were being separated from the wagons. This meant that the cargo in their truck was either destined for Minsk or was to be diverted from Minsk.

It was broad daylight. If they tried to get out from the roof aperture they would almost certainly be seen but if they sat tight they could end up in Kiev, Tambov or even Vladivostock. Their best chance they decided was to hope their truck was left where it was for the time being.

Li and Gennardy took turns at keeping a lookout through the various apertures in the flawed structure of the truck. At mid-day they shared another of their precious jars of food. The day dragged on endlessly until the light began to fade. They then packed up their precious possessions of survival and returned them to their respective bags before making their exit through the roof.

Minsk was no warmer than Moscow. Everywhere was covered in snow that had frozen solid. The Minsk goods yard appeared deserted but Gennardy knew that security guards employed to protect goods in transit were probably keeping themselves warm and playing cards to relieve the boredom of yet another uneventful and dreary day.

He also knew that they would be delighted to relieve the boredom by arresting anyone seen sneaking around the yard; and that was exactly what he and Li were doing. No chances could be taken.

Gennardy was very familiar with the yard and with Minsk in general so evading the guard was not too difficult even if they were patrolling. Once out of the goods yard they made their way to the central underground station next to the main station. They bought tickets separately and sat apart on the tube train until it reached its furthest destination where they got out and Li followed Gennardy to a nearby bus stop.

The bus took them to within half a mile of his

Grandmothers little house in the village of Brot five kilometres from Minsk. Gennardy knocked and shouted 'Nana. It's Genna. Open the door please.'

The old lady opened the door and let them in. Gennardy embraced his Grandmother lovingly. 'You look well Nana. Have you been looking after yourself? May we have a drink, Nana we are choking with thirst?'

The old lady poured them both a glass of milk saying 'I will make you a hot drink soon. It is so good to see you but you look exhausted and who is this fine young lady you have with you.'

They all smiled at each other and Gennardy's Grandmother got out her cherished cutlery and crockery and prepared the best meal she could manage with what was available. Before, during, and after the meal the three never stopped talking, mainly because the old lady never stopped asking questions.

It was strange, thought Li, how human expectations and standards could change so swiftly.

Since their arrival they had been welcomed and fed. After their experiences over the last twenty four hours what they were now enjoying was a feeling of relative security and yet this security was really a sensation only.

How was it, she asked herself, that she could be wrenched from the boring security with which she had become so familiar over the months and years in the employment of Plakinov to a situation where relative tranquillity and peace of mind, and hope, could be found in the tiny home of an elderly peasant lady who had made her welcome.

Gennardy's Grandmother insisted that her guests should sleep in her bed.

'That bed was made with my husband's own hands.' she advised them.

'I will be very comfortable in my rocking chair by the fire.'

Having eaten, Li and Gennardy just wanted to sleep.

Taking nothing off except their boots they pulled the homemade woollen blankets over them and fell into a sound sleep side by side.

All through the night the old lady dozed, tended to her stove, and returned to her chair from where she would look across and watch her two young charges sleeping like babies.

When Gennardy awoke the next morning he was stiff, partly from sleeping so soundly and partly because of his fall from the train.

Li woke up and seeing an empty room enquired where Grandmother was.

'Probably gone to get some milk; I think.' Just then his grandmother returned with ham, milk and eggs.

Li asked if she could undress and wash herself as a first priority and so it was agreed that they would eat a feast of a breakfast after they had both attended to their needs.

As Li and Gennardy sat down to breakfast they both felt so good and refreshed. They both laughed easily as they related some of the minor incidents about the journey to Minsk. Gennardy had told Li that the authorities were bound to get round to visiting his Grandmother at some time so the less she knew the better and therefore Gennardy told his Grandmother that they were making their way south via Kiev and they would be boarding a train from Minsk that night. He pointed out that Li had no identity papers and they wanted to borrow hers.

'Of course.' was the reply.

'I never go out of the village anyway so no one ever asks me for them.'

Gennardy said that he had to go into Minsk to do a

little business and left.

He told Li and his Grandmother that he would be back about dusk and that Li should be prepared to leave.

Gennardy walked out of the village towards Minsk and stopped the first bus to come by. He then took the tube and stepped off at the nearest station to the apartment block where his actor friend Alexander shared an apartment. Alexander was called Sacha for short like most other Alexanders in Russia.

Sacha would almost certainly be in bed. Like most actors and entertainers who performed in the evenings it took time to wind down from a performance and so going to bed in the small hours of the morning was a way of life.

A dishevelled young woman came to the door in response to Gennardy's prolonged knocking. Sacha was sitting on the floor smoking a cigarette with his blankets around him.

Yes Gennardy could stay there for the night. Gennardy expressed his gratitude to Sacha and said he would get some food for them. He returned with some meat and vegetables and began making a stew in the tiny cooking area that Sacha shared with others. Sacha was grateful and savoured the smells as the food cooked.

Gennardy told Sacha nothing of his adventures except to say that he had done some work in Moscow and he had stayed with Irena. Sacha smiled knowingly; he got on quite well with women but Genna always seemed to have that edge over him; he wondered why.

When the meal was ready Gennardy broke into a bottle of Vodka and gave Sacha a generous glassful. They finished every morsel of the meal and Sacha sat and sipped another glass of vodka that Gennardy had put at his disposal.

After the meal Gennardy said he wanted a nap and Sacha agreed that it was a good idea. Within minutes Sacha was fast asleep and Gennardy went looking for Sacha's identity card and papers and found them together with Sacha's roubles. Gennardy stole the identity papers but did not take the money. Talking to himself Gennardy said 'Hopefully you will think you have lost your identity papers. I'm sorry my friend but I am desperate.'

Gennardy left a note to say that he had called his office and been sent on an urgent job. Two hours later Sacha awoke and on reading the note thought nothing of it. It would be some time before he realised how he'd been used.

As Gennardy had predicted he was back at his Grandmothers by dusk, after more food and a prolonged farewell Li and Gennardy left. His Grandmother had obviously enjoyed her unexpected guests and Gennardy left her dreaming her own pleasant dreams which, he felt sure, involved him, his father, and his grandfather. They were the pillars in her life.

Gennardy and Li walked along the unmade road talking about the knowing looks Nana had been giving them during their stay.

'I think that she thinks we are lovers.' said Li.

Gennardy laughed and said. 'Maybe we should be but not now. My soul preoccupation is to get the bus to the underground station and get on that train. Each extra metre I distance myself from Moscow makes me feel better.'

Li shuddered from fear and the cold as she hurried along beside him.

Before they were out of sight Gennardy turned

around several times in the direction of his Grandmother. He could see the light from the oil lamp that she held in her hand. Then the road curved and took her out of sight.

The six o'clock passenger train from Minsk to Warsaw was the train that Gennardy had targeted. They boarded the train with time to spare and sat in separate cushettes in the same carriage.

This train would be at the Polish, Belarus border by 11pm. It was important to travel in the dark; if things went wrong they could get an opportunity to slip away in the night.

Chapter 12

Gennardy knew he was taking a chance using a passenger train. They should have been in Warsaw by now. It was just bad luck that the goods train was split in Minsk. Going back to his Grandmother's had been unscheduled but he felt better for his overnight stay there.

Li sat in a cushette in a different carriage to Gennardy. They had reasoned that the authorities would have passed a message to look for a man and a woman together so it was prudent for them to be apart.

They took comfort by stepping into the corridor every forty minutes to stretch their legs. Just the sight of one another was very reassuring; especially to Li.

During one of these periods of apparent excercise Gennardy entered into conversation with the attendant who was putting more coal on the stove which provided the heating for the passengers travelling in his carriage.

'You must be looking forward to the spring comrade.' declared Gennardy.

'Everyone looks forward to spring.' the man replied unhelpfully.

'I find it difficult to sleep on the train at night.' Gennardy went on. 'It makes the night very long.'

'My sleeping clock can no longer tell the difference between night and day.' said the attendant.

'You would do well to sleep now if you can; we have a long unscheduled excercise when we get to the Military camp at Brest.' he went on.

'Oh what's that for comrade?'

'Some boss wants the train searched as though we were in an emergency situation. I suppose it's to keep us on our toes. All the attendants were called up to the restaurant car just after the train left. We were told not to check the papers of the passengers because they will do that before we cross the border - the military I mean. We had the same palaver before the train left Moscow. Some of the passengers were embarrassed by some of the things found in their bags. Black market things mainly but they didn't bother with them. Arrest them or anything '

'That's unusual' Gennardy said. 'Not arresting them I mean.'

'It mustn't have been what they were looking for.' the man volunteered.

He yawned before advising Gennardy. 'I am just filling the stove up before I get some sleep in. You should try to do the same.'

'Sounds like good advice.' replied Gennardy who was suddenly on full alert. Gennardy's mind was in overdrive trying to imagine how the authorities would go about catching them. At the appointed time he met Li in the corridor and stated that they must talk despite their earlier arrangement. Li listened intently as Gennardy restated his conversation with the attendant.

Gennardy ended the explanation of his conversation with the attendant by saying: 'It has to be us they are looking for and even if it isn't a detailed examination of my Grandmothers papers will reveal her date of birth and and give you away. Then there's the name they are looking for; Mardosov.'

They were standing in the corridor together each staring out of the dirty window. All they could see was their own reflection and the dirt on the outside of the glass.

Li responded. 'It is more than twenty four hours since we left Plakinov's bunker. They must know all about that by now. Plakinov will be wild. He will be threatening all of his top people. They will be desperate to find us. What time would this train leave Moscow?'

she ended.

'Let me think! It would leave Moscow at noon. We have already passed through Smolensk and it is now 21.40 so we have about an hour before we roll into the wheel sheds in Brest. They will not wait till the train gets to the border they'll board us in the wheel sheds so as not to hold up the train. It usually takes about two hours to get the wheels changed so they will have plenty of time for a thorough search. We must get off the train about two miles before the sheds.'

The rail guage in Poland is the same as the rest of Western Europe unlike the rail guage in the Russia which is slightly wider. Because of this every railway wagon and carriage has to have the wheels disconnected from the body. The carriage or wagon body is then lifted off the wheels and the wheels are pulled away whilst another set of wheels with the appropriate guage is rolled in and the carriage or wagon is then lowered and reconnected to the new wheels.

It was this difference in rail guages which contributed so much to limit the German advance on Russia in World War 2. As the Russian army retreated to Moscow they took all of their wide guage rolling stock and spare wheels with them. They destroyed what they couldn't take.

Without the appropriate wheels for the Russian railway system the German supply lines were limited to a small proportion of what was needed. Road vehicles travelling over unmade roads or snow and ice could not make up the deficit.

The failure to deliver supplies as they were required played a significant role in slowing the German advance before the winter set in bringing the advance to a halt.

The story of Russian and Western railway wheels

was familiar to every schoolchild in the USSR and the railway guage difference created a physical and phsycological barrier between East and West.

Li and gennardy had little interest in the political semantics of railway guages and concentrated their thoughts on their own survival. Fortunately for them they were educated in the geography of the Eastern Bloc countries. Gennardy's knowledge of the railways was invaluable to their aspirations.

Through an open window on the carriage door Gennardy could suddenly see the lights from the wheel changing sheds outside of the ancient town of Brest. About a mile from the other side of the sheds was a large glow of electric light from a major military camp. Thousands of conscript and regular soldiers of the Soviet Union were billeted there.

Li and Gennardy met again in the corridor just before Brest and and on Gennardy's signal they both returned to their respective cushettes, picked up their bags, and without explanation to the other passengers they met at the junction of two carriages. The train was travelling slower and slower as it navigated the long slow bend in towards the sheds. Gennardy opened the door at the end of a carriage and told Li to jump when he shouted. Fortunately no one came past them.

From the light of the train Gennardy could see the terrain a few yards ahead, a large heap of snow appeared, Gennardy pointed to it and seconds later shouted 'Now.'

She hesitated and so he pushed her and followed himself with his bag in his hand. Li had inadvertently released her bag on being pushed. Gennardy's selected place for the jump was fortuitous. The top layer of the snow bank was covered in a crust of ice. Their fall was broken as they landed and the crust broke. Their fall was soft and even pleasant as their hands and knees plunged into the snow beneath.

The train trundled on as they extricated themselves from the snow. When the train had passed Gennardy went back for Li's bag. Having recovered it the pair set off south away from the army camp and the sheds. It was not the most direct way to the Polish/Belarus border but in his view it was the safest.

The night air was freezing their breath as they walked along the side of a track before turning east to follow a snow covered unmade road used by the few farmers and locals who lived in the vicinity. The snow was deep in places, difficult and exhausting to walk through. Sometimes their feet broke through the ice crust making walking quickly very tiring. In other places the snow was not so deep and they had to be careful not to slip on solid ice. Both conditions slowed them down.

Gennardy reckoned that it would take them up to three hours to cover the ten kilometres which would get them to their immediate destination.

Half an hour after leaving the train Li was struggling. Her bag seemed to be ten times heavier than it was when they set off and despite the exertion her toes were frozen. They stopped and sat on their bags in the snow.

'How much further' Li gasped.

'Not far now' he lied.

Gennardy reckoned that they had travelled almost two kilometres. He opened his bag and found two winter vests and some cord. He wrapped a vest round each of Li's feet and tied them on with the cord.

'Your feet will soon be warm once you start walking again.' he told her.

He didn't believe what he said and neither did Li but

somehow it made them both feel better and Li had got her breath back. After a while it became easier when they found that the snow had been flattened by the passage of tractor and lorry wheels.

They had found that by passing their arms through the loops which formed the handles of their bags they could carry their bags on their backs. They were now making better progress and Gennardy felt happier.

Towards the end of their march Gennardy pointed out that they were walking parallel with the river Bug which they were to cross. In the distance they could see the silhouette of a building against the night sky. Gennardy pointed at the building and said. 'When we pass that farm we cross the river.'

'Why here.' said Li. 'because the river is shallow here at this time of year so if we go through the ice we will only be up to our knees'

'How do you know?' she asked.

'My father brought me here when he was stationed in Brest. I remembered it when I was making my original plans.'

'Why can't we walk over where the river is frozen solid.' she panted.

'Because the thickness of the ice varies and if we go through phu...ttt.' he waved his hand dismissively besides there is a lookout tower every two kilometres. Sometimes they are manned and sometimes not. At this point we are about midway between the towers.

Li didn't ask any more questions.

A quarter of an hour later they reached a narrow snow covered pathway leading to the edge of the river. Like so many other places they had passed over the previous two hours the sides of the river and the pathway were populated with silver birch trees. The trees never grew to any great stature since they were chopped down and used as soon as they got to a certain size.

When they reached the end of the path they stood on the river bank and surveyed the river. At this point it was shallow but fast flowing in places. Where the flow was slow ice formed and then broke away in flakes which were carried along until stopped by an obstacle to which they attached.

Gennardy pointed. 'Over there is Poland. All we have to do is to get across.'

Li looked at Gennardy. Although their eyes were accustomed to the darkness and they were close together they couldn't really see each other's faces yet they looked in each others direction as they talked.

'Dont tell me that we are going to walk through that water?' said Li.

'When we get to the other side we'll be in Poland.' Gennardy replied.

Li didn't answer she was now totally dependent upon this strange and kindly man who just seemed to know what he was doing. It was as though everything had been rehearsed.

After a while she reponded with a sigh and; 'whatever you say Comrade Mardasov.'

'Hold on to me.' said Gennardy as they carefully negotiated their way into the freezing waters.

Li needed no encouragement. She had warmed up during their long walk but as they entered the river the cold seeped into her feet and legs making her gasp.

Two incongruous silhouettes shuffled their way across the stony uneven river bed. The water depth varied from ankle deep to past their knees. The transit took no more than five minutes but it seemed that that far river bank would never come.

The feeling of jubilation when they reached the opposite bank was not celebrated in any way. Both were numb with being in the water so long. There teeth chattered. Gennardy linked arms with Li and they forced one foot in front of the other till the silhouette of a farm on the Polish side appeared when they cleared the silver birch trees lining the Polish side of the river.

As they approached the farm a dog growled from somewhere in the distance.

They walked round the farm at a distance and the carefully made their way to a barn and went inside.

The barn was a long shelter made from roughly hewn wood with one central double door to give access. This system kept as much cold out as possible. The barn housed a horse, several cows, and over a dozen pigs. Chickens and ducks also huddled together in groups at either end of the barn. The smell was sharp in the cold night air.

By the light of a pencil torch Gennardy explored the barn. The animals were unperturbed by his presence and the only movement came from a shuffling sound as some of the animals changed position slightly. Gennardy returned to the door where Li stood with her body trembling uncontrollably from the cold. Opposite was a large stall filled with loose straw. They climbed over the straw and made a hole in it at the back of the stall away from the door. Gennardy couldn't undo the knots in the cord which held the vests to Li's feet. He slid the cord along until it came off her feet and then removed her boots and filled them with straw. Li stretched her legs out and tried to wriggle her frozen toes. It was painful. Gennardy rubbed her feet with his hands which were also very cold and some circulation returned to both his hands and her feet. Gennardy then spent ages removing his own boots as Li held the torch. They pulled out one of the body bags and Gennardy got in after wrapping all the other clothes in the bag round his feet and the feet of Li.

'Get in beside me.' Gennardy said as he pushed his way into the body bag. Li didn't argue but she was sure there was no room for her. She got her legs down beside Gennardy's and they did up the zip as far as it would go. Gennardy put his arm around her neck and she snuggled next to him. Eventually warmth came and they were surprisingly comfortable. The heat from their bodies was trapped in the capsule they had created. As soon as warmth was not such a priority Gennardy opened one of the jars of food and they shared it before snuggling together again. Li soon fell into a sleep whilst Gennardy dozed fitfully. Every time an animal changed position he was wide awake.

Before dawn a cockerel from elsewhere on the farm went through his ritual and the stirrings of the other animals increased. Gennardy lay wondering what this new day would have in store for them. Li was awakened by the cockerel and they lay silently in the straw wondering what would happen next.

As daylight seeped through the gaps in the timbers of the shed Gennardy could hear footsteps outside. They didn't come near the barns.

Gennardy was grateful; grateful that they hadn't been discovered, grateful that he didn't have to act without having some plans or a strategy for what to do next. By talking things through with Li and by having a contingency plan for each step of the way they were amazingly still free and still on target to find their way to England.

They may not be as comfortable as they would wish but their discomfort was easily bearable and for the time being at least they had a possible future. They talked quietly as they lay side by side. They were now both in their own body bags.

Gennardy's plan was for them to make their way to Lublin, the Capital of Lublin province, in south east Poland. Lublin boasted two universities and it had a long history. Gennardy had been once before and he had liked it there.

Being in Poland gave them a major advantage. Although they did not know the names of leaders or particular individuals they both knew that since 1980 a new movement had developed in Poland. It was called Solidarnosc (Solidarity) and it was an independent trade union movement with the leadership based in Gdansk. The power of the Solidarnosc movement was so effective that the Polish Communist Leader, General Jaruzelski, had imprisoned its Leader, Lech Walesa, in December 1981 and declared martial law. He was then forced to release him to avoid a major confrontation with the Polish people and Walesa remained at the head of a huge underground movement and was openly supported by the Catholic Church. Gennardy intended to make his contact with Solidarnosc through the Catholic Cathedral in Lublin.

They lay in the straw in their respective bodybags and talked endlessly throughout the day. Conversation only ceased when the farmer, or his wife, or another man had come into the barn to feed and water the animals or milk the cows.

A small dog which followed the Farmers wife everywhere had barked and barked at the straw in which the pair lay. The Farmers wife shouted at the dog; 'Shut up and stop barking.' as though the dog could speak. The dog continued to bark; 'Stupid animal;' she shouted, 'it's only a rat.'

The barking gave way to a discontented growl as though the dog felt cheated by not receiving some appreciation for his discovery. Eventually the woman left the barn with her pails of milk followed by her devoted dog. After a sigh of relief when the woman was out of earshot Li and Gennardy laughed at the little pantomime they had witnessed.

As darkness approached the two escapees shared another jar of food and carefully packed their bags. Li told Gennardy how much she missed her bathroom in Plakinov's apartment and he had told her how lucky she was just to have known the experience. 'When we get to England we'll have a bath every day. Three times a day if you like.' he said to cheer her.

They came out of the straw and stood in the moonlight going over each other picking off pieces of straw from their clothes. Satisfied that they were as presentable as possible they left the farm and made their way along a track. They passed no one and the only sign of life was the smoke coming from the chimneys of distant farmsteads along the way.

Eventually they came to a much better and bigger track which in turn led to a road. After walking for about half an hour a bus came along and they waved it down. The few people on the bus were watching the couple all the way into Lublin. It was unusual to see strangers at night in this part of the countryside.

Gennardy asked the driver to stop the bus for them half a kilometre before the main Lublin bus station which the driver dutifully did. Gennardy paid the driver in roubles because he had nothing else. Paying in roubles in Poland wasn't usual but it wouldn't normally create any problems. To ease any anxiety felt by the driver Gennardy said. 'This is what our Soviet masters paid us with.' Gennardy knew that Solidarnosc was thought to have enormous support in the countryside and Walesa had boasted that rural Solidarnosc had as many as one and three quarter million members. Poland was definitely more comfortable after the driver shared the sentiments of his passengers.

As soon as the bus stopped Gennardy and Li made their way to the great cathedral church. Gennardy hoped that some sort of service would be taking place and after about an hour they watched as people began making their way through a small door in the great main entrance door. The people were mainly women and all were wearing headsquares folded into a triangle and knotted under their chin.

Gennardy and Li had never been into a church before and both were filled with awe at the architecture. They were also impressed by the obvious commitment of the congregation. The atmosphere in the church was so different from anything within their previous experience.

Although they did not understand the service they copied the rest of the congregation as best they could. They stayed in their pews whilst others took communion. No one seemed to bother that they didn't go forward and they felt that the place posed no threat to them.

As the service went on they both felt as though they weren't there. It was as though they didn't exist on earth and they were watching from elsewhere. 'Were the last few days real? Were they dreaming? Were they real or was this all a fantasy?'

Li was tempted to to put her hand on the arm of Gennardy to see if he really was there; she did; and he was. Gennardy looked at her reassuringly.

After the communion the singing in the church seemed to become more fervent. It was also beautiful. When it all ended the congregation became little groups of people greeting one another as they left. Then the little groups melted away until Li and Gennardy were left in the empty cathedral.

One of the three ministers who had conducted the

church service came towards them. His long gowns made him look as though he was slowly floating down the stone aisle floor.

'May I help you before you leave?' he enquired.

Without hesitation Gennardy replied; 'We are here because we need your help.'

The Priest looked at this unusually clad couple before instructing them.

He said. 'Follow me.' and they obeyed. Picking up their bags they followed the Priest through an arched, wood panelled, door at the side of the altar. Inside was a long wood planked table with forms to sit on at either side. Another Priest joined them then the two priests sat at one side of the table with Li and Gennardy sitting on the form on the other side facing them.

The first Priest opened the conversation with: 'And how can we help you.'

Gennardy knew they would be suspicious if he told the full story but on the other hand the story was so farfetched that they would probably think he was a crank.

Undercover operations to get information on Solidarnosc were a constant threat to the organization so they would also be suspicious in case the Russian intelligence services were attempting to infiltrate Solidarnosc.

As the first Priest watched Gennardy gathering his thoughts he spoke again:

'Perhaps we should introduce ourselves. I am Father Ignatius and this is Father John, my colleague.'

'Gennardy Mardosov and this is my ...' Gennardy suddenly realised that he was not sure what status Li and he had between one another. He looked at Li before saying; 'And this is Li Saric, my friend.'

'Li does not speak very much Polish.' he added.

The four looked at each other as Gennardy

hesitatingly told the Priest that they were on the run from the secret intelligence services. He explained how they had made their way to Poland to get help from Solidarnosc; the only organization that they could trust to help them. Gennardy explained that it was in the interests of Solidarnosc to help them.

Father Ignatius stood up and said. 'We are Priests and we know nothing of Solidarnosc but we can see that you are in some discomfort so we can offer you hot food and we will prepare you each with a room for the night and facilities to wash. If you would come with us please?' he enquired.

Gennardy turned to Li and nodded as they all stood up and left the room through a door leading to a courtyard. They crossed the courtyard and entered another door leading to the accomodation used by the clergy who served in the cathedral.

They were then taken down a staircase into a corridor with doors either side.

'Please leave your bags in your rooms and I will show you where you can wash' said Ignatius pointing to two doors.

'When you have washed we will have some food ready for you and perhaps we can talk later.'

Gennardy nodded in agreement and said 'Tac' (yes) in Polish.

Li and Gennardy luxuriated in the warm shower which they used in turn. They went to their respective rooms opened their bags and changed some of their clothes before both sat on the edge of the bed in Gennardy's room which, like Li's, contained only a bed and was windowless. The two talked for a minute or two before Father John returned to invite them upstairs to eat.

In a large warm kitchen they ate some delicious soup with black bread before being presented with some pork and steaming potatoes by a large middle aged lady with an agreeable disposition and a kindly smile.

The two guests devoured the food gratefully.

When they had finished three men entered the room one holding Gennardy's bag and coat and another holding Li's bag and coat. The hair stood on the back of Gennardy's neck and Li oozed anxiety.

'You will come with us. Put your coats on.' Gennardy realised that it would be unwise not to comply. They exited the building through a different door and found themselves outside on a main street where a large van was parked. The men ushered them into the rear of the van before joining them. The van was driven slowly away. It trundled along for about twenty minutes before stopping. The doors opened and all five got out in a farmyard. Gennardy could see that they were somewhere on the outskirts of Lublin city. There was darkness all around. The lights of Lublin flickered right across the base of the skyline.

It was spartan inside the farmhouse which was furnished by a large wooden table in the centre of the room surrounded by a dozen chairs. A large open fire fuelled by logs was the only other feature apart from a couple of religious pictures hanging on the wall.

Gennardy suddenly felt much better. At least he knew that his captors were almost certainly Solidarnosc. It was almost just as certain that he and Li were considered to be potential Russian infiltrators.

The leader of the group gestured to Li and Gennardy to sit which they did. The man then opened their bags and removed their handguns holding one in each hand.

'I suppose you know nothing of these?' he questioned.

'Only KGB specialists get these. Which one is yours young lady.'

Li looked at the man and then at Gennardy and lowered her gaze. She was terrified and tried not to show it.

Gennardy put his hand on hers to reassure her and replied on her behalf.

'These are not our guns really. We picked them up to protect ourselves when we found ourselves in great danger.'

The man resisted the temptation to be facetious and said: 'Tell us how you got them and whilst you are about it tell us how you each came by two sets of identity papers. Then tell us about your rail tickets from Minsk to Warsaw.'

Gennardy realised that their bags and coats had been examined when they were having the meal they had enjoyed so recently.

He felt that anything but the truth would be counter productive. The files, what about the files? The man hadn't mentioned them.

In an attempt to promote some confidence in him and Li Gennardy said 'and the files; what about the files.'

'Ah! The files, what about the files?' questioned the man.

'Those files are our passport to the west said Gennardy. Our story is difficult to believe but it is still true. Where are the files?' he asked.

'Safe.' said the man shortly 'your story please.'

Gennardy was not sure where to begin. He didn't want to tell his story in Polish either in case Li later contradicted him. The man by this time was aware that Li's Polish was very limited and so he insisted that Gennardy speak in Polish so that his colleagues could understand also.

The time was passing quickly and the man's two colleagues were tired of standing so the seats were rearranged. The three captors sat at one end of the table with the guns and the papers and Li sat side by side with Gennardy at the other. One of the men went out of the room and came back shortly afterwards with a jug of beer and five mugs. They all took a drink as Gennardy related his story.

Occasionally the leader or one of his accomplices would ask a question. As Gennardy spoke he felt less and less threatened as his captors looked at him and Li with a mixture of doubt and incredulity.

They were now into the early hours of the morning and the leader stood up and declared; 'That's enough for now. We will have to keep you in a secure place. Do not try to escape. We will shoot you dead if you do.' the statement was made in such an off-handed way that Gennardy believed him without doubt. One of the men lifted a hatch in the corner of the room and the two prisoners were ushered into the cellar below.

The cellar was exactly the same size and shape as the room above but not as high. Gennardy's head just avoided colliding with the joists when he stood up to his full height.

'Not much chance of escaping from here said Gennardy shrugging his shoulders.' he spoke in Polish and so he had to repeat it in Russian for Li.

The cellar contained a dozen bunk beds in six groups of two, one above the other, against three of the walls. The only other furniture was a container beneath the staircase which they were to use as a toilet.

Chapter 13

The lady who had heard the muttered conversation at the door to Plakinov's apartment began to feel uncomfortable as she sat on her chair at the entrance to the apartment block. It was half an hour now since Sergei the guard had gone upstairs to investigate the voices she had heard in Plakinov's apartment. She didn't want to create a fuss unnecessarily but what with the disappearance of Li, mutterings in the apartment when it was supposed to be empty and now the fact that Sergei had failed to return she felt insecure and frightened. After all, she reminded herself, she had sat in the entrance for eight and a half years and there had never been an incident of any kind. Something must be wrong now. She decided to telephone Sergei's headquarters.

To her surprise Sergei's boss Colonel Visinski arrived within ten minutes and asked for a quick explanation. The lady explained that Sergei had gone upstairs to investigate the noises she had heard in Plakinov's apartment and he had failed to return.

Visinski beckoned to two of his men and the three ran up to the door leading to Plakinov's apartment on the first floor landing. Visinski withdrew his pistol from its holder and entered the apartment followed by his two soldiers each with their machine pistols at the ready.

Each room in the apartment was searched. Nothing was found and everything appeared to be in order. The only thing that was odd was the fact that all of the electric lights were on.

The Colonel felt that it would be unwise to enter Plakinov's office without his presence or instruction so he decided to do the prudent thing and telephone

Plakinov on his special number. The call went directly into the emergency unit and was put through to Plakinov.

The security guard, Cheslav, accompanied Plakinov. The two were driven directly to his apartment in his big black limousine. On arrival at the entrance to the building Plakinov felt so anxious and so ill that he had to hang onto the railings beside the front door. Having rested for a moment he had to muster all of his strength and resolve to avoid passing out as he walked across the foyer and up the staircase. At the back of his mind was a nagging recollection that he had familiarised Li in detail about the workings of his bunker.

No! He told himself. No! It could not be! Surely not! She wouldn't dare?

As he entered the apartment Plakinov ordered the two soldiers to stand outside in the corridor.

He then looked at Visinski who saluted and said 'I have checked the apartment Comrade Plakinov and everything appears to be in order. The only place I have not checked is your office.'

'Then check it' barked Plakinov.

Visinski still had his pistol in his hand. He walked up to the office door and turned the handle asking. 'Is the door locked or....'

'Find out.' shouted Plakinov.

Visinski turned the handle and the door opened. He thrust his pistol forward and switched the light on with his left hand. Looking around he said. 'There's no one here Comrade.'

Plakinov rushed in followed by Cheslav to find his precious box lying open on the floor by his desk. His heart sank. He felt sick.

Suddenly Visinski said. 'What's that noise?'

'Noise?' said Cheslav. 'Listen. There it is again.'

As they listened they heard a distant whine. All three looked at each other and Plakinov nodded to Cheslav who went to the panel and pushed it open stepping quickly to one side as he did so. The noise was clearer now and quite pitiful.

Plakinov flicked a switch beneath a window near his desk and the empty apartment below became illuminated in bright light. At the same time a small orange light flashed on a wall panel opposite Plakinov's desk and in the foyer at the entrance. Plakinov pressed an intercom switch and spoke to the lady in the foyer telling her to ignore the flashing light.

Cheslav peeped cautiously into the empty apartment to see the guard staggering towards the concrete staircase groaning and whimpering with his leather belt tied round his head and between his teeth.

Cheslav stepped lightly over the panel threshold and down the staircase pistol in hand. Not seeing anyone else he ignored the guard and made his way to the bunker entrance door and peered in. Seeing no sign of life, he shouted 'There's no one here. They've gone.

Visinski went to help the guard. He quickly removed the man's belt from his head and mouth. The man was desperate to get out of the place.

As he attempted to move up the concrete staircase he jarred his injuries. Free from the restrictions of the belt between his teeth he shrieked his agony.

By this time Plakinov was at the panel door void looking down in disbelief whispering quietly, No! No!......No!

As the guard shrieked Plakinov put his hands to his ears and went to his office desk chair and dropped into it. He then picked up his telephone and barked instructions into the mouthpiece.

He then examined his box to check the contents only to discover that two of the files were missing. One of those files was the UBAC plan and the other was his file on agents and officers working with the KGB on their operations in Great Britain.

Plakinov was now in a seething cold rage. He wanted revenge. He wanted Saric and Mardosov as his prisoners; they would wish that they had never been born.

It was now more than twenty-four hours since Goodchild had first sent the warning. Goodchild had telephoned several times since hoping to hear that the fugitives had been apprehended. Embarrassed by not being able to confirm their capture Plakinov had not answered.

Plakinov took a call at his desk. Could he speak to Adria? He responded by saying that he wasn't available and that Adria was to be given the message that everything was in hand. He didn't want Humphrey Goodchild on the telephone every five minutes; it was better for the time being if Goodchild believed that all was well.

One hour later the injured guard was full of morphine in a hospital bed feeling very sorry for himself and wishing that the two men at the side of his bed would stop asking questions and go away so that he could be overwhelmed by sleep. 'I have told you everything I know.' shouted the guard. The Doctor suggested that he should really get his patient prepared for the operating theatre and the two interviewers eventually agreed to leave. They returned to Plakinov's special KGB unit and reported back. The gist of their report stated that Li Saric and a man called Gennardy had left the empty apartment shortly after the guard had come upon them. Each had left with a bag. Each of them had a gun. Li Saric was given the handgun taken from the guard by the man called Gennardy.

The major emergency procedure was now in full swing throughout Moscow. Passengers and drivers in every means of transport were asked for their papers and their destination.

People in the Soviet Union thought little of being asked for their papers but this was different. If the man looked to be in his thirties or if he was carrying a bag his questioners subjected them to a search and their bags were emptied and examined. If the female being questioned looked as though she was in her twenties with natural black hair or if her hair was dyed she was also given a full search and her bag was to be emptied and the contents examined.

Contact was made with Gennardy's office in Minsk and his boss was ordered to be on call twenty-four hours each day until further notice. Any calls for Mardosov were to be intercepted and the details reported to Moscow immediately. All details of any matter, no matter how trivial, related to Gennardy Mardosov were to be communicated to the emergency operations unit in Moscow. Everything on file regarding Mardosov was to be despatched to Moscow that night. In response Gennardy's quaking boss reported back that Mardosov had last been in the office the previous week and had received his pay together with rail travel passes to Leningrad and Murmansk.

The Secretary to Gennardy's boss with the red-lipped oval mouth was despatched by plane that night from Minsk airport to Moscow with all of the files and photographs that she and her boss could come by. She was the last person to have seen Mardosov. On arrival at the KGB centre the officers who interviewed her gave her a very hard time in an attempt to extract any morsel of information which could provide a lead or a clue. After two hours the only two snippets of information they had was a reference to Gennardy's friend, the actor, Alexander Gabets (Sacha), who Gennardy had casually mentioned in the past, and the fact that Gennardy lived with his Grandmother in a small village just outside of Minsk.

News from the hospital confirmed that the condition of Andrei was critical. He had undergone a surgical operation to remove a blood clot from his brain. Plakinov was infuriated at the lack of intelligence and the lack of progress. He ordered that Alexander Gabets and the Grandmother of Mardosov were to be found immediately and they were to be interrogated ruthlessly to ensure that there was no chance of them withholding information.

Plakinov was convinced that his quarry was still in Moscow. After all where would they go? He kept saying. It was only last night that they were last seen, he pointed out to the members of his emergency think tank. He did not dwell on where they were 'last seen' and no one in the room was prepared to ask for further details of the last sighting.

Just in case he was wrong Plakinov ordered a rigorous search of all trains en-route to Murmansk and Leningrad.

To cover the real purpose of the search in Moscow from his Kremlin rivals Plakinov issued a photograph of Gennardy Mardosov to all Police. Moscow television news transmitted a story explaining how a mental patient was on the loose with a young woman after murdering two male Moscow citizens. The man was very dangerous and the public should be on their guard. All citizens providing information leading to the apprehension of the two fugitives would be rewarded.

Sacha had woken from his, vodka induced, slumbers feeling the worse for his over indulgence.

'Drank too much of that damned vodka.' He muttered to himself as he examined his features in the bathroom mirror.

He was splashing his face with cold water when the door to his apartment was subjected to an unusually loud knock. Apprehensive at the continuous door thumping Sacha made his way to the door shouting. 'Yes, yes! I'm coming! Who is it?'

As soon as he slipped the door bolt a huge Officer from the Minsk arm of the KGB pushed the door wide open and pointed a pistol at him. Sacha was wide eyed with fright as the big man pushed him in the chest with the palm of his hand.

'What's going on.' gasped a protesting Sacha.

'Is your name Alexander Gabets.'

'Yes! Of course it is.'

Two armed policemen had entered the room behind Sacha's assailant and they too pointed their weapons at their hapless victim. Sacha was terrified. He had heard rumours of people being removed by the authorities and never heard of again.

'Your papers?' demanded the big man.

'In my jacket I think.' whimpered Sacha.

'Show me.'

Sacha sidled across the room to his jacket and went through his pockets tearing at them as the papers failed to appear.

'They were here.' He said weakly. 'They must be here. I must have misplaced them. Please let me look.'

The big man turned to the two policemen and said. 'Turn this place inside out. I want everything searched and I want news of anything I should know about immediately.'

Looking again at Sacha he said. 'You will come

with me. You will be no trouble if you want to be alive in the morning.'

Within a few minutes Sacha had been transported to Minsk prison. He was told to sit in a chair in a windowless room where his interrogation began.

A knock on the door roused Gennardy's Grandmother as she sat dozing in her chair by the fire.

'Who is it?' she shouted as she eased herself out of her chair and slowly made her way to the door.

From behind the door she shouted again. 'Who wants me at this time of night?'

'I have news for you about your Grandson, Gennardy Mardosov' came the reply.

The old lady then knew exactly who was at the door.

'Wait a minute' she said as she undid the bolt.

'What can I do for you? What do you want?' she said as she made her way back to her chair.

Whilst her passage was slow her mind was racing through the possible reasons for the visit and she decided that these men would not be here if Gennardy was in Police custody.

'Ah. Three young men come to see me.' She gossiped as the men closed the door behind them and made their way towards the little fire.

The men were glad to enter the tiny room that was a refuge from the bitter chill outside.

'Three young men, Eh, I would be happy with one.' she said mischievously.

The three men looked at each other and then the man in the plain clothes cleared his throat and said. 'What did your Grandson say to you before he left?'

The old lady looked at him directly. 'My Grandson, you know my Grandson?' she smiled.

'We understand that he called to see you and it is

important that we contact him' said the Officer as the two uniformed policemen looked on.

'Who called to see me?' said the old lady.

'Gennardy Mardosov called to see you. Has he been here?'

'Has who been here?'

'Your'e Grandson, Gennardy Mardosov. May I see your papers?' said the exasperated officer.

'He's a fine man. Like my husband. Of course he's dead now.' The old lady went on.

'Who's dead?'

'My husband, he's dead, for too many years now.' said the old lady.

She knew that Li and Gennardy had left only hours before and she was determined to delay these men as long as possible. Every moment she could keep them in her little home would be a bonus for Li and Gennardy. She may be getting on in years but she had a brain and a very long memory. More than that Gennardy carried the family seed and every second of their time that she could waste was a tiny piece of revenge for the fact that she had been without a husband for all these years. Furthermore she was enjoying these moments when she could get a little of her own back on this awful system that they had all endured for so long. If Gennardy was successful perhaps she would have Great Grand children growing up in an atmosphere free from the hardships and injustices that were all too familiar.

The old lady gave away nothing. She continuously offered the men refreshments and dodged their questions by asking them questions about their marital status and their children.

Eventually the officer decided that the old lady had lost her memory and didn't know what she was talking about. She had gone to look for her papers and couldn't find them telling the men that she hadn't seen them for years. The men left after she said that she thought the last time she had seen Gennardy was about three weeks earlier. She wasn't sure.

Late that evening Plakinov's headquarters received two reports as a result of the visits. The first stated that the visit to Mardosov's Grandmother had produced no information as to his whereabouts or recent activities. The old lady had no papers and her mental health was in question.

The second report stated that Mardosov had visited the flat of Alexander Gabets. Gabets papers had disappeared whilst he had slept after a meal and vodka provided by Mardosov. His inquisitors were convinced that Gabets had nothing more to offer and had willingly told everything he knew. It was obvious that Gabets was not part of any plot or plan involving Mardosov.

This information gave some confirmation to what Plakinov's think tank had already concluded: That with Mardosov's parentage and knowledge of railways and his fluency in Polish the route he would take would be the one that he knew most about. Poland was his immediate target. Link that with the open unrest in Poland and it was the obvious place for a defector with his background to look for allies.

They further concluded that Mardosov was in hiding in or near Minsk awaiting a chance to get to Poland or he was already on his way either by road or rail. If he had left Minsk directly after leaving the Gabets apartment the earliest train he could take to Poland was the 6pm which would be arriving at the wheel changing sheds at Brest that evening.

Plakinov had already ordered that every security officer on every train leaving Moscow for whatever destination now had three different photographs of Gennardy Mardosov. Every passenger was to have their papers examined and their hand baggage searched.

The Commander of the Military camp at Brest was ordered to send two hundred armed troops to the wheel changing sheds at Brest to support the normal security personnel. No one was to leave the sheds until the fugitives were found or until ordered to do so by Plakinov's headquarters.

Having issued his instructions Plakinov sat in his private office and waited for the telephone to ring with the message he longed to hear.

Half an hour before midnight he eased himself from his desk and poured his favourite Laphroig single malt whisky into a large tumbler, savouring the aroma and rich peaty taste but he found little comfort on this occasion. He was sipping the last drops when the clock opposite him showed Midnight and no call had come. He went to pick up his telephone receiver then changed his mind and looked at the clock again. Suddenly he began banging his fists on the desk in a frenzy of temper and frustration. Never had anyone made a fool of Plakinov. Why couldn't the telephone ring with a message saying that his quarry was captured? Never, in his life had he longed for anything more.

Just after midnight the telephone did ring but it was not with the message that Plakinov wanted to hear. The Security at Brest had reported that two passengers, a man and a woman, answering to the descriptions of the two people being hunted had disappeared from the train. They had left their seats with their bags just before Brest and had not been seen since. They were definitely not on the train and they were not in the sheds. No one had seen them actually leave the train.

The two had not sat together on the train and the

passengers sharing their compartments had confirmed that they had left their seats and taken their bags with them into the corridor a few minutes before the train arrived in the sheds. The guards all along that section of the line had been alerted and a search had started.

Plakinov went into his outer office. The eyes of all his personnel were on him. He walked up to the map.

'Here!' He shouted. 'I want every available man out now to search this area. They have to be on foot. They cannot walk far in these conditions and they cannot cross the river without help.'

Striding into his private office Plakinov picked up the telephone receiver and shouted into it.

'Get me General Jarulzelski in Warsaw.'

As the titular head of government in Poland and also the leader of the Polish Communist Party Jarulzelski was under pressure from the Russians to destroy Solidarnosc at a time when Solidarnosc was enjoying massive support from the people of Poland who wanted more freedom from Russian domination.

Jarulzelski was in bed and woken from a rare sound sleep when the telephone rang. He was having enough sleepless nights as it was with Solidarnosc. What on earth could the KGB and Plakinov in person want with him at this time of night?

Plakinov asked for immediate assistance to find and apprehend the two escapees. He explained that it was essential that the two were caught dead or alive and that there was a chance that they were on the Polish side of the border in the Bug River area of Lublin province. Full details of the two escapees would be in Warsaw first thing in the morning. A courier had already left.

Jaruzelski agreed. He had no intention of falling out with the Russians over what he saw as a relatively small thing, however, he decided to himself that it could wait till morning. He pulled the sheet over his head and slumbered on.

By noon the next day over three hundred Polish troops were involved in a search along a ten kilometre stretch of the Polish side of the river Bug. If the troops had gone a further half kilometre to the south they would have seen footsteps in the snow among the birch trees that Li and Gennardy had passed through ten hours before.

Chapter 14

The two prisoners each selected a bunk bed. Their cell was cold but dry. On each bunk bed lay a selection of home made, hand knitted woollen blankets. They each took blankets, made up a bed, and lay down. At first they could not sleep and they lay talking.

They congratulated each other on their achievements going over the different situations that they had found themselves in since the incident in the park just six days ago. Gennardy was satisfied that they were as safe as they could be for the time being. Their captors would want confirmation of their incredible story. They may also want them as a bargaining tool. Gennardy was under no illusions; desperate people do desperate things and Gennardy himself was living proof of that. As he lay contemplating the underside of the bunk above him he smiled to himself and gave his head a little shake as he thought of the adventures they had packed into such a short space of time. Eventually Li did not respond to his latest contribution to their resume`. Gennardy looked across the cellar. She was sleeping.

The next morning they were awakened by the sound of heavy boots walking across the uncovered wooden floor above. Although their cellar was large it was still oppressive with the light from one low power electric light bulb hanging from a joist. They discussed at length how they would react if they had an electrical power failure that left them in total blackness. Gennardy was always anticipating something going wrong.

Every so often the sound of the boots would cause their

eyes to be uplifted towards the top of the steps at the entrance to their dungeon.

As the day developed Li had a terrible headache and her throat was dry. She could hardly swallow. At first she did not mention her predicament but as her thirst intensified she told Gennardy. He went across to her and put his hand on her brow. He realised she had a temperature. She was shivering. 'Would they give us a drink.' she said referring to their captors.

'I will see.' said Gennardy going to the steps so that his head was immediately beneath the hatch.

Gennardy stood in silence for a few minutes and listened. He heard chair legs scraping against the floor and then the sound of the boots at which point he banged on the hatch with the side of his fist. The footsteps stopped and then started again but they were getting fainter as they left the room. The footsteps returned and this time they were the steps of more than one person. Gennardy continued to bang on the hatch.

The hatch lifted and Gennardy looked up to see one of the men who had sat with them the night before together with another man. The second man shouted down to Gennardy.

'You were told not to make a noise.'

'Li is ill.' said Gennardy. 'Can you give us some warm water please?'

The second man called to a woman in an adjacent room. He then told Gennardy that they would be fed in the middle of the day.

The woman who had responded to the shout arrived with a jug of hot water and a mug. She handed them down as he asked; 'how long will we be kept here?'

The first man replied with; 'When we know a lot more. We will know what to do.'

Gennardy realised that they probably had no idea how to handle this unique situation. He heard the hatch close into place as he went to Li.

Li was obviously ill. Gennardy propped her up and poured some water into the mug. He held the mug as she sipped. The water came into contact with her inflamed throat making her grimace at the sharp pain. Then she sighed as the discomfort subsided as she lay slowly sipping the hot liquid.

'It will not be long before we get some food.' Gennardy told her. 'It cannot come quick enough.' To pass the time he told her about traditional Sunday Lunch in England. About roast beef and Yorkshire pudding with roast potatoes and mashed potatoes and cabbage and carrots and peas and roast parsnips. 'You cannot imagine how much I enjoyed this food.' said Gennardy. 'When I had finished I had eaten too much and I had to lie down I was so full. I will never forget roast beef and Yorkshire pudding as long as I live. My friend Tony Harthill was laughing at me because I enjoyed it so much.'

Li looked at Gennardy and told him that they may both have roast beef and Yorkshire pudding in the near future. Gennardy hoped and hoped that she was right.

To fill the long hours they talked always of England and Tony Hartill and incidents that Gennardy remembered from his trip. The more questions Li asked the more he thought about it and the more vividly he remembered. The more he talked about it the more Li wanted to hear and the more she wanted to improve her ability to speak English.

At mid-day the hatch opened and Gennardy was told to collect the large dish of steaming stew together with two bowls and a plate of black bread. After three trips up and down the steps Gennardy had placed the food on the small table in the middle of the room. The smell of cooked food was a heartening experience and Gennardy set about serving it. Li had sipped all of the warm water provided earlier that day and she looked forward to again feeling the ease that the hot juices from the stew would bring to her throat glands. She wanted only the liquid and a small portion of the black bread. Gennardy tucked into what was left save for a small amount of bread and stew that he kept for later in case that was all they were to get that day.

After eating they both felt much better and both lay among their woollen blankets and slept awhile before resuming their conversations and endless speculation.

'I think of you only as a brother now.' She said to Gennardy.

'A brother' Gennardy questioned.

'You know when we met in Minsk?' Li said. 'Well I enjoyed that night and when I saw you again I was thrilled. You see! I really believed that you were attracted to me. When I look back now I realise how vulnerable I was. I was so lonely.'

Gennardy responded with. 'Lonely! I had to go to England to realise that I had been lonely ever since my parents died. Disappeared! Or whatever happened to them.'

He shrugged.

'You don't understand!' said Li. 'I thought that you wanted me. You went to all that trouble to find me and talk to me and your intention was to use me.'

'I didn't really know you then.' said Gennardy apologetically.

'Perhaps you didn't but you were prepared to sacrifice me for your own ends.'

Gennardy did not answer. He knew that she was telling the truth.

Li had broached this same subject more than once.

Whenever she felt a bit low she went over it again. Gennardy resented the fact that he had punctured her illusions.

Their situation was suddenly changed again. The hatch opened and they were asked to come out. Gennardy was also asked to bring out their makeshift toilet facility.

Li was unsteady on her feet and feeling poorly. Gennardy helped her out of the cellar and explained her situation to the three men who had brought them to the farmhouse. The three lent a hand and Li was given a chair by the fireplace. Gennardy went back for the toilet container and he was shown to a drain outside where he was to discard the contents. Darkness had fallen about an hour before and Gennardy could again see the lights of Lublin to one side of the farm and the darkness of the countryside on the other.

Gennardy took the container back into the cellar and returned as he was instructed. He was then told to sit at the table and his three captors sat opposite him.

The leader of the three seemed a little more relaxed than on the previous night. He offered Gennardy a cigarette and Gennardy declined saying that he had never smoked. 'No bad habits friend' said the leader 'except of course making trouble for the big bear. Not many people make trouble like you do Comrade Mardosov.'

The man had Gennardy's precious files lying before him on the table. He watched Gennardy's eyes looking at them.

'I wish to talk to you about these files friend. But first I think we talk about how you got here. Is this satisfactory for you friend?'

'Of course.' replied Gennardy who was looking

straight into the eyes of his interrogator and thinking that the man was anything but Gennardy's friend at this point in time.

'You will start your story again from the beginning when you were in England. Not many people from the Soviet Union get to England. Why are you so special?'

Only the truth and the actual story would suffice Gennardy decided. That way he couldn't make mistakes. So he began all over again to tell the man and his two colleagues his long convoluted and incredible tale.

Before starting his story Gennardy expressed his concern about Li who was obviously feeling very ill.

'I would be very happy to answer all of your questions but first I must tell you of my concern for Li. She has had an arduous experience and she is exhausted and ill. You will find out that we are telling the truth and I must ask you for some medicine for her.'

'This is already being taken care of friend.' was the response 'the lady is to be taken elsewhere where she can be better cared for. A woman is coming for her shortly.'

Someone outside banged on the door.

'Ah! That will be them now.' said the man

One of the men went to the door and opened it to the lady who had served them with their food at the Cathedral in Lublin. The woman went straight to Li and seemed genuinely concerned for her. Gennardy told Li that she must get well and to co-operate with the good lady who was to take her away.

Li looked at Gennardy saying, 'Tell them to promise I will see you soon.'

Before Gennardy could speak the leader intervened.

'You have nothing to worry about. This lady will take care of you. You will be well in a day or two and then we shall see what to do. You must understand that we must take precautions. You wanted to contact Solidarnosc and you have done so. It is up to us now.'

'We can only trust them Li. I know we will be safe.' said Gennardy.

Their eyes met and Gennardy nodded to her saying in Russian, 'Roast Beef and Yorkshire Pudding.' She smiled a little smile and nodded in return.

'What is this Roast Beef and Yorkshire Pudding.' said the leader, first in Russian and then in Polish. 'No more talking.'

Li and her adopted nurse left the room and a few seconds later the noise of an engine was audible from the farmyard. The noise got weaker as the vehicle distanced itself from the farm.

Gennardy was uneasy as he looked to reply to his interrogator.

The man obviously thought that Roast Beef and Yorkshire pudding were code words between his two prisoners and he was clearly concerned. Gennardy went to great lengths to explain that it was an innocent remark and he went over the conversation he had had with Li as they had sat in the cellar earlier that day. Eventually the man seemed satisfied and the night went quickly as Gennardy told his story again. Whenever he was thought to have deviated from his explanation of the previous night one of the three men would stop him and say he was contradicting himself. Gennardy stuck rigidly to his story.

The leader gave an instruction to one of his colleagues who returned with some ham, cheese, bread and a bottle of vodka. Whilst the leader ate heartily he did not touch the vodka. Gennardy also took advantage of the food and felt better. He then relished the large glass of vodka that had been placed before him earlier.

In the early hours of the morning the leader abruptly stood up and said. 'Enough.'

He beckoned Gennardy to the hatch with the words. 'We will speak again soon.'

Gennardy asked about his files and the man said, 'They are in safe hands. I think we will talk about this next.'

As Gennardy and his interrogators had sat at the farmhouse table that night Polish police assisted by Polish based Russian soldiers dressed in Polish army uniforms raided the homes of hundreds of people who were thought to be Solidarnosc sympathisers. The exercise was largely cosmetic in reality because Polish intelligence was aware of the level of support for Solidarnosc who always seemed to be a step ahead of them.

During almost the whole of 1982 the country had been run under martial law in an attempt to quell the popularity and effectiveness of the movement. When martial law ended and the leaders of Solidarnosc were released from prison in December 1982 the movement had become an underground movement claiming up to 10 Million members with Rural Solidarity claiming over 1.5 million members. Even some very senior personnel in every part of the Polish administration were thought to be sympathetic to the movement.

The raids went on for a week and uncovered nothing of any consequence. General Jarulzelski's office passed on reports daily to KGB headquarters detailing the raids and identifying individuals thought to be in leadership positions within the movement. These unfortunate individuals were arrested and given a hard time being questioned by Polish police with the help of KGB officers.

Those arrested and questioned were usually released within a few days and then de-briefed by Solidarnosc about their experience. From the resulting information it became clear to the Solidarnosc leadership that the raids were prompted by the belief of the Russian hierarchy thought that two Russian defectors were in Poland. The Russians desperately wanted to detain the two who they believed were using Solidarnosc to get to the west.

A Solidarnosc sympathiser who was a senior officer in the Polish Police in Warsaw informed Solidarnosc at the highest level of the reason for the manhunt. He also gave detailed descriptions of Gennardy Mardosov and Li Saric.

Gennardy spent seven nights and days in 'the hole' as he now called it. Each evening he would join his original captors and sit around the table whilst he answered questions. His story captivated his small audience who loved the idea of anyone putting one over on the Russians.

Despite the fact that Poles and Russians were in the same communist camp there was little love lost between them.

After a week living in the hole Gennardy was brought out on the evening of his seventh day and advised that he was to meet a special visitor from Solidarnosc who wanted to talk to him. Gennardy asked about Li and was told that she was well again; the special visitor had spent the day talking with her.

Li was feeling well again. The lady had given her a comfortable single bed in a small room heated by logs burning in a grate. She was constantly plied with hot drinks and given good food each day. Her temperature was normal and her throat was much better. Conversation between her and her kindly nurse had been difficult because of the language problem. Each spoke a little of the other's language but not enough to have a good conversation. The lady who nursed her was called Karina and today she was very excited. She brought clean, simple clothes for Li to wear together with a head square to keep her head warm and a scarf to keep the chills from neck and chest.

The two women sat in the main room in a farmhouse similar to that in which Gennardy was being kept. They sat at a table before a large log fire that heated a cooking range waiting for their visitor. Just before noon a very tall man wearing the rough country clothes of the Polish peasantry joined them. He had heavy boots, baggy pants and a heavy knitted jumper beneath an ill fitting jacket. Li decided immediately that this man was no farmer. The clothes did not match the disposition and the natural authority of the man. Besides his hands were not those of a farmer.

A smiling Karina chatting happily in Polish introduced him to Li.

'This is Aleksander.' She said.

The man inclined his head and gave a brief smile to Li before shaking hands and sitting opposite to her at the table.

'I see you have been well taken care of.' he said in Russian.

'You speak Russian well?' enquired Li.

'I do.' he replied shortly.

Karina removed four warm plates from the range and served a rich stew thick with vegetables. The other man who had arrived with Aleksander joined them and they ate with appreciation. Outside it was another raw day.

When the meal was finished Aleksander told Li that he was going to see Gennardy. He told her that her friend was well but before he went to speak with him he wished to speak with her.

Karina and the other man left the room and Aleksander said. 'Now we can talk freely and first I want you to tell me who you are! Tell me where you were born and start from there.'

After a stumbling start Li began her story whilst Aleksander hardly took his eyes from her as he listened intently. Occasionally he would interrupt with a question and Li would respond before going on with her story. Twice Karina came in with a hot drink for them as they talked and suddenly it was dark. They got up from the table to stretch their legs and Aleksander conversed with the man who had arrived with him. Another man, Karina's farmer husband, joined them. All five returned to the table to be fed once more.

After the meal they all sat in the warmth of the room as Li and Aleksander continued their conversation in Russian. 'Now tell me about Mardosov. How did you meet him.' said Aleksander.

Once again the dialogue continued. The two appeared to be oblivious to the three who occasionally talked to each other in low tones.

After about one hour Aleksander told Li that he thought her story had to be one of the strangest tales ever to come out of the USSR. Li agreed before asking 'What will become of us? What will you do?'

Aleksander looked earnestly at her before saying, 'We will do whatever is required to free our country from Russian domination. We will also do nothing that will provoke the Russians. We will help you if we think it will be to our advantage. We need all the help we can get from the West. We may be able to use you and your friend and we may be able to help you.'

'Now tell me about the files you stole.'

Li responded; 'Gennardy needed evidence to give to the British. When he saw the United Kingdom Embassy file he thought we were finished. He realised that Jeremy Smart was reporting to his boss who was working for the KGB. How else could Plakinov have found out about us'

Aleksander was looking past Li thinking aloud and saying 'Anyone caught with those documents or copies of those documents is dead. I have not seen them but I have been told of the content. If this UBAC plan works it will end any hope of the Poles shedding the yoke of the Big Bear but it is so far fetched to think that Britain could become part of the Soviet Bloc.'

'Plakinov doesn't think so.' said Li realising that the man was no ordinary Pole. He was well educated and in possession of a wide knowledge of the cat and mouse game played between the Russians and the West.

Aleksander stood up and declared his intention to leave. Li stood up and asked, 'When will I see Gennardy?'

'Soon, I think.' said the big man who smiled and shook hands before offering his Goodbyes. Shortly afterwards Li could hear the sound of the lorry engine getting weaker as it was driven off in the night. A thoughtful Aleksander sat in the passenger seat staring ahead deep in contemplation.

Gennardy was sitting at the table in the farmhouse with two of his captors come inquisitors. Like Li he was feeling the benefit of enforced rest and regular meals.

All three heard the sound of an engine in the distance and one of the men went upstairs to look out of the bedroom window. He switched the bedroom light on and then off. The headlights of the lorry immediately dipped twice whereon the man flicked the light switch on and off again. Two minutes later the lorry pulled up in the yard and Aleksander entered the room where Gennardy was sitting by the table. The four Poles exchanged handshakes and greetings before joining Gennardy.

Aleksander and Gennardy looked hard at one another across the table as Aleksander said 'I hope you have been treated well Mr Mardosov.'

The voice confirmed Gennardy's suspicions. The man he was talking to was the Colonel in the Polish Intelligence Service who he'd shared a compartment with on the train journey from Moscow to Minsk. The Colonel had stayed on the train bound for Warsaw.

Gennardy decided not to declare the fact that he recognised the Colonel.

The Colonel surprised his colleagues by asking them if they would leave him with Gennardy for a few moments. The men left immediately and went into an adjacent room.

When they left the Colonel said, 'I am known to these people only as Aleksander. You have a habit of turning up in surprising places Mr Mardosov. How did we come to share a compartment on the train from Moscow?'

'I have to tell you that sharing that compartment was a fluke. I could have gone anywhere on that train. As you say I seem to get myself into some strange situations.'

'You certainly do.' came the reply. 'My identity is now compromised. I must ask you to refer to me only as Aleksander and we never met before.'

Gennardy was worried. Once again he was in danger through an innocent encounter.

He replied, 'I never met you before Aleksander.'

The others were ushered in and Aleksander said. 'Mr Mardosov's friend Li asked me to give him a little message.' he paused and looked at each of his colleagues before adding, 'in private.'

They all laughed and felt a little more comfortable after the explanation when one of the men said 'I like your taste in women my friend.'

Gennardy was then asked to go over his story. Again he related his extraordinary tale as his small audience listened intently. After about one hour Aleksander began asking questions and then he stood up. 'Your lady friend told me the same story. It is quite remarkable!' he commented.

'And now...' said Aleksander. 'Mr Mardosov has some files which I need to study.'

His captors had returned his files to him so Gennardy immediately went down the hole and took them from under his bedding. He handed them to Aleksander who drew up a chair by the fire and began reading.

Gennardy sat round the table with the others as they chatted over mugs of home made beer.

Well over one hour later Aleksander suggested to his colleagues that they turn into bed for the night whilst he and Gennardy discussed the files.

Before they went Aleksander told them 'I do not think we need to worry about Gennardy and his lady friend. What they have told us appears to be true and they have made themselves very important people. The massive search for them laid on by Jaruzelski at the request of the Kremlin is further evidence that they are genuine defectors. They have information that could be very important to Solidarnosc. The details of that information must be kept to a minimum number of people so I ask you all to trust me to see to it that only

231

those at the very top of our organisation be advised. It is in everybody's interest.' The men nodded their understanding and left the room.

It was now late in the evening and Aleksander yawned, stretching his long limbs out as he did so.

'Tomorrow I will return to my office. During the next few days I will see how we can help you to help Solidarnosc. Very few people know where you are and it must stay like that but any farmhouse or home can be subjected to a surprise call from the Police and the internal security intelligence services. They will follow any scrap of information. Most people are with us but that still leaves significant numbers of people prepared to do anything to ingratiate themselves with the authorities for a quick gain. I will get some sleep in the cellar for two or three hours before I leave. If the farm is raided we will have ample warning to slip away in the darkness.'

With that Aleksander went down the steps followed by Gennardy. The two men stretched out in their respective bunks with the hatch open. Gennardy went to sleep feeling better in all respects.

Three hours later Aleksander swung quietly out of his bunk bed. He then went upstairs to wake his colleague, and the pair drove off. Gennardy was awake the moment Aleksander stepped out of his bunk. He lay awake listening to their departure before dozing off again. No one came to close the hatch.

The following morning the elderly farmer and his wife who ran the farm entered the room and Gennardy came up through the hatch to join them. The farmer's wife busied herself making the breakfast. The three men who had brought them to the farm originally joined them and they all sat down to eat.

As they ate they broke into conversation and

Gennardy was told that the leader of the three men was called 'Witold One' and he was the son of the elderly couple. The two younger men were his cousins and they were called Witold Two and Witold Three respectively. All three worked the farm that was code named The Witold Cell, within Solidarnosc.

In Moscow the only useful scrap of information coming from the arrests, the enquiries, and the searches in Lublin Province confirmed that a bus driver had picked up a man and a woman, who were together, in a remote area near the River Bug. The two people had paid their bus fare in roubles and they had got off the bus in the centre of the City of Lublin.

Plakinov was coming to terms with the idea that his quarry was in the hands of Solidarity in Poland and concluded that the most likely route to England would be by sea from Polish seaports of Gdansk or Gdynia. The Russian intelligence services were well aware that British Intelligence was very active with Solidarnosc in both ports.

Plakinov had called off his emergency exercise within the USSR and congratulated everyone on the overall efficiency with which the operation had been carried out. In the newspapers and on television a story was conveyed of how a mock emergency exercise had been held in the interests of the national security. The explanation was designed to satisfy potential critics in the Soviet hierarchy for some of the recent events.

Humphrey Goodchild was contacted and a meeting was arranged in the National Hotel in Moscow. Plakinov explained what had happened. He explained that the fugitives were almost certainly in Poland and that all efforts were being made to find them.

This was not what Goodchild wanted to hear. If

Mardosov and Saric escaped to the West their story would expose the connection between the British Embassy and Plakinov. Without proof of that connection an inquiry could do no more to cast a shadow over him.

He knew that for the British to prove that he was a traitor would be almost impossible. The evidence would be only circumstantial and in any case he had diligently passed on information that the British had considered to be very useful. The British were not to know that most of the information passed on had been with the approval of the KGB.

It was only when Plakinov told him that his own personal files had gone missing and that they were with Mardosov in Poland that the full implication became clear. Humphrey Goodchild went white.

It was in these circumstances that Goodchild agreed to use his best offices to locate the whereabouts of Mardosov and Saric using British Intelligence through their contacts with Solidarnosc.

Goodchild knew that if he was recalled to London the game was up. He would not be seriously suspected of being a double agent unless there was evidence. So a sudden recall would mean that to escape a British prison he would have to spend the rest of his life in the USSR. Whilst this meant safety and some comforts it would not be the lifestyle of his choice. He was resolved to do his best to have these two upstarts from spoiling the plans he had made for his declining years.

To ensure that he was above suspicion Goodchild immediately sent off a signal informing London that Mardosov and Li Saric had gone missing and that a major manhunt had taken place. He ended his message with the speculation that missing may mean dead since neither had been seen since two days after Mardosov's meeting with Jeremy Smart when it had been confirmed that Mardosov had been seen with Saric outside the Moscow library.

At the same time that Goodchild was telling London his version of events, the Solidarnosc leadership was receiving a verbal report from Aleksander. The leadership agreed to assist Mardosov and Saric to get to England together with their files. In exchange for this Solidarnosc exacted a price agreed with MI6 in London. Both parties acknowledged that Mardosov and Saric were to be killed if there was a likelihood of them being captured and turned over to the Russians.

Shortly after this Li and Gennardy were re-united in the farmhouse that had been Gennardy's place of residence for more than two weeks. The farmer's son, Witold One collected Li from Karina's farmhouse. Before leaving Li thanked Karina and kissed her on each cheek promising that if she ever had the opportunity she would express her appreciation by doing something for Karina and her husband to return their kindness.

The journey from Karina's to Witold's farm was only ten minutes in the lorry. They left just after dark and Li was transported in the back so as not to be seen. Her meeting with Gennardy was celebrated with a hug and large smiles all around. They were told that they were to be ready to move at short notice.

Once again Gennardy and Li shared the dungeon beneath the farmhouse. They were out of sight of the rest of the world and spent the days and weeks that followed talking about England and their future. To improve Li's English Gennardy spoke in English whenever possible. Her dedication to learning and her progress was a surprise to Gennardy. Each day she would learn more nouns and construct sentences containing them. Sometimes she would attempt to relate her life story or an experience shared with Gennardy so that he knew what she was attempting to relate. Because of the intense learning process the time passed fruitfully as the spring arrived and the weather improved.

One afternoon Witold One beckoned them to sit at the table. He advised them that they were to be moved elsewhere.

'You will be transferred separately.' he went on. 'We go tomorrow at first light in separate vehicles. It will be safer to travel in daytime. You will travel in the passenger seats and you will both have papers.'

'If we are stopped by the Police or army people' He went on, looking at Li. 'I will tell them that I picked you up in Lublin after you approached me for a hitch to Warsaw. I never saw you before tonight. You understand.' Li nodded.

He continued 'I know nothing about your business. I gave you a lift. You gave me your body.' You understand? He repeated.

She nodded.

Looking at Gennardy he said 'another lorry will come for you. Your papers will say that you are a farmer like me. Your Polish is perfect. There should be no trouble. You will travel with my cousin. You will call him Ari. He is Karina's son and he travels to farms delivering chemical fertiliser. One last thing and very important: Aleksander told me that contact with genuine Solidarnosc or with the British will be by the word UBAC and you will spell out the word YOU and if your contact is genuine he will spell BACK. You will then shake hands and say 'You-back' together the English way.'

Before first light the following morning the two lorries left, half an hour apart. They headed due north on a predetermined route avoiding Warsaw by travelling through the flat countryside to the east. By nightfall they had travelled halfway across Poland. To reach their destination, a safe house on a farm situated a few kilometres distant from the ports of Gdansk and Gdynia.

Once again Li and Gennardy found themselves as lodgers of another farming family. Again the farm had been chosen because the farmer and his wife had a grown up family. There were no children who could inadvertently expose them to the attention of the communist administration.

Li was given a small room with a single bed next to the bedroom used by their hosts whilst Gennardy was given a bunk bed in a room usually shared between their two sons. Both young men were in their early twenties and very conscious of their visitors.

Apart from their own papers and the papers they had obtained from Sacha and Gennardy's grandmother neither had any luggage apart from the two files that Gennardy kept with him always. They both believed that these documents were essential to their success in attaining a place in England. With the exception of the files everything they had brought out of Moscow had been burned on the instructions of Aleksander.

All eight residents sat round the large, all purpose table in the middle of the main room of the house and tucked into hot food. There was limited conversation and all were aware of some tension. They were playing a dangerous game and the nervousness showed. Li and Gennardy were told to stay in the house at all times.

Witold advised them that Aleksander would make contact with them at any time over the next few days.

After the meal they all watched state television on a small black and white receiver. A news bulletin claimed that coal miners in Great Britain were on strike and many were starving. No one in the room made any comment. Gennardy later assured Li that no one in England would be starving.

'People only make revolution when they are at the limit of their endurance.' He told her. 'In England, even people who have no jobs and do no work eat better and live in better houses than our people. This is more lies. Do not believe!' he implored.

Chapter 15

Wherever Tony Hartill went he was taunted. Those who couldn't understand why he was not in favour of support for Markham constantly taunted him whilst at the same time he was constantly badgered by those who were furious at the way they had found themselves locked out of the pit by their own work mates. Never before had the miners been split like this and for Tony the split was ominous. Because of the split, because of the lack of support from other unions and because of public opinion Tony concluded that Markhams policy could not succeed and the miners and their families were to be subjected to months of unnecessary hardship. The futility of it all left Tony and tens of thousands of other miners in despair and yet those despairing found themselves marginalised by Markham and his supporters so that they were watching helplessly as the game was played out nightly on television.

To make things worse the split as perceived by Tony was endorsed only too vividly by the formation of a breakaway Union mainly centred in the Midlands and led by the Miners of Nottinghamshire. The irony of the split was not lost on Tony who was well aware of the thousands of Northumberland Miners who had transferred to the Midlands, and particularly Nottinghamshire.

Tony could only lament the loss of all of those who had left Northumberland to go elsewhere in the sixties and seventies as the pit closure programme in Northumberland had been at its peak.

In those days Northumberland was considered the most moderate area in the country. The moderates had gone to the Midlands.

As a union official Tony threw all his energy into alleviating the hardship which was already evident. He knew that greater hardship was to come the longer the dispute went on.

Most of the Union officials shared Tony's concern. They knew that help from relatives and friends was unlikely because they too relied on the mining industry.

A meeting of representatives from the seven pits in Northumberland met to organise a more efficient system for collecting donations of cash and tinned and food.

Initially the plan had got off to a slow start with many people and organisations believing that the miners should put their union into order and get back to work then a deal could be thrashed out with the board of British Coal Industries, the Government and the CMU.

Most of the miners and the general public seemed to believe that an agreement of some sort would be cobbled together but as the dispute rolled into weeks and months the problems increased and the perception of the dispute changed. This change was reflected in the increase in donations, because, whilst there was little support for Markham's policies the public began to understand the dilemma faced by the Miners.

Tony was aware from the outset of the lack of public support. In the early stages even within the coal mining communities there was scepticism about the dispute but as time went by shopkeepers and those in work began to contribute more generously and more regularly. Like the other volunteers within the CMU Tony collected from twelve shops in one section of Ashington on a weekly basis. Every other week he and two others would go to Morpeth, the rural capital of Northumberland to do a tour of the shops asking for donations. Licences were obtained from Winsbreck

District Council and other local authorities for street collections to help the Miners Hardship Fund. Duty rotas were organised to collect the various types of donations.

Like most of the other volunteers Tony hated the collection duty. The collectors saw themselves as proud men and women who were ill equipped to go round the doors begging. Many of the shopkeepers were polite but reticent to assist because they saw their contribution to the miners as a contribution to Markham's cause.

Others wanted some identification from the collectors to ensure that their contribution went to needy families and not to those posing as miner's representatives and pocketing the cash.

By mid-May the dispute was well into its third month. As usual, every other Wednesday, Tony went to the Miners Union Hall to pick up four collectors for the trip to Morpeth. Inside the hall were two were middle-aged women who were married to miners and two miners both in their early thirties. After some good natured banter Tony checked to make sure they all had their identification badges and a letter authorising them to collect on behalf of the Northumberland CMU.

As he was talking to the two miners Tony became aware of the heavy, unmistakable smell of beer from their breath.

'You cannot go collecting when you're stinking of beer.' said Tony forthrightly.

'Who says we cannot.' said Donny McIntyre the taller of the two. 'All we've had is a few cans.'

'Don't be so bloody silly. People aren't going to give you money for food if they think you've been on the beer all day.' Tony replied sharply.

'Look smart arse.' snarled McIntyre 'If they don't want to help us cos we've had a couple of beers that is

241

their fuck'in hard luck. They're just a heap of Tory bastards anyway. Think they're fuck'in it.' They can keep their do-na-tions.' he continued.

Donny McIntyre looked at his mate and said, 'Ho'way, a'm not stoppin here. The other man looked at Tony and then at McIntyre and the two stormed off.

Tony Hartill's heart was pounding with anger and anxiety. Donny McIntyre was unpredictable under the influence of alcohol. He looked at the two women and appealed to them; 'Are they stupid or what? Where do they get the bloody money from anyway to be drinking at this time of the day?

'They've been in the union offices all morning.' said one of the women. 'The union sends cases of beer in there for the lads.'

'You've got to be joking.' said Tony disbelievingly. 'What the hell do they think they are playing at? You mean to tell me that they're gett'in stoned while we are going round the doors begg'in.'

'My man doesn't go.' volunteered the other woman. 'He reckons that there's a couple dozen of them gett'in into the Union offices regularly through the day and going home legless.'

The two women nodded their agreement at each other.

Tony walked out of the hall with the two women and after locking up the three went to Tony's car to find Donny McIntyre and his mate waiting for them.

'What are you after now?' enquired Tony.

'We changed our mind.' said McIntyre. 'It's wor turn so we'll gan to Morpeth.'

'Don't argue with them,' said one of the women. 'It'll not do any good.'

With his four passengers Tony drove to Morpeth and reluctantly gave the two Miners a list of shops to call on. When he asked them to watch what they were

242

doing both men stuck two fingers up to him. Tony wanted to bang their heads together. Instead he and the two women made their way to the other end of the main street and proceeded to call at shops and businesses as they worked towards the rendezvous in the town centre.

The collections had been better than usual; especially the amount of cash they had received and Tony was pleased to think of the relief it would bring.

When the collection was almost finished a torrent of abuse shattered the quiet dignity of the market place.

As Tony swung round he could hear the unmistakable voice of McIntyre directing awful abuse at the female owner of a hardware shop that was an institution in the town. The middle aged lady who owned it, had inherited the business from her father and grandfather, was at the door of the shop shouting; 'Go away you nasty man.' with a gentility that seemed incongruous considering the torrent of expletives to which she was being subjected.

'Stupid old cow.' shouted McIntyre as he and his colleague sauntered towards Tony and the two women.

'For God's sake get back to the car.' said Tony through gritted teeth as he ran towards the hardware shop.

'I'm very sorry Miss Simpson. Some of the lads just can't seem to cope with things the way they are. I do apologise. I know how kind you have been. I hope that one stupid man isn't going to make you think we're all like that. You've been so generous in the past.'

'No excuses can make amends for ill manners. Said Miss Simpson primly with her hands held together before her and her head nodding to emphasise her statement.

'I know that.' replied Tony, 'just ignore him he's not typical and he's full of stupid prejudices.'

To Tony's surprise Miss Simpson invited him into

243

her shop and handed him ten pounds.

'I know the miners Mr Hartill and for the most part they are the salt of the earth. Do not think for one moment that that oaf can colour my experience.'

Not knowing quite what to say Tony said nothing for a while and then sighed, 'I just wish this was all over.'

'Everything comes to an end.' pronounced Miss Simpson with absolute certainty.

Tony put out his hand towards Miss Simpson and as her hand gripped his they looked at each other for a moment before releasing hands simultaneously.

Miss Simpson was a very special person decided Tony.

As Tony reached the door of Miss Simpson's shop on his way out an unfamiliar female voice floated towards him with the words. 'My! My! You do have a way with women Mr Hartill.'

Looking round he saw a young woman with dark luxurious hair framing fine features. Her dark blue eyes danced mockingly above her confident smile. Her lipstick enhanced an already beautiful mouth.

Realising that he was staring at her without saying anything Tony responded with.

'Erh! What do you mean?'

Realising what he had uttered he could have kicked himself. Although he hadn't a clue who she was he would have felt much happier if he could have said something more appropriate, something that would have impressed her; but the moment was lost.

He held the door for her as she walked past him on her way from the shop. Tony felt that her voice was as beautiful as her face as she said, 'You were obviously very upset by the actions of your colleague. What prompted all that?'

As she spoke she looked across at Tony. His mind was preoccupied by the desirability of this woman and at the same time he was aware of the recent incident and his obligation to get his collectors back to base as soon as possible.

'Look!' he said suddenly, 'I don't know who you are. A lot of strange things are going on these days. I sometimes wonder if I'm dreaming. To tell you the truth I sometimes think I'm having a nightmare as well.'

'That's wonderful.' she responded. 'I need to know all about your dreams and nightmares.'

'Am I being set up for some television show or something, what are you on about: My dreams and my nightmares.' said Tony frowning.

'Well you can believe it or not but I had just arrived in Morpeth and parked my car outside the Queens Hotel, where I'm staying, when lo and behold! I witness my first evidence of the spin off's and consequences of the miners strike even before I have time to get my pen out.'

'You're a reporter?' was Tony's response.

'Ten out of ten Watson.' she replied cheekily.

Her vivacity and intelligence was not lost on Tony who suddenly felt slightly inadequate confronted by her natural self-confidence.

In an attempt to balance his perceived inadequacy Tony said, 'Well the first thing you got wrong was the idea that this is a strike. This is not a strike, unfortunately, it's a dispute between those miners who want to work; because a strike is futile, and those miners who are determined to keep the pits shut. And by the way please do not, repeat; do not write about what you have just witnessed. McIntyre, who caused all the bother, is a nutter by any yardstick when he has had a few drinks but that doesn't make the rest of us nutters.'

'You're a very sensitive man, Mr Hartill, and you obviously bruise very easily.'

Tony was embarrassed, 'And you're very bloody patronising. Anyway how do you know my name?'

'I asked one of your two concubines. You know the two ladies you left by the car when you went to rescue your colleague?'

'You're a cheeky bugger aren't you?' Tony said smiling for the first time.

'And you really are full of compliments; Mr Hartill.' she said with a big friendly smile.

'Look! Can we start again? I'm Pippa Glendinning from the National Telegraph. I'm up here to do some pieces on the effects of the strike.. er.. dispute, and I would love it if you would help me.'

'Tony Hartill at your service Miss Pippa Glendinning, Sir.' replied Tony with a sardonic smile as he offered her his hand.

Pippa responded with a little gurgling laugh and shook his hand warmly saying; 'Where can we meet?'

When Tony returned to his parent's home late that afternoon his first words to his mother were, 'Don't bother making me a meal for tonight Mam I'm going out.'

Tony stood in front of his Mother and teased her with a parody of words he'd remembered from somewhere, saying; 'I am going out to dinner with a gorgeous singer to a little place I know down by the shore. Her name is Patricia. I call her Delicia and the reason isn't hard to see.'

They both laughed as Tony's Mother said. 'I hope you know what you are doing.'

'Look Mother I'm not exactly a teenager you know.'

246

'Never mind, you just be careful.' she went on.

Tony looked in the mirror and wished that he had been a few years younger.

He went back to Morpeth that evening and met Pippa in the cocktail bar of the Queen's Hotel. The lighting was subdued but sufficient. As he walked across to her she rose and smiled.

She wore a simple close fitting black dress that was low cut without being in bad taste. Tony was thinking that it was the sort of dress that women called a cocktail dress. He was pleased that he had put a tie on - he could always take it off he had reasoned not knowing what to expect.

'Welcome back to Morpeth.' declared Pippa.

'Welcome to Northumberland.' he replied; pleased with his response.

'What can I get you to drink Mr Tony Hartill?' she asked.

As he looked at her he saw how well groomed she was. Her perfume wafted in hints of delectable fragrance.

He couldn't help thinking that the whole atmosphere and the scene reminded him of an American movie and he smiled at the thought.

She was watching him and said, 'What are you smiling at? You look like the cat that stole the milk.'

'I would like a beer please.' he said.

'No beer until I know what you are laughing at.' she insisted pointing a finger at him and frowning in mock admonition.

'I'm laughing at us; this; it just strikes me that it's like what you see in the movies.' he explained.

'Havn't you been in here before then.' she asked.

'A couple of times; years ago, when I was just a kid, we used to come over here looking for posh birds.'

'And did you find any?' she said and then placed a

cherry in her mouth drawing the cocktail stick from between her teeth.

Tony was watching every detail. He paused a moment to remember what she had said and then answered. 'Er! Yes. Once or twice, couldn't afford to come over here that often though. This place has all been done up since those days and we thought it was posh then.'

About an hour later Pippa said. 'Well I'm bloody starving. We'd better eat and I feel like something hot and spicy' she said teasingly 'so what about the Indian in the square? The barman says it's excellent. Do you like Indian Food?'

'Love it!' replied Tony astounded that an hour had elapsed since his arrival.

As he rose to leave he suddenly realised that the cocktail bar had filled up. He was aware of the glances from customers, of both sexes as Pippa and he walked across the room to the door.

The Indian restaurant was busy. They were shown to a table for two by a window overlooking the market square. Pippa had obviously booked the table. Again Tony was aware of the glances. 'Hardly surprising,' he thought. 'She is attractive.'

The waiter had given each of them a menu that Tony glanced at before saying. 'Look I can eat most things. Just order what you fancy and I'll get stuck in as well.'

'I'm having raw crocodile toes.' She replied, shrieking with laughter.

Tony was aware of the other customers smiling at them. He felt embarrassed at the attention her loud laughter brought but he couldn't help laughing too.

'I think I know what we should do.' she said. We'll

have a bit of everything. We'll order a thali.'

'Never heard of it!' he replied.

The food was delicious and they didn't stop talking.

Tony was suddenly aware that the restaurant was almost empty. The waiter was topping up their cups with more coffee. He couldn't remember when he had enjoyed himself so much. He was in another world.

'I had better get the bill.' she said looking at a large watch face on her slender wrist.

'In the movies that's the man's job.' Tony pointed out.

'You must watch old movies.' she replied. 'My paper pays for all of this and I freelance for television.'

Tony walked her back to the hotel and said. 'Well, I have to say that today has been definitely different. And thanks for the food. It was excellent.'

'So!' he went on. 'I'll see you tomorrow as arranged and introduce you to one or two people. Show you round. OK!'

'Fine.' she replied. 'You can come in for a coffee if you wish.'

'It's late,' replied Tony. 'And I don't want to take advantage of your generous hospitality besides I'm giving the food vouchers out in the morning.'

'Suit yourself.' she said. 'It's been fascinating.'

As Tony drove back home he pondered the evening: It was ages since he had enjoyed himself so much. She was great company and they had got on really well. Should he have chickened out of going into her hotel for coffee? Was she just asking him out of politeness or did she fancy him? Tony was doubtful. After all he was much older and he couldn't imagine any bloke not fancying her. No doubt she has somebody; he thought.

Nevertheless she had seemed to enjoy herself and he

had had a great time. It had been invigorating.

Tony's thoughts turned to their conversation and the more he thought about it the more he realised that he knew very little about her but, by contrast, she could probably write a book on what she knew about him.

What she had done was to re-awaken his interest and desire for a woman. Especially, he thought, a woman as desirable as her.

It was half past midnight when he let himself into his parent's house. As soon as he got inside the door he heard his Mother at the top of the stairs saying in a low voice 'That you Tony.'

'It's a good job it is.' he laughed. 'You'd get the shock of your life if it wasn't.'

'Cheekie Charlie.' she gently scolded.

The next morning the Miners Union Hall was busier than ever. A long queue had formed waiting for vouchers and food parcels. Tony explained to his union colleagues that a reporter was coming to see how they were doing things and it was agreed that Pippa could come into the hall and watch the procedure. At a few minutes to ten Tony went to meet Pippa as arranged.

As he walked up to her she smiled broadly. She wore a plain grey straight skirt with a white blouse and a black jacket. Gone was the glamour of the night before and yet she was still very eye catching.

'So this is your Ashington.' she beamed.

'This is it!' he replied smiling happily.

'There is a big queue this morning. It gets longer every week. Pride surrenders to necessity as this bloody feud goes on.'

'Where did you read that?' she asked.

'Read what?' he queried.

'Pride surrenders to necessity.'

'I don't think I did read it, it just came out.' said

Tony looking at her.

'Don't think that because we're coal miners we're all bloody half wits.' Tony said angrily.

'I wasn't being patronising Tony. I simply felt that it had a lovely ring to it. That's all. Bit touchy you Miner's! I have to say.' she said apologetically.

'Wouldn't you be? Touchy, I mean, if you were portrayed the way you and your colleagues portray us. You always look for the worst elements and hold them up as an example of what we're like. Television is the worst.' Tony explained.

'So that's the way you see it!' she replied.

'That's exactly how it is so far as I am concerned.' Tony said with finality as he let her into the rear door of the hall.

Tony introduced Pippa to his colleagues and she shook hands with several and listened to the friendly banter. 'What's a bonny lass like you do'in here? You should be mak'in pictures with a face like that.'

'Watch him.' they would say pointing at Tony. 'He's a dark horse wi' the women is Tony mind.'

Tony returned the banter with a smile 'Just ignore them.' He responded good humouredly. 'Bloody workie tickets the whole lot of them.'

Everyone gave a friendly smile.

The food had been divided and placed into about one hundred and fifty bags. Much of the food was from shops that had donated it because it was close to the sell by date.

To guard against problems every item had been closely scrutinised to make sure that everything distributed was satisfactory and only sound products were issued.

Items included bags of sugar, flour and porridge.

Some of the bags contained fruit that was given because it would go off if it wasn't used immediately.

When the doors were opened the people moved into the hall and were directed along a line of tables where they were handed a bag. They immediately looked into it to examine the contents.

Non of the recipients was overwhelmed with the contents of the bag they were given and the hall was soon full of people, mainly older women, many of whom were arguing with the distributors about what they'd received.

'How are we supposed to survive on this lot?' was a common complaint.

Not many extended any gratitude and a few accusations were floated suggesting that the distributors were keeping the best for themselves. When each person had received a bag there was still a few left over. Some of the people who'd stayed to the end received a second bag.

Pippa sat in a corner at the back of the hall and watched the whole procedure. When the last of the people had gone several of those doing the distribution picked up a bag each for themselves from the room at the back of the hall. Their share was the same as that contained in every other bag except that they had picked out the better quality items. This was their reward for helping with the distribution.

When it was all over Tony sat at a table with the rest of the Union men and volunteers discussing the process of food distribution and how it could be improved. It was generally agreed that the system was far from satisfactory and that many of those with young families who most needed help were not getting it. Delivering bags of food to families that the Union officials considered to be in most need caused problems because some people didn't like being singled out for assistance and others complained that the people who were singled out were not as much in need as others. The impromptu discussion ended with a decision to call a meeting of all the interested parties from each of the pits to see how things could be improved. Differences between pro and anti-Markham factions were set aside within the food distribution network.

No one minded Pippa listening in on the discussion.

When they finished Tony walked across to Pippa saying 'Right then. What do you want to see now?'

'Well I now know where Ashington is and where the Town Hall is and the Trade Union Hall so I would like to familiarise myself with the town and the other nearby coal mining communities. Get my bearings as it were' declared Pippa. 'We can use my car.'

As they walked to the car Pippa said. 'The other thing I need to learn is the language. I could hardly understand a word that some of them said. You are about the only one I can understand first time.'

'I suppose that's because of my time in the army and Military police.' said Tony. 'You've no idea the stick I took when I first joined up. You'll love the patter when you get used to it. The humour is in a class of its own. The miners love taking the mickey out of each other.'

They drove the few hundred yards from the Town Hall and passed the pit entrance gate where a handful of pickets stood, and sat, around their makeshift shelter. It was a fine day and some had their shirts off; most waved as the car passed.

'Are they waving because they recognise you or do they wave to everyone?' Pippa asked

'They just wave at everyone and hope they get a blast of support from the car horn.' replied Tony. 'If they recognised me they wouldn't be waving, they'd be shouting abuse of one kind or another.'

'Why is that?' she went on.

'Because they've heard that I'm involved with a breakaway Union.' Tony answered.

'And are you?' Pippa asked.

'I'm one of the originals. It started as an attempt to get a proper ballot. When that failed we felt we had no choice. It's a tragedy.' he lamented.

'We've gone from being, probably the best Union in history to this shambolic mess.'

Her questions came thick and fast and each answer from Tony seemed to prompt another question as they drove around for an hour or so.

As they came past a field Pippa said. 'Why is it that the wooden fence rails are sawn off in so many of the fields? That's the third time I've noticed it.'

'Most of the miners have coal fires and they have no coal so they come in the night and saw a couple of rails off for firewood.' Tony advised her.

'But that's barbaric.' she said screwing her face in distaste.

'What would you do if you had no heat? It's not exactly tropical weather up here even in the summer.' he replied.

'My God it's all so depressing.' Pippa said and then for the first time she fell silent.

To break the silence Tony said, 'Well where to next?'

'To eat.' she declared with a beaming smile.

'I haven't eaten a thing since last night. What are you doing for lunch? Where can we get something light and delicious.' she went on.

Tony thought this over for a moment and realised

that, fish and chip shops apart, he couldn't think of anywhere in Ashington that would be open at lunch time despite the fact that it had a population of nearly thirty thousand people.

Slightly embarrassed by the realisation Tony said. 'Well.... I would say that your best chance would be in Morpeth again. They have a Pizza place that is supposed to be tops.'

'Ideal.' declared Pippa. 'There's nothing like some food and a drink to lift the depression.'

'Just drop me off in the town centre, if you would.' said Tony.

'Can't you come with me?' she appealed not waiting for an answer.

'We'll both feel much better when we have imbibed.'

'Aye why not.' replied Tony. 'I could murder a nice thick pizza.' he paused for a moment before adding 'on condition I buy them. It's a deal.'

Tony went for the pizzas. Pippa picked up a couple of things in the shops and they met outside the Queens Hotel.

'Let's eat them in my room.' said Pippa walking off without awaiting a reply.

Her room was large with a separate bathroom.

They each sat on upright dining chairs on either side of a coffee table and tucked into a huge pizza with the grand name 'Royal Italian.'

'This is the best one they do.' said Tony as he munched 'Top of the range; pricy, but good Uh.'

'Yummy.' said Pippa between chews.

As Tony munched through his second piece of pizza Pippa stood up declaring 'Mmm. that was lovely.' she picked up a plastic bag and went to the bathroom saying. 'I'll just get cleaned up and get us a drink.'

Tony finished his second portion and decided that Pippa had had her fill so he ate the last portion then picked up a copy of the National Telegraph that was lying on the bed together with copies of the Times and the Guardian. As he browsed through the pages he wondered how anyone had time to read all of any one of the daily heavy newspapers let alone three.

He was beginning to wonder what on earth she was doing in the bathroom when the door opened and Pippa walked out wearing a short chinese patterned, silk dressing gown. In one hand she had two tumblers each half full. Her other hand held the two sides of her dressing gown together.

Tony sat upright in the straight chair setting the newspaper aside. As she approached him she released the front of her dressing gown to take a tumbler in each hand. The front of her dressing gown opened a few inches revealing her naked body. She stopped before him with one foot either side of his chair. Tony' mouth was open as he slowly lifted his head until their eyes met.

'Chardonnay, M'sieur.' she said looking down on him as she passed the tumbler.

An instantaneous explosion of energy burst into his loins. He was aware only of her body, her voice, that incredible perfume she wore and the acute, delectable constrained discomfort in his trousers.

As he took hold of the tumbler she hooked her hand, still holding the tumbler, round Tony's arm and tilted the tumbler to her lips. Entranced he responded likewise.

'To pleasure' she toasted sitting on his knee at the same time.

They stared into each other's eyes as they emptied their respective glasses.

'Oohargh.' cried Tony. 'Stand up for God's sake

before I become permanently crippled.'

Pippa shrieked with laughter as she stood up and watched him rise to undo his trousers.

'Ooargh.' cried Tony again tearing at his trouser belt. 'Ooargh Oh that's better.' he laughed as his pants hit the floor.

The laughter stopped as they embraced. Three hours later Tony Hartill left the hotel with a new perspective.

Chapter 16

Ignace Diwinski was the Gdansk Harbour and Ports Manager. He was sixty years of age. For all of his life his country had been struggling to retain its identity and to find some self-determination free from foreign interference. Poland's long history was really all about an ancient nation reborn again after the First World War and Ignace was named after Ignace Paderewski who had signed the Treaty of Versailles on behalf of a new Poland in June 1919.

In August 1939 the Russians invaded Poland from the East whilst at the same time the Germans invaded Poland from the West. Against such odds and the prearranged treachery of Germany and Russia the Polish resistance quickly collapsed.

Like many young men who were students in Warsaw in 1939 Ignace had heeded the call to arms only to be captured by the Germans days later. He spent the rest of the war in a Labour camp near Warsaw until the summer of 1944 when he and his fellow prisoners were released after the people of Warsaw rose up against the Germans. On hearing of the uprising the Russian advance was stopped and the Russian army waited whilst the Poles fought heroically for 63 days before they were crushed and their city flattened by the Germans. The Russians then continued the advance happy in the knowledge that they had allowed the Germans to destroy the Polish resistance army making it that much easier to impose a regime acceptable to the Soviet dictator Josef Stalin.

Before the Russians arrived Ignace had made his way to Gdansk and joined the Communist Party. He told his friends and family in Gdansk that he had simply escaped from a German Labour camp. He made no mention of his part in the Polish resistance knowing that many of those Poles, who had survived the battle against the Germans were later summarily shot by the Russians.

Outwardly Ignace was a good communist. He had worked hard to rebuild his country and he had a responsible position. Secretly he was working with Solidarnosc. He had become a founding member in 1956 after the people in Poznan had staged a revolt demanding bread, freedom and the departure of the Russians. He was also the father of Colonel Josef Diwinski who was known to the Solidarnosc leadership as 'Aleksander.'

Ignace was expecting his son that night to discuss the best way to handle the problem of the two renegades from Russia who had been at the farmhouse outside of Lublin for too long and now that they were near Gdansk he wanted rid of them as soon as possible.

Gdansk was considered to be the home of Solidarnosc. Operating an underground movement was difficult anywhere; the problems in Gdansk were even more difficult because of its interface with the west and the consequent concentration of informers.

Ignace cycled from his work in the port and across Gdansk making his way to his small apartment where he lived with his wife. A military van was parked just outside the entrance to the apartments. This meant that Josef was home.

Josef always brought something with him and this time it was a bottle of very good Romanian red wine that he shared with his parents over a meal prepared by his mother

After the meal Mrs Diwinski left her two men to talk.

She was well aware of their sympathy for Solidarnosc but she was never advised of any operational matters in case she was picked up and interrogated by the Secret Police. She went to bed feeling the effects of the wine. Aleksander and his father each updated the other before they got down to the tricky bit about getting Gennardy and Li to England.

'We must get them off the farm as soon as possible.' said Ignace. 'Our people are obviously concerned that they are discovered. They worry for the future of their sons if things went wrong.'

'What have we got in the way of shipping.' asked Aleksander.

'They are nearly all coal carriers bound for Teesport in England. They are going out on a daily basis. It is our biggest source of revenue at the moment.' was the reply.

'Are the ships registered in Poland or Britain.' questioned the son.

'That's not really relevant. It's about the crews. Half of the British ships are sailing under flags of convenience. Many of them with British Officers and crews from one or more other countries.' replied the Father. 'We have few problems getting them onto the ship once they are in the port. Several of the ships have British agents aboard who know the *YouBack* greeting. The difficulty is in getting them into the port and the woman poses a special problem. Her features are difficult to disguise. The whole port is on the lookout for them and it's the same in Gdynia.' he went on.

'They must be made aware of the dangers. The couple I mean.' said Aleksander.

'Solidarnosc is too important. We cannot allow them to be caught alive if things go wrong. So we must keep them within our own control at all times. They know too much. The lives of too many of our own people could be at risk. KGB techniques would ensure that they told everything that they know. Besides Mardosov is under no illusions, he has said that he will do anything to avoid him and Li being caught alive.'

The older man looked at his son and said 'easier said than accomplished.'

That same night the farmer hosting Li and Gennardy took a trip to Gdansk to visit Ignace and receive instructions regarding the departure of his guests.

Josef had left his father earlier. The farmer knew of Aleksander but he had never met Ignace's son Josef. He was unaware of the connection.

On his return to the farm the farmer passed the message to Gennardy and Li that they were to be dressed like port workers and they were to be ready to leave at any time. When questioned about their chances he seemed vague.

'I have told you to be ready. My instructions are to advise you to go when I tell you. We have to get you through the shipyard gates. The security is very strict. You must do as we tell you. I will soon get the order to move.'

A crestfallen Gennardy asked the farmer if this was the best plan his colleagues could come up with. The farmer pointed out that he did not make the plans, he was simply helping. Gennardy wanted more information and he wanted to go into detail and to draw a plan as best he could of the port and all of the ways in and out. Gennardy questioned the man on his knowledge of the port. On many of the points he could not give answers.

Gennardy wanted to know about local fishermen, how many ships came in and out of port, what their cargoes were. The man told him; not to worry, everything would be taken care of.

Eventually asked if he could question his wife and two sons and the farmer brought them into the conversation. Between them they drew plans of the port, where the ships berthed, where the sailors went when they were ashore, how many ships went to England and what was their cargo.

As they talked Gennardy's mind was refreshed. He had been to Gdansk many times before but the better they prepared the better their chances he argued.

A clear picture began to emerge in his head.

When the farmer's wife and sons were ready for bed Gennardy said. 'Thank you for everything you have done. I realise the risks you take for us and for your movement. Tell your contact that we are ready to go. We will do everything that you tell us. Tell him to advise us of the names of which ships we should look for or which ship we have to get aboard, and when, and leave the rest to us. Remember that we must board the ship after midnight and it would be better if the ship sailed soon afterwards.

The farmer replied. 'I cannot see him again until tomorrow after dark. I will tell him what you say.' with that he went off to bed leaving Li and Gennardy to talk things over.

'We go now.' said Gennardy to Li as soon as they were on their own.

'Now, how now, I thought you just told the farmer that you would do everything he told you.' she questioned.

'They are in a difficult position. They want us out of here but there is no easy way. They cannot allow us to be caught alive in case we expose their people. They plan to get us through the security at one of the gates, probably with some false papers. If we are stopped we will be shot to stop us falling into the hands of the KGB.'

Gennardy finished his statement then leaned back in his chair taking a deep breath before confirming; 'We make our own arrangements.'

Picking up his precious files Gennardy handed them to Li saying 'Put these behind my back between my vest and my shirt.' Li did so and they made their way to the door to select the warmest and least cumbersome clothing they could find. Gennardy then picked up a half litre bottle of Vodka and they left the farmhouse.

From the information they had gleaned from the family Gennardy new that the railway line into the port was less than a kilometre away. The sky was crystal clear and a late sharp frost chilled the air so they walked briskly towards the glow in the night sky that emanated from the busy Polish port.

Within half an hour they were walking alongside the railway line and a few minutes later they could here the sound of a train coming from behind travelling towards Gdansk. The pair slipped behind a bush hedge until all the wagons had passed. The wagons were laden with coal. Just as they came out from behind the bush another train with empty coal wagons passed them on the way from Gdansk to the Polish coal fields. Within an hour they were close to the port perimeter.

They could see the security position dead ahead of them. There was a large wooden shed on either side of the railway line. In each shed was a port security man and an armed guard wearing the uniform of the Polish army. As the trains came in and out of the port the Engine Drivers were obliged to stop the train and exchange papers and signatures with the port security man. The shed on the side of the line carrying the inward traffic was elevated so that the guard could see over the top of the wagons. This left a blind spot between the high point of the coal in the middle of the coal wagon and the side of the coal wagon.

Gennardy and Li stood beneath a leafless tree about three hundred metres from the checkpoint awaiting the next incoming coal train. They ran on the spot and swung their arms to keep themselves warm until they heard the rumble of an approaching railway engine.

Gennardy had counted thirty six wagons on each of the two trains they had seen earlier. They selected a position about two hundred metres from the checkpoint. When the Engine Driver stopped his train to exchange papers Gennardy helped Li up on to the narrow platform between the thirty fourth and the thirty fifth wagon then followed. They then climbed up a short steel ladder welded to the end of the wagon and lay on the coal at the side of the wagon furthest from the observer on the elevated platform; in this way they were hidden from the lookout by the mound of coal in the centre.

As the train began to move and the wagons jerked back and forth Gennardy was pushing coal along with the heels of his boots to make a furrow to improve their concealment. As soon as they had the best position they could make in the few seconds available they pressed their bodies into the coal and hoped.

Each of them covered their faces with their gloved hands. As they passed the security sheds they could see the glow from the electric lights above the sheds illuminating the wagons. The glow became brighter and brighter. The heartbeats of the two fugitive passengers intensified. The increasing illumination seemed to last for long minutes before suddenly the brightness began to subside and then they were in darkness again.

The pair took advantage of the darkness to slide across the coal and down the ladder on to the platform. They were almost shaken off as the wagons came to a juddering halt. As soon as the train was stationary Gennardy leapt off and helped Li down.

The illumination in the coal yard was poor. The blackness was pierced only by the light from ordinary light bulbs fixed beneath steel dishes fastened to wooden posts. 'We must get to where we can see the ships.' Gennardy whispered. 'Stay close behind me. Just walk normally as though you have every right to be here.' They made their way from the poorly lit coal yard towards the bright lights placed on pylons around the jetties. Walking between two rows of long sheds they suddenly found themselves on the quayside. Coal was being loaded onto several ships. Each ship lying at a different depth in the water depending upon how much coal had been loaded.

Few people were about at that time in the morning and Gennardy felt free to look for the red duster of the British merchant navy with the union flag in the corner. He counted six ships loading. The flag flying from the stern of the first ship was not one he was familiar with. He walked past the gangplank of a second ship riding high in the water that had just begun to load. He saw the word '*Welcome*' in English at the top of the gangway and he made his way to the stern to check which flag it was flying. Suddenly Gennardy stopped. Something had just registered. Without realising it he was running back to the gangway of the ship and he saw it all. The word *Welcome* was painted on a strip of canvas that was roped between the hand rails on one side of the gangway. On the other side of the gang way was the word '*Youback*'.

Li had run back with Gennardy. He turned to look at her, jubilation all over his face. 'What is it Genna.' he heard her say.

He noted that she had never called him Genna before, then he dismissed the thought because what he was to show her was more important. 'Look Li!' he said in English. 'Look.' he shouted.

Li looked and said 'What is it? What is it?' her eyes were searching everywhere.

'*Youback*' he shouted.

At the same moment another voice shouted. 'Halt!'

The pair stood as if frozen. Each of them turned their heads slowly to witness a lone security guard walking towards them undoing the catch on his holster as he did so.

'What are you doing here.' said the guard in Polish.

Gennardy's thoughts were racing. He gathered himself together and said in English. 'I am having a walk on dry land my friend.'

'Your papers please.' said the guard in English. It was obviously a phrase he had learned.

'I have left them on the ship.' said Gennardy pointing up the gangway as he spoke.

It was obvious that the guard was not impressed. He looked them over and his brow was knitted as he did so. His hand was resting on the handle of his handgun. Gennardy could almost see the man's mind working. The guard pulled out the gun and waved it in the direction of the cabin from which he had emerged.

Gennardy was frantic and furious with himself for alerting the guard with his premature burst of joyous jubilation. He could do nothing and he could see no one near only a lone sailor watching proceedings from a ship two berths away.

The guard followed them into his shelter, placed the gun on a shelf at the side of the little counter behind which he stood.

'Your papers please' he said as he went into his own pocket and pulled out his papers, pointed to them, pointed to himself, and then pointed to the papers again, before pointing at Li and Gennardy. Gennardy stood up and as he did so the guard picked up his gun from the shelf. Gennardy shook his head and indicated that he was going to put his hand into his coat to comply with the request for papers. Li's hands became little clenched fists when the guard picked up the gun. She stuck the gloved fists into her mouth and drew in breath noisily. The man looked at her and began to speak to her. Gennardy leaned back against the wall and switched off the light with his shoulder.

The guard swung around in the darkness as Gennardy chopped the the man's neck with the side of his hand. The man staggered and Gennardy missed with his fist so he rammed his knee into the man's groin. The guard's head came down as a result allowing Gennardy to bring his other knee full into the face of the unfortunate guard who dropped the gun and was now holding both hands to his face.

The guard was shouting in Polish. 'Help, Maniac!' Gennardy grabbed his collar and told him to keep quiet in Polish. The man was left in no doubt about the terms of the request.

Having recovered the gun Gennardy carefully opened the door of the security cabin and looked out. No one was coming. He closed the door and switched the light on.

Li was standing jammed in the corner still with her teeth biting into her fists.

The guard was covered in blood. It streamed through his fingers as he continued to hold his hand to his face.

Once again Gennardy used the belt from the man's coat and also his trouser belt. He told the guard to sit on the floor and then he fastened the man to a wooden member by passing the belt round his neck. He then used the coat belt to tie one of the man's arms to the same wooden member before using his own belt to secure the other arm.

'I did not wish to harm you my Polish friend but desperate men do desperate things. This I have learned. If you move I shall shoot you dead.'

The unfortunate guard, who had never before thrown a fist in anger, or seen any noteworthy incident in his fifteen months as a port security man, stared wide eyed at Gennardy through his bloodied face and nodded in compliance making him cough and splutter sending a spray of blood across his cabin.

Gennardy and Li left the cabin light on and closed the door. Li was shaking.

'Please Li, I do not feel good either but we must go on.' said Gennardy.

'I will Try.' whimpered Li who cleared her throat and repeated in firmer tones; 'I will be fine. Do not worry about me'

'Good.' said Gennardy. He stuck the hand gun in the pocket of his overcoat and took her by the elbow.

By this time it was Gennardy who needed reassurance. He was putting a brave face on things but he kept wondering if the sign of recognition was really no more than a coincidence. If he got it wrong it was likely to have disastrous consequences. After all *Welcome you back* may be something unrelated, a coincidence?

The British were always doing humorous things. They were so different; less serious, yet deadly serious, it seemed to Gennardy that everything that the British did had to have a funny side to it or they were not interested. Was this sign for him? It had to be.

Steering Li gently by the elbow Gennardy made his way past the ship displaying *Welcome Youback*. He couldn't see anyone on the ship despite the fact that coal was pouring into a hold from a conveyor belt suspended by a crane.

The man Gennardy had seen standing on the deck two ships down the quayside had witnessed the guard, Li and Gennardy, enter the security cabin.

He was the Chief Engineer Officer of the Motor Vessel 'Amada' which was a twenty thousand ton freighter plying the coastal ports of Europe. The ship had a Panamanian registration and sailed with British Officers and an Indian crew. There were three Deck Officers, three Engineer Officers and a crew of twenty including cooks, stewards and deck and engineering staff.

The Chief Engineer was called Jon Oppick who was born in 1942 after the marriage of his Lithuanian Father to his English Mother. His Father had made his way to Britain in 1940 after Hitler's Germany allowed the Russians to take over the Baltic countries.

Jon Oppick had also seen the '*Youback*' code painted on the other ship this immediately advised him that another agent was working on behalf of British Intelligence and it was almost certainly the ship's master. Only the ships Master could have authorised the professionally prepared canvas declaring the words *Wecome-Youback.* 'Ingenious bastards these British.' he had muttered to himself when he first saw it.

Oppick made his way along the quayside. He was almost at the security cabin when Gennardy emerged with Li. 'May I speak with you.' he said as he watched Gennardy steering Li along. Gennardy looked quickly across at the man who looked at the gangway and said.

'You appear to have received a nice welcome.' Gennardy was suspicious. Who else had seen them? Was his thought before he responded with 'Every one likes to be made welcome dont 'you' think.' he said with a heavy emphasis on the YOU. 'I suppose you want to get BACK' the man replied. The two men looked at each other before both said 'YOUBACK' in unison.

Gennardy wanted to laugh hysterically but retained his self-control remembering the cost of his last outburst.

'I am the Chief Engineer of this other ship. It leaves at first light. Follow me please.'

They made their way to the other ship and as they got near it Gennardy said. 'This ship, it has no British Flag, why no British flag?'

'Flags of convenience, I will explain later. We are sailing for Hull in England.' said the Chief who went on; 'Just trust me. You must do as I say.'

Li and Gennardy obeyed and within minutes they were aboard the Amada. The only person who had seen them come aboard was the Indian watchman on the bridge. It was none of his business if the Chief Engineer brought people aboard.

All three stepped through the bulkhead steel door opening into a passageway with doors either side. They went to the door at the end bearing the legend - Chief Engineer. All three passed quickly inside into the spacious cabin living room.

'I suggest the lady has the bedroom and you and I share the living room.' he said as he swept his hand around the room that had fitted settees against two of the bulkheads.

'Please make no noise. You may rest or take a shower. I must go now we will be leaving in about one hour. The last cargo hold has been filled and we will soon have clearance to sail.' Jon Oppick instructed them.

Gennardy and Li nodded. When they sat down they suddenly felt very tired indeed.

Li looked at Gennardy and caught her head in her hands as she laughed and said 'Gennardy, Roast Beef and Yorkshire Pudding!'

Gennardy smiled and said. 'Not too soon! What if they find the guard?'

Li frowned.

Gennardy switched the main light off in the cabin and went to the forward bulkhead to look out of the line of portholes. The engine room and all of the crew accommodation was situated at the rear, or aft end, of the ship. The portholes in the Chief's cabin gave a clear view across the decks and over the bow of the Amada and on across to the aft end of the ship in the next berth. Having got his bearings Gennardy looked out of the portholes on the side giving a good view of the jetty.

It was about fifteen minutes since he had been arrested and ten minutes since he had met the Chief Engineer and it seemed like a million years ago.

During the night the wife of the farmer who had hosted Li and Gennardy awoke. She always slept badly. The farmhouse was in silence. It occurred to the woman that she had not heard Li go to her room and out of instinct she got up to check.

Li's room was empty and moreover when she looked downstairs there was no sign of either of her guests. She didn't want to wake her husband. He worked too hard as it was. After debating for a few minutes she shook him gently. 'What is it?' he asked.

'Our guests, they have gone.'

'Gone, what do you mean gone?' he asked as he threw back the blankets and pulled on his trousers. It was so cold he could not get his clothes on fast enough.

After a quick look around the house he woke his two sons to tell them that Gennardy and Li had left. He gave one of his sons the address of Ignace and told him to cycle there as fast as he could with the message.

Ignace immediately telephoned his good friend who

271

was an assistant Chief of Port Police and a Solidarnosc supporter to tell him that he needed to see him urgently. He then dressed and went to his office where his Police friend awaited him. Ignace pointed out the names of the two ships currently in port that had British Intelligence contacts and the fact that Gennardy had not yet been told which they were.

They deduced that he was obviously making an attempt to get into the port and therefore the risk of he and Li being caught was high; if this happened both had to be shot dead resisting arrest. Under no circumstances were they to be captured.

One hour later Gennardy was looking through the side ports. The ropes that tied the Amada to the quayside were being lifted off the steel capstans as a senior port policeman walked briskly along past the side of the ships. He went past the Amada and Gennardy sighed with relief. Several other port officials had come and gone in the minutes before the ship had cast off and Gennardy felt a little safer as he heard the big diesel engine of the Amada burst into life edging the freighter into the main channel at dead slow ahead. As the ship turned Gennardy saw the port Police Officer go into the cabin where the guard was tied to the cabin wall and then he could see nothing as another ship excluded his view. The tension in the breast of Gennardy made his chest ache. He felt for the bottle of vodka that he had taken from the farmer, removed the top and took a deep swig.

Chapter 17

The Amada was over an hour out of Gdansk when she dropped the Pilot. Gennardy and Li watched anxiously from the portholes of the Chief's quarters as the Pilot Cutter came alongside. The Pilot went down the steps that had been lowered into place for him. He disappeared from view and then reappeared on the deck of the Cutter as it drew away from the side of the ship. At the same time the engines of the Amada changed tune as the revolutions moved up in response to the full ahead instruction.

The Amada was heading into the Baltic. Gennardy and Li were heading for freedom.

In Gdansk things were slow to unfold. Ignace's Port Police friend was disbelieving when he opened the door of the quayside security shed. He saw this poor young man covered in his own blood sitting on the floor with his back to the wall and his arms stuck out. The man gurgled in pained relief when he saw his boss.

A few minutes later the injured guard was sitting in a van on his way to the hospital. At the same time the boss of Port Police was calling in all available manpower and making repeated requests to speak to the Commander of Polish and Russian troops in Gdansk.

It was over an hour before the Commander finally arrived in the port to hear about the incident. All port police and forces, brought in to ensure the security of the port, had been specifically told to look out for a man and woman and each duty cabin had their pictures displayed.

The Commander felt sick when he heard that a man and a woman had been apprehended and had escaped. He was certain of the humiliation to come since it was he who had guaranteed the security of the port. His instructions had come from the very top. He remembered giving reassurances that this port was more secure than the Kremlin. That claim was certain to rebound upon him.

Every available person was brought into the port and instructions were issued that every vessel, irrespective of size, was to be thoroughly searched. All vessels leaving port were to be stopped, boarded and searched.

By this time Amada was in the Baltic Sea and outside of the territorial limit. She was bound for the North Sea and Britain after passing through the Skagerak and the Kattegatt. She was out of reach.

In Gdansk the search was called off after forty-eight hours and weary men trudged back to their barracks and homes. The port was to remain on full alert but no one held out much hope. The birds had flown.

No less a person than Jarulzelski reluctantly advised Plakinov directly. He was paid no compliments.

When Plakinov put the phone down he was seething. This upstart Interpreter had made a mockery of the whole Soviet system. He himself, Plakinov, the head of the mighty KGB, had harboured a traitor who had joined forces with this devil who used belts to muzzle and bind his victims. This man couldn't be a Russian. No Russian would even think of doing that. His frantic thoughts jumped about; the UBAC plan; that was started - at least that had started. Britain could become a Communist republic and then where would they go? How he would relish that: Mardosov and Saric his prisoners in London. Too far ahead he decided, as his crazed mind returned to reality.

All the information he was prepared to disclose was put before his think tank and he was advised that his quarry had obviously had a great deal of help in Poland and that the Gdansk security had been without imagination or good intelligence. A list of all vessels known to have left Gdansk was placed before Plakinov. One of those vessels was the Motor Vessel Amada. It had just escaped the net and was bound for Hull in the United Kingdom. Plakinov sent details of the Amada to the Russian Embassy in London. The Russian Embassy in Stockholm was also sent details of another freighter, which had left about the same time, bound for Malmo, but all bets were on the Amada.

Plakinov then contacted Humphrey Goodchild.

Humphrey Goodchild left the National Hotel after his meeting in Plakinov's suite. He and Plakinov had been at one in exhibiting the cold, dangerous, calculating rage of the thwarted. The two men had sat in the dark leather chairs exchanging thoughts on the implications of the events of recent weeks. Each word and sentence of the conversation was carefully weighed and thought through. Both men knew that the other would not divulge all he knew. The trick was to get as much information as possible.

They were so used to this thought process and the implied subterfuge that right and wrong and fact from fiction were not really relevant. What was relevant was what affected them.

In London a coded radio message was received from Jon Oppick stating that he had aboard the two fugitives from Moscow. The message read "Samson and Delilah en route to the promised land."

The message prompted a meeting of three men in British Intelligence. The oldest of the three, George Norman, had a file before him that told an incredible story:

It started with a report from the British Embassy in Moscow telling of a 'walk in' called Gennardy Mardosov making contact with Jeremy Smart.

Whenever someone 'walked in' to offer their services as an informer, Intelligence Services personnel world wide looked askance. Penetration of the secret services was most usually attempted by 'walk-in's who were always under suspicion from the moment they walked in.

George Norman was fascinated with the information he had to hand which was in three communiqué's. The first was from the interview conducted in Moscow with Miss Smith and Jeremy Smart. The second had come from Humphrey Goodchild and the most amazing and fascinating of all, from Solidarnosc in Poland. The news from agent Jon Oppick was even more amazing. These two people had abandoned Solidarnosc and made contact themselves; the *Welcome.Youback* idea had played a part in a way not intended. The files and the escapers were on their way to the United Kingdom.

George Norman had struck a deal with Solidarnosc in Gdansk. He had, at the same time, agreed with Ignace that he could only confirm the accuracy of the information in the files with Mardosov and/or Saric if they were in attendance. He accepted the fact that the two were dispensable should the KGB or their agents get too close to them. It was essential to preserve the integrity of Solidarnosc.

Ignace had informed Norman that one of his best men had read the documents and had insisted that they were very important to Britain even though the proposals in them were unlikely.

Having been in the espionage and intelligence business for almost thirty years George Norman believed that nothing would surprise him any more. However this tale certainly had. He had two theories in this case: The first was that this was a crude attempt to persuade him and his department of some unlikely plan they may or may not fall for. The method of delivery of the plan was so crude that British Intelligence would possibly fall for it because of its lack of sophistication and professionalism. The second theory had more appeal but was less likely: Some young Russian Idealist actually gets so angry and frustrated that he risks everything, including his life, because he feels threatened and because of some limited contact with a few Geordies in a remote corner of England.

Sitting before the two agents that he had called in, George Norman decided to say as little as possible to them. He started by saying; 'I want you two to go to Hull and pick up two.... .....refugees, political refugees.....', he shrugged, call them what you will, and bring them back here. They are arriving in Hull on Friday morning or thereabouts aboard a coal carrying freighter called Amada out of Gdansk. Our contact is the Chief Engineer. His name is Jon Oppick, any questions?'

The two men looked at each other. Both were in their early thirties both had receding hair. The one with the lighter hair was about six feet tall. The other, the darker of the two, about five feet eight inches tall. Both were very average looking and neither had any distinguishing features. Mark Benson, the shorter and darker of the two, said to his colleague Tim Graham. 'Up to Hull pal, meet the people. Welcome them to dear old blighty. Come to see your Uncle George then, have you?'

They both nodded to each other and then at George Norman, who gave a wry smile and responded with;

'facetious bastards, both of you.'

George Norman admired his protégé's. They worked well together and exhibited their shared humour at every opportunity.

'What's the catch.' said Tim Graham.

'I really don't know' said George Norman. 'In all honesty I do not know.'

He went on, 'What I do know is that these two are full of tricks. They say, and their claim has been supported, that they have information we should know about. I want you to bring them here to this very house that we are sitting in and I want you to tell them that they are safe here and that they will be looked after whilst we listen to their story. When you get them here you will contact me and you will stay with them until further notice.'

Tim Graham and Mark Benson then began to take an interest in their surroundings. They were sitting in the lounge of a semi-detached furnished house in Barnet, North London. 'Where did you get this place from then George.' said Tim Benson.

'From an Estate Agent in Barnet that I have known for a long time, don't worry every thing is taken care of. You won't have any visitors. No men to read the gas meter. Nothing like that! Besides you will only be here for a few days.' he leaned across to each of the two men in turn and gave each a key for the front and back door.

'I'll leave you to it then.' said George Norman.

At the same time as George Norman was meeting his two man team a similar meeting was taking place in the Soviet Embassy in Belgravia, London. Apart from the Ambassadors room, and the entrance and the hallway leading to the beautiful staircase, everything else was shabby. Only the parts that the visitors saw looked the part. The rest of the embassy was in need of decoration, refurbishment and repair.

The Ambassador, who was a long standing supporter and friend of Plakinov, was in one of the shabby ground floor rooms with two of the embassy 'staff.' The three sat on fifties style low chairs with sloping backs and wooden arms. The two well trained KGB men sat opposite the Ambassador. The Ambassador gave each of the men a photograph of Li and Gennardy and went on to tell them that these two people were almost certainly on a ship called the Amada bound for Hull out of Gdansk. The man, Mardosov, was particularly dangerous and resourceful. Both of them were to meet with a fatal accident. Hopefully an accident in which they and anything on them would be incinerated and no trace of them nor anything they carried, was to be left for inspection. Above all it had to look like an accident that took place shortly after their arrival in Hull and no evidence was to be left suggesting Soviet involvement or anything untoward. British Intelligence would almost certainly be looking for the same people off the same ship.

One of the two men listening to the instructions was Cheslav; Plakinov's personal bodyguard, who was still seething at the humiliation inflicted upon him and his colleagues. His friend, the unfortunate Andrei, was making a very slow recovery from the head injury received at the hands of that madman Mardosov. He was also seething at the way the KGB had been embarrassed and the searing lecture Plakinov had subjected him to. The future of Plakinov was, to say the least, uncertain and that meant that his own future could also be jeopardised.

The Russian Ambassador to London who was addressing Cheslav and his new colleague was unaware of the events that had led up to this assignment. All he knew was that Cheslav and his fellow officer, Nicolai, were to be provided with adequate funds to fulfil their mission and they were to return to Moscow on completion of their task.

Rosario the Goanese Steward who looked after the requirements of Jon Oppick was quite put out for the first twenty four hours after the Amada left Gdansk. He and Jon Oppick got on well and Rosario liked the genial, good humoured Chief who was happy for Rosario to keep his cabin clean and carry out his other duties as and when it suited Rosario. If the Chief was not prepared to get changed and go into the saloon for his meals Rosario would bring food to the cabin and the two men would often chat. It was the sort of working relationship that Rosario cherished.

As the Amada was leaving Gdansk the Chief gave instructions to Rosario that he was not to enter his cabin under any circumstances. 'What about your room Sahib.' asked Rosario.

'Don't you worry about my room or my washing or anything else.' had come the reply.

Rosario hated mysteries and he wondered if the Chief suspected him of stealing or dishonesty. Another mystery was the change in the habits of the Chief. He was having all of his meals in the Saloon and then forever ordering tea and biscuits or coffee and biscuits or sandwiches, platefuls of sandwiches, and dishes of fruit. The Chief was always sitting in his lounge on his own whenever Rosario went in. Rosario had to knock on the cabin door and then put the tray on the coffee table in the middle of the room, pick up the empty tray from his previous visit, and leave. The Chief didn't talk to him much either during his brief visits and the bedroom door was always closed. Normally it would be open.

A ship is an island, a small world where people work very closely together, where each person is part of a team and life can turn sour and very uncomfortable if doubts and uncertainties between individuals develop. After only twenty-four hours at sea Rosario didn't like the atmosphere that had developed.

On the second morning after leaving Gdansk the Chief had his breakfast in the saloon and then he ordered a bowl of fruit for his cabin. Rosario filled a large dish with bananas, apples, grapes and pears and promptly delivered it to the Chief's cabin. 'Rosario thinks you will soon be a very fat man like Rosario Sahib. Rosario thinks that something is very wrong with you.'

Rosario put his small hands on his clean white jacket that covered his ample belly and waited for a response. He looked anxiously into the face of Jon Oppick who knew what was troubling his shipmate.

'Rosario.' said the Chief.

'Acha Sahib' replied Rosario to confirm he was listening to every word.

'Nothing is wrong. I am not angry with you and I know you are a good man. Do you trust me Rosario?' he asked.

'Acha Sahib' replied Rosario with his head going from side to side.

'Fine then.' replied the Chief. 'If I have any news you will be the first to know.'

'Acha Sahib.' responded Rosario who was then directed from the cabin.

An unhappy Rosario heard the cabin door close as he left. He walked down the alleyway talking to himself at speed with his head rocking in rapid little sideways movements. He was very unhappy he told himself as he racked his brains to think how he could possibly have offended this man he had got on with so

281

well.

Whenever there was a knock on the cabin door Li and Gennardy would step out of the cabin lounge and into the bedroom gently closing the door behind them. Then they would sit quietly listening to the noises and exchanges that took place before they would hear the outer cabin door close and John Oppick would open the bedroom door to give the all clear. After Rosario left the cabin on that second morning Jon Oppick gestured to his two guests to sit in his lounge.

Now that they were well into their voyage Oppick told them that he would have to tell the ships Captain about his two passengers.

'What will he do?' asked Gennardy.

'Blow his top.' replied the Chief. 'That means that he will probably be angry with me.' He went on in explanation.

'What will happen to you? Will you be arrested?' queried Gennardy.

'No of course not, he will radio ahead to tell our company headquarters who already know that you are here.'

'How do they know?' asked an uneasy Gennardy.

'Because I sent a radio signal to advise my boss in British Intelligence telling him that you are onboard, they will have cleared the matter with our Ship owners and the Immigration people.' said the Chief who then explained the procedures he had followed.

Chief Engineer Jon Oppick didn't have a very high opinion of the Master of the Amada. He had been on many ships in his time and he was of the opinion that Martin Arkle was probably a good seaman but out of his depth as a sea Captain. The reason for this opinion was Arkle's obsession with minor events that he would attempt to make an issue of in order to confirm his position as Captain. There was an atmosphere of insecurity about Arkle that seemed to be emphasised by his tall gangling body that was hunched at the shoulders making his head stick out above his chest. The crew felt that their boss was a bit of an officious and pompous man and throughout the fleet he was known as Captain Ahab. The title was partly attributable to his habit of shaving his top lip and around his mouth whilst leaving the rest of his beard to grow. Arkle hated the title Captain Ahab.

The two men sat opposite to each other in Arkle's cabin situated behind the bridge of the ship and they commented on the progress of the Amada in a casual way before the Chief addressed the reason for his being there. 'This trip has turned up something which I can now tell you about Martin.' declared the Chief. 'What do you mean asked Arkle quizzically knitting his brow and sticking his balding head and bearded chin out even further.

'I took two people on board this vessel in Gdansk and I have harboured them in my cabin since we left.' Arkle looked at Jon Oppick as though he wasn't there and he was dreaming. 'What on earth are you talking about.' said Arkle unravelling his long body to stand up as he spoke.

Jon Oppick repeated his statement. He then went on to say; 'I know that this is very unusual but I was under instructions to look out for a man and a woman in Gdansk and to use this ship to transport them to the U.K. if I came into contact with them.'

Arkle's mouth opened before he sat down again looking at Oppick to see if this was some prank. 'Is this some sort of joke; do you know the penalty for smuggling illegal entrants into the U.K.'

'This is not smuggling. I am under instructions from

the authorities to bring them back and I have them on board. The owners of the Amada have given permission unofficially to my bosses for me to act in this way. Before we get to Hull you will get a message from head office asking you to co-operate fully with me in seeing that the two people in my cabin are handed over to the right people.'

'What the bloody hell are you up to.' said Arkle; his head shaking with incredulity. 'Bring who back? Who the hell have you got here on my ship? I'm the bloody Captain and I'm having no smart arse using my ship like a bloody.........'

'Before you go any further I would ask you to confirm with head office that you're aware of your two passengers and that you await their instructions.' said a very calm Chief Engineer. 'I am advising you, now that we are in open sea, which is what I was told to do. My instructions were to find them and get them on the ship. Finding them was a pure fluke. I can assure you.'

'What the hell has been going on behind my back.' shouted Arkle.

'Please! Settle down! Nothing! Well I couldn't tell you before. I was under instructions not to' said the Chief spreading out his fingers from the palms of his hands and indicating for Arkle to calm down.

Eventually Arkle and the Chief went into the radio room to send a message. Before any message could be sent Arkle was suddenly struck with the thought that it was a trick to make a fool of him. 'No.' he said to the Chief. 'I want to go down to your cabin and see for myself.'

'No problem' replied Jon Oppick.

Whilst their host was advising Arkle that he had guests, Li and Gennardy were working out their situation. After the elation of escaping from Gdansk and time to wash, bathe, eat good food and rest themselves the two escapees spent much of their time contemplating their future. Gennardy was concerned that British Intelligence may have more people than Goodchild in their ranks working with the Russians. The files that he carried had information about several other KGB agents who were working in the West. The information they had was invaluable to the Western Intelligence Services but could they trust the British to offer them asylum or could they be handed back to Plakinov and company as part of some deal?

Li was more optimistic pointing out that Gennardy had out thought their pursuers from that day in the Moscow Park that had changed her life forever. Her instinct, she told Gennardy, left her with a feeling of confidence.

'Everything will be all right, you will see Genna.' Li had told him.

Li had never seen the sea before and she was bemused when there was no sight of land. During the day she would stand looking out of the forward ports in Jon Oppick's cabin watching the bow break through the waves and watching the spray fly across the flanks of the Amada. She was also enjoying the improved lifestyle and once again she could spend hours in the bathroom luxuriating in the warm water and the perfumed soap she had found there. The wife of Jon Oppick sometimes joined the ship for a short voyage and all her toiletries had been made available to Li who experimented with the shampoos, lotions and face makeup. She applied a selection of perfumes all of which she considered to have wonderful fragrances. The overpowering smell of these perfumes permeated every part of the Chief Engineers accommodation and it was also a source of great concern to Rosario who wondered why his Chief had taken to perfuming his cabin.

For Gennardy the enforced idleness, the perfume and the intimate presence of Li was too much to ignore. Several times he made advances to Li and each time he was repulsed.

'What sort of woman are you?' He asked in frustration. 'Tree trunks have more feelings! Are you not human?'

'Only too human, you animal, but not for you, we are thrown together like this because you wanted to use me' she snarled 'Partners yes, nothing else! Concentrate on our safety. Tell me about your friend, Tony.'

Gennardy narrowed his eyes in exasperation and his lips tightened.

'Alright, alright, one day you will see, you have to take what you can when you can!'

He then began to answer Li's questions about England, Tony Hartill, shops, what people wore and much else.

Li and Gennardy evacuated the lounge for the bedroom on hearing the key being inserted into the cabin door. Captain Arkle entered behind the Chief to exclaim: 'Bloody hell! It smells like a whore's handbag in here.'

The Chief closed the cabin door and explained that Li was using his wife's things. Arkle frowned and wished he had kept his mouth shut. He had a habit of saying the wrong thing and his timing usually left a lot to be desired.

The Chief then opened the bedroom door and ushered Li and Gennardy into the cabin lounge.

'I suggest we all have a seat.' said the Chief indicating the seating around the cabin. All four sat down and then stood up again as the Chief made the introductions. The atmosphere was tense as Arkle surveyed his uninvited guests.

'Do you have any papers?' asked the Captain.

Gennardy confirmed that he had papers in the bedroom. He rose and went to get the papers and handed them over.

Arkle couldn't read a word of Russian. He looked over the papers and said. 'I'll hang on to these then till we get back to England.'

'Will that be necessary?' enquired the Chief.

'I wouldn't have asked for them if I did not feel it was necessary came the curt reply.'

Jon Oppick frowned. Li and Gennardy were ill at ease and it showed.

Arkle looked over the two strangers again and declared.

'From now on you will eat in the saloon with me and my officers. You will be locked in your cabin during the hours of darkness. I don't want you people wandering around my ship as and when you please so if you want to look around; ask.'

With that Arkle left and went up to the radio room to make contact with his head office.

'I think this man believes that we are a threat to him.' said Gennardy in English. He then repeated his view in Russian for Li who told him that she had understood in English.

Jon Oppick said. 'Don't worry about him he will receive his instructions from head office in London and everything will be all right. I just want you to relax and enjoy your cruise on this coal barge and when you get to England the authorities will take care of you.'

Gennardy didn't like the word 'authorities' and said as much to Li. He asked Jon Oppick if he had a map of Great Britain and the three took time to pore over the geography of Hull and the North East of England.

287

The word England stirred great feelings in the breast of Gennardy. He found it difficult to understand how it was that this tiny nation which would fit into Russia a hundred and fifty times over could have had, and continued to have, such a significant influence in the world. What was abundantly clear was the fact that England was very important to Plakinov and what was also very clear was the importance of England to him and Li. Gennardy told Li that he had to pinch himself every so often to be sure that he was real. Li felt much the same. Every now and then they would have a fit of the giggles just as excited children do. Their days were a mixture of anticipation, elation and uncertainty.

As they looked over the map Gennardy showed Li where Ashington was and where Newcastle was. He told her again about the shops and the cafes and the pubs. Li kept telling Gennardy that he exaggerated whilst he insisted that he was telling the truth. 'Is it like the pictures in the magazines I have read?' queried Li.

'Better.' Gennardy would reply.

'It cannot be.' Li would insist.

'Better.' Gennardy would repeat with his hand on his heart. They would then look at each other and giggle like excited children.

When the giggling was over a deadly serious Gennardy would look over the maps again and again as the Amada made its way around Denmark and into the open reaches of the North Sea. For the crew the two unexpected passengers became the subjects of endless speculation.

For Rosario contentment returned and all his unhappiness dissipated as he again went about his business with the air of a man, content with his lot. Rosario told the Chief that he didn't like mysteries because they created suspicion and speculative allegations.

The Chief amused himself listening to Rosario attempting to communicate the questions of his endless curiosity to Li and Gennardy. It was obvious that Li, Gennardy and Rosario were getting along together very well.

The second half of the journey to England was, in the main, a very enjoyable experience, not only for Li and Gennardy, but also for the Deck and the Engineer Officers but also for the Indian crew.

The Stewards and the Cooks who looked after the Officers were Goanese Roman Catholics from the former Portugese colony of Goa whilst the Deck and Engine room crew were Mohammedans who practised the teachings of Islam.

No matter what their station, or religion, every man on the Amada was taken by the great beauty of Li who enjoyed the endless attention.

Captain Ahab frowned with his displeasure whenever he witnessed his off duty Officers in the company of Li helping her to improve her English.

Gennardy spent most of his time talking to the 'Serang', or Engine room Foreman, who spoke good English but with a heavy accent that Gennardy gradually became attuned to.

The Indians laughed heartily as Gennardy winced and blew in and out attempting to cool his mouth after sharing in their curry dishes that were so hot that Gennardy found it difficult to comprehend that these men ate such hotly spiced food daily.

The Indians found Gennardy to be friendly and answered his endless questions about what they did ashore in England, what they bought, what their wages were, how they got ashore, who supervised them and where they went.

Throughout the daylight hours of each day Gennardy mixed freely with the Indians laughing and joking with them and refusing their hotly spiced food every time he was offered it. This refusal brought about inevitable hoots of laughter from the Indians as Gennardy acted out his first and only experience with their curried dishes.

Dusk was upon the Amada as the first sighting of the English mainland was made. During the voyage Li and Gennardy had complied with the orders of Captain Arkle and remained in the Chief's cabin after dark. On this occasion they did the same and watched through the darkness as the Amada entered the Humber estuary and made its way to the coal docks. As the ship was tied up they could see the longest suspension bridge in the world to the west of the City of Kingston upon Hull spanning the river Hull. Lines of light from the vehicles crossing the bridge moved across the span showing off the amazing structure to the onlookers. Li was very excited whilst Gennardy was preoccupied with his thoughts and apprehension.

Li would regularly put her hand on the shoulder of Gennardy and reassure him. 'It will be all right Genna' she would say. He would look at her, remain silent, and nod to her with a small thin smile.

As soon as the ship was tied up the Captain signalled 'Finished with Engines' and preparations were made to unload the cargo and prepare the ship for port conditions. Most of the ship's company was busy as Li and Gennardy came out of the Chief's cabin. They walked along the alleyway without seeing anyone and down two flights of stairs to the deck that accommodated the Goanese stewards. Rosario was waiting for them in an alleyway below and ushered them into a cabin. Li and Gennardy then sat side by side at a shallow desk with a mirror above it and immediately applied brown shoe polish to their faces and hands, behind their ears and on their necks. They then dressed in clothes belonging to Rosario's colleagues. This took about five minutes during which time Rosario was watching the quayside through a porthole looking for the arrival of customs and other port officials. As soon as the gangway was properly secured the party of officials boarded the Amada and made their way up to the bridge. Rosario handed the identity papers of two of his fellow Goanese stewards to Li and Gennardy.

One genuine and two Goanese impostors left the accommodation section and stepped out onto the deck. The ship was illuminated in patches by rings of yellow light from the ship and floodlighting from ashore. All three walked purposefully towards the gangway and descended onto English soil. As they walked away from the ship Rosario was chatting away in Portugese. On seeing the main gate Gennardy's heart sank. There were two men in a glass sided security cabin with a clear view in all directions but what worried Gennardy was the lighting which was almost as bright as daylight. As they walked up to the gate they stopped and Rosario took the papers from Li and Gennardy. 'Remember' Gennardy reminded Rosario, 'if the guard is suspicious or he will not let us through I will threaten him with the gun. If I do, you go back to the ship and we will take care of ourselves.' Rosario nodded and handed the papers into the security guard together with his own.

The guard sitting behind a desk accepted the papers though a hole in the glass and shouted. 'You three are soon off the mark.'

'My friends are ill and the Captain has made arrangements for them to go to Hull General Hospital for examination. Can you get a taxi for us please?' The head of Rosario was going from side to side as he spoke and Li and Gennardy joined with a little head shaking.

The bored guard hardly looked at them. He handed the papers back saying. 'You'll get a taxi just around the corner.'

What appeared to be three coloured ship's crewmen walked around the corner from the port gates and entered a Hackney cab, 'Take us to City centre please. Thank you.' said Rosario as the driver started the engine.

As the cab drew away two KGB men sat in a large black Mercedes saloon car on the opposite side of the road observing everything and everybody who came out of the port gate. They saw the three Indian crewmen pass through the gate and enter the cab without realising that their quarry had simply walked past them.

The three sat in silence as the cab took the ten minutes necessary to reach the middle of Hull. 'Where do you want to be off.' shouted the taxi driver. Gennardy had little idea of where he wanted to go so he opted for the railway station as a safe bet 'beside the railway station.' Gennardy replied.

The three alighted from the cab and Gennardy gave a ten pound note to Rosario who in turn handed it to the driver. The driver fiddled, taking his time looking for the change, hoping for a tip. Rosario waited patiently and took the change. The driver drove off muttering about ungrateful Asians never tipping anyone but always looking for a bargain or a bonus themselves. Gennardy, Rosario and Li all stepped into a shadowy doorway where Gennardy handed Rosario one hundred pounds that he had stolen from the cabin of Jon Oppick.

'Thank you my friend,' said Gennardy, 'and thank you're friends for the loan of their papers.' Rosario's head went from side to side as he said 'I will put their papers back and maybe they will never know that we borrowed them. Many of us have relatives living in England and sometimes we have to get another relation in if they cannot get through immigration. Sometimes it works and sometimes...' Rosario shrugged his shoulders and made his way back to the ship.

Li and Gennardy stood in the doorway looking at each other. 'I cannot believe it.' Gennardy stated as he slowly shook his head to express his disbelief.

'I know! I Know!' Li responded. 'What do we do now.' she said with her fists clenched in excitement.

'Now I must telephone my friend Tony Harthill.' said Gennardy. 'I have his telephone number in my head forever. Number 01670 858858. But first we must get this shoe polish from our faces.'

The pair made their way into the Gents toilets in the railway station. Li followed Gennardy who walked up to the wash basins filling the basin before him by pressing on the taps. Li watched him and at the same time through the mirror above the basin she watched the backs of the men as they came in and urinated against a stainless steel panel.

On completion of their relief most men walked across to the wash basins to rinse their hands looking askance as Gennardy removed his jacket, rolled up his sleeves, and began to wash his face and hands. When he had finished he stood before the hot air dryer and dried off before telling Li to do the same. Li removed her hat and coat that she handed to Gennardy. He was watching the clientele around him stopping abruptly in shock as they saw a coloured person with well formed breasts, long black hair and a trim waist undoing the buttons of a mans shirt exposing smooth white skin

293

between cleavage and neck. Li was aware of the glances and sidelong looks as she went about washing off the boot polish as quickly as she could.

A passing voice with a thick accent remarked; 'Aye they dont make fella's like that where I come from.' To which an anonymous respondent replied. 'You're bloody right pal.'

As soon as most of the polish was removed Gennardy held her coat urging Li to get into it quickly. She dried her face on her sleeves as Gennardy hustled her out of the toilet to look for a telephone.

In Russia telephone calls were free of charge. Gennardy and Li were inside a telephone kiosk reading the instructions when Gennardy realised that he needed some coins. The only place open was a News stand. Gennardy walked over towards it and asked the young woman for some 'telephone money'. The woman looked quizzically at what she took to be a young tramp before asking. 'What do you want then'?

'Telephone money.' repeated Gennardy.

'I know that.' said the woman. 'What sort of telephone money?'

'I must telephone my friend and I do not know what money's I must use.' pleaded Gennardy.

'Oh. Your not from here then.' said the woman taking a renewed interest in her customer.

'No! I have come to see my friend and I must telephone him. Tell me what to do please.'

The woman examined Gennardy's face for a moment and then switched her eyes to the twenty pound note he had in his hand.

Gennardy was looking at the display of chocolate bars. He looked up to the woman and said. 'Ah! Yes. I will take two of these to eat. You will give me these and some telephone money and I will give you this money. I think this is a good idea. Yes?' he questioned.

The woman looked at him; followed his instructions and complied with the words.

'There then! Here's your change and plenty of ten pence's for you telephone O.K?'

A smiling Gennardy took the chocolate and the change and walked back to Li. How he loved England he thought.

Gennardy and Li stood inside the telephone kiosk munching their chocolate and commenting on how delicious it was before Gennardy telephoned the home of Tony Hartill.

Tony Hartill's wife, Maggie, was watching television on her own in the lounge of her terraced home in Ashington. The air in the room was hazy from her chain smoking habit. The noise of the telephone jarred her from her thoughts. She rose lethargically from her chair and walked across to the small telephone table and lifted the receiver.

'Hello.' said Maggie.

'Hello, Hello!' said an excited voice with an unusual accent. 'May I speak with Tony please'?

'Tony does not live here.' said Maggie mournfully.

'But he must.' said Gennardy. 'I have this telephone number. He lives there.'

'Tony has left. Who is that?' said Maggie.

'It is Gennardy! Tony's friend from the Soviet Union, you must remember me.'

'Oh! Gennardy from Russia; Tony lives with his mother.' Maggie volunteered.

'Then I must telephone him. You will give me the number please.' said Gennardy.

'Eight one four one three one' Maggie responded.

Gennardy repeated the number several times looking at Li as he did so. They both repeated the numbers several times as Maggie listened.

Having secured the number in his head Gennardy said 'How are you Mrs Hartill, Margaret.'

'I think you should speak to Tony.' was the reply. 'Goodnight.'

Maggie bit her lip, put the telephone receiver down and returned to her seat facing the television, lighting a cigarette as she did so, lost in her own thoughts.

The short telephone call with Maggie had not provided the response that Gennardy had imagined and anticipated. Li could see that he was put out.

'Ah.well, I will telephone this number now.' said Gennardy reassuringly to Li.

Chapter 18

Tony Hartill was feeling depressed at the way things had gone over the last few months. He and so many of his colleagues were fed up with being kept from work. They were all deeply concerned at the financial implications as savings disappeared to pay for mortgages and hire purchase commitments. Many miners were Council tenants and they knew that the Council would not insist on payment of rent. This caused further strains between those miners who were buying their homes and those in accommodation rented from the Local Authority which was broadly in support of Markham. Few had any money coming in and there was no end in sight. The feeling of helplessness was the worst part of it.

Reflecting on his personal life Tony had mixed feelings about leaving Maggie. On the one hand he found the life at home with Maggie unbearable and at the same time he felt that he had betrayed her and his family. On the other hand he knew that coal mining as he had known it was dead and he didn't want to be tied to a life in a dying community with all of the prejudice and bitterness that would flow from Maggie's family and others. The wounds would be very slow to heal, if they ever did.

Since leaving Maggie he had talked through his problems with his two younger sons when they came home. They had both listened and had not taken sides. It had been such a bonus for him to share his situation and find them sympathetic. They had shared the same discussions with their mother and had not argued on either side. They had simply confirmed their love and commitment to their parents and their brother Kevin. Nothing, however that his brothers would say could reconcile Kevin with his father.

Against this background Tony concentrated his energies on alleviating the increasing hardship among the miners and at the same time doing what he could to get the miners into the pits and get some meaningful negotiations started.

The miners would certainly feel the pinch over the summer months. For many, those with allotment gardens or large gardens at their homes, the late summer and autumn would not be so bad. They could grow most of the potatoes and vegetables that they needed. The real crunch would come in the winter if the dispute went on that long. Without money for fuel or food to compound the escalating debts that so many miners had, life would be a test for the most resilient. Tempers would really begin to break and events were sure to get uglier than they were already.

A freak event was to embroil Tony in another situation he could not have anticipated. His friend, Bill Robinson, had called at the home of his parents asking to speak with him. Mrs Hartill had welcomed Bill and made him a cup of tea whilst they waited for Tony. Bill sat and chatted happily with Tony's Mother who took a keen interest in his family. She always asked about their school and their interests whilst at the same time recalling events from her own experiences as a Mother and a Grandmother.

They chatted for a while before Tony came into the room with a hearty, 'You two having another heart to heart again. I hope you're not talking about me. You mustn't be otherwise my ears would be burning.' They all smiled at one another in the cosy confidence that comes from long friendships.

Mrs Hartill left the room and immediately Bill said.

'Tony! One of my Technicians answered a call to

repair a photocopier at the headquarters of the CMU in Newcastle. He couldn't repair the thing on their premises so he was told to take it to the workshop, do the repair, and return the machine in the morning. They didn't want him on the premises. There was a document in the machine that I think you should see.'

As Bill slipped the locks on his briefcase he lifted the lid and handed the document over saying. 'It was the Technician who brought it to my attention.'

'I need specs to see fine print these days.' said Tony squinting at the document and getting to his feet to find his reading glasses.

'You'll need specs alright when you read this. It's from Markham to Mullaney and a few others in Markham's magic circle.'

Tony sat down wearing his glasses and addressed the first page which read:

Our battle for a true Socialist state is well under way. Again we need the perfect sacrifice of our dedicated Brothers and Sisters to smash a system which is dedicated to destroy the CMU and then the Trade Union movement. It is only a matter of time before our Brothers and Sisters in Road Tranport, the Railways, the Power Stations and even the Armed Forces join us in this great revolution to bring a true Socialism that will link us with our Socialist Brothers and Sisters throughout the world. We will be the example that Socialism needs to bring world Socialism to every Brother and Sister....... And so it went on.

Tony raised his head saying to Bill. 'You know! I can just picture Markham spouting this bilge to those miners who turn up at his rallies. The trouble is that many of them are taken in by all this garbage. Tragic isn't it.'

'It gets worse.' said Bill.

Tony looked at the document again and read on:

The next major incident planned for in our strategy is to be put into operation in the Northumberland area. Our plan is to be implemented with immediate effect. Blyth Power station is to be decommissioned by whatever means necessary using your most loyal comrades. Success will serve as a model and as an inspiration to our comrades in other areas. At all times you must ensure maximum press coverage insisting that the actions of our comrades have been provoked by Police Brutality........ The document then went on to give a detailed explanation on how and when the press and electronic media were to be used to serve the cause.

Tony looked up again at Bill who had not taken his eyes from the document since Tony had resumed reading.

Bill's thoughts were imagining the confrontation s between Police and Miners. He could easily picture Mullaney before the cameras manufacturing the stories. Stories designed to incite the relatively small band that hung on to his and Markham's every word and at the same time cast doubt and uncertainty in the minds of the uncommitted.

Like Markham, Mullaney was adroit at fomenting hatred in the breasts of the vulnerable by playing on their well -entrenched prejudices.

The two men looked at each other for long seconds before Bill said, quietly, in a low voice.

'What do you think then? What do we do?'

'Wish I knew' replied Tony. 'What amazes me is how so many things have found their way to us. It's uncanny.'

Tony leaned back in the upholstered lounge chair and sighed. 'To tell you the truth I am just sick of the whole bloody mess. I seem to be sticking my neck out all the time and I sometimes wonder if it's for good reason. Why can't those silly sods realise that they are just being used as fodder by Markham and Mullaney and the rest. They're not going to save the pits by following Markham. He'll just make things worse and they'll foot the bill. They pay that bill with their own bloody hardship. It makes you weep.'

Tony finished his involuntary statement with a look of anguish on his face, anguish born out of frustration and exasperation at the futility of the unnecessary hardship that was going to get even worse.

There was a pause and Bill said quietly; 'Yeah! The trouble is though that those stupid sods, as you call them, will always believe Markham and company. Not because they are right or wrong or any other reason except that it is what they want to believe. You cannot blame them when you think about what will be left when the pits shut. They cannot imagine any other life.'

'They're not silly sods Tony, and you know it. They're just frightened. And because they are frightened they are vulnerable and gullible.'

Tony listened to Bill's words before saying. 'I know you are right Bill. But what do we do? We haven't much time either this is all scheduled for tomorrow.'

'That's why I came here straight away.' said Bill. 'We have to do something now.'

The two men looked at each other in silence as they contemplated their thoughts each man thinking through their next action.

Eventually Tony said, 'Has the copier gone back?'

'No.' replied Bill. 'It will be returned at 9.00am in the morning as promised. The Technician just had to take a roller out and drop another one in. The daft thing is that they didn't want him in the office for security reasons. The original document is under the cover where it was found. What you are looking at is a photocopy.'

They both smiled a little smile of irony as Tony said. 'Couldn't be handier could it. To take a copy I mean.'

Then they both smiled broadly at one another.

'I'll tell you what Bill. I am going round to see Jackie Richards. Remember him?'

'Of course I do.' Bill replied. 'He's a sergeant now. Been in the Police for years and he was always a straight sort of bloke. I'll come with you.'

'Better not.' said Tony. 'You never know who's playing tiggy with who? It might just look a bit heavy if we turn up together. I'll let you know what is happening.'

Tony's Mother entered the room as the two men stood up before Bill left.

'You going now Bill, I was just going to make you a cup of tea. Is everything alright?'

Mrs Hartill looked on with a smile as Tony patted Bill on the shoulder. When they reached the front door Tony said. 'Good of you to go to all of this trouble Bill.'

'Suppose we've all got to do the best we can.' Retorted Bill as he smiled and acknowledged Tony's Mother with a wave of the hand.

'What are you two up to now?' said Mrs Hartill with a quizzical look.

Jackie Richards was just getting out of his car as Tony arrived at his home.

'Hello Tony!' he hailed.

'How are yi' gettin' on?' replied Tony.

The two men were well acquainted over many years and had often enjoyed a pint of beer together in the club.

'Oh all right. I just wish all this bloody nonsense was finished and done with. I'm gettin` it in the neck

302

from my younger brother and from the wife's brother about being in the force. A'm sick of the buggers.'

Tony knew the two men referred to and sympathised with Jack's distress. The mining communities had been so harmonious. Life had felt secure and dissension was usually marginal but this situation had tainted all aspects of life. The involuntary explanation that Jackie had just delivered was typical of how everyone in the area was affected and how they wanted to vent their anguish whenever it seemed safe to do so.

'Anyway, what can I do for you?' asked Jackie.

'It's about the strike Jack! I have some information and I want your advice.'

'Hell not more bloody trouble! I would ask you in but the wife'll go off it if she hears us going on about the strike in the house. We've never had so many bloody row's I'm sometimes not sure what's right and what's not.' said the Policeman in a deprecating way.

Tony was certain that Jackie was never more certain about what he thought was right and what wasn't as he said to him. 'There's a big confrontation planned and I think the Police should know about it.'

'What! Here you mean in Winsbreck?'

'Aye in Winsbreck' Tony replied.

'The lads here'll never get involved in anything over the top. A few hot heads maybe, but not that many.' said Jackie as he considered the proposition.

'The big problem will not be from our lads Jackie. The plan is to bus in hundreds from Scotland Durham and Yorkshire.' Tony answered in measured tones.

'You've got to be fucking joking.' replied the policeman in disbelief. 'Anyway how do you know all this? After all you're not exactly big mates with Mullaney and his crowd. He went on.

Tony proffered the photocopy he had received from Bill towards the Policeman who said. 'I believe you

Tony! I don't need to see it and to tell you the truth I don't want to see it. My boss will be home now. I've just left him. Tell him you have spoken to me O.K.'

'O.K.' Tony replied.

Jackie announced the telephone number of Superintendent Brian Welsh from memory. As Tony wrote down the numbers Jackie Richards wife was looking out of the window to see why Jackie had not gone in the house. The two men saw her looking and Jackie muttered 'She'll want to know what you want, your not the most popular man on the block at the moment with Mullaney's boys.'

'Tell me about it.' said Tony as he walked off half turning as he departed with 'By the way. Thanks.'

Superintendent Welsh accepted the telephone call from Tony and the two men met half an hour later in a car park. Tony emphasised that he didn't like what he was doing but he wanted to help in avoiding bloodshed. The thought was at the back of his mind that his own son would almost certainly be involved.

As the Superintendent read the photocopied document he murmured, 'The hypocrisy of these guys! We had a meeting with Mullaney just yesterday and he was telling us how hard he was working to keep the men in check. We wanted an assurance that some of the scenes we'd witnessed on television would not be repeated here.'

'It's just too easy for him.' said Tony. 'I just don't know what it will take to get the lads to realise that they are being led down the garden path.'

'Just leave this with me if you don't mind. We'll do everything we can to keep the peace. The trouble is that we are often asking a lot of our boys in blue to keep their heads. Sometimes the intimidation is terrible, especially for the one's imported from other forces. As soon as the Pickets here a different accent they go all out to get our lads to boil over.'

Before parting the Superintendent and Tony shook hands: 'Thanks for the information. Believe me we are very grateful. We had heard some rumours; that's why we had the meeting with Mullaney. I'll speak to the Chief Constable right away and hopefully we can keep the whole thing low key.'

The following morning all was normal outside the Blyth coal fired power station. There was only the usual number of Pickets asking drivers not to pass through the gates. As 11am approached six buses loaded with Miners from Scotland, Yorkshire and Durham came together in a line on the trunk road adjacent to the power station. When they got to the point on the road nearest to the power station the buses stopped on the hard shoulder of the road and the miners poured out, climbed up an embankment and ran the three-quarters of a mile, over the fields towards the gates of the power station.

As soon as the Miners had disembarked the buses were driven off the hard shoulder back onto the trunk road and made off. Five minutes later a convoy of forty lorrys came along the trunk road with their cargoes of coal covered with tarpaulins. The lorrys had wire mesh mounted on a steel frame to protect the windscreen and glass windows at the sides of the driver's cabins. The convoy was led by a Police patrol car. Two Police outriders on motorbikes brought up the rear.

The Police had erected vehicle check points on all the roads leading from the trunk road to the power station and they were caught completely unawares by the tactics of the imported pickets who had timed their arrival over the fields to perfection.

The Police decided to allow the lorrys to complete

their journey to the power station otherwise the trunk road would be blocked.

Almost two hundred Police reinforcements were standing by in a car park almost three miles away awaiting a call and hoping their presence would not be required.

When the Police car leading the lorrys arrived at the power station gates over seventy pickets, linking arms and standing in three lines were blocking the closed gates. The Police car had to stop as the driver's assistant repeatedly shouted into his radio pleading for immediate assistance and all the reinforcements available.

The drivers of the convoy of lorrys had no choice but to stop and mayhem followed. Other pickets carrying pickaxe handles lined the road up to the gates and charged the stationary lorrys. They lashed the wire mesh on the cabins whilst others got on top of the vehicles and cut the tarpaulins away exposing the coal. They climbed on top of it and pushed it over the sides with their feet. A few miners had crow bars and wire cutters that they used to free the panel at the rear of the wagon allowing the coal to spill onto the road.

Acting under instructions the Police reinforcements arrived via a different route and the front line of Police in riot equipment held their shields side by side and made their way forward. Behind them came the majority of the Police in normal uniform with truncheons.

The Police Superintendent in charge bellowed at the miners over a mobile loudspeaker telling them to withdraw. Few could hear very much above the din of shouting and the banging of pickaxe handles on the wire cages protecting the cabins of the lorry drivers.

The drivers were terrified and doing all they could to ensure that their cabin doors were secured. Despite the mesh few drivers had a windscreen left intact after five minutes into the melee.

Unable to get a reaction to his overtures the Superintendent ordered his men forward and the battle began between Police and Miners.

Mullaney's aides had tipped off the local television networks. Their film crews were standing by a couple of miles away not sure where their story would be filmed. As soon as the Police reinforcements arrived they were told the precise location and within minutes they were filming the battleground. The road was covered in coal and hundreds of Policemen and Miners were laying into one another with sticks and batons. After ten minutes the Police had the upper hand and the Miners took to their heels and made off over the fields towards the trunk road with the Police in pursuit.

Scores of Police and Miners were injured though none sustained serious injuries. Several of the lorry drivers had been pulled from their vehicles and dealt some nasty blows. All of this was recorded in the television camera tapes for the news that day and for several days to follow.

Tony Hartill was collecting food and distributing parcels when the power station battle took place. He arrived back at the home of his parents later than anticipated.

'You've been away ages and your dinner will be ruined.' said Mrs Hartill. 'I'll have to heat it up. I hope it will be all right. You should tell me if you are going to be late. Your Father and I had ours ages ago.'

'Don't fuss.' said Tony's Father. 'He'll just have to take it as it comes.'

'He should tell me if he is going to be late.' came a slightly wounded reply.

'You're quite right Mam. Sorry.' apologised Tony.

'I don't suppose you've seen the news then.' Said Tony's Father as his son appeased his Mother.

'No! I haven't' said Tony. 'What's fresh?'

'Fresh! They've had a real ding-dong at Blyth Power station today lad. Dozens injured on both sides and loads of Miners arrested.' advised his Father.

'But I thought the Police would have…' Tony corrected himself. He hadn't told anyone about the photocopy apart from the Police. 'I'll see it on the next news on BBC.'

Tony had his meal and sat before the television set to watch the media version of what had taken place.

He was astonished at the scale of the operation and how it came across on the media. It was undoubtedly a marginal propaganda victory for Mullaney who had the final word demanding an enquiry into Police brutality. He made no comment about the sixty-three Miners arrested for a variety of offences who would have to accept the consequences of the events for the rest of their lives.

'The whole business just makes you sick.' said his Father. 'The sooner this is all over the better.'

Tony agreed. He was also shocked that the information he had given had not prevented so much grief and injury.

For the rest of the night he sat watching television to pick up any new news about the strike. Everyone was waiting for a breakthrough and Miners and public alike switched from channel to channel in the hope of hearing fresh developments.

It was after Nine O Clock when the telephone rang. 'I'll get it.' said Tony.

Having lifted the telephone receiver Tony tensed on hearing the voice of his wife Maggie.

'Hello Maggie.' he replied. They had been parted

from each other for several weeks and Tony felt a tinge of guilt and remorse as he listened to her voice.

'I'm just phoning to tell you that that Russian fella called Gennardy phoned wanting to speak to you.' She said waiting for a response.

'Gennardy, from the Polish Miners visit you mean, what does he want?' mused Tony.

'Don't know.' replied Maggie. 'I gave him your Mother's number.'

'Well I haven't heard from him. He said he would try to keep in touch.' Tony continued. 'Did he give you his number in Russia?'

'Number, I didn't ask him for a number.' said Maggie in a distant voice.

Suddenly Tony decided that Maggie's call was a ruse to have a talk with him and that Gennardy's call was probably an invention.

'How is everybody Maggie?' he enquired.

'Fat lot you care. We may as well be on the bloody moon…..for all you care.' Replied Maggie angrily.

'Look Maggie I just want to know that the young un's are O.K. Is everything all right?'

'We're the same as everybody else, struggling. While you're enjoying your home comforts I bet.' snarled Maggie.

'Maggie! Surely you didn't phone to go on like this. I didn't ask for all this trouble and bad feeling no more than you did. I'm just as sick of it as you are.' As he spoke the words came out quickly and his voice was rising in anger.

'I should never have phoned.' shouted Maggie. 'Go and talk to your Russian pal or that tart from London that you've been busy with' she shouted before she clashed the phone down.

The telephone was in the sitting room and his parents had heard his words to Maggie. Tony's Mother looked at him anxiously whilst his Father looked away.

'What's wrong now Tony? Maggies bound to be upset living on her own. You must see that. Couldn't you have been a bit more helpful' said Mrs Hartill who couldn't bear altercation of any kind.

'It's all right Mother' said Tony. Putting his hand on her shoulder and patting her gently. 'It's all right.' As he did so the light caught the strands of his Mother's hair that had turned silver in colour. She looked younger than her years. His Mother had never smoked and Tony concluded that the ever-increasing dependence on the cigarette tobacco addiction of Maggie and her sisters had aged them prematurely.

Twenty minutes later the telephone rang again. Tony walked across the room and picked up the receiver sighing. 'What now?'

'Hello!' Tony declared.

'Hello Tony! Tony Harteel' Gennardy shouted Tony's name as his voice raised by an octave in anticipation.

'Yes! Who is that?' replied Tony.

'Eet eez your good friend Gennardy Mardosov, Oh Tony I am so pleased to hear from your voice. I have been thinking many times that I would not see you again. I can now really believe that I am een Eengland.'

'England? How are you in England?' asked a bemused Tony.

'Tony. I have much to tell you and so many problems and now, at last, my friend I am in Hool.'

'Hool, where's Hool.' enquired Tony.

'No! No! Not Hool. How you say it by spelling is aich yoo el el.' Gennardy replied.

'You mean Hull in England, the seaport?' Tony asked.

'Yes! Yes! I am here now and Tony I need your

310

help very much. I have information which you must have because I think that some English people are doing very bad things for your country and I do not know who is good and who is very bad.'

'Go to the Police Gennardy and they will look after you and then perhaps…..'

'You do not understand Tony. You must come here and help us….' Gennardy interrupted.

'What do you mean us?' questioned Tony. 'How many is there?'

'There are only two of us who have escaped from Russia, from KGB, from everybody. We need your help to stay here Tony.'

At this point the line went dead as the time paid for in the kiosk expired. Tony looked at the telephone receiver in his hand in wonderment before replacing it.

'Who was that Tony? That was a funny conversation.' said his Mother.

'You're right there.' He replied repeating himself. 'You're right there.'

Just then the telephone rang again. Tony picked up the receiver with a tentative: 'Hello!'

'Ah Tony, the machine it wanted some more money. Can you come to bring us Tony? We are not sure where we are and we need somewhere to stay. You must help us my friend.'

In Gennardy's voice Tony could feel more than a hint of desperation.

'Gennardy.' came his reply. 'There is a number on the telephone box you are speaking from. Please give me the number and I will telephone you. Then I will begin to know where you are O.K.'

'O.K.' replied Gennardy who related the numbers

'Fine' said Tony, now replace the receiver, the telephone.'

'You promise to telephone again Tony?'

311

'I promise.' came the reply.

Gennardy looked at Li as he slowly replaced the receiver. The two continued to look at each other in silence as their thoughts and doubts raced through their minds. This tenuous link with Tony Hartill was all they had.

Gennardy and Li were both startled when the telephone rang. Gennardy grabbed the receiver and shouted into it. 'Hello Tony my friend?'

A relieved Gennardy heard Tony say. 'Yes Gennardy! Now listen carefully. I need time to think. I will telephone you in two hours. Leave the telephone box and return in two hours. If you have problems telephone me again at this number.

'I think we cannot telephone you from here Tony. I must phone you, in two hours time. We must leave here now.'

'I will be at one of these numbers.' Tony said as he gave Gennardy his number again and the telephone number of Bill Robinson.

Gennardy and Li made their way from the railway station and began walking around Hull avoiding the main thoroughfare but constantly coming back to it so that they did not get lost.

Eventually they went into a busy pub and ordered two beers. They sat talking anxiously about their prospects and their hopes until the barmaid announced that it was time for last orders. Apart from some strange looks because of their attire the experience in the pub was incident free. Feeling more confident Gennardy asked a man sitting nearby what last orders meant and on explanation they left and continued their walk until they found another telephone kiosk near the station but off the main thoroughfare.

Once again Gennardy telephoned Tony who

confirmed that he was making some arrangements and he would let him know how he proposed to pick them up from Hull.

After speaking with Gennardy Tony had immediately telephoned Bill Robinson.

'Hello Bill.' Tony greeted as Bill answered. 'I know it's late but you'll never believe this.'

Tony related Gennardy's story for a few minutes before Bill said. 'Look, why don't you pop along and have a chat.'

Tony left immediately and cycled the two miles to Bill's house in the nearby coastal village of Newbiggin by the Sea.

Bill Robinson lived in comfort. His home was a large stone built detached house standing in three acres of woodland. Inside the house was furnished in a comfortable way without appearing to be lavish or ostentatious.

Tony was greeted at the door by Bill and his wife Kate who ushered him into the lounge where they chatted politely about the call from Gennardy before Kate said: 'Why don't you two pop into the snooker room and I will get you both a drink. What do you fancy?'

'A beer would be lovely' said Tony, smiling.

'Same for you Bill?' queried Kate.

'Aye that'll be fine thanks.' Bill replied. 'You're a good'un.'

'And you are spoiled, Bill Robinson' said Kate with an impish grin.

Tony had always got on with Bill and Kate but Maggie had always found an excuse for turning down invitations to their home. This had been a great source of irritation for Tony over the years. He would dearly have enjoyed their company.

Bill Robinson was aware of the situation as was Kate but they never mentioned it and were never affronted when Tony declined their invitations.

The two men sat in the conservatory at one end of the snooker room that had views around the woodland. Bill had planted thousands of daffodil, narcissus and tulip bulbs in the grounds. He and Kate took great pride and pleasure from the results, particularly in the springtime.

Now that summer was imminent the trees were covered in leaves and Tony commented on the views over the woodland that was illuminated by electric light.

'You want to see it in the daytime.' said Bill. 'Far from the madding crowd I call this spot. Kate and I have enjoyed living here.'

'Pity you have to take so much stick just because you put yourself out and earned a few bob.' Said Tony alluding to the many times he'd heard disparaging comments on Bill's good fortune.

Looking across at Tony he said. 'Anyway what's all this about Gennardy; Sounds like one of those spy books. You know' The spy that came in from the cold or something.'

'Exactly.' retorted Tony 'except of course, it's true! I checked the dialling code for Hull and sure enough it matched the phone number he gave me. So he is there.'

To their surprise they realised that they had been talking for over an hour. Bill looked at his watch and said. 'It'll not be long before he phones again we had better decide what to do.'

'I don't want to find myself in trouble with the law.' said Tony. 'He's very anxious to get out of Hull and of course he'll not know where else to go. Then, of course if we bring him back here he'll have to stay somewhere.'

Kate came into the room again saying. 'I'll have to go to bed. Are you two going to sit here all night?'

'Look Kate.' said Bill. 'It's about Gennardy ……..' he went on to tell her the story and what their plan was.

'I am going to look like a real party pooper if I disagree.' said Kate.

After all the obvious questions had been asked and alternatives explored Kate agreed to accommodate Li and Gennardy whilst they got things sorted out.

The telephone call from Gennardy came exactly on time and Tony left with Bill in his Jaguar bound for Hull railway station.

Left with at least a further two hours to spend in Hull, Gennardy knew that he would have to find a refuge until Tony arrived. He was sure that there would be hundreds of people searching for them and therefore it was imperative that they were not wandering the streets.

He left Li in a doorway not far from the railway station and went to the taxi rank and took a cab. The cab driver was instructed to collect Li as Gennardy guided him to where he'd left her. As soon as she was safely in the cab Gennardy asked the taxi driver to take them for some inexpensive food.

The driver's response came in such a strong dialect that Gennardy could barely understand the man. It took some time before the Queen's English attuned the ears of both men in mutual understanding.

An examination of the clothes and accent of Gennardy persuaded the Taxi driver to suggest a roadside café on the outskirts of Hull approaching the M62 Motorway. Having seen sight of a twenty pound note the man agreed to take them there and the deal was struck that the taxi driver would stay with them until it was time to drive back to the railway station. On seeing evidence of further twenty-pound notes the driver was happy to oblige.

'The food is good at this place pal' said the taxi driver as they journeyed to the café. 'You'll not get better value anywhere. Open twenty four hours a day it is, famous with all the truckers running in and out of Hull; loads of them about at the moment leading coal from abroad to the power stations.'

Speaking in Russian Gennardy explained to Li what was happening and why it was necessary to keep the Taxi driver with them until it was time to go to the station.

As they sat side by side in the cab Li smiled at the resourcefulness of Gennardy and the usefulness of the money that Gennardy had *borrowed* from Jon Oppick.

'I hope that one day we can send Mr Oppick his money back.' She said in Russian. Gennardy smiled back.

As soon as the Amada was "Finished with Engines" Captain Arkle had gone to his cabin as normal to go through the formalities with customs, immigration officials and other authorities with paperwork to complete. On this occasion he had been instructed by his Head Office to deal with the two officers from British Intelligence accompanied by a Police Inspector. The Police Inspector had papers authorising him to take Li Saric and Gennardy Mardosov into custody and hand them over to the two men accompanying him.

Arkle sent the First Mate to fetch the two 'escapees' as he called them. At that time he did not realise how accurate his word of description was.

Ten minutes later the Mate returned to announce that he was unable to find them. All four men stood looking at the First Mate until the message was absorbed.

'What do you mean? You can't find them. Where's Oppick.' shouted Arkle.

'He's going round the ship looking for them.' replied a subdued First Mate.

'Well they can't get off the ship…..' the words trailed from Arkle's lips.

The two officers from British intelligence looked at each other momentarily and then at the Police Inspector.

Mark Benson shouted. 'The gate, I'll get the gate.'

To the Inspector he said. 'Can you order a search of the yard? Right now!' and to Tim Graham he said. 'He may still be on the ship or over the side. You see what you can find on the ship with Captain Arkle. I'll be back as soon as I've checked the gate.'

All five hurried off to fulfil their allotted task.

The two KGB men sat in their Mercedes car outside the main gates of the port of Hull observing the inactivity which suddenly ended when a breathless Mark Benson arrive at the gate office and entered. They could see an animated conversation between him and the two security men before Benson left in a hurry and disappeared out of sight into the port.

On the ship Oppick had overseen a thorough search of the whole vessel. The only thing he could confirm was the fact that there was no sign of the passengers and Rosario was missing.

Arkle ordered the whole of the ship's crew to assemble in the crew mess room immediately.

A check of personnel confirmed that Rosario was missing.

Mark Benson explained to the crew that the two passengers who had joined the ship in Gdansk had slipped ashore with Rosario dressed like Indians. He then asked if anyone had knowledge of the unexpected departure and if they had seen the three leave the ship. There was no response.

He then explained that three Indian crewmen had left the Amada and passed through the gates but there was only one crewman missing. Again there was no response from his audience.

Arkle instructed that no one else was to leave the ship until further notice.

Back in Arkle's cabin The Police Inspector together with Jan Oppick, the First mate and the two agents from British Intelligence made some phone calls and concluded that whilst their quarry had ingeniously eluded them they would soon pick them up.

'After all' said the Police Inspector. 'They'll stick out like sore thumbs in those clothes and besides what will they do for money? They have to eat somewhere and sleep somewhere.'

The mention of money sent an uneasy feeling through the body of Jan Oppick' sending him off to his cabin to find that £380.00 in twenty pound notes had disappeared from his writing desk.

'This guy's full of little surprises. Isn't he?' said Tim Graham. 'I'm beginning to understand how he made it out of Russia.'

'You're right there! Let's get out of here. We'll not find them in the Port of Hull. That's certain.'

A few minutes later the two KGB men sitting in their car outside the port gate watched as the Police Inspectors car swept out of the gate closely followed by a Ford Granada driven by Mark Benson with Tim Graham in the passenger seat.

Nicolai went to the gate house and asked the man

where the two cars were headed. 'What's that got to do with you' asked the man.

Taking a chance Nicolai said. 'We've been waiting here for them and they drove straight past us before we knew what was happening.'

'So what do you do?' asked the gateman.

'Immigration' said Nicolai.

Suddenly the aggrieved gate men were more than forthcoming. 'Well you want to be more bloody careful Pal. Those buggers can hardly blame us. We checked the papers of those Indians and they were all in order. How are we to know that they aren't who they said they were? None of them looked like a woman to me. Anyway they all look the same in the main. The Indians I mean.'

The man paused before saying 'Anyway how did they get off the ship in the first place? That's the question they should ask.' His colleague nodded in agreement.

Nicolai nodded his agreement to the two men and made his way back to the car.

'You'll not believe this Cheslav but it looks as though those three Indians we saw included Comrades Mardosov and Saric. Let's get down into the town and find them before the Police do.'

In the roadside café Gennardy treated Li and the Taxi driver to a full English breakfast. They were all hungry so no one said much as the three tucked into their meal but as soon as the Taxi driver put down his cutlery he began to ask questions.

In the bright light of the café Gennardy and Li looked dirty and dishevelled with patches of brown around their eyes and ears.

Li couldn't understand much of what the man said because of his strong accent. She listened as Gennardy avoided his questions by telling the man that he had a friend who was coming in his car to meet them. I am looking forward to staying with him. He has a friend who lives in a big house and sometimes we play snooker. My friend and I are working in England for him.

'But you're not English.' The man insisted.

'How do you know this?' said Gennardy.

'Because ya don't talk English' insisted the taxi driver.

'Maybe you have adopted me.' teased Gennardy.

'Your friend must be coming a heck of a long way' said the man trying a different tack.

'He is coming from Newcastle upon Tyne.' replied Gennardy.

After a while Gennardy amused the man by asking him questions, many of which were sources of amusement to the taxi driver. Questions such as; 'How many wives do you have?'

At 1.20am they left the café and when they were near the railway station Gennardy said. 'Please! You will stop here until my friends come for me?'

'Aye, O.K. then, no problem.' came the confirmation.

Gennardy took up a position diagonally opposite to the railway station where he could look into the canopied area that heralded the station entrance. Cars coming in to collect or leave passengers using the railway station had to come this way. He watched carefully but there was little to see at this hour of the morning. The station was very quiet.

His attention was drawn to two men. They had appeared and gone two or three times. Both men were well dressed in suits and coats, neither appeared to have any luggage. One would walk into the station and a few minutes later he would reappear under the canopy and occasionally he would walk up to another man and talk for a minute or so. Then the other man would stroll into the station out of view then they would meet up again and stand together talking.

After a while a uniformed Police officer walked up to the two men and they all had a short conversation before they went their separate ways.

Gennardy felt sure they were looking for him and Li.

Across the street from the station entrance was a black Mercedes car. The man in the driver's seat was smoking a cigarette with the car door window open whilst the other was sleeping in the front passenger seat with his head resting on a cushion.

Just before two-o clock a spotlessly clean, Juniper Green Jaguar XJ6 gleamed its way under the station lights heading for the canopy. It moved slowly and silently stopping short of the canopy. Wisps of steam wafted from the dual exhaust system. The registration number was VRG23T. That was the plate number Tony had given Gennardy on the telephone.

Feeling uneasy about approaching the Jaguar himself Gennardy made his way back to the taxi. He persuaded the taxi driver to approach the Jaguar and tell the driver that Gennardy was round the corner. The taxi driver pocketed the keys for his car and did as he was asked.

Walking up to the jaguar he knocked on the driver's window. Bill Robinson wound down the window saying; 'Yes! What is it?'

'I am a taxi driver and your friend Gennardy is sitting in my cab. He has asked me to get into your car and show you where the cab is so that he doesn't have to come into the railway station. Bill looked at Tony and they both nodded their assent whereon the taxi driver got in the rear seat and the Jaguar purred through the canopy and into the main street.

'Along here.' said the taxi man. 'First right then first right again.'

Cheslav noted the Jaguar since the activities going on there was all that was happening. He woke Nicolai as the Jaguar slid past him. 'I have a hunch we may be on to something.' He said as he started the engine and swung the car round in a half circle. By the time Cheslav had turned the car to face the opposite direction the Jaguar had gone. The next opening was on the right so Cheslav took the turn. As he did so he could just see the tail end of the car and the wisps coming from the exhaust as the Jaguar disappeared up another right turn. As he took the second right he just caught sight of his target taking his third right turn. He followed and stopped the Mercedes just before the third corner where Nicolai jumped out and peered up the street. The hunch was right. The Jaguar was stopped alongside a taxi. Both rear doors of the taxi were open and one of the rear doors of the Jaguar was being closed as it pulled away.

Whoever had switched cars was in a hurry.

Nicolai watched the taxi driver look at a piece of paper in his hand before pocketing it and walking round to close the rear doors. By the time the taxi driver had closed the doors and got into his driver's seat a large black Mercedes had pulled alongside of him

Chapter 19

Sitting in the back seat of the Jaguar with Li a tense Gennardy watched out of the rear window as the car purred through the empty streets of Kingston upon Hull. Wet roads and pavements reflected the street lighting. They made their way towards the A19 road heading North. About ninety minutes later they were passing through the Tyne Tunnel. Twenty minutes later the Jaguar pulled up outside of the home of Bill Robinson.

The manner of their coming together and the exit from Hull railway station was so quick and unexpected that the atmosphere in the car was eerie.

Apart from the few simple instructions spoken as Li and Gennardy had transferred from the taxi to the Jaguar and the transfer of money to the bemused taxi driver no one had said anything. Gennardy was fearful. His anxiety was infectious. All four looked out of windows and in mirrors in anticipation of some impending incident.

Only when they had cleared Hull and reached the dual carriageway did Gennardy turn to sit comfortably in his leather seat.

'I am so pleased to see you my friend Tony. I am so very worried that perhaps we are followed. No one seems to be following us. I think there were men at the station looking for us. We cannot even believe in the British authorities, Tony, believe me some of them are working for KGB...'

'Please Gennardy!' declared Tony, as he and Bill Robinson exchanged sideways glances.

'Please, you must not worry. We aren't being followed. All we have to do is to get home and get something to eat and then we can decide how best to help you. Don't you think you should introduce us to your friend?'

Li had sat by Gennardy in silence. She could see little of the two men in the front seats. Her eyes flicked from the back of their heads to Gennardy and then out of the door window next to her and then to Gennardy and then through the rear window. Their arrival in England was not what she had imagined. She felt just as anxious as ever and then Tony Hartill, of whom she had heard so much, had answered Gennardy's garbled outburst and suddenly she felt reassured.

His voice was deep, quiet and comforting. It was clear and pleasant. She liked it and it made her feel more secure. She had listened every day for months to Gennardy telling her about the owner of that voice and she was not disappointed.

In answer to Tony's request Gennardy replied. 'Please again, please forgive me. You must understand I am all the time worried. Tomorrow I will explain to you.'

'I think its tomorrow now.' said Bill as he watched the road ahead. They all laughed a little nervously.

'Why don't you two just sit back and relax' suggested Bill. 'When we get back to my home we can have a snack and then we will all get some rest. Tomorrow we can talk at leisure when we are fed and rested.'

Gennardy lay back as his host suggested but sleep would not come for him. By contrast Li was sleeping soundly. She had nodded off and her head had come to rest on his shoulder.

As the taxi driver watched the Jaguar pull away and disappear into the night he switched on his radio to contact his office. A voice came over the noisy receiver in a thick accent; 'Where the hell 'ave you been.'

'Just cleared that last fare a few minutes ago, queer set up if you ask me.' As the taxi driver spoke he saw, in his mirror, a big black Mercedes coming slowly up the street towards him from behind.

'There's another bugger just pulling up alongside of me in a big black Merc. I'll leave the set on; OK.' said a very nervous taxi driver.

Cheslav's companion Nicolai wound down the window of the front passenger door of the Mercedes and smiled at the taxi driver as the car came to a halt. Cheslav got out of the driver's seat and walked round to the taxi driver's door. The taxi driver wound down his door window and waited till Cheslav spoke.

'Your passengers that have just left, we think they are friends of ours and we have just missed them. Can you help us?' asked Cheslav as Nicolai listened.

'Never seen them before last night mate, all I know is that they're foreigners. Myself I would say that they're a couple of Ruskies. Their friends of yours ah take it?' queried the driver.

'Yes, that's what I said.' answered Cheslav. 'They're friends of mine. We were to collect them from the railway station and give them a lift in our car.'

'They've got a fair few friends I would say.' said the taxi driver. 'They've just gone off.'

Cheslav put his hand in his pocket. The taxi driver watched nervously until he was shown a ten-pound note.

'Perhaps you can help us to find them. Do you know their destination?' asked the KGB man politely.

'Aye, Ah do that. They said they wuz headed for Newcastle. I would say that the two blokes who picked them up were a couple of Geordies so it sounds about right.'

'Jordiz; what is 'jordiz.' came the reply.

'No not Jordiz; Geordies!' emphasised the taxi man

who was beginning to wonder if this night was really happening.

'Do you know their names?' asked Cheslav deciding not to pursue the Geordies mystery.

'Aye, I do.' said the man eyeing the ten pound note. 'Eeh were called Genna and she were called Lee, sometimes she called him Gennardy and sometimes Genna.'

'This is what I need to know.' responded Cheslav pressing the money into the hand of the man. 'Goodnight and thank you.'

As Cheslav returned to his car the taxi man wound up his window and said into the radio microphone. 'Did you hear all that then?'

'Aye I did.' said the controller, 'That lot might have something to do with two illegal immigrants that the police are looking for. We had them on last night asking for us to keep an eye out for them, never thought to mention it to you, you having that open fare. I'd better phone police.'

The taxi driver replied 'you know ah thought there was someth'in fishy about those two but a'll tell thee this. Those two that's just left are a bloody sight fishier, could be into drugs or something. He didn't even know what a Geordie was.'

Half an hour later a policeman advised the two British agents who were still waiting around the railway station. They were told that a call had been received from a taxi company. Initial information suggested that the two illegal immigrants had gone.

Ten minutes later the two agents and a police inspector questioned the taxi driver for half an hour before thanking him and advising him that they would prefer him to keep his information to himself.

At the same time the Soviet Ambassador in London had been awakened from his sleep to take a telephone call from Cheslav and Nicolai. Having listened attentively to their story the Ambassador immediately contacted Plakinov who in turn summoned Humphrey Goodchild.

Goodchild couldn't believe his ears when Plakinov advised him that the interpreter and Li had arrived in England and been met in Hull before being driven off. He was ordered to return to England immediately.

'How can I do that.' asked Goodchild.

'Simple.' replied Plakinov. 'You will be taken ill in one hour from now. You will be taken to a hospital in Moscow and the doctor there will tell you that the reason you were so dizzy and unwell was because you have blood pressure problems requiring immediate attention. The Doctor will give you letters in Russian and English explaining his findings and confirming that you can travel under medication prescribed by him. You will telephone your boss and advise him of this problem and tell him that you are taking the next plane out to get private treatment in England. The rest you make up as required.'

Before Goodchild left Plakinov emphasised; 'To the best of our knowledge this lunatic, Mardosov has my files. Those files will not only condemn you they will also expose the whole of the arrangements to finance Markham and the UBAC plan. We know that Mardosov has those files because you would have been recalled to London if Solidarnosc had taken them from him and passed them over to the British or the Americans.'

Plakinov paused and went on to point out. 'Furthermore my advisers have concluded that Mardosov will be unwilling to pass those files to anyone other than someone he trusts implicitly. Why?

Because he knows that the British contacts he made in Moscow are reporting to you. And he knows from the files that you are working for us.'

Goodchild looked at Plakinov open-mouthed.

'We made a pact that you would be my only contact and that my involvement with the KGB was known only to you.' He shouted

'My friend' said Plakinov. 'When you have helped us to dispose of Mardosov and the files are recovered or destroyed the people in KGB who know about you will also be disposed of.

'I am a man of my word. On this occasion I have been forced to "make some adjustments" as you say in England.'

Plakinov shrugged his shoulders before continuing; 'I am sure you must see things my way. Besides; I know how ingenious and resourceful you can be when you are in difficulties.'

It was almost daylight by the time that the Jaguar arrived back at the home of Bill Robinson. Bill's wife came downstairs with her dressing gown over her pyjamas and began to make them all a hot drink and a sandwich. Gennardy was so pleased to see her again.

'I have longed to see you again Mrs Robinson. Do you remember me?' Tony Hartill and Bill Robinson looked at each other in mock shock saying; 'You don't waste any time Gennardy.'

Gennardy looked across at them as they laughed at him. He shook his head looking embarrassed when he realised what he'd said to Mrs Robinson. Then he too laughed with them saying 'I think I should change my words. I don't mean that I have longed just to see you but also your husband Beel and Tony, my friend Tony, also. Sometimes I think that I am dreaming that I am here. I am in Eengland. Tell me that I am in Eengland for sure.'

They all laughed again despite their weariness.

Bill's wife laughed a little too but she was nervous about the whole exercise as she had made plain to Bill before he had left for Hull.

She became more nervous when Gennardy went on. 'I must tell you that we have many problems with everything. This is why I am so careful. You must understand that we had to escape from the ship, the Amada, because we do not know who may be waiting for us. Maybe they will be good for us, and maybe, not so good. Our information will be good for your country but some of your officers are working for KGB. We know. I will show you.'

Receiving another anxious look from his wife Bill said. 'I think you must be very tired. We will show you to your rooms and, after we have slept, perhaps we can all sit down together and see where we go from here.'

Tony waited until Bill and his wife had shown their guests to their rooms. On their return he said, 'Right then I will go to my mother's now and tomorrow, well today; I mean, we can decide what to do. I don't want to get you out again Bill so perhaps I can borrow your bike.'

'Good idea.' agreed Bill smiling. 'The fresh air will do you good.'

With that Tony cycled off after agreeing to telephone no earlier than 11am so that they all had time to sort themselves out.

As soon as Tony left Bill's wife asked him a barrage of questions. She felt ill at ease.

Bill poured a generous whisky and went to great lengths to assuage her concerns as he sipped his drink.

Although he too was uneasy Bill said, 'Don't worry! We can sort it out in the morning and it will just be another little story. I must get some sleep, I'm knackered!'

That same morning, acting on the instructions of Plakinov, the Russian Ambassador sent an aide to give instructions to Owen Williams at his flat in Islington.

Ninety minutes after receiving the call Owen Williams was on a train to Doncaster. Albert Markham stepped out of his car in West Street near Doncaster railway station and caught up to Owen Williams as he walked along. The two men talked as they walked around the town for some forty minutes before parting company. Williams was on his way back to London. Albert Markham walked to the end of the street before hailing his driver.

Markham was incredulous at what he had heard from Williams. Of all the things that could have gone wrong he had never, even in his worst nightmares, imagined a possibility like that explained a few minutes ago; Plakinov's assistant in England with an interpreter who had seen him and Owen Williams in Minsk?

As the car pulled into the kerb Markham instructed his driver to take him home. He then telephoned his office to cancel all engagements for the day. He needed time to think.

George Norman left the Central tube station in London. As he walked towards his office in the bright morning sunshine he felt good. As always the nearer he got to work the more his mind focused on his priorities for the day. On arrival he was surprised that there was no message from Mark Benson and Tim Graham confirming that their two charges from the Amada were safely tucked away in Barnet. It was his plan to go up there about lunchtime.

His Secretary called him on the telephone; 'Mark Benson for you Mr Norman.'

'About time, put him through.' came the reply.

Before Benson could speak Norman said. 'You all having a long lie in, you lazy buggers.'

'The news is not good I'm afraid.' said Benson. 'We are still in Hull. Our friends have disappeared.'

'What are you talking about, disappeared.' responded George Norman.

'Exactly that.' came the reply 'It seems that they conned their way out of the dock dressed as Indian crewmen. We found this taxi driver who spent half the night with them before someone in a Jaguar car picked them up.'

'What about our contact on the ship? How did they get away from him?' asked Norman.

'They stole £380.00 from him before departing. It is obvious that he had not anticipated the escape. It all takes a bit of believing. Eh.' Quipped Benson before continuing 'What is of greater concern is our conversation with the taxi driver who reckons that two well dressed gentlemen with good English, spoken with a foreign accent, were also looking for them.'

The conversation between George Norman and his two agents went on for a further twenty minutes. Afterwards Norman opened up the file on Li and Gennardy. As he did so he picked up the telephone and contacted his boss.

'Hello George! What can I do for you?' came a jolly greeting.

'I think we should talk. Can I come up right away' asked George Norman.

'Just for a couple of minutes I must leave shortly.' replied the boss.

After a quick account of what had taken place the two men agreed on the course of action that George Norman suggested. He was just about to leave when the boss observed.

'It's all happening this morning. I've just had a message to say that one of our men in Moscow; one Humphrey Goodchild has had a bad turn. He's on his way back to get treatment over here. Heart trouble or something like that.'

Tony Hartill arrived at the home of his parents, secured Bill's bicycle, and entered the house quietly so as not to disturb his sleeping parents. As he got to his room his mother came to the bedroom landing asking if Tony was all right.

'Of course I am' he whispered. 'I wish you wouldn't worry about me. I'm a big lad you know.'

The fact was that Tony Hartill was worried. It seemed that fate was drawing him into situations that he could never have thought of.

Despite being so weary sleep would not overtake him for some time, there were so many thoughts passing through his head. So many questions he needed answers to. He was also concerned that he was involving Bill Robinson and his family. He was taking advantage of them. What was Gennardy talking about with KGB and British Intelligence?

The following morning he was back at the home of Bill Robinson before 11 0 clock to find Bill's wife and Bill sitting at the large table in the kitchen. They had all breakfasted and each was sitting with a mug of tea before them. Tony joined them. The little furrows of consternation between the brows of Mrs Robinson did not escape his notice.

'Right then' said Bill; 'Now that we are all refreshed and fed I think we should have a little chat to see what's what.'

All eyes were on Gennardy who stood up, lifted two files from his chair, and put them on the table before resuming his seat.

'These files are from the headquarters of KGB boss Yuri Plakinov. Li was his assistant before we had to come to U.K. to become safe and free. These files are to help us to make sure that the British Government will let us stay here.' pronounced Gennardy with a firm nod of the head. Li nodded in assent.

The hosts and Tony all exchanged looks before concentrating their attention once again on Gennardy.

'I need your help to make sure that this information is given to people who will help us. The British Secret Service man I made contact with in Moscow was reporting to his senior officer who is working for KGB. These are files from Plakinov's office. He kept them for no one else to see. I have read these files and looked at the pictures many times. I know many things some I do not understand.' Looking at Tony he said. 'Albert Markham is in this file. I saw him in Minsk with Plakinov and Owen Williams.'

Again quick glances were exchanged. Tony pulled the files towards him and looked inside. There was a picture of Markham and also one of Owen Williams. They were the only two he recognised. Most of the file was in text, obviously Russian.

Tony looked up saying 'Gennardy, I think we had better start from the beginning and decide how best we can help. I know someone who may be able to advise us. We should really call in the police and let them deal with it.'

'No please.' retorted Gennardy. 'I want you to understand everything. No Police; please I must explain.'

Bill Robinson had listened intently to every word before saying; 'Look! I think we are out of our depth and this could be serious stuff. I don't want to let anyone down but we cannot conceal your presence and if what you say is true we could find ourselves in serious trouble with the Police.'

'But it is true.' blurted Gennardy.

'I'm sure it is.' said Bill. 'But you must put yourselves in our shoes. I have a wife and family and whilst I am prepared to help I want to know that I am doing the right thing.'

'Look Bill' Said Tony, 'you have been wonderful and I agree with you. Gennardy and Li can't stay here. I have an idea to give us time to think this through properly and leave you with peace of mind.'

'What are you thinking of?' said Bill.

'Well! If they were staying in a caravan on one of those out of the way country sites we could listen to this story properly and decide what to do. Whatever way you look at this story it's bloody amazing. I know someone who would love to hear it and at the same time offer some impartial advice on how we get this file translated and how we use it to help Gennardy and Li. We just have to accept what we are told; at least for the time being.'

Gennardy listened and nodded his approval. 'Who will come, Tony?' He asked.

Someone I think we can trust. Someone who knows where we can get the files translated and then her boss can make contact in high places to ensure that you get a fair deal.'

When their guests were out of earshot Bill said. 'Your talking about your journalist friend aren't you.'

'Exactly' replied Tony.

'Look let's not waste time.' urged Tony. 'I will get my car and take them up to a caravan site where they'll be safe and where they can recuperate in a beautiful setting with all the food they can eat and lots of exercise and fresh air.'

'I'll drive you round to your mother's Tony whilst

you make a little parcel up for them.' said Bill looking across to his wife.

'Of course.' she replied before looking at Li and Gennardy saying 'And what sort of things do you like to eat.'

As the two men drove off in the Jaguar Bill said. 'Thanks for that Tony. The wife is worried sick about spies and Russians and furtive trips to Hull in the middle of the night. Let's face it, these things don't exactly happen every day.'

'Don't thank me old lad. I'd have been lost without you. It's funny though how our paths always cross in unusual circumstances and situations.' Tony replied.

'Aye, I've been thinking about that lately too. Now't like a good adventure though; is there.'

Tony smiled and nodded his agreement.

As Tony expressed his thanks again Bill reached into his wallet and pulled out five twenty- pound notes.

'Here.' He said. 'Take this and give them a good feed. They have had a rough time whatever their story is and it's quite obvious that Gennardy is scared stiff that something is going to go wrong.'

'You sure'Tony said knowing full well that Bill was sure.

'I'm not hard up Tony. You know that. I'm just glad to be able to help. Imagine if the roles were reversed.'

'That's what my Father always says, put yourself in Gilligans place. That's how he expresses the sentiment.'

'Well said! I like that. See you back at my place in a few minutes O.K.'

'O.K.' replied Tony.

Half an hour later Li and Gennardy were sitting in Tony's car heading North out of Ashington towards the

Cheviot Hills of rural Northumberland.

'I will take you to this beautiful place.' said Tony. 'It's called Rothbury. At this time of the year there are lots of visitors and many of them are foreign so you will not seem out of place. Tonight I will stay with you and you can tell me your story. We'll get some drinks and have a little party to celebrate your arrival in England, how about that!'

'This seems wonderful to me Tony. You have no idea how many times I have thought about being in England and talking to you like I did when I was with the delegation.'

Li got the gist of the conversation and said slowly; 'All the time when we are hungry he tells me of Roast Beef and Yorkshire pudding.' The two refugees laughed together and Tony felt the tension within them ease.

'Roast Beef and Yorkshire pudding it shall be. Tonight we will eat in a small hotel and they are sure to have Roast Beef.'

Li and Gennardy giggled like children.

Within three miles of leaving Ashington they were in open countryside heading towards the Cheviot Hills lying to the south of the border with Scotland. Apart from the two small villages they passed through the only other communities evident were hamlets or farmhouses. The rolling landscape occasionally gave way to woodland as the road wound round and across the river winding along the bottom of the valleys. They followed the road until suddenly they came off a hillside and before them was the picturesque country town of Rothbury built on either side of the river Aln. The buildings were all built in the local sandstone giving the area its unique appearance.

Having found a luxurious six-berth caravan to stay in they watched television as each in turn washed and dressed. Bill's wife had provided some clothes for Li whilst Tony had found some suitable garments for Gennardy. As the pair went through the hastily gathered wardrobe their excitement and joy was evident. Humour in Russia was largely extinct by comparison to Britain and Gennardy wanted to indulge in the happiness and joking he recalled and harboured from his former experience as a guest at Tony Hartill's house.

As Tony sat in the caravan he shared in their investigation of their new home. They were both fascinated with this new experience and obviously enjoying it. Every door and cover was opened or removed to see what the next revelation was before they decided to prepare for an evening out. Li used the bathroom first and she took ages before emerging. Tony and Gennardy took turns in knocking on the bathroom door to tease her.

'Thees ees teepical Eenglish humour' Gennardy was shouting and laughing.

When she appeared from the bathroom Tony was immediately struck with her beauty. Her slender body moved with grace. She had let her hair down. It was shoulder length and it framed her face. She was wearing tight fitting jeans, borrowed from the wardrobe of Bill's daughter, with a fine woollen 'V' neck jumper from the same source. She was without make-up. Her eyes were joyful and shining. It was obvious that she felt good. As Tony and Gennardy looked at her she lowered her eyes and looking at them sideways in a fashion Tony found endearing.

There was a short silence before Gennardy clapped his hands and shouted 'Bravo'. Tony joined in then they all laughed. Tony was captivated.

At six thirty that evening they arrived in the bar of the Lamb and Garter hotel a small establishment in terms of accommodation but it had a large reputation for food. They all ordered a drink of lager and then Tony asked what they wanted to eat. They all laughed as they said in unison 'Roast Beef and Yorkshire pudding.'

They made their way into the self- service Carvery where the assistant cut large slices of beef off the joint and laid it on their plates together with a Yorkshire pudding. Gennardy was gleaming with pleasure as he placed vegetables upon his plate and returned to the table assigned by the waitress. Li and Tony joined him and all three sat down to enjoy the meal that Gennardy had spoken of so often during the long journey from Moscow.

As they ate Tony was quite embarrassed by the noises and grunts as Gennardy tucked into his meal.

'Do not worry Gennardy' said Tony 'No one is going to take it from you.'

They all laughed as the waitress brought a bottle of red wine and poured it for them.

Gennardy was the first to clear his plate. He sat back and thanked Tony before turning to Li who was making steady progress.

'This is good. Eh!' asked Gennardy.

'Da, Mmh, I mean Yes. I am eating in English and thinking in Russian.' They all smiled.

When the meal was finished they returned to the bar where Tony ordered a brandy for each of them.

'Now then, Gennardy, perhaps this would be a good time to tell me about your journey. We are safe here. No one knows where we are.' he said reassuringly.

'Ah! Tony my friend! You are so kind.'

He looked across at Li before continuing, 'Is it not just like I told you it would be.'

'Da, Da, Yes Yes.' replied Li. We are having much good fortune with you Tony.' She went on.

Gennardy paused and looked at Tony before beginning his story. After an hour Tony suggested that they return to the caravan. On the journey back Tony bought a couple of bottles of red wine.

In the caravan they toasted one another and sipped their wine as Gennardy continued his tale. Li too listened intently and occasionally she would remind Gennardy of something or ask him to explain to her in Russian.

Suddenly it was one-thirty in the morning. Both bottles of wine had been consumed and the tale was still unfolding. When they turned in for the night Li and Gennardy were explaining their reception in the Lublin Cathedral in Poland.

Tony knew that this story was so detailed and complete that it was true. Before going to sleep he lay in a pull out bed in the lounge area of the van staring at the ceiling trying to imagine the scenes described to him.

In the morning Li and Gennardy emerged from their respective rooms to greet their friend Tony.

Over breakfast Tony advised them of his intention to bring his friend Pippa Glendinning to see them and to hear the story from the beginning. After some explanation Gennardy and Li agreed.

Before leaving Rothbury they all went shopping in the little town and bought provisions to last them a day or two. Tony assured them that he would return within three days.

As he switched on the car ignition to leave Gennardy came up to the car and thrust his hand through the open window of the driver's door. 'I hope you can return soon my friend.' said Gennardy. Then Li shook his hand. Their gaze lingered for a moment then the two stood aside and waved Tony off until they could see the car no more.

It had never occurred to British Intelligence that they would fail to pick up Li and Gennardy from the Amada and interrogate them. Now that they had failed in this simple task George Norman went over the file and it was not difficult to conclude that Tony Hartill was the common denominator. The two failed agents had returned from Hull to London immediately after reporting their failure. By the time they returned to George Norman's office he had a detailed file on Tony Hartill including his army service record.

'This case is too weird for words.' said Norman. 'First of all the Russians do not allow their people, no matter how discontented, or ingenious, or lucky, to simply walk out of Russia with Plakinov's files and deliver them to the U.K.'

He stared at his two subordinates as he thought of his next statement. 'Secondly we are in the middle of the most dangerous industrial dispute that this country has ever been involved in.' He paused looking at each man in turn before going on. 'And thirdly the story we got from the Moscow Embassy could be true. The story we received from our Solidarnosc accomplices shows no contradictions. This man Mardosov could be genuine. If so! Why does he escape from the Amada? Why not deliver himself and his colleague to the British authorities in Hull. He's obviously wily, he's obviously bright and he's also very violent if his tale is true: Any comments?'

His audience of two shook their heads slowly from side to side. They showed none of their usual bonhomie and casual jocularity for which they were renowned within the department. Their failure to bring Mardosov and his companion back from Hull had not been well received.

George Norman stood up 'right then! Get yourselves up to Ashington and find them. Start with Mr Hartill and see what comes up. I'm sure that it has not escaped your notice that others will almost certainly have been set the same task. I'm talking about the two gentlemen in Hull; the two with the foreign accents.'

In response to the instruction Mark Benson and Tim Graham looked across at each other and stood up. The two then looked across at their boss who said. 'Well! What are you waiting for'

'Arms, you know guns and things. Do we have a fall back position?' enquired Mark.

'Unwise I think to go up there armed. Keep in touch. You know you can contact me at any time. Meanwhile I'll alert the Chief Constable of the Northumbria Police Force and let him know that you are in the area making a few enquiries; just in case you need their help.'

Shortly afterwards the two agents were at London's King's Cross Railway Station boarding a train for Newcastle upon Tyne.

Humphrey Goodchild did not bother to go home to his wife and Daughter. Instead he telephoned them to say that he had returned from Moscow on Doctor's advice and he would be entering a health farm. He said he was suffering from stress and high blood pressure but there was nothing to worry about.

His wife asked 'What if some one asks for you, where should I say you are?'

'I'll let you know where I am when I find a place. I'm getting in touch with an old chum to see what's available.'

Goodchild unknowingly boarded the same train as

Mark Benson and Tim Graham at King's Cross. When the train stopped at Peterborough Goodchild disembarked and took a taxi to a small hotel in a nearby village owned by an old school friend.

The proprietor was surprised to see his old friend and asked what he'd done to deserve this unexpected visit.

Goodchild went straight to the point. 'I'm here because I need some bloody peace. My Doctor has sent me home on leave whilst I have a check up and so on. It's all a nuisance really and I don't want to alarm the wife etc. Can I book a room here for a while? It means that I can go up to London quite quickly and see my man in Harley Street. I don't suppose I'll spend that much time here. It's just that if I can give my wife your telephone number..... If anyone needs to contact me; well; I can phone you if I'm not here and take messages and return their call if I want to.'

Goodchild's host was vaguely aware of how his guest made his living.

'No problem' he replied 'delighted to be of service to an old friend. If anyone phones I'll take the number and you can take it from there.'

'Splendid. You've been very understanding and I do appreciate it. I shall be going up to London in the morning and I'm not sure when I shall return, depends upon the tests. They may wish to keep me under observation for a day or two. Can we have a couple of drinks together this evening? It would be nice to chat over a small tipple.'

His host agreed and Goodchild telephoned his wife with the telephone number.

The following morning Goodchild took a taxi to Peterborough railway station and bought a first class return ticket to Newcastle upon Tyne.

The two Russian Agents stayed in Hull awaiting instructions from their embassy in London. Each day they telephoned every four hours beginning at eight in the morning. The last call of the day was at midnight.

The noon phone-call was made to a public call box not far from the Russian Embassy in Belgravia. The KGB used public call boxes to avoid bugging. Their instructions came directly from Plakinov via the Ambassador himself. Within minutes of making the call they too were making their way to Ashington. The district of Winsbreck had no hotels and within a period of twenty-four hours the local tourist information offices had three separate enquiries asking for accommodation in a large well appointed hotel in Ashington or nearby. The enquirers were advised that there were no large hotels in Northumberland. All three enquirers were advised to contact the Queen's Head hotel in nearby Morpeth.

Pippa Glendinning was at her desk in the London office of 'The National Telegraph' newspaper. A nearby telephone rang. Someone picked it up and shouted 'It's for you Pippa.'

She swung her chair around and picked up the receiver. 'Pippa Glendinning.'

'Hello Pippa' he responded with an instantly recognisable voice.

'Hello you, this is a nice surprise. What can I do for you then? Or shouldn't I ask that?'

Tony Hartill smiled as he listened to her voice. 'You're a she devil.' He replied.

'Well if I am I know someone who gets along with them very well' she answered.

The tone in the voice of Tony changed. 'Look Pippa I need your help urgently.'

Pippa was about to say something flippant then

changed her mind. 'What's wrong?'

'I need your help: Urgently. I have a story you will find difficult to believe but I know it's true. You remember me telling you about a Russian guy who came to stay with Maggie and me?'

'Vaguely, wasn't he the interpreter who wanted to empty all the boxes in the supermarket to see if there was anything in them?'

'That's him. Well he's here.'

'Where?' asked Pippa.

'In Ashington, well not exactly in Ashington, they're in a caravan.' replied Tony.

'Who are they, then?'

'Look Pippa it's all too complicated to explain over the telephone. You must come up here now.'

'Just like that' she replied. 'I have a deadline to meet this afternoon. I also have an assignment to follow up which is very important.'

'This could be the assignment of your life' stated Tony emphatically. 'If you miss this you will rue the day.'

'Good as that'

'Good as that' repeated Tony.

It had not occurred to Tony that she would not come immediately. He had assumed that it was such a tale and Pippa had got to know him so well that she would drop everything and come. The thought that she wouldn't come left him alarmed. He didn't want to go to the Police just yet. He suddenly spoke in a more subdued voice.

'Look Pippa! I promise you that you will not regret this and time is short. We need help and you can provide it. You need a super scoop. We need help.'

'Give me a telephone number where I can reach you in the next couple of hours and I'll come back to you when I've seen my boss. And by the way this had better not be a ruse to get me into bed.'

'Never even thought of it' he lied.

That evening Pippa Glendinning was on the British European Airways flight from Gatwick to Newcastle airport where she was met by Tony.

Chapter 20

Tony Hartill took Pippa directly from the airport to the caravan at Rothbury. As the car progressed along the country roads Tony outlined the story that Gennardy had told him. Pippa was incredulous.

'Are you sure?' she asked. 'This bloke does a James Bond with his beautiful girlfriend in tow and cheats the whole of the Russian apparatchik, KGB and all, then ends up in a caravan in Rothbury. Not even Popeye would believe it.'

'I know.' replied Tony. 'I have to pinch myself to remind myself that I'm not imagining the whole thing. It's just so fantastic.' He paused before saying. 'And by the way she's not his girlfriend. So he says. They certainly don't give the impression that they're, well you know…'

'Do you mean to tell me that this bloke goes to all that trouble for a woman he's not hopelessly in love with?' replied Pippa turning to look at him.

'Well! From what I can gather Gennardy is no slouch with women, he reckons that without them Russian men wouldn't survive the winter cold.'

Pippa snorted 'typical chauvanist pig.'

When they arrived at the caravan Li and Gennardy were sitting inside absorbed by the television programmes. Li saw the car pull up and as Tony step out she shouted to Gennardy and they both rushed to the door to welcome him.

After an elaborate introduction and greeting ceremony they sat in the lounge of the caravan to make their arrangements. The discussion ended when Pippa spoke to Li and Gennardy saying 'If you don't mind I would like to talk to each of you in turn. Each of you has a fascinating tale to tell and I am just itching to hear it all. Why don't we begin right now?'

The other three looked at her and each other before agreeing. Tony shrugged his shoulders saying 'Why not?' Li and Gennardy copied him.

'What about the files.' said Gennardy passing them over.

'Tony told me about them. My boss has a friend who speaks fluent Russian and who does a bit of work, I think, for the Security people. They were in the army together in the fifties. Both know a great deal about the cold war. I'll ask him if we can go to Durham University in the morning to see if he will organise a full translation and then we'll see about getting someone to identify all the pictures.'

'Can we trust him' asked Gennardy thrusting his head forward.

'Who said it was a him?' returned Pippa. 'Women do things too you know.' she said before changing the subject.

'And now, I'm starving. Let's get some food and then Gennardy can take me for a long walk.' With that she gave a bright smile and everyone concurred.

Li and Tony cooked bacon, eggs and beans whilst Pippa and Gennardy talked. After the meal they went for their planned walk. Tony asked Li what she would like to do.

'I think I would like to go into the town to the pub.'

'O.K I go to the pub with you. O.K.' she smiled.

'Wonderful!' Tony responded. 'Why don't we walk there it's not far.'

That same evening the proprietor of the Queens Head Hotel in Morpeth was very pleased with the unexpected attention his establishment was enjoying. He had let five of his twelve rooms that day. Two large and very athletic looking foreign gentlemen had booked in for an indefinite period and another two English Gentlemen secured rooms for a week. That lovely reporter, Miss Glendinning, had also booked a room for a week and then phoned in to say she was staying with friends for the time being, could he retain the room for her in case she needed it, all bed and breakfast, and all at the full rate. This was good business for a change at a time when the Miner's dispute was having such a damaging effect on businesses everywhere in the region. As the man contemplated his good fortune the telephone rang and a voice that sounded like an Etonian cabinet minister enquired about accommodation before he too booked a room. The voice belonged to Humphrey Goodchild.

The two British agents were the first to arrive that night. As soon as they were allocated their rooms Mark Benson and Tim showered, had a meal and returned to their rooms to rest. The following morning they drove their hire car to Ashington.

Maggie Hartill was washing the windows at the rear of her immaculate little terraced colliery house when a man with a south of England accent introduced himself as Tim and said he had some information for her husband.

'What sort of information.' said a suspicious Maggie.

Two nights before she had attended a packed meeting in the Miner's hall, the meeting was addressed by Ray Mullaney who told the 'Friends of the Miner's' group that the Tory Government was working in collusion with the Directors of the British Coal Industry. He claimed that they had agents in the area who were looking for 'traitors' within the coal mining communities who would betray the striking miners and discredit Albert Markham and the other heroes of the class struggle.

At the end of the meeting Mullaney gathered Maggie and others of her family to point out that he had accurate information from headquarters confirming that Tony Hartill was a scab and he was working with the enemy. 'He has to be found and quickly' urged Mullaney.

Mullaney's words were ringing in her ears as she looked hard at the man now standing in her yard.

'Well! As a matter of fact my colleague and I wanted a chat with him. Is he about?' came the answer.

'What sort of information.' repeated Maggie.

'Is Tony here Maggie?' said Tim using her name to confirm that he was speaking to Mrs Hartill.

'How do you know my name' snarled Maggie.

'Tony told me. He often talks about you.'

'Does he now' smiled Maggie suddenly changing her attitude. 'Just a moment and I'll phone for him to come.'

She went into the house and picked up the telephone receiver. As she talked she watched Tim Benson through the kitchen window who had been joined by his colleague. When she returned to the rear door she said. 'I'll just put the kettle on while your'e waiting.'

The two men looked at one another and thanked her.

Five minutes later a dozen men suddenly appeared in the lane behind them. Two of them were the Yorkshire men who were Mullaney's bodyguard. They stood in the front with two young, well built, local men who were carrying pick axe handles. Messrs Benson and Graham had been in some very difficult situations but they quickly realised that this was potentially very dangerous.

Knowing that there was no escape both men attempted to enter into a dialogue to delay the inevitable and gain time to think. Neither man did anything to provoke an attack.

From the back a voice barked out; 'give it to the bastards.' A chorus of 'Ayes' followed.

One of the four in the front said. 'So what are you two after; what do you want Tony fucking Hartill for.'

'Well if we could speak to him he would let you know. He's a friend of ours.' said Tim confidently.

'That clinches it pal cos he's no friend of ours.'

It was only time before something triggered conflict. Some of the men had obviously been drinking and they wanted action.

In the row of terraced houses opposite a friend of Tony Hartill stood back in his bedroom and watched through the window what he knew was the prelude to bloodletting. He recognised the mob from Mullaney's headquarters and called the police.

By the time the police arrived ten minutes later a lopsided battle was raging. The mob had received a shock from the two defendants who were accounting for themselves very well despite the odds. The arrival of the police was in time to stop them being completely overwhelmed.

Nine men including the two security men were arrested and herded into two police vans. All were driven off to the Police station in Ashington and placed in cells before each was interviewed.

Two hours later two badly bruised security men were seated opposite the duty shift Police Inspector. A few telephone calls later the two men were released and on their way back to the Queen's Head hotel after a check-up at the District Hospital.

The Police gave the two very sore agents the address of Tony Hartill's parents. The following morning they set off to try to get information from them to help locate

350

their son.

As they approached the street they saw a thin line of people watching as the fire brigade were recovering their gear after having put out a fire at the house they had planned to visit.

An onlooker told them that the elderly couple in the house had been taken to the local hospital for a check up but they were thought to be uninjured. No they had not seen Tony Hartill and no one knew where he was. The fire had been started by a petrol bomb pushed through the letterbox.

As the two agents sat in the car watching the scene Tim Graham said. 'You know! This is a bloody war zone.'

'Your right there' said his colleague 'when we started with this thing. It seemed just about the simplest job you could get. Let's get back to the police station and see what we can pick up there.'

'Just a minute.' said Mark from behind the driving wheel. 'Isn't that the Geezer staying at our hotel, he was just going out from breakfast as we went in this morning.' The Geezer was Humphrey Goodchild.

Unknown to the two British Agents the site had also been visited that morning by two Russian gentlemen who had breakfasted in their rooms at the Queen's Head Hotel.

At first Pippa Glendinning could not sleep after her walk with Gennardy. His story seemed preposterous and yet she knew it was true. As she lay in the bed that Gennardy had slept in the night before she felt guilty that he should be sharing the caravan lounge with Tony. After all he'd been through he had a right to some comfort. She liked him. He was quiet, easily abashed and yet very, very dangerous. She decided to do all in her power to help him. And what a scoop this was.

At breakfast the following morning she announced the plan for the day. It didn't occur to her that someone would wish to demur.

'Right then, the files! We'll take them to Durham this morning, the sooner we know what's in them the better, I've already telephoned my boss and so it should be in hand before the end of the day.'

'How long before we get them back?' asked Gennardy. 'Perhaps they can take copies so that I can retain the original. It is very important for us. Yes?'

Pippa placed her hand on his. 'Do not worry.' She reassured him. 'I am sure that all will be well and you will all live happily ever after. Just like a fairy tale.'

'You are making fun of me.' said Gennardy. 'Even when it is so serious you make jokes with me.' He smiled and shook his head.

Dr Anton Hawkins of the Dept. of Russian Studies greeted them on their arrival at Durham University and managed to get them all into his tutorial office where they enjoyed a cup of tea before departing. The visit was long enough to give Hawkins 'a feel' for the people who had thrust this project upon him so suddenly.

It was Wednesday and he had asked Pippa to telephone him, mid-morning, on Saturday.

When they were back in the car Tony said 'right then, what do we do until Saturday?'

'Well I know what I am doing.' She said looking at Gennardy. 'I want to spend the next two days listening to Gennardy Mardosov.' Then turning to look at Li and Tony she went on; 'You won't mind will you.'

They were all in good spirits when they returned to the

caravan. Pippa put a notepad in her bag. Slipped on her most durable shoes and went off with Gennardy for a walk in the surrounding hills. Tony looked at Li and shrugged saying. 'And what would you like to do.'

'We too can walk; maybe. Will this be O.K.' said Li happily.

'I know!' said Tony. 'I will take you to see the most beautiful castle in the whole world.'

'In the whole world.' answered Li joyfully.

Tony Hartill had been whisked away into a dreamland. He couldn't remember a time when he had been as happy as this. They had driven across Northumberland to Bamburgh and on up to the magnificent castle standing high on top of a granite rock outcrop.

They parked the car and entered the castle gate and walked through and up the castle rooms and stairs. Eventually they reached a stone tower and walked up the winding steps inside. They emerged on the round battlement at the top from where they had a wonderful view over the North Sea to the east and over the wild rolling Northumberland countryside to the west.

The sky was clear and the air was full of sunshine. A stiff breeze from the sea lifted Li's hair. She grabbed at it as though it would blow away. 'Tony!' she shouted. 'This is so beautiful. I cannot believe I am here. Tell me that I am here please.'

Tony laughed. 'Of course you are here.' He shouted. 'Four days ago you were on a ship coming from Poland across the North Sea to England just out there.' He pointed.

'Coming to England to you Tony'

Suddenly they were looking at each other earnestly. All Tony could see was a countenance beautiful to behold. It appeared as though through a mist. He stood motionless looking at her. Everything else in the world had ceased to exist. Her lips moved and he heard a voice say; 'Why do you not hold me Tony.'

His arms went around her as she pressed her body close to his. He had never experienced a moment so exquisite. They held each other without a word passing their lips; suspended by a moment that neither would ever forget.

Eventually they disentangled and stood looking at each other again before embracing once more before Li said. 'I want to stay here forever.'

'So do I' he whispered.

'I mean here forever with you' she insisted.

Tony blinked rapidly for a moment. He put his hands on her shoulders and looked at her before saying. 'I think we should go now.'

Li smiled openly at him, radiating her happiness, as she nodded in assent.

They returned to the car and began the journey back to Rothbury. After a few seconds Li said. 'What will be happening now if we return to the caravan?'

'I'm not sure.' Tony replied.

'Why can't we stay here for longer?' She urged.

'What would you like to do?'

'I would like to eat something in the town of Bamber and just walk and look.

Tony was tickled by her pronunciation of Bamburgh but didn't comment.

They found a small café and sat outside overlooking the village green with an ancient church in the background.

Li surveyed the scene and sighed. 'I think this must be the most beautiful place on....' She paused and suddenly the words, translated inside her head into English, rushed out 'anywhere in all of the earth.'

She went on. 'Until I met you I thought that places such as this were in western magazines only. You make dreams come true Tony.' His hands rested on the top of the table and as she spoke she placed her hands on his and gently squeezed them.

Tony was alarmed. He looked straight at her speaking slowly. 'Li, I think you should not misunderstand. You are very young. You know very little about me. I want you to!' before he could continue Li gently interjected.

'You are incorrect.' she said, squeezing his hand again. 'I know so much about you. When Gennardy and I were escaping together we would talk about you all of the time especially when things were very bad. Tony told me all about your wife and your family and your friend, Bill Robinson, especially. He told me about the house of your Mother and Father and about your kindness and so many things. When we left Hull Gennardy and me; we were so anxious. It was just as Gennardy told me. I would feel so much better when we met. When we were in the car coming from Hull I heard your voice. It was making me feel good, so much better. Now I know I have come home.'

Tony listened to her little speech, extricated his hand and patted hers. 'We will just not think about anything else at the moment. We will just share this experience together and make the most of it. We have some big problems to overcome. I want you to be safe. I want Gennardy to be safe.'

Despite the words he found himself saying, Tony knew that, for him, to be apart from Li would not be easy. That sensation of desire had to be balanced by what he considered to be Li's illusion of him and his world. He didn't want the illusion to be punctured, for that would be too cruel; he wanted it to dissolve in painless realisation.

That evening Li and Tony returned to the caravan

blissfully happy in the company of one another. Tony couldn't remember any day in his life with which to compare it.

Reality, however, was suddenly hard on his heels. A note was attached to the caravan door with a message to telephone Bill Robinson immediately. He did so from the site manager's office.

'Tony!' Bill declared. 'You had better know that someone is gunning for you.'

'What do you mean for Hell's sake?'

Bill replied. 'Don't do anything until you have thought this through. A lot has happened since you went up there.'

'Like what Bill?'

'Two blokes called to see you at your house. Maggie must have phoned Mullaney's hit men. There was quite a battle and these two visitors were too good to be amateurs, they gave as good as they got. The police arrested most of Mullaney's mob including the two visitors. Apparently the visitors were released.'

'The rumours are endless.' He went on, 'You are working for the Government, MI5, MI6, MI93 and any other organisation real or imaginary. I have been to see your Mother and Father they are fine. But Tony things are pretty serious; their house was badly damaged after a fire bomb was put through the letterbox.'

There was a long pause while Bill awaited a response.

'The bastards, the bastards, how could they do that? I'll be down there right away Bill.'

'That's just it!' said Bill. 'Do you think you should? Someone is trying to smoke you out, literally'

'What about Mum and Dad.'

'They're fine Tony but pretty upset as you can imagine.'

'Where are they now?'

'They are staying with your Aunt Lily for the time being.'

'Look! I'll come down right away Bill. I'll see you in ab….'

Before he could finish Bill said.

'Tony. I think you should think this through. I don't think you should rush down here. I think you should stay there. This is serious stuff Tony. You have to ask yourself if this is to do with the overseas visitors. Does someone else know about them? I think they do. Why not phone your parents then sit down with the others and have a look at who could know?'

'Thanks Bill. You're right. I'll do that. I'll be in touch.'

Li knew from the expression on Tony's face that something was wrong.

Her anxious voice murmured; 'What is the problem Tony.'

'I thought that if I went out of the way there wouldn't be a problem. But I was wrong. Someone is on to us. They have been to my wife's, Maggies, house. They have also been to visit my parents; with a petrol bomb.'

Li's hands lifted involuntarily in horror to cover her mouth.

'Oh. Tony!'

'I can't leave them where they are. They'll be past themselves. My Mother will be worried about everything; me in particular.'

'Can you not bring them here too Tony. They would be safe here perhaps.'

'That is a good idea. My Mother would feel better if I was close at hand. That would make my Father feel better.' He replied with a weak smile.

Li and Tony sat in the caravan until sunset waiting for

Pippa and Gennardy. The two walkers came bursting into the caravan. Pippa threw her bag down and slumped onto a long seat.

'I don't think I have ever walked so far and talked so much, ever, in one day. It's been marvellous. Hasn't it Gennardy.'

Like Pippa, Gennardy was full of himself until he saw the expressions on the faces of Li and Tony. His smile disappeared. He realised that something was wrong.

'There is a problem please?' he enquired.

Tony looked at him and Pippa who sat silently waiting for him to speak.

'We have a big problem. Let me explain.'

The caravan was silent with the exception of Tony's voice as he related the details of his telephone call.'

He finished with. 'Li and I have had time to think since Bill phoned. I think we should go over everything to see how deep this thing goes. The only thing that we know for certain is that no one knows we are here with the exception of Bill.'

'How do we know that Bill has not told anyone else?' asked Pippa.

'Because he would have told me, when we arrived here and settled in I phoned him confirming the site telephone number in case of emergency. Rather than telephone me he wanted to tell me about my parents so he drove up here. We were out, of course. So he left the message on the door and another with the site manager asking me to contact him. That's the sort of bloke Bill is.'

Pippa said. 'Look I'm going to phone that bloody boffin in Durham to see what he thinks.'

Gennardy went with her to the site manager's office and after several calls she located the man at his home.

Back in the caravan Pippa advised her audience that

the information in the files was, in his opinion, genuine and that he would be contacting her boss first thing in the morning.

'Furthermore.' she added. 'He thinks that the Russians will go to any lengths to retrieve it, especially if it has not been in the hands of British Intelligence as yet. I would also guess that he is ex-Intelligence Services himself. He may be involved now.'

Looking at Gennardy and Li she said. 'And you two had better tell us in detail all you can remember about what was in those files.'

The four talked well into the night. As the time went on Tony and Pippa began making the linkages that could explain the events in Ashington.

Eventually Pippa said. 'It all adds up really. Just as Gennardy said, except that it was so unlikely that we didn't take him seriously enough. Owen Williams and Albert Markham are working directly with Plakinov to overthrow the British Government making Britain into a European Cuba. Gennardy comes along makes contact with Mr Smart and Miss Smith in Moscow. They pass Gennardy's story to a Mr Goodchild who is working with Plakinov. Goodchild cannot withhold the story and so he passes it to London where the Intelligence Services treat it with suspicion because no one walks in off the street in Moscow with that sort of information. They pass it off as a bizarre diversionary plot by the Russians or just a story from some crazed Russian trying to get into the U.K. It gets left on a shelf.'

Pippa stretched her tired body before continuing. 'However Gennardy Smartypants here links up with Li and comes all the way to the United Kingdom with Plakinov's original documents which seriously incriminate our Mr Goodchild. Presumably the Brits don't know about Goodchild, however Goodchild knows that the information that Gennardy and Li have will finish him.'

Tony asked. 'What I don't understand is why the Solidarity lot in Poland didn't use it to ingratiate themselves with the Ruskies or why they didn't keep it.'

'This is simple.' said Gennardy. 'Solidarnosc took great risks in harbouring us. They did this because they wanted to strengthen their links with the west. Any mention to the KGB of these files could have helped to tip the balance. The Soviet leadership was split. Some wanted to bring the whole might of the Soviet army in to Poland to smash the Solidarnosc movement. The only advantage the Poles saw was in helping the British to overcome a workers revolution in Britain. That would have crippled their ambitions. They would like to have a democracy like Britain. They helped us but if they thought that we would jeopardise their prospects they would have killed us. That is why we took such a chance in escaping from them and finding a ship in Gdansk. If they could have got us to Britain without trouble they would help. Any problem and they would kill us. Two dead Russians is little price to pay for the success of Solidarnosc.'

The matter of fact explanation offered by Gennardy created a silence of understanding. Not only had he reinforced his story he had also confirmed the desperate circumstances of his flight to the west; and it wasn't over yet.

They all went to their beds.

Ray Mullaney had been in his bed for hours. Despite several large whiskies he was unable to sleep. He went into the kitchen and filled the electric kettle with water. It was the only thing he could think to do.

Markham had paid him and his two minders a visit and explained to them the importance of the treachery of Tony Hartill to the movement; he had persuaded them that the livelihoods of thousands of miners was at stake and that Hartill was the key man in the North East working for Maggie Thatchers stooges. Then Markham told them that two Russian traitors had been smuggled to the West by British Spies in Moscow. The Russian traitors had been told to report directly to Hartill with papers exposing the financial and political links between the CMU and the Soviet Union. Hartill had been chosen to make the disclosure to the national press and hence the miners, through the newspapers and television, precisely because he was a CMU official.

It did not occur to Mullaney that Markham's explanation was completely fabricated. He accepted every word. What had chilled him were the parting words of Markham. He had passed over photographs of a man and a woman.

'That is Li Saric and that is Gennardy Mardosov the man you entertained on an exchange visit I believe. They have to be with Hartill. I want them smoked out and disposed of and the papers they have must be recovered.'

Mullaney had never seen Markham in such distress.

'Smoked out' and 'disposed of' were not terms that Mullaney could live with. He might be a hypocrite and a parasite but physical violence, arson and murder were not things he could rest easy with.

As usual he had decided to go along with events but those two Yorkshire lunatics had firebombed the home of Hartill's parents just because they said that they didn't know where their son was. The consequences of that event had been too close for comfort. The police had been to his home twice asking questions. Each time he had to wipe the perspiration from his brow as he denied any knowledge of the incidents and promised to pass any information he came by.

Each day at an appointed time Goodchild telephoned a call box near Belgravia. He received and passed information to his contact who in turn kept him informed of the reports from Cheslav and Nicolai.

The fracas triggered by Maggie's phone call had revealed the presence of two British Intelligence agents. Mark Benson had lost his wallet in the battle and the contents clearly identified his role in life. The wallet had been handed to Mullaney who scrutinised the contents with his two minders photocopying all documents for Markham before passing the wallet to the Police.

Mullaney went to the Police station in person to hand over the wallet advising the Police that one of his lads had handed it over to him and he had brought it over immediately. He also took the opportunity to add that he had no idea what had prompted the disturbance in the first place.

On his return from the Police station Mullaney faxed copies of all of the documents in the wallet directly to Markham who in turn advised the KGB Head in London. He was directly responsible to Plakinov co-ordinating the activities of his three unlikely intelligence units.

At the request of the KGB man in London Markham was asked to use his contacts in the Ashington area to find out if Tony Hartill knew anyone with a green Jaguar car. Markham contacted Mullaney who provided the name and address of Bill Robinson. There were very few Jaguars in the district of Winsbreck.

Within twenty-four hours Cheslav and Nicolai had each

hired a car and parked them about one hundred and fifty metres away from the entrance to the driveway leading to the home of Bill Robinson. His house was under surveillance.

Although Anton Hawkins had told Pippa Glendinning that he was planning to telephone her boss in the morning he had already telephoned Sir Hollis Baker-Jackson KG. MC. who was the man directly responsible to the Defence Minister and the Prime Minister as co-ordinator of all Intelligence Services.

The following lunchtime a large military helicopter arrived at Newcastle airport. The three passengers included Baker Jackson, George Norman and his boss. Anton Hawkins knew them all so there were no introductions when they met in the V.I.P. lounge which had been set aside with special security for their arrival.

Hawkins explained how he had come by the files. He then presented Baker-Jackson with a synopsis of what he'd read. 'There is a great deal of information in these files and I have no doubt that it is genuine.'

'What's the gist of it.' asked Baker-Jackson.

'In a nutshell Ivan (the Soviet Union) is in a mess. Their economy is in tatters and they recognise that, for them, time is short. They need a spectacular victory against the Western alliance. To achieve that they have thrown everything into the European Cuba plan: ie The Soviet Socialist Republic of Britain.'

'This is nothing new.' Baker-Jackson commented. 'They have been whittling away at Britain since the last war and whilst we have had our problems in the heavy industries with a few well documented Soviet sympathisers it seems that apart from the present situation, namely the Miner's and our friend Markham, there plan is a non-starter.'

Hawkins nodded his assent. 'I would agree except

for the information in here which suggests the introduction of millions of U.S.Dollars worth of cash being funnelled into the country for Markham to bribe and buy to create absolute chaos. The details are not in this document they have been worked up by Markham and his Republican contacts in Ireland.'

Hawkins paused before going on. 'Believe it or not but this file' he said tapping the document 'even gives us the details of all the account numbers and details of how the money is to be transferred to Markham. The amounts are staggering.'

He paused again to allow his listeners time to absorb the ramifications.

'The implementation of that plan is already in hand but behind schedule. By now a Markham led General Strike should be in its third month. They must be desperate for this is obviously their final throw.'

The four men sat for an hour and a half discussing the implications of what Plakinov had titled the UBAC plan.

Some sandwiches arrived as George Norman said 'and what about the people who delivered this. Our information at this moment is that they are with Tony Hartill. The report from the Moscow 'walk in', Gennardy Mardosov, indicated that Hartill was the only contact he had in Britain. Events since his arrival with Plakinov's assistant bears this out. Yesterday the home of Hartill's parents was letter bombed and the day before two of my agents were waylaid by Markham's heavies. Hartill's wife blew the whistle would you believe. Hell hath no fury etc.'

There was a silence as the sandwiches stimulated an enforced period of contemplation.

George Norman was the first to speak after a swig of coffee.

'We have to find these two Russians and Hartill

before someone else does.'

'I agree.' Baker Jackson confirmed. 'It's obvious that everyone who needs to know knows that they are not far from here and their lives aren't worth a thing to the KGB or their sympathisers. We have to get to them first.'

Hawkins revealed his arrangement with Pippa 'Told her I'd ring her boss this morning. She's no doubt itching to get this into the press.'

Baker-Jackson immediately responded. 'Leave her boss to me. The press mustn't print this lot. Not just yet anyway. Besides who would bloody well believe it even though it is all true.

Markham would have a field day telling the press it was all a capitalist plot. We'd look stupid, Reds under the bed and all that sort of thing.'

'And what about Goodchild and Owen Williams.' asked George Norman.

'Nothing!' said Baker-Jackson. 'Nothing, just leave them to me.'

By mid-afternoon the three visitors were in the air on their return flight to London. Hawkins was on a train out of Newcastle central station on the way back to Durham.

Chapter 21

Preoccupied with the plight of his parents Tony resolved to get them out of Ashington; at least in the short term. He also wanted their home refurbished to obliterate as far as possible the dreadful effects of the fire. Waking from a fitful sleep he rose early the next morning and dressed. As he did so Gennardy woke to ask what he was planning to do.

'I must see my parents. They will be so worried. I would like to get them away from Ashington. I must go to see them.'

'Should I come with you?' said Gennardy.

'No. It will be better if I am on my own.' Tony answered.

'I have money Tony. Look!' Gennardy stretched across to where his trousers were lying and pulled out a bundle of £20.00 notes.

'Where did you get all the money? Tony asked.

'From my friend Jan Oppick, I think he has very much money.'

Not wanting to ask Gennardy to explain this act of generosity Tony accepted the statement as given.

Money was of concern to Tony despite the fact that he was being paid a basic wage as one of those technically back at work after the attempt to break the picket at Ellington. Maggie and Kevin would not accept any financial help from him and so he gave it to his parents who each passed on a £5.00 or £10.00 note to them two or three times a week. The recipients never queried the source of the money.

Escaping from his thoughts Tony responded to Gennardy's offer.

'No you keep that Gennardy. We have a long way to go and we may need every penny.'

'I want you to have something my friend.' said Gennardy.

'O.K I'll take something towards the caravan. Give me £40.00.'

Gennardy duly obliged and Tony went off. The two women woke when Tony closed the caravan door as he left. By the time they got out of bed Tony was in his car headed for Ashington.

Forty minutes later he was knocking on the door of the home of his Aunt Lily who was his Mother's sister. Her house was a neat privately owned terraced house a short walk from where his parents lived. It was almost identical to the house that Tony had shared with Maggie.

As was customary Tony went to the back door and as he opened the yard gate he could see his aunt in the kitchen window. She smiled instantly on seeing him then he could see her speaking as she moved to open the door. The two sisters greeted him together then Lily made her way back into the kitchen to make some tea.

Tony put his arm round his Mother, asking. 'You all right Mother?'

'I'm a lot better for seeing you'

His Father was sitting in a chair by the fireplace. He'd been reading the morning paper. 'It's a right carry on this mind you.' He said.

'I'm pleased you're both all right Dad. I wanted to come down right away, thought better of it. A lot of things have happened since Bill and I went to Hull.'

'Why on earth would anyone want to do such a dreadful thing to us? The whole house could have been burnt down.' said Mrs Hartill.

'I'll tell you, it was something to do with those two fella's that came round looking for you.' 'They're two of Mullaney's pals. You never saw two nastier pieces

367

of work in your life.' stated Tony's Father.

'Would you recognise them then Dad?'

'Course I would! One of them was Yorkshire. The one who did all the talking; I've seen him on the street with Mullaney.'

'I think I know who you mean.' said Tony.

All four chatted solemnly over their cups of tea for twenty minutes before Tony said.

'Look. I think that I am indirectly responsible for what happened. But, I have to say that I never dreamt that it could come to this. Why don't you pack some clothes and we'll get away into the country for a couple of weeks. You can't go back to your house until it's sorted out and anyway you haven't had a holiday for ages.'

'Ah'm not really one for holidays. What do you think?' said Mr Hartill looking at his wife.

After a detailed discussion it was finally agreed that Tony's parents would join him and his friends in Rothbury. Tony was very relieved.

At the insistence of their son the Hartill's were on their way to a holiday in the country. Mrs Hartill's mind was in overdrive trying to think through all of the logistics of living in a caravan. But Tony insisted that he would slip back to their house if necessary to get their mail and whatever they needed. Having telephoned to cancel the daily milk delivery Mrs Hartill had completed the last of her tasks and they set off.

By lunchtime they were back at the caravan site where Tony secured a caravan to accommodate his parents for two weeks. Their unit was situated within a few yards of Tony's. Li, Gennardy and Pippa all came to meet them and suddenly the thoughts of Tony's parents were diverted from the awful events of the previous day.

Having left Mr and Mrs Hartill to make themselves comfortable Tony and his unlikely colleagues went back to their caravan.

As soon as they were inside Pippa said to Tony. 'Gennardy told me about your conversation this morning. About money! Well you don't need to worry for the time being. My paper is sure to contribute for a scoop like this. What's more, Gennardy and Li could make a fortune for their story. What I'm saying is this: If you have any problems in that direction in the immediate future let me know. I'll see that all this is paid for.' She went on, gesticulating with a sweep of her hand.

'Well as a matter of fact my mate Bill helped out. I do have some savings but I wouldn't be surprised if Maggie hasn't got her hands on that. I'll have to check. You're offer has to be helpful. Thanks very much.' Tony replied relieved that at least he wouldn't have any immediate worries with money.

Pippa then changed the subject. Shouting for Li and Gennardy to join them Pippa said. 'What about the rest of the day. Why don't we organise some lunch and then I would like to put some more time in with Gennardy. Is that all right Gennardy?' she asked smiling down on him.

'This is fine.' He said. 'I am very happy.'

Tony had his suspicions as to why Gennardy was so happy but he kept his own counsel.

Mr and Mrs Hartill joined the party for lunch. It turned out to be a very pleasant experience for Tony's parents who were both very curious to see Gennardy again and interested in the roles of Li and Pippa.

After the meal they all chatted together and shared the terrifying event experienced by Tony's parents. It was Pippa who took the lead and after a while the Hartill's were talking freely of their ordeal after which they seemed much happier in their new environment. Sharing their experience seemed to alleviate some of the aftershock of such a dreadful deed.

The lack of sleep and the tension and trauma had made the elderly couple tired. In the middle of the afternoon they took their leave and went for a nap.

When they were gone Tony said. 'This is all very serious and I think we should simply call in the Police and let them do whatever they have to do. I am familiar with a senior Policeman in Ashington. He will talk to the right people and I feel sure that everything will work out. How long before we are found anyway?'

Pippa responded with; 'As long as the Russians think that there is a possibility that those files have not yet been handed over to the British authorities there is the possibility that they will pursue them. Then there's the other point. The files themselves are maybe worth a lot less if Li, in particular, is not there to confirm their origins and the British are sure to have copies supplied by the Poles, which brings me to another point. When the Intelligence Services make contact with us they will probably keep you three apart for days and maybe weeks on end whilst they question you to see what they can discern to confirm that the files are genuine or otherwise. It wouldn't do to arrest Goodchild, Williams and the rest then accuse them, together with others, of spying and treason only to find that the Russians set this whole thing up for some other reason completely removed from anything that we are aware of.'

'But everything we tell you is true.' stressed Gennardy.

Li too stressed that the files were genuine.

'I have no doubt about that.' Replied Pippa; 'But the Intelligence people trust no one. They take nothing for granted. They will find out that it is true so I don't think you need worry. I just think that you should be aware

370

of what will happen.'

'We must get in touch with the Police right away.' insisted Tony. 'The people who did that to my parents were determined to frighten them and bring me back immediately. Once they had me they would have a better chance of discovering the whereabouts of Li and Gennardy.'

Tony stared into space for a moment. He was afraid. He was also calculating the possibilities of what could have happened to his Mother and Father. The whole house could have evaporated if the fire had come in contact with the gas system.

'Thank goodness again for Bill Robinson. If it hadn't been for him I would have gone racing down to my parent's home there and then. That's what they would expect me to do.'

'Well! We are all safe where we are for the moment I think. So let's not do something that we may later regret. It's a beautiful day and we should make the most of it then tonight we can take Mr and Mrs Hartill out to dinner and in the morning we'll have another talk to see how we all feel about things.'

'There's a wonderful spot called Cragside' said Tony. 'It's only a couple of miles from here, wonderful gardens and woodland, with the most fantastic house to browse through, full of inventions and things. What about it?'

They all agreed immediately.

'Good.' said Pippa. 'I'll leave a little note for your parents telling them not to eat. The National Telegraph is taking them out to dinner this evening.'

Tony was grateful for the gesture to his parents. He felt relaxed again and looked forward to making the most of the day.

Cragside was a blaze of rhododendron flowers as they

drove along the narrow lane through the woods towards the big house standing on a crag at the side of a ravine. From whichever way it was approached it was spectacular. After parking the car they made their way to it and marvelled at the towers and arches all built in cream coloured sandstone. They marvelled too at the imagination that had gone into the conception.

'What a wonderful place' said Pippa.

The sun was shining brightly through tall trees and the scents and smells of Mother Earth created an atmosphere enhanced by light and shade and colour.

On arriving at the house they stood opposite the main entrance inside a waist height wall with their arms resting on the top as they looked down, along and over the ravine.

'We can go down there?' asked Li.

'Yes of course.' Tony replied.

'And you?' Gennardy asked Pippa.

'Rather not.' She replied. 'Why don't we have a look at the lake.' she patted her bag containing her fat notebook. 'And I'll fill in a few more gaps of this thrilling story of yours.'

'See you soon!' said Tony as they parted company. Li copied his gesture. 'See you soon!' she confirmed.

That morning whilst Tony was in Ashington Li and Pippa had bought a top and a jumper for Li in a small drapers shop in Rothbury. Li was wearing both garments. As they went down the tiny path into the ravine she slipped off her jumper and hung it over her shoulders with the sleeves tied under her chin. Tony was struck again with her elegance as she walked lightly over the stones that made up the walkway. She was like a dancer with her bare, slender arms outstretched and her hands fluttering to keep her balance as she went quickly along stepping lightly from stone to stone. She stopped and turned on a small plateau at the bottom where a stream gurgled and chuckled over the stones with lights flashing as the sunbeams caught the movement of the waters.

Stretching her arms out, she declared. 'Thees ees so lovely, I thought that Bamber-ra was the best place in the world but I think that this is also.'

'I love this place.' said Tony. 'I have been here several times and each time is better than the last. This time is definitely better than the last.' He said as he stopped in front of her.

'And why is this please?' she said knowingly with a big smile. Her face was alive with happiness and her eyes dancing like the water splashing over the stones in the stream.

'You make me feel so good.' said Tony.

Her voice dropped almost to a whisper as she replied. 'And how do you think you make me feel? You make me feel so good too.'

Tony's arms went towards her and they moved together looking straight into the eyes of one another. 'If they separate us I may not see you for many weeks.' she said quietly.

'Whatever happens you will always be part of me' said Tony. I can hardly understand that we only met such a short time ago. I seem as though I have known you always. It's incredible!'

They stood together in a long firm embrace before finding each other's lips. Their lips lingered gently together and then more firmly and with more intent. They drew away from one another as Tony said. 'Let's find a place that is ours.'

Li put her hand in his and they stepped across the stream away from the path and away from the direction of the house. They made their way up the other side of the ravine stepping over the leaf-strewn earth in

373

shadow from the canopy of the trees above. Suddenly they were in a small clearing and they stopped at the base of a Scots pine tree. The sun shone on them with warmth as they stood facing one another. They stood looking at each other for long moments, then, as though on a signal, each undid the buttons of the others shirt and top. Both garments dropped to the ground together. They embraced and came down on the warm grass. Time stood still and two people oblivious to everything except each other made love. Forever more Li and Tony would remember that afternoon. Li told Tony that they were like the dewdrops captured in the deep long grass during the darkness and now they dazzled and sparkled when exposed to the sun for the first time.

As time slipped by the shadows moved slowly over them as the day blended into early evening.

Pippa and Gennardy had been back to the car and the big house several times looking for their colleagues. They were standing by the wall overlooking the ravine where the two couples had parted company hours before when Gennardy pointed saying to Pippa. 'Look there they are.'

In the distance Tony was walking along with Li each with their arms round the other. 'It looks as though it's been a good day all round' declared Pippa to no one in particular.

Back at the caravan Tony's parents were all dressed and ready for food.

'Where on earth have you been till this time?' Mrs Hartill scolded. 'We've been ready for ages. We couldn't think what happened to you.'

'Cragside is quite bewitching Mrs Hartill.' replied Pippa looking towards Li and Tony with a mischievous grin. 'Spellbinding I would say' she went on.

An hour later they were all washed and changed and ready to eat.

Inside the same restaurant that they had used on that first night in Rothbury they selected their choice of food. Once again Gennardy opted for roast beef and Yorkshire pudding to the amusement of all. Mr and Mrs Hartill enjoyed listening to the story causing the amusement. They smiled warmly at the animated rendition of the story given by Li using the English language in her special way. She was quick to note also the expression on the face of her son as he watched and listened entranced.

Having returned to London Sir Hollis Baker-Jackson set in train a number of enquiries; the first was to the home of Humphrey Goodchild. His wife answered the telephone.

'Hello!' said the voice. 'I'm enquiring after Humphrey. It's his London office. I do hope he's not too poorly. May I talk with him?'

'He isn't here' replied Mrs Goodchild.

'Oh! I see!' The voice went on. 'Where can I contact him; is he well?'

Mrs Goodchild concealed the embarrassment she felt at not knowing exactly where her husband was. In reality she didn't care very much but it was necessary to keep up appearances.

'Well, as you know he has been unwell. If you leave me your number I will ask him to telephone you or you can contact him at this number.'

The man on the other end of the telephone line took careful note of the number as it was dictated and thanked Mrs Goodchild for her help.

The same man made another telephone call and within ten minutes he had the name and address of the Lamb and Garter in Peterborough.

Shortly afterwards the proprietor of the Lamb and Garter received a telephone call. The caller was a woman enquiring after Mr. Goodchild.

Goodchild had advised the proprietor that the only person likely to telephone was his wife and so the proprietor answered on that assumption.

'Humphrey isn't here at the moment Mrs Goodchild. I shall tell him you called.'

'Would you know where I can contact him?' asked the female voice.

'I'm afraid not, he said he would call from time to time in case there was any messages. I can tell him that you called.'

'Oh! It's nothing urgent he'll probably be in touch himself. Thank you for your help'.

The lady who had telephoned the Lamb and Garter sat at a conference table opposite her male colleague who had spoken to Goodchild's wife on the telephone. At the end of the table sat their boss, Baker-Jackson.

'Well what have you made of this business.'

'We've done a report on the movements of our man Humphrey Goodchild and some things are perhaps.' He paused, searching for a word, and then said 'Significant, for instance; timing.'

'Let's see what you have then.' said Hollis Baker Jackson.

'Goodchild was on leave when Mardosov approached Jeremy Smart in Moscow. That was the first contact. Several days elapse and the Russians are apparently oblivious to the contacts between Mardosov and our Moscow embassy people. Goodchild returns to Moscow. A copy of the transcript taken from the interrogation with Mardosov is on Goodchild's desk on his return to Moscow. The following afternoon Li Saric is apprehended by KGB people she recognises. Mardosov rescues Saric and knows that someone has tipped off the KGB. How could they know? The KGB I mean.' The man stopped and looked at his small audience.

'Go on.' said Baker-Jackson politely.

'I don't think that anyone is in any doubt now that the files brought out of Russia by Mardosov are other than genuine. Gennardy Mardosov would know who had tipped off the KGB. He saw Goodchilds picture in the file. Then he realised that the Brits he was talking to were reporting to Goodchild, a KGB informer. I believe Mardosov is telling the truth right down the line.'

'As far as the Russians are concerned Mardosov and Saric left Minsk and disappeared from the train at Brest. On the Russian side nothing is heard of them for months and suddenly a guard with a broken nose and his mouth muzzled by his own belt is found in a hut on the quayside in Gdansk. The belt is Mardosov's trademark. The Russians have clear confirmation from the injured guard that his assailants were Mardosov and Saric. They would show him photographs of the two escapees. Then Goodchild is back in the U.K. at about the same time as the Amada is docking at Hull.'

'And Goodchild knows he is doomed if the file gets into the hands of the Brits.' commented Baker-Jackson.

'Worse than that' came the reply 'our friend Humphrey knows too much. If we discover that he is a traitor then he has to go to Russia for sanctuary but that is not what he would get. When the Russians find out that we know all about their man, he becomes a liability to the KGB too. Suddenly he has no friends, nowhere to run.'

'How on earth have we failed to spot Goodchild all these years.' Baker-Jackson ruminated.

'I'd like to throttle the bastard with my own hands' he went on as he leaned back in his chair and stared at the ceiling before continuing with; 'We have to find him before he finds someone else.'

His two companions nodded their assent and the woman said. 'Goodchild knows that his only hope is to recover those papers before they can be passed to us. He obviously believes that we haven't seen the original papers yet. He will make that assumption because he hasn't been arrested and to the best of his knowledge no one is looking for him from our side.'

'He knows who has the papers and he knows that he will find Mardosov and Saric when he finds Hartill. That means that we know that Goodchild is in the Ashington area.' Baker-Jackson concluded. 'So get a photograph of Goodchild to George Norman and tell him to get his men to concentrate on finding Goodchild and make arrangements for his arrest. When Goodchild is arrested we'll pick up the Honourable Owen Williams MP.'

The two Russian agents, Cheslav and Nicolai found Ashington a drab place devoid of restaurants and pubs. They had taken turns at looking out for the green Jaguar car that came and went from the home of Bill Robinson, in nearby Newbiggin by the Sea, but they had not had sight of Tony Hartill, Li Saric or Gennardy Mardosov.

Their instructions were to wait until they had a sighting or until they received further instructions. Each night they returned to the hotel in Morpeth where they ate and drank before returning to their rooms for sleep and then more boring surveillance the following day.

They made a point of keeping themselves to themselves despite the casual questions asked by staff serving them in the hotel or the shops they visited to make the odd small purchase.

Questions such as 'you on holiday?' or 'where are you from then, you don't seem to come from these parts?' were very common and unlike the cultivated indifference from most of the people they had come into contact with in Greater London.

The consolation that they both enjoyed was the fact that they were very comfortable and they enjoyed their food and the beer. Every four hours they telephoned their London contact. Each call was concluded with a curt. 'Continue surveillance, no further instructions just now.'

The after effects of their battle in the yard of Tony Hartill's home had left Mark Benson and Tim Graham sore and in shock. They needed time to lick their wounds and refresh their aching bodies. After witnessing the Fire Brigade outside of Tony Hartill's home they had returned to their hotel to bathe and sleep before taking further orders from George Norman.

On the second day of their rehabilitation the telephone rang in Tim Graham's hotel room. It was George Norman.

'There's a lady on her way to see you with the photograph of a man we wish to apprehend. It's your job to find him and to make arrangements with the local Police to arrest him and charge him. I have already spoken to the Chief Constable of Northumberland Constabulary who will make two plain clothes men available at your request. I do not need to remind you to read the instructions you receive with care.'

'You have already reminded me' quipped Tim Graham.

'How do you feel after you twenty four hour holiday?' asked George Norman.

'Much better' came the reply 'I have to say though that those bloody miners were meant. Mark and I have so many wheals and bruises that we look like abstract oil paintings.'

'You two'll never be oil paintings.' retorted George Norman laughing at his own riposte.

Just after lunchtime a taxi arrived outside of their hotel. The businesslike young woman stepped smartly out and went to the hotel reception where she enquired for Mr Graham and Mr Benson. The attendant telephoned their rooms and a few moments later Mark Benson slipped down the staircase and took her to his room where Tim was waiting.

The woman looked at them both for an instant and then handed over an A4 sized envelope. 'The boss asked me to give you this.' She said then as Tim accepted the envelope she went on.

'I recognise both of you though you won't have seen me before. And that is all I have to say except Good Luck and Goodbye.'

'I'll see you out.' Mark suggested.

'Don't bother. The taxi is waiting for me.' She smiled and departed.

The envelope contained the photograph of Humphrey Goodchild. As soon as he saw the picture Mark Benson said. 'Hey! That's the geezer that we saw outside of the Hartill's house. He's staying here.'

'So it is.' said his colleague. 'That's a stroke of luck, him staying here. At least we'll not have to look far for him.'

Chapter 22

Saturday morning arrived much too quickly. The four campers awoke in their caravan to the sound of the English countryside. It had rained through the night. The rain had given way to bright morning sunshine and the air was warm and rich with the smell of the damp vegetation.

The two couples had abandoned any pretence. Gennardy and Pippa had shared the double bedroom whilst Li and Tony had shared the lounge.

Pippa and Gennardy entered the lounge where Pippa chided Tony. 'Come on its time to welcome a new day. You are not allowed to stay in bed all day no matter how much you want to.'

'Why don't you go away' said Tony.

'Because you two would stay here all day' came the reply 'besides there's your parents to think of.'

'Oh all right.' said Tony as he sat up yawning and stretching.

Together with Mr and Mrs Hartill they all sat in the sunshine and breakfasted. The smell of cooked bacon blended with the natural ambience to whet appetites.

When they had eaten Pippa said 'I'll telephone Durham and then we can see what is what.'

Accompanied by Tony, Pippa made her way to the site office and telephoned Anton Hawkins.

'I've been waiting for you to call.' said Hawkins. 'The files are very interesting. I have a transcript now so you can call for them, you realise of course that the intelligence services have a copy of this from the Poles.'

Pippa replied 'I'll come down right away.'

'Will you be on your own?' Hawkins asked.

'Why?' came the reply.

'I took the liberty of speaking to an old pal of mine about the files and his people are anxious to have a talk with your friends' said Hawkins guardedly.

'Can I phone you again in a few minutes?' Pippa enquired.

Hawkins had been asked to help to arrange for Li and Gennardy to be apprehended and taken into custody. He had also been told to do nothing that would cause them to be alarmed. If it was possible he was to invite all four to his office to discuss the files and if they agreed arrangements would be made for Mark Benson and Tim Graham to be there with the police.

The previous day Mark Benson and Tim Graham had called at the home of Bill Robinson who had had denied any knowledge of the whereabouts of Tony Hartill. The two agents didn't want to cause unnecessary concern by bringing the Police so they had left the house after leaving him a telephone number to contact them if he subsequently found himself in a position to provide them with information. After seeing their credentials Bill said he would contact them if he had any news. When they left he immediately tried to contact Tony but no one was answering the telephone at the site office.

Bill Robinson was unaware that his telephone had been tapped or that a window cleaner had also been that day leaving several tiny listening devices stuck to the window frames beneath the lintels. The visit of the two agents had confirmed the effectiveness of the listening devices as well as making a first contact with the Robinson household.

Tony's Aunt Lily also received a visit by the two British Agents. Lily explained that she had seen Tony when he had called to take his parents into the countryside for a holiday after their ordeal. Tony hadn't said where he was taking them.

Aunt Lily's telephone was also tapped.

Pippa and Tony left the site managers office and stood outside while Pippa related her conversation with Hawkins.

'I knew he was connected to the security services. He has obviously told them that the files are genuine. He wants us to get Li and Gennardy to his office. He said they, his friends that is, were anxious to talk to our friends. I'll just bet they are' she mused.

'We can't just take them there without telling them.' Tony replied. 'They have had enough of an ordeal. We have to make it as easy as possible for them.'

Just then Bill Robinson rolled onto the site at the wheel of his green Jaguar and saw Tony and Pippa deep in conversation outside the site manager's office. Bill stopped the car, wound down the window, and shouted across. A few minutes later Li and Gennardy were seated in the caravan with Bill, his wife Kate, Tony and Pippa.

Pippa explained her telephone conversation with Hawkins emphasising that she had told him she would phone back in a few minutes. Bill explained the visit he and Kate had from the two Intelligence Officers.

'Well I know the whole story' said Pippa 'each day I've posted my notes to my boss so an independent source has a comprehensive version of this remarkable tale. I can go myself to get the files from Hawkins but if I do, I will no doubt be followed. We may as well leave them where they are.'

'But these files are our ticket to get into U.K.' said

Gennardy.

Bill Robinson chipped in. 'We had two blokes from the security services at our home yesterday it's just a matter of time before they find you. I think we have all done everything we can. You don't have anything to worry about. The sooner you hand yourself over to the authorities the sooner you will be free to live a normal life.'

'What about these British people working with KGB' replied Gennardy.

'If the authorities have the evidence then they will be arrested. The sooner you and Li substantiate the evidence in the files the better it will be for you.' said Tony.

'O.K I do as you say.' said Li. 'we have to believe, what about you?' she went on, looking at Gennardy who answered. 'O.K I too agree. How do we do it?'

'Well why not come back to our place and invite the authorities along. That way we will all be witness to the event and we will have met our obligations to our recent visitors from the MI5 or whatever they're from.' said Kate unexpectedly.

Bill Robinson looked at his wife slightly surprised and said. 'That's a good idea.'

As Tony Hartill and Pippa walked across the caravan site to advise Hawkins of their plans for the immediate future they were unaware of Cheslav sitting in a hired car parked fifty yards away. He had followed the distinctive green Jaguar carrying Bill Robinson and his wife from their home to the hideaway in Rothbury.

After a brief farewell to Tony Hartill's parents Bill and his wife set off for home. Cheslav did not follow them. He sat in the car fascinated by the sight, at last, of his quarry. He continued to watch as Li and Gennardy sat round a small table outside of the caravan drinking tea with four others.

Unaware that they were being watched Tony's charges and parents sat in the late morning sunshine discussing their future.

'It'll all be a bit strange I suppose when we actually get to your friend Bill's, have our dinner and then wait for the Police to come.' said Pippa.

'For God's sake, you make it sound like the Last Supper.' Tony responded.

'What is this Last Supper?' asked Gennardy.

'We are just making a joke about when we meet the authorities' answered Tony.

'Joke, joke, joke, all the time joke and we are to be arrested' sighed Gennardy shaking his head.

They all laughed nervously. Everyone could feel the tension. Gennardy was especially edgy.

They all said their farewells to Mr and Mrs Hartill before storing their possessions in the boot of Tony's car.

As Tony manoeuvred his way out of the caravan site Cheslav started the engine of his vehicle and followed from a discreet distance.

Kate and Bill Robinson had been busy since they returned to their home. Bill insisted that they prepare a special meal so that their Russian charges could enjoy some Northumbrian hospitality. Bill was aware of Tony's concern for Li and he wanted the party to be special so he arranged a barbecue and set down a couple of bottles of champagne on ice.

It was mid-afternoon when the guests arrived.

There were smiles and handshakes and hugs all over again as guests and visitors mingled outside the front door of Bill's home. They all removed their bags from Tony's car and brought them into the house.

'None of us knows exactly how things will turn out so if you leave everything here in the hall. If anyone wants a wash or the bathroom or anything there's one here.' said Bill.

Kate contributed by saying 'and there's another at the top of the stairs if that one's busy.'

They all made their way through the house to the snooker room and the conservatory. The doors of the large conservatory were wide open. The view across the large garden was eye catching with patches of cream and yellow narcissus, areas of bluebells and stretches of dark red tulips all around the edge of the lawn. Young apple and cherry trees punctured the newly cut lawn in clouds of blossom to compliment the stunning art of nature.

'This is my sanctuary.' he said as they emerged from the conservatory 'and this for me is the best time of the year.'

'It is so beautiful' Li responded 'you didn't describe the colours to me Genna.' She went on turning to look at Gennardy.

'I didn't see it at this time of the year.' He replied.

'Everything else is just like you described it. You do not realise how much Gennardy told me about all these things. When we were making our journey to England I learned to improve my English very much talking about Gennardy's visit to your country.'

They all listened enchanted by her voice and there was a short silence before Tony said. 'Perhaps England will soon be your country too.'

Bill poured glasses of champagne and they toasted one another.

George Norman was disappointed that his men had not

attained their objective of taking Li and Gennardy into custody. Apart from the owner of the green Jaguar and Tony Hartill's Aunt Lily there was no other link that would locate their host Bill Robinson.

Having arranged the phone tapping he persuaded the local police to find an empty property as close as possible to the home of Bill Robinson to base the receivers that would pick up the transmissions from the listening devices. The police had obtained access to a small semi-detached house that was for sale and situated less than one hundred metres from the garden wall surrounding the home of Bill Robinson. The street was a cul-de-sac terminating at the garden wall.

Two men arrived to take up their station in the upstairs bedroom of the temporary listening- station. Their task was to listen in on the Robinsons until the location of Tony Hartill and the Russians was known. As soon as they had their equipment working they realised that they were listening to a conversation among the very people they were there to find. They immediately communicated their news to George Norman's office.

When Pippa had telephoned Anton Hawkins the source of the call registered on a display in a special centre that had been set up to assist the intelligence services during the Miners Strike. George Norman knew that Hawkins would receive a call on Saturday morning so he had used the facility to intercept Hawkin's telephone calls. On receiving the address from where the call had come, Benson and Graham immediately contacted the local Police.

By mid-afternoon the two intelligence agents, supported by two policemen were talking to the caravan site manager who confirmed that he had let a caravan to four people as described and they had left the site just an hour earlier.

'Do you reckon some one's having us on.' said Tim Graham. 'This lot's like Scotch mist.'

'Bloody uncanny.' answered Benson.

'D'you think they'll be back.' he asked the site manager.

'Can't say really they put some bags in their car; but on the other hand they paid two weeks rent and they've only been here a short while. Why don't you ask the couple who came here a couple of days ago, they're Mr Hartill's parents?'

Mr and Mrs Hartill weren't in their caravan either so they made a telephone call to George Norman.

'Sorry Boss, we're too late again.' said Benson.

'It's alright, we've got them' came the reply. 'They're at the home of Mr and Mrs Robinson and they're having a bloody party would you believe.'

'Are we invited?' asked Benson.

'I've just had the listening boys on the phone and they're telling me that the party is a prelude to them giving themselves up.'

'And when do they plan to do that?' asked Benson.

'That's what we're waiting to hear.' Norman answered. 'Get back and sit in with the listening boys and wait for further instructions. I will make arrangements with the Police so that we don't tread on too many toes. Put someone on the front of the house to make sure that we see if anyone else enters and if anyone tries to leave stop them.'

'Bloody bureaucracy' muttered Benson.

Having followed Tony Hartill's car back to Bill Robinson's house Cheslav communicated the fact that they had found Mardosov and Saric to their London contact.

'At last!' sighed the Ambassador, who took all the

details with some relief.

'What do we do now?' asked Cheslav.

'We need them both dead and we also want the files.'

'What happens if they leave?' said Cheslav.

'They don't. You go in and keep them there. Someone will join you as soon as I can make contact. You will take your instructions from him. It is important that he interrogates them.'

Cheslav made his way back to Nicolai who confirmed that the green Jaguar and Tony Hartill's car were still at the front door of the house. The two men then recovered two machine pistols from beneath the front seats of their car and discussed their plans as they sat in the vehicle checking the weapons out of the line of sight of any passers by. Cheslav went off to reconnoitre the home of the Robinson family. Before leaving he instructed Nicolai to drive the car across the entrance gates that accessed the short driveway to the front door of the Robinson house if he saw anyone preparing to leave.

Within the Robinson household hosts and guests sat and chatted enjoying the warm evening sunshine outside the door of the conservatory as they sipped their drinks. The atmosphere was subdued but pleasant.

'You know I have to remind myself all the time that I'm not dreaming.' said Tony after a long reflective lull in the conversation. 'Whenever fate pulls Bill and I together things seem to happen, sometimes the most unexpected things' he went on, looking across at Li.

Li smiled across at him without replying.

Pippa picked up the conversation with 'I must have one of the best stories a Journalist could ask for and I must agree none of this seems real. I have to pinch myself from time to time. It's all so far fetched and yet

I know that it is all true.'

'Eet all seems very real to me' Gennardy offered 'we have come so far and now that we are here I feel more worry than I did when I was in Moscow. They couldn't send us back? Would they?' he asked.

'Of course not' Pippa responded. 'Your story will be in every newspaper in the Western world. I expect you to be rich and famous, me too' she said pointing to herself to emphasise the point. Then she continued; 'They will almost certainly make a film of your exploits and I will write the book.'

'What will we do if we stay here?' asked Li. 'Will we be able to get work with payment and live in a big house like this.'

'I hope so' said Bill 'but I have to tell you that it took me most of my lifetime before I could afford to live like this.'

'I would be happy if I have a house like you in a terrace in Ashington. For me this would be good.' said Gennardy. 'Then maybe we can buy some beer in the pub sometimes eh! And maybe sometimes we play snooker and we get a little drunk or maybe we get very drunk.'

Everyone laughed and Gennardy's unease seemed less intense.

'Let's have some music and do a little dancing.' Bill suggested and followed up by bringing a mobile music centre out of the snooker room. He inserted a tape of music and addressed the company.

'And this tape is called; *Songs for swinging lovers,* so take your partners.'

The slow rhythm of the music supported by the sighing melody filled the conservatory and overflowed into the garden. Tony and Li stood together on the marble floor and moved about slowly and gently as the voice of Frank Sinatra spoke the universal language of new love.

Cheslav returned to the Mercedes and slipped into the passenger seat. 'They must use this drive entrance for everything.' He advised his colleague. 'The wall goes right round the house. There is another door on the other side but it looks as though it hasn't been used for years.'

'What do you suggest we do now.' asked Nicolai.

'Well they're all on the other side of the house, in the garden. You can see them over the wall from the other side, through the trees.'

'How many?' said Nicolai.

'Six I think. They're having a party. You go now and check it out before we report back.'

Nicolai left the car and Cheslav transferred into the driver's seat to await his return.

Twenty minutes later Nicolai was back and the two men sat in the car discussing their plans.

They compared observations and agreed their plan for moving into the house and holding their quarry.

Tim Graham left the semi-detached house listening house, got into the large van parked outside and drove it the short journey to a spot that gave him a view of the entrance and drive leading up to Bill Robinson's house. The Mercedes was parked immediately opposite to the drive entrance and Tim Graham watched as Cheslav got into the car and Nicolai got out a few minutes later. Recognising them he used his two way radio to call Mark Benson who was enjoying a cup of tea in the listening house.

'Got a couple of old friends in my sights' he declared 'remember the two big boys we saw outside the home of the Hartills after the fire?' before Mark could answer he went on 'They're doing a surveillance job on the Robinsons place.'

'Yeah, I know who you mean, funny how the same faces keep cropping up' sighed Mark.

'They are up to no good and I reckon we had better get in there quick and sort something out. We don't want another cock-up.'

Tim Graham involuntarily nodded to himself saying 'Get in touch with the boss pronto and see what he says.'

Tim Graham was on edge waiting for Mark to call back. He saw Nicolai return to the Mercedes and watched as the two Russian agents had an animated conversation.

'Come on Benson!' he said to himself. 'What's keeping you?' then 'Christ!' as he watched another car draw up further along the road and the pink face of Humphrey Goodchild preceded his large body as he emerged from his car and made his way to the Mercedes.

Tim picked up his radio and called Mark Benson. 'Our man Goodchild has just arrived too. The three of them are in the black Merc. What's the boss say?' The words rushed out.

He's making arrangements with the police and some bugger higher up. Says he'll call back in a few minutes.

'Awh shit' exclaimed Tim as he watched the three men step out of the Mercedes.

'What's wrong?' asked Mark Benson.

'The bastards are going in and they're not ice cream cornets they are hiding under their jackets. They've taken off their jackets and they're hiding machine pistols under them. They are going around the back from either side and Pinky is going up the drive, he has his jacket on so you can bet he's carrying something smaller. These buggers are meant. We'll have to go in

392

ourselves and surprise them before there's a bloody slaughter.'

Mark Benson listened to the commentary of his friend as he redialled George Norman. It seemed an age before the receiver at the other end was lifted and a female voice said. 'Who's speaking?'

'It's me Benson. Tim Graham has just watched the two gooks going into the Robinsons house and they're armed to the teeth. What's more Pinky is making his way up the path and that bastard wont be delivering the milk. I must speak to the boss.'

'He's in the building but he's not here. It'll take me a minute or two…..'

Before she could finish her sentence Benson said 'cant wait, me and Tim are going in, the listening boys will keep you informed.' Whereon he slammed down the receiver and gathered his jacket as he ran from the house.

Breathless from his exertions Mark Benson arrived at the van and jumped into the passenger seat.

'Couldn't get through to the boss he's going through all the bloody bureaucracy.' he gasped.

Tim Graham looked at him saying 'What do you reckon? We have no weapons. We can't just go in there and say – now look fella's don't be naughty and just give yourselves up'

'Don't I just know it' Benson agreed.

Tony and Li were swaying gently encouraged by the words of and music while Pippa, Gennardy, Kate and Bill sat watching them when the sound of chiming bells punctured the tranquil scene. The chimes were in response to the button pushed by Humphrey Goodchild as he stood at the front door of the house.

All six stopped and looked towards the source of the

sound. Bill stood up and said, unnecessarily, 'It's just the door bell.' as he walked from the conservatory, through the snooker room and into the hall with Kate close behind him.

From the hall Bill could see the silhouette of a large man through the transluscent glass panels in the porch doorway. He opened the door with 'Yes?'

Goodchild was at his most charming as he smiled and said. 'Good evening. Would you mind if I came in and had a word with you? I am from the security services. It's rather important.'

Bill looked at Kate whose face was the picture of anxiety. Turning back to Goodchild he replied.

'I don't see why not. Would you come into the dining room? We have some friends with us. Will it take long?'

'Nothing to worry about' replied Goodchild 'just a formality really'

All three went into the dining room that lay across the hall from the snooker room and the conservatory. They all took a seat around the dining table.

Goodchild opened the conversation with 'You have a lovely home Mr Robinson.'

'Yes well! We think its fine.' Then turning to look at Kate he went on 'Don't we?'

Kate was sitting bolt upright in her chair. The pallor in her face was grey. 'Are you alright?' asked Bill.

Cheslav and Nicolai had each scaled the wall at either side of the house and made their way unseen towards the back of the house. They were at either side of the conservatory each within a few yards of the open double doors that led to the garden. They heard the sound of the chimes through the sound of the music and watched as Tony and Li stopped dancing and Pippa and Gennardy stood up.

Cheslav nodded to Nicolai and the two men moved quietly and swiftly into the conservatory each with a machine pistol in their hand.

'Stand absolutely still.' Cheslav shouted in Russian then in English he said 'do not move.'

Gennardy's head swung round in response to the demand. Screeching with rage he moved across the conservatory towards Cheslav who was looking away. He was almost reached him when Nicolai pulled the trigger on his weapon. Two of the hail of bullets caught Gennardy, one in the thigh and one in the hip turning him in the air as he collided with the big Russian.

Nicolai shouted at the top of his voice. 'Stand absolutely still. Do not move.'

A shaken Cheslav got quickly to his feet and cocked his weapon. 'You.' he said to Tony 'sit there facing out of the window.'

Tony did as he was asked after first glancing at Li.

Then to Pippa he said. 'You, sit there' pointing to a seat on the other side of the conservatory. 'Turn the chair around and look out of the window. Do not turn around.'

An ashen faced Pippa did exactly what she was told.

Walking across to Li Cheslav grabbed her by the upper arm and spat in her face before pushing her into a chair saying 'It's been a long time my treacherous little friend all that effort and all for nothing.'

In the dining room all three occupants jumped at the sound of the burst of gunfire. Goodchild immediately pulled a handgun from inside his jacket and pointed it at Bill. 'You will sit here whilst your wife and I investigate.' said Goodchild. 'Should you decide to ignore my instruction your wife will be the first in line. I'm sure you understand.'

For Bill Robinson the events were so unexpected

and terrifying that he decided to do exactly as Goodchild ordered until he could think straight.

Using Kate as a shield Goodchild left the dining room and crossed the hall entering the snooker room before looking into the conservatory where Cheslav was pulling a distraught Gennardy across the floor. Gennardy was groaning involuntarily through gritted teeth as the pain from his wounds seared through his body.

'Pull him in here' instructed Goodchild. Pointing to the leg of the snooker table he went on 'Sit him on the floor with his back to the leg and remove his belt.'

Cheslav did as he was asked and then Goodchild said 'Put the belt between his teeth and fasten the buckle behind the table leg. Mr Mardosov has a taste for such things I believe.'

Cheslav gleefully followed his instructions as Nicolai moved into the doorway to witness the procedure.

Gennardy's position looked as cruel as the pain he felt. Kate looked at Goodchild with disbelief written all over her. 'He'll die. He's bleeding to death.' She said slowly as she pointed to the blood seeping into the expensive woollen carpet.'

'Put some clean linen over his wounds to stem the bleeding a little. He'll be all right for the time I need to talk to him' sneered Goodchild who then turned to Nicolai instructing him to bring Bill Robinson from the dining room.

'On the floor' Goodchild ordered as Bill entered his snooker room to witness the plight of Gennardy.

'God, he needs treatment. You can't leave him like that.' Bill blurted.

'On the floor and shut up; I will remind you that you are completely expendable so do exactly as I ask.'

Bill had no doubts that his captor meant what he

said. The charming man he had seen at his front door a few minutes earlier was undoubtedly a sadistic monster.

In the listening house the noise of the gunfire startled the operator.

'Fuck'in Hell' he shouted to his colleague. I've just heard someone speaking a foreign language, Russian I think, and then gunfire. Nearly blew my ears out.'

'Jesus' came the reply from his mate. 'I'll get on to George Norman. Tell those two in the van to keep their heads down. We're in a bloody war zone.'

Messrs Benson and Graham were just getting out of the van when they heard the faint but unmistakable sound of small arms rapid fire.

'Oh my God' exclaimed Benson.

A moment later the two way radio bleeped and the operator in the listening house conveyed his news.

'We heard it.' said Graham. 'We're going in to have a look see.'

The two men ran around the outside of the garden wall and after making sure that there was no one watching they dropped into the garden and concealed themselves behind the new foliage that covered the many trees and shrubs in the garden.

The day had given way to early evening and the sun dipped below the horizon. The two men had a clear view of the inside of the conservatory. They could see Li, Tony and Pippa sitting in chairs staring out of the windows. Occasionally they caught a glimpse of the occupants of the snooker room through the open door and the secondary glazing at the back of the conservatory.

As they watched they saw Li then Pippa and then Tony Hartill taken one at a time into the house.

Curtains were closed in two of the upstairs rooms and the lights were switched on inside, the two agents sat in the bushes witnessing the lines of light where the curtains were not completely closed.

'There's no easy way to do this.' Said Benson 'get inside I mean. What do you reckon?'

'One of us better get back to the house. We need someone to put that van across the driveway at the first sign of anyone trying to leave. They have the two cars in the drive and that Mercedes standing in the street; theres nine of them all together so they'll need all three cars to get everyone away.' Tim Graham replied.

'Maybe not.' said Benson sombrely. 'Perhaps one car will be enough.'

'For God's sake don't say that.' replied his mate.

George Norman sat in London assembling a picture of the events in the Robinsons house. The telephone tap picked up a call from the house made to London by Goodchild. The conversation was held in Russian.

'Careful bastard isn't he?' said Norman to his assistant who also spoke fluent Russian.

The two listened intently as Goodchild reported that the two fugitives were caught at last but there was no sign of the documents. The respondent in London said that a furniture van would arrive at the house as soon as it could be arranged and the prisoners and hostages were to be put in it and taken to a safer place where there was time for a thorough interrogation.

Goodchild finished the exchange with 'Get the van here in the next hour or two at the latest. The Brits must be very close behind us.'

Ray Mullaney couldn't believe his ears. It was eleven O' clock at night and Albert Markham was on the telephone.

'Get that furniture van out right now and get it to Hartill's pal, Robinson's place.'

'At this time of night' Mullaney queried.

'Right now we've got Hartill and company and we want them out now.'

'What's going on?' Mullaney protested.

'Look Ray. Get this done or you will never get anything else done in your life. I mean it. All you have to do is to ensure that the van gets there pronto.'

There was a pause as Mullaney failed to respond.

'Do it now. It's been arranged as part of the contingency plan for days. Just do it. I'll make a couple more phone calls to make sure you do.'

Reluctantly Mullaney got into his car and went to see the man who owned a house contents removal business. The man had been paid a handsome retainer to transport miners past the vehicle inspection points at any time he was asked. He was to drop everything he was doing if a request came through and one of the vans had to stand in his yard readily available at any time.

As specified by Markham, Mullaney handed over an extra £200.00. The man was suspicious but he complied on seeing the colour of the money.

Chapter 23

Kate attended to Gennardy's injuries by placing large pads of clean linen over his wounds and securing them with a bandage to limit the bleeding. He was weak from the blood loss and the after shock. Kate's attempts to have the belt removed from his mouth went unheeded by Goodchild who insisted on no concessions. Gennardy looked grotesque with his face screwed up by both the pain and the distortion to his features caused by the belt.

Tony was transferred from the conservatory and taken to the dining room. His instructions were clear and forcefully put by his captors.

'You will not attempt to move from this room. If you do the consequences will be dire and not just for you. Remember we have nothing to lose. Understand?' Goodchild stated.

Tony nodded.

'Now about this other woman; who is she?' was the next question.

'Which one'? asked Tony.

'The English woman of course' Goodchild said deridingly.

'A friend that's all.' came the reply.

'She is a journalist who works for the National Telegraph Mr Hartill and from now on when I ask a question I want the right answer and quickly. I consider my time valuable and it will all be very civilised for you if I enjoy your full co-operation. If not.....' Goodchild shrugged and smiled menacingly.

'I will leave you to consider this while I talk to someone else. You will not move from where you sit erh... unless you want your head blown off.'

Having made his point Goodchild closed the curtains across the window and went off. Tony watched and listened as his inquisitor left the room closing the door and stepping across the hall. His footsteps echoed on the parquet floor until he stopped and picked up the telephone.

Tony could hear Goodchild's voice clearly but he couldn't understand a word. The conversation was in Russian.

Li and Pippa had been taken upstairs to separate bedrooms at the rear of the house. Goodchild had made his intentions very clear when he told them 'When I ask questions you will answer them and be accurate in every detail. If you do not do so the first time I can assure you that you will the second time.'

Pippa was very surprised when she realised how much he knew about her and decided that this man was no fool and he was prepared to pursue his aims with ruthless determination and

Li knew that any pleading on her part would fall on deaf ears.

Li was distraught for Gennardy who had brought her through all those hazards and tribulations only to be thwarted with his dreams almost in his grasp. She wished she had been kinder to him. Goodchild resisted her attempts to be allowed to see to Gennardy's wounds.

'He may die!' she told him.

'Then we shall turn all our attentions on you. Particularly when we get you back to Mother Russia.' said Goodchild.

'You will never do that.' said Li scornfully.

'Do not be so sure.' said Goodchild with certainty. 'The British are famous for doing deals to save their own people.'

Li's jaw dropped at this as she watched him leave the room.

Pleased that everything had gone so well Goodchild went downstairs, looked in on his prisoners and then told Nicolai to check the gardens outside. He then went into the kitchen where Kate was. She had been allocated the kitchen and been told to stay there.

'My husband, please, you do not need him.' said Kate.

'Just ensure that you follow your instructions and nothing will happen to your husband.' Goodchild replied speaking in German.

'You see I know much about you. How your family fled from East Germany, how you met your husband and also the fact that many of your family are still in the German Democratic Republic. Now then! You do not want anything unpleasant to happen to your husband and your relations; do you?'

Kate did not reply. She had had a bad feeling instinctively ever since Gennardy and Li had arrived at her home. She was also well aware of that Goodchild meant every word of what he said.

Goodchild finished with; 'you will do everything I say.'

Kate nodded slowly.

Tim Graham had just rejoined Mark Benson in the garden after slipping over the wall and reporting back to the listening house.

'What's fresh?' queried Mark.

'The boss has phoned up to say that Pinky has phoned for transport. There's a bloody furniture lorry coming to pick them up.' Tim answered.

'What about us?'

'The boss has to clear the red tape. In the meanwhile

402

we're on our own.'

'Shush' said Mark suddenly putting his hand on Tim Graham's sleeve to caution him.

'Might be a chance on here if we can do something with him' he continued as they watched Nicolai enter the garden from the conservatory.

'He's a big'un. What do you think?'

The two men held a short whispered conversation and then separated.

Stepping into the garden Nicolai stood for a moment breathing in the fresh air. The only sound to be heard was the gentle rustling of leaves and the engine noise from cars in the distance. The air smelled good.

Nicolai was glad that this mission was almost at an end. He had liked what he had seen of England but it made him feel uncomfortable to think that he could have qualms about the way in which the United Kingdom was portrayed in his country. From what he'd seen even the striking miners were better off than most of his own countrymen.

He wondered what Cheslav thought. Cheslav was very deep and very loyal to mother Russia. He could understand and relate to Cheslav but he didn't care for Goodchild. He wondered if there were traitors like Goodchild betraying his country.

The night was quiet and peaceful as Nicolai strolled around the gardens of the house. He breathed in deeply. He was tired and he wished that he could rest but that could not be. It was going to be a long night.

Nicolai had almost completed his check of the gardens when he heard a sound like that of a twig breaking. He stiffened. Suddenly he was acutely alert. He stood silently in the half-light.

Another sound came to him. It was the sound of breathing; could it be some animal?

He made his way in that direction. The sound was coming from behind the bush in front of him. He crouched and went forward. A man jumped up before him in the gloom startling him so that he stepped back slightly. As he did so a heavy weight crashed upon his head and shoulders. Nicolai staggered under the weight of the blow until he crashed to the ground with a thud.

Tim Graham and Mark Benson were so pleased their plan had worked. Despite his size and strength their man had succumbed to the blow received from the cricket bat. Whilst their man was stunned they pulled his hands behind his back and snapped hand cuffs on him rendering him helpless. From Bill Robinson's garden shed they took a ball of twine and used it to secure their victim to the base of a tree. On completing the job they took a couple of minutes to regain their composure and decide their next move.

Having secured the first of their targets the two men moved around the garden to the side of the conservatory and hid behind the thick foliage of a large shrub to wait for a further opportunity.

After a few minutes Cheslav came from the snooker room into the conservatory. He placed his machine pistol on a table and then stepped out through the conservatory doors and into the garden.

Cheslav too was tired. It had been a long day and it was far from over. He flung his arms back and sucked the evening air into his lungs. He was tense. His hopes and thoughts meandered through his weary mind; the sooner the van arrived to take them all away the better. Plakinov would be pleased to know that Sarich and Mardosov were once again under his control even if he didn't have direct contact. Cheslav reflected on how Plakinov might express his gratitude when he was back in the USSR.

As he stood in the garden Cheslav looked around for signs of Nicolai. He wasn't alarmed at not seeing him. Nicolai could take care of himself. He must be around the side.

Cheslav stretched his arms again and breathed deeply. The last hour and a half had been stressful. Everything was in hand now. All they had to do was wait for the van.

After a few minutes stretching the big Russian went to look for Nicolai.

As soon as Cheslav was out of sight Tim Graham moved silently over the short distance and entered the conservatory picking up the machine pistol and returning to join his colleague.

'They mustn't have a clue that we are onto them.' Tim said.

'Arrogant bastards aren't they.' commented Mark Benson.

'What now? We have to take him out now before he finds his mate.'

After a few words the two men moved silently round the house in the opposite direction to Cheslav who was half way round the house and passing the front door when he began to feel uneasy. There was no sign of his colleague.

'Nicolai.' He called in a suppressed voice.

There was no response. As soon as he was past the front door and in the shadows Cheslav took his handgun from the holster beneath his jacket and moved quickly to check the other side of the house. When he was around the corner he could see movement at the base of a tree. He moved cautiously towards it with his gun at the ready.

'Do not utter a word.' said a voice in Russian as he got to within a few yards of Nicolai.

Cheslav froze.

'Who is that? Nicolai?'

In the half-light Cheslav realised that the writhing body at the foot of the tree was his partner. Alarm bells banged in his head and he swung around ready to shoot.

A single bullet thudded into Cheslav's shoulder spinning him around. With some difficulty he retained his balance then he winced through gritted teeth as another single bullet hit him just above the elbow grazing his arm and entering his chest. Cheslav fell to the ground and with great agility and strength rolled over and was back on his feet in a second despite his wounds. Mark Benson was at him instantaneously from behind chopping at his neck as Tim Graham stepped out from behind a bush and barked a command in Russian.

'Stand absolutely still or this will cut you in two.'

Gasping for breath a wide-eyed Cheslav obeyed as he stared at his own machine pistol.

'Over here by your colleague.' came the order in Russian.

Again Cheslav complied with the request. A few seconds later he was securely fastened to the same tree as Nicolai. Each man had a handkerchief stuffed in his mouth with his head secured to the tree with twine and his hands tied behind his back.

The two British agents were sweating profusely from their exertions and from the tension and danger of their exploits. Again they took a few moments to restore their composure before moving in on the house.

'And now for Pinky!' exclaimed Tim.

'Too fucking right' confirmed his colleague as they covered the distance over the rear of the house to the door of the conservatory.

With their weapons at the ready the two men entered

the conservatory and crossed the floor to the door leading to the snooker room.

As they looked in they saw Gennardy attached to the leg of the snooker table. His eyes opened and rolled before he closed them again. Saliva trickled down his chin. His twisted face was grotesque with pain, anger and discomfort. A mixture of blood and urine soaked his trousers and the floor where he sat.

'Poor bastard' commented Tim.

Before they could help him they heard a voice from the hallway. It was the voice of Goodchild speaking in Russian.

'Cheslav, where are you? Is Nicolai there?'

'Da'? Tim Graham answered the affirmative in Russian.

Goodchild entered the room full of himself. He was about to speak then he saw the machine pistol and the man who held it standing immediately in front of him. Goodchild could hardly believe his eyes. Tim Graham, who had been standing out of sight at the side of the door, came into view. The body of Goodchild sagged as he realised how the tables had turned.

'Sit in this chair.' said Tim.

Goodchild obeyed and sat on a low chair situated in an alcove by the door.

'More twine required' quipped Mark Benson to his colleague. 'We may as well nail this slippery bastard for the time being.'

Tim Graham left to recover the twine from the garden as Mark Benson watched Goodchild.

'What a treacherous bastard you turned out to be,' Said Benson before continuing 'and where are the others? Speak up man but not too loud.'

Goodchild spoke quietly. 'They're in different rooms.'

'Who's where? And they'd better all be in better

shape than this poor sod.' said Benson.

'The two women are upstairs. The wife of our host is in the kitchen.' came the reply.

'Where's the other bloke then?'

'In the dining room' sighed Goodchild in fretful resignation.

Bill Robinson lay on the snooker room floor tied to the snooker table leg diagonally opposite to Gennardy. He had watched as Benson and Graham had come into the room. His brain was frantically trying to work out what was going on. Like his captors these blokes were also speaking in English and Russian.

'Who are you?' ventured Bill.

'Don't worry pal we're on your side. We'll have you clear in a couple of minutes.' replied Mark Benson.

'Do you hear that Gennardy?' shouted Bill Robinson at the top of his voice.

Gennardy made no response.

'Kate. Kate!' shouted Bill again at the top of his voice. 'Get me out of this tangle.'

'Kate walked cautiously from the kitchen, across the hallway and looked gingerly into the snooker room.'

Mark Benson saw her approaching. 'Don't worry we're on your side. All will be well shortly.'

Kate looked at Goodchild who stared at her with a face filled with menace as he said. 'You are very fond of your husband Mrs Robinson. Anyone can see that.'

Kate Robinson looked quickly in the direction of her husband.

'What's he ranting about.' said Bill.

Without warning Kate Robinson began to close in on Mark Benson.

'No! No! No!' she shouted 'You do not understand.'

'What the hell!' exclaimed Benson as he found himself struggling with this woman who had obviously taken leave of her senses.

Goodchild was off his chair in seconds. His speed and agility defied his size, weight and years as he made the three steps to the snooker table, picked up the handgun left by Tim Graham and swung it round firing as he did so. The first bullet missed Benson and drilled into the back of Kate who was thrown across the room with the impact. Mark Benson caught the next two bullets causing him to release the machine pistol. The room erupted with screams and shouts in the confusion.

Bill Robinson was shouting 'Kate! Kate! What are you doing? Kate.'

Mark Benson was shouting at Kate as she closed in on him again despite her wound.

Goodchild barked out a few words in German and Kate immediately looked around at him with wild eyes.

Reverting to English Goodchild said. 'Thank you Mrs Robinson. You will sit in this chair now and be very quiet.'

Kate Robinson's body suddenly sagged and she fell to the floor.

'Very well lie there and do not move.' said Goodchild.

Mark Benson was sitting on the floor using a corner of the room to prop himself up. He was not in a position to do anything.

'Fucking woman' he cursed at Kate.

Bill Robinson watched the scene open-mouthed. As Kate fell to the floor he was screaming at Goodchild who ran across to him and kicked his legs shouting 'Shut up! Or I'll finish the job.'

The effort and anxiety made him sweat profusely. Small rivulets ran from his neck and temples. His eyes darted from one person to another as he summed up the situation.

Outside Tim Graham had just recovered the ball of twine from where Nicolai and Cheslav were lying when he heard the sound of shots. The sounds were definitely the sound of muffled gunshots. Alerted by what he'd heard he started back to see what was happening. He entered the conservatory just as Mark Benson's body jerked from the impact of the bullets striking his body. Through a side window between the conservatory and the snooker room he saw a clear silhouette of Goodchild with a gun in his hand. Instantaneously he decided to withdraw whilst he collected his thoughts. There was little point in barging in only to be shot.

For a few moments he stood with his back to the wall of the house next to the conservatory to gather his thoughts. He concluded that Goodchild could not have turned the tables on an agent as experienced as Mark so he decided that he must get some help. He had to get to the listening house as soon as possible. Having made the decision he made his way to the garden wall and leapt up turning round at the top to let himself down, as he did so two pairs of hands grabbed him pulling him to earth. As he hit the pavement on the outside of the wall a large hand covered his mouth jerking his head back while another pair of hands pushed his hands behind his back.

At first Tim Graham struggled mightily but the strength of his handlers was focussed and determined. He could hardly breathe. He was almost suffocating so he used all his will power to stay still. After a few seconds the pressure of the hand on his mouth eased and he breathed a little easier. By this time his assailants had turned him over. In the gloom he saw a police marksman wearing a bullet proof vest with his index finger to his lips indicating that he expected Tim to stay quiet. Tim nodded as best he could and the hand was completely released allowing him to gulp the night air with an appreciation only understood by those who have almost suffocated.

'Don't you make a sound pal.' said the other man.

'I'm with British Intelligence.' gasped Tim. 'I must get to the house up there, the listening house. There's body's all over the place in there.' He went on pointing in the direction of Bill Robinson's home.

'Just relax pal till we get checked out.' came the reply.

'Relax, relax you daft bastard. My mates in there full of fucking bullets. Get some help for Christ's sake.'

'When we know who you are' came the curt reply, as strong fingers dug into his arms and he was frog marched up the street.

Hearing the sound of muffled gunshots Tony Hartill was sure that someone was using the machine pistols he had seen fitted with silencers. Deciding that he had nothing to lose he ran to the window of the dining room and frantically tried to open the hinged section. It would not move. He then picked up a chair and dashed it against the window. The window remained intact. In his exasperation and frustration he shouted to himself 'Damn you Bill Robinson; I might have known you would fit toughened glass.'

Abandoning attempts to escape through the window Tony ran for the dining room door flinging it open and falling over a chair that Goodchild had left on it's side to thwart any noiseless departure from the room.

Tony's body flew headlong into the wall on the opposite side of the hall splitting his head as he impacted. Impervious to the pain Tony was instantly on his feet and bounding up the staircase as fast as he could with blood pouring past his ear and onto his shoulder.

Goodchild heard the noise as Tony had crashed the

dining chair into the unyielding glass but he wasn't sure where the noise was coming from. He walked around the snooker room eyeing his prisoners then entered the conservatory ears cocked. It was at that moment that he heard the crash in the hall. Retracing his steps he made his way to the door joining the snooker room with the hall only to see Tony leaping up the staircase.

Goodchild swung the handgun up with arms fully stretched and pulled the trigger. As he did so Tony had reached the bend in the staircase. For a moment he was convinced that he had eluded the bullets and then his foot flew sideways as though it had been struck with a cannon ball. He shrieked in pain but continued to the top of the staircase.

In the bedrooms Li and Pippa had sat or paced up and down not knowing what to do. The cries from Tony brought both to the door of their respective bedrooms as Tony reached the landing.

The two women grabbed Tony and pulled him into Li's room then the three of them toppled a wardrobe over to jam the bedroom door.

Goodchild had moved to half way up the stair case where he shouted, 'That's alright you won't be going far from up there.'

Knowing that the furniture lorry was due at any moment Goodchild went into the snooker room and looked down on his forlorn prisoners. His eyes were wild with effort, anxiety and fear. Everything was as he'd left it.

'Good he said. Just like good little rabbits. It's not over yet.'

As he spoke there was the distinctive whine coming from the engine of a large vehicle. Goodchild ran into the hall and through the glass in the front door he saw a furniture van slowly navigating the bend as it turned into the drive. Before it had completed its turn there was a sound like a minor explosion at the rear of the house. Goodchild rushed anxiously to discover the source of the noise only to see a huge mechanical digger crashing through the garden wall.

Goodchild rushed back into the hall to take refuge with his allies in the furniture van. As he watched it coming up the drive he realised that it was accelerating and approaching the front door at considerable speed there was no way that it could stop in time; fifty yards from the house the driver opened his door and leapt out. Realising that the van was about to impact on the front of the house centring on the front door Goodchild made his way up the stairs for protection.

Six men dressed all in black with their faces blackened ran up the drive behind the furniture van. The three in front carried aluminium ladders. As soon as the furniture van had shuddered to a halt the ladders were leaned against the roof of the crashed vehicle. The men who had carried the ladders held them whilst their three colleagues rushed up them onto the roof of the van, over the top and through the shattered windows of the two bedrooms that Li and Pippa had sat in pondering their future just minutes before.

Li, Pippa and Tony lay on the floor of the Li's room with their backs against the wardrobe that barricaded the bedroom door. Tony was attempting to remove his shoe and sock so that he could tend the ankle wound. His shoe was filled with blood.

Tony had only been in the room for a matter of minutes. The threat from Goodchild had subsided temporarily and the first priority was to tend to Tony's wounds until they heard the furniture van coming up the drive. Pippa switched the electric light off and watched the van as it accelerated up the drive. As she watched the driver leap from his cabin she realised that the intention was to crash into the house.

'Oh! My God!' she shouted to the others 'they're going to crash.'

As her words filled the room she dropped to the floor shouting to the others to lie as flat as possible. The words had barely escaped from her lips before their ears were filled with what seemed like the noise of a nuclear explosion.

Pieces of building, splinters of wood and glass flew all over the room. They all instinctively covered their heads with their hands and stayed like that for a few seconds until a voice shouted through the clouds of dust and the darkness 'Don't Move! Identify yourselves!'

The three couldn't see the source of the voice but Pippa and Tony responded in unison.

'Only one of you speak' said the voice; then 'Quickly.'

Tony answered 'I'm Tony Hartill with Li Saric and Pippa Glendinning.

'Switch on the light.' ordered the voice.

Pippa stood up and flicked the switch whereon the settling dust was illuminated and the room was visible through the haze.

'Move across the room, away from the door' said the voice and as they did so the man that the voice belonged to emerged through the fog of dust with an automatic machine pistol in his hands saying 'Put your hands on your head and stay like that.'

The man then backed out of the room, across the remains of what had been a veranda and into the room that had been allocated to Pippa. He then followed his two colleagues carefully down the staircase.

Goodchild's perception of his prospects had gone from jubilation when he'd first seen the furniture van to

414

despair as he realised that the vehicle had obviously been stopped and Special Forces had taken it over. His quick brain instantly advised him that the authorities had been on to him for some hours. For him the game was up unless he could evade capture and find his way to Switzerland. Even then assuming that he got there he would be pursued forever more by both sides in the East/West game. He smiled grimly as he thought of Plakinov who'd sent him on this fruitless and futile mission. His vanity had precluded him from refusing Plakinov's demand to take the mission on. Plakinov had played on his vanity, not for the first time but certainly for the last time.

Goodchild walked into the snooker room that was filled with his victims. They were all alert and ashen faced as they lay helplessly on the floor where he'd left them.

'Congratulations to you all.' He said politely as he passed through the door into the conservatory where he stuck the handgun in his mouth at a carefully placed angle and pulled the trigger just as Tim Graham came bounding through the door.

Epilogue

The day after the rescue Pippa Glendinning was joined by George Norman in her room at an army hospital in North Yorkshire.

'How are you feeling.' he asked.

'Disbelieving is the right word.'

'That just about sums up the whole story' Norman replied.

'How are the others and when can I see them?' said Pippa with little of her natural exuberance.

'There's something I wish to tell you!' Norman went on. 'You probably won't like
this but, officially nothing happened.'

Pippa gaped at him filled with apprehension as he went on. 'All four wounded are in
some discomfort but there is nothing life threatening or anything like that'

'Phew! I didn't know what you were about to say! Well that's a relief, when can I see them! What do you mean nothing happened?' Pippa's words tumbled out.

'I'm not explaining myself very well. I suppose we're all in a bit of shock! You can
see them all soon briefly. Then I must ask you not to say anything about this.'

'Why ever not?' questioned Pippa.

'Because officially the incident never happened.' replied Norman.

'Never happened? All those people are shot and nearly killed and nothing happened?'

'That's right.'

'What about my story?' Pippa enquired.

'What story' said Norman 'your Editor will not print anything and neither will anyone else, officially nothing happened'.